WITCHCRAFT

KATIE M JOHN

www.katiemjohn.com

Little Bird Publishing House

London

ISBN-13: 978-0956739551
ISBN-10: 0956739555

To Charlene
Wishing you a magical read!
love Katie [illegible]

DEDICATION

Roo & Boo
x

"Fair is foul, and foul is fair."

W. Shakespeare. 'Macbeth'

ACKNOWLEDGMENTS

To all my readers and cheerleaders, thank you. To the amazing fans of 'The Knight Trilogy' – you guys rock. Your belief and passion has allowed me to write this series. I love you all x

1

Jeremiah Chase looked in the mirror, smoothed his hand through his dark brown hair and straightened his tie. His cold, blue eyes flashed back at him and a wicked little smile danced over his lips. He ran his fingers down the length of his black trouser-braces and pulled them out in front of him with his thumb before snapping them back in place.

He was to spend his evening as guest of honor at one of his great Aunt Penelope's dreary dinner parties. Even though he'd only been in the country for a month, he was already tired of the stuffy English supper party custom. He shared a mock yawn with his reflection and cocked an eyebrow, admiring the way that the shadows played over his strong jawbone. He knew he was handsome; there had been many girls that had told him so. He shrugged his shoulders dismissively. He would not apologise for having been given certain *talents*, even if they were the main reason his parents (well, his father to be more exact) had exiled him to England, believing a stint in English society would curb his "wild" and "scandalous" behaviour. They hoped that Jeremiah would return home to New York a "gentleman."

The final straw had come when he'd been photographed by some Wall-Street-Paparazzi-

Scum, kissing the face off a woman twice his age. Unfortunately, that wasn't the only scandal about the clinch; the woman also happened to be his college professor at his incredibly over-priced, private, red-brick college. Jeremiah allowed himself an indulgent smile at the memories of their afternoon extra-curricular sessions. She'd been a particularly good teacher – in all things. The young and impressionable Miss Scarlet, (yes, you can imagine how the journalists clapped their hands with sheer glee when they'd discovered her name) had been his philosophy teacher. The term's topic had been "The Question of Ethics." You can see how it all inevitably unraveled. She wasn't really to blame; Jeremiah was hardly an innocent under a predatory influence. In fact the poor girl didn't really ever stand a chance. Jeremiah knew he had a certain charm.

Jeremiah Chase: wealthy heir to his father's company, just as he was heir to his father before him, and so on and so on until the history of America goes all native and therefore not considered worthy of note. He'd always found it best not to think too long on how their family wealth had germinated; grubbing around in the dirt, chasing after gold like a desperado, and shedding the blood of those who were born from the land they'd invaded. *Time goes on*, he thinks, *the new generation can't be held accountable for the sins of the fathers – they have their own to commit.*

As he stands, Chase Enterprise (a cutting-edge pharmaceutical company) is worth several billion dollars. Jeremiah's father had sent his son to

England with the threat that unless he sorted himself out, he would be disinherited and his father would leave it all to the ass-licking younger Chase brother, Uncle Jason. Jeremiah could not stand his Uncle Jason any more than he could really stand his father.

Aside from his mother and sister, Lucia, there was only one other family member Jeremiah felt any particular fondness for: his father's eldest brother, Daniel. Daniel, the true blood-heir of the Chase Enterprise empire, who had given up his multi-billion dollar birthright for one simple principle – good. Uncle Daniel had always sagely said, "It isn't a man's strengths that define him, but his weaknesses." (Jeremiah suspected the proverb was not Daniel's own invention.)

"And if you're going to have a weakness," Jeremiah says to the reflection in the mirror, "then surely love is the best of them."

Jeremiah takes one last look in the mirror as he puts on his dinner jacket and offers up a silent prayer for something – some*one* – interesting to cross his path. He's already been in England for almost a month with nothing to distract him apart from fields, trees, and visits from his great aunt's elderly neighbours. Jeremiah feels like he might possibly internally combust from boredom, which would at least be a slightly interesting event. *At least college is due to start in less than a week*, he thinks as he rummages around his piles of textbooks looking for his cell phone. (He still struggles to call it a mobile.)

He is expecting a text from Lucia, as she has spent the day in New York trying out for the New

York Ballet Corps. He is expecting good news because he can't believe that there is any way they will turn her down; not only is she absurdly talented and beautiful, but it will also secure the kind of patronage from their father that the arts can only dream about. Nevertheless, sweet Lucia has spent months worrying herself sick about it. No one can ever question the tenacity of a Chase.

He is also desperate to hear from Daniel about his latest adventure and had hoped his e-mail notification would flag a message. Daniel left for Mexico just before Jeremiah's exile to England. He's in pursuit of a coven linked with the disappearance of several young girls from one of the mountain villages. Jeremiah hasn't been overly concerned about his Uncle's lack of contact, for he is a seasoned Witch Hunter.

The thought of Daniel's job title still makes Jeremiah smile wryly. In the world of Chase Enterprise, the thought of something so quirky and medieval as a Witch Hunter does not fit easily. However, Daniel is less your zealous nineteenth century Presbyterian minister and more your Indiana Jones turned Special Investigations FBI agent; and he is the best in the business – or so his incredibly wealthy employers believe. Not that Daniel can ever name exactly who his employers are. (But there is the not-so-secret secret that they live in a very big "house" in Rome, and have enough wealth to pay Daniel a very healthy seven-figure salary for his services without flinching.) Mind, there is no way you'd guess such a salary from the cockroach-infested apartment Daniel owns in Brooklyn.

Jeremiah finds his phone just as the dinner-gong sounds. "For Christ's sake, who still has a dinner gong?" He muses before heading down the stairs like a good little puppy in training. He has the hope that if can fool his crazy old aunt into believing that he has been instantly reformed from the shock of everything, then he might be allowed to go back home sooner rather than later.

*

Coldstone House was the kind of English Country House that you see on the front of ghost story collections. There was absolutely nothing endearing about it. Hewn from grey, unwelcoming stone (hence its apt name) it squatted in a clearing of ancient English woodland, with a scar of park land that sprawled out down the hill towards a man-made lake that was now pitch black apart from on the sunniest of English days, when it turned an unattractive shade of slime-green. His great aunt Penelope had inherited Coldstone House from her mother's line. Unusual, as such things normally ran down the male lineage. However, due to the tragedy of the First World War, in which all the direct male lines of inheritance were killed in the trenches at Ypres, a special legal loophole had been "found." The house still clung to the tragedy of the family loss and everyone who visited it had the uncomfortable feeling that the house was still mourning. Jeremiah had felt it too, from the very moment he had arrived.

On his first guest tour around the house, the discovery of the nursery (untouched since the last children had lived in the house over sixty years before) had given Jeremiah the creeps so badly that he swore for the first few nights he'd heard the sound of music boxes going off in the middle of the night and the giggling of children as they scampered past his door.

As he'd been put in one of the furthest rooms away from his Aunt's living quarters, it meant he had to pass the weird little room several times a day. Thankfully, his imagination had calmed down a lot since he'd taken the key from the nursery door and shut it up nice and tight. The key now sat in a little cedar box on his dressing table, and that was where it was going to stay.

Despite having been at Coldstone House for a month, Jeremiah had not properly explored the whole house and wasn't in a rush to. Even his aunt, who had lived there for the last fifty years, acted more like a suffering custodian than mistress of the house. At least his aunt's regular supper guests made the house appear a little warmer, if only for a few hours, and he was surprised to find himself almost letting out a sigh of relief when he entered the warmly-lit library, now full of the village's wealthiest, and most ancient and eccentrically dressed, inhabitants.

Aunt Penelope sat in her wingback chair, a glass of champagne in her ring-heavy hand. She flashed a smile at Jeremiah and nodded her approval at the effort he'd made over his dress. As manners dictated, he approached her and reached for her hand, which he kissed. She flushed with a momentary pride before introducing her "handsome and talented American nephew" to Lord Faris-Jones, neighboring estate owner and Head of the local hunt.

Jeremiah flashed his most charming smile and swallowed down his instant dislike of the man. He wasn't sure if was his yellow plaid trousers or the fact that he was Head of the Hunt that disgusted him the most. Unfortunately, Jeremiah's Aunt appeared to have given Lord Faris-Jones an account of every aspect of her nephew's education and upbringing (obviously with the exception of the most interesting parts) and now Faris, who was far too fat for the pretty Queen Anne dining chair, ensnared him in a web of ridiculously inane questions. Jeremiah managed five minutes of polite endurance before he found his eyes roaming around the room looking for rescue. *Same old, same old*, he thought heavily. His cell phone vibrated in his pocket.

"Excuse me," Jeremiah said, flashing the old man his most charming smile, "I'm expecting a very important business call and I'm afraid my cell is…"

Lord Faris-Jones offered a tight smile and waved his hand as if suggesting that it was no offence, when in reality, Jeremiah knew he had just committed the equivalent of a loud fart in polite society. He escaped through the open French windows and out onto the balcony, answering as he went. It was Lucia and she was very excited.

"Jay, I bloody did it! I got in! I aced it!" Lucia's voice lilted with breathless excitement.

He smiled and breathed in deeply. Homesickness swept over him as he thought on how he'd like to take her in his arms and twirl her around like they always did when they shared good news.

"That's fantastic, Luce." He was grinning so wide that his mouth hurt. "Totally freakin' awesome!" He knew how much it meant to her, and even though the grueling pressures of being a prima ballerina filled him with concern for her, he couldn't help but be totally infected by the passion of her dream.

"I start rehearsals next week for Swan Lake. Swan Lake, Jay!" she said it with the excitement of her five-year-old-self, dressed in her ballet outfit.

"That's brilliant, Luce. I'm so proud! I can't wait to see you on opening night."

Her voice dropped at the realisation of the distance between them. "Do you think you'll be able to come home to see me?"

"No question," he said, not entirely sure he wasn't about to make a promise he couldn't keep. "Wild horses couldn't drag me from your opening night. You're the very best of us, Luce."

"Don't be silly, Jay. You just haven't found your way yet."

"Careful, you're beginning to sound like dad."

"Sorry, I didn't mean to…"

"It's alright, Luce, it's quite fun being an outcast. You really shouldn't give me a second thought. Things are wild here. I'm having a total blast!"

"Really? You always were a terrible liar. How is the old crow?"

Jeremiah laughed despite feeling a little disloyal. "Our dearest Aunt Penelope? Yes, she's quite a charmer when you get past the cobwebs, the sourness, and the six-foot wall of snobbery."

Luce snorted out a laugh and he couldn't help but grin. "So when does college start?" she asked.

"Next week, thank God! Mind, I've got no idea where the hell I'm going or what I'm doing. They call it sixth form."

"Sounds all very Hogwarts," she said, giggling.

"Yeah well I haven't got a clue where I'm at. Dad's signed me in for the start of A-level courses. Apparently it means I'm going back a year but you can't start the courses half-way through."

"Sounds complicated. What classes you got?"

"Lessons, you mean!" Jeremiah laughed. "Aunt Penelope has been tutoring me in speaking properly."

"Sounds fun!"

"Yeah!" he said, lacking conviction. "Dad's signed me up for, History, Literature, French, Physics, and Maths."

Lucia let out a low whistle. "The curse of being a boy genius, brother! Clearly our dear father wants to keep you from having too much time on your hands."

"Yeah, something like that I guess."

"So how many English girl's hearts have you managed to already break?" Lucia gave him no time to respond. "Talking of which, I bumped into Ms. Scarlet at the bookstore the other day – she was very keen to know how you were getting on; she wanted to know if I'd heard from you."

"Luce, I really don't want to talk about Rachel."

She continued as if she hadn't heard his protest. "She was looking rough! Aged about ten years, I'd say. I heard through Fabian's sister that they've sacked her, and her boyfriend has dumped her – mind you, I guess he would, wouldn't he. I mean who would want to go out with a cradle snatcher? It's all quite a scandal," her voice glittered.

Jeremiah's mood was souring and he didn't want to fall out with her. He knew she was playing; she had no real understanding of the connection he'd had with Rachel. She had meant more to him than some foolish afternoons of fun.

"Luce, I've got to go," he said, cutting her off before she had a chance to say anything else stupid. "They've called us to dinner."

"Oh, okay, I'll ring you later then. We're going for dinner at Chi's to celebrate."

The thought of them all out at Chi's deepened his homesickness. Chi's was the family's favourite restaurant; a Chinese they'd gone to for all major family milestones since he could remember.

He forced his voice to sound cheery, "Well, have a good time, then. Talk to you later."

"Laters bro!"

Jeremiah switched off the phone and looked out across the dark grounds. Far in the distance he could see the little yellow lights of the village; they looked like ship-lamps far out at sea.

"Can I get you a drink, sir?"

The voice of a girl startled him and he turned, slightly flustered from being caught off guard. As soon as he'd heard her, hope ignited that she would match the attractiveness of her voice. He wasn't disappointed. He greeted her with his most flirtatious smile. He saw immediately from her blush that he wasn't the only one to have been caught off guard. She dipped her eyes from the intensity of his curious look.

"Why, thank you," he said, holding out a hand to receive a flute of champagne. She returned her eyes to his and he saw that there was a sparkle of defiance in them; it was as if she was daring herself to look at him. Suddenly he felt uncomfortable, and for a rare moment he felt his usual rock-solid confidence crack. She was tall, tall enough to subconsciously stand with one knee bent behind her other leg in order to drop an inch from her height. Her dark, blonde hair was scraped back into a utilitarian bun and secured with a large black velvet bow, which had the effect of lifting her eyes so that their natural feline properties were accentuated. They were lined lightly with kohl. He examined her face and noted that she wore very little make-up. She was very pretty, in the same way as a wildflower; her eyes were corn-flower blue. His eyes roamed freely over the rest of her. If she knew what he was doing, she didn't show it, and he wondered if she were doing her own appraisal of him. It felt like she might be. In a strange and curious way he felt like she might be rummaging around his soul.

Her waist was nipped in by a large black belt that joined the crisp white of her fitted blouse to the snug fitting black knee-length skirt. Her toned legs were sheathed in sheer stockings.

"My name is Jeremiah," he said, extending his free hand. "My friends call me Jay."

She glanced down at his hand and shifted the weight of the drinks tray so that she could reach out an unsteady hand in return.

"My name is Fox."

"Fox?" he replied, nodding his head. "That's certainly an interesting nickname." He threw her a teasing smile. "Any particular reason why?"

"It's not a nickname, it's my birth name." She shifted uncomfortably.

"Oh," he replied, lifting the glass of champagne to his lips and looking at her over the top of it. He watched Fox flush under the intensity of his eyes' wicked sparkle and he smiled. *It really shouldn't be this easy*, he thought.

"Anyway," she nervously cleared her throat, "Lady Asquithe asked me to come and call you to dinner."

"Does my Aunt always insist that you call her by her full title?" he asked, tipping his glass up and draining the last mouthful of expensive vintage champagne.

"It's what's expected," she shrugged dismissively.

"And do you always do what is expected, Fox?" he asked stepping towards her with a complete awareness that he was about to invade her space without invitation. It was a move of dominance, a test of her boundaries.

"That depends on who is doing the expecting," she said sharply, stepping back. She flashed him a warning stare and Jeremiah was surprised by the sudden flare-up in her spirit. He stopped his advance and pressed his lips together, nodding with approval. The flash of venom had intrigued him: he'd underestimated her.

He waved the champagne glass in the air, signaling that he wished to put it down on the tray, but before he had a chance she'd turned and left, leaving him hanging.

"Touché!" he said under his breath. Far from her cold rebuttal calming his interest in her, she'd just kindled a fascination in his brain like he hadn't felt since he'd taken the challenge to seduce Miss Scarlet.

"There's no such thing as impossible, son!" he said into the night air, bitterly mimicking his father.

*

Dinner was only made tolerable by the momentary flashes of Fox as she carried in the dinner dishes. However, it was clear that the usual Chase Charm was not having its normal effect. She barely made eye contact with him for the rest of the evening. Jeremiah knew he was an arrogant son of a bitch, he'd come to hear the insult enough from his sister who took great delight in mocking him whenever she had the chance, but up until now, it seemed to have served him well. His arrogance had ensured he usually got what he wanted. And besides, it wasn't arrogance, it was confidence, he told himself as he watched Fox flit from guest to guest.

Girls liked a boy to be confident – or so he had been tutored to believe. His education in the art of charm had started young; at the age of fifteen, when his mother's friend, Gabriella, had come to stay for a while whilst she battled a bitter divorce from her husband. Gabriella had been made for an adolescent's wet-dream, and Jeremiah could not believe that her fat, balding (and ridiculously wealthy) husband could possibly find anything more in any other woman. Gabriella didn't steal his innocence, he'd been with several girls his own age before, but Gabriella took Jeremiah on as a sort of pet project – and she had enjoyed the role of tutor as much as he enjoyed being her student.

Although he had no real regrets about any of his past, he had come to understand that Gabriella had, in a way, spoiled him. She had left him with a deluded and slightly warped sense of human relationships. He had discovered too much too soon, and found he couldn't really connect with girls of his own age; and he had certainly bypassed the wonderful experience of true first love.

His only socially acceptable relationship (in his parents' eyes) had been with Harper, High-School-Prom-Queen-Twenty-Thirteen. With her expensive highlights, perfected elocution, and virginal Victoria's Secret lace, she had almost been his first taste of a wholesome relationship. In the end it had ended miserably because there was only so much chatter about the various love interests of the cheerleading squad he could stand before wanting to take out his own eyeballs. It had all ended in a lot of tears and unattractive public scenes in restaurants.

He sighed. The lack of interesting company was making him far too reflective. He'd spent more time having to face his own behaviour in the last few weeks than he'd ever had to before. He wasn't sure he liked what he saw.

Maybe Luce had had a point when she'd rather ceremoniously placed a copy of Oscar Wilde's *Dorian Gray* into his travel bag. He smiled at the thought of how she had wrapped it in a large red-satin bow. Luce always had had a taste for the dramatic.

At last, Fox came over to him so that she could take away his dinner plate. As she reached out her hand, he reached out his as if innocently heading for his wine glass but then let it drop so that it "accidently" brushed against Fox's fingers. She flashed him an acidic look that told him quite clearly she wasn't falling for his cheap tricks. The heart-stopping sound of shattering bohemian crystal filled the room.

"I'm so sorry, Lady Asquithe. I'm so sorry!" The waitress, Amber, was already crying as she crouched down to try and retrieve the broken shards of the dozen wine glasses that had toppled from the silver tray.

"You stupid, clumsy, girl!" Lady Asquithe rose from her seat, her hand against her chest, which was puffed out in full force, giving the impression of an angry peacock. “Do you have any idea how much those glasses are worth?” she screeched.

Amber let out a small “ouch” as a shard of glass bit deep into her finger, adding to the general sense of chaos. After flamboyantly discarding his napkin, Lord Faris was on his feet and placing a soothing arm on Lady Asquithe’s elbow. “Now, Penny, old gal – the child didn’t mean it; it was just an accident.”

At the sound of a champion, Amber was wracked with sobs. She fled the room repeating between gasps of air, “I’m so sorry!”

Jeremiah couldn’t help but break into a bemused smile as the Victorian-style melodrama unfolded in front of him. Aunt Penelope collapsed back into her dining chair and fanned herself with her napkin as if suffering an attack of the vapours. Lord Yellow-Trousers, red faced, took charge, shouting at various staff to move into action. The rest of the guests did their chattering-best to calm Lady Asquithe down and reassure her that things weren’t like they used to be.

Jeremiah slid his eyes towards Fox, who was stood watching the scene as if it were taking place in a different world. Feeling his eyes on her, she turned and blushed, before putting down his plate and rushing over towards the scene of the crystal carnage. Jeremiah watched as she knelt down and threw her white linen serving cloth over the mess. She gathered the cloth up and impossibly pulled from underneath it, ten of the dozen goblets. They were perfectly intact. She placed them back onto the table one by one, as if they had simply, by some miracle, survived the crash. The rest of the glass shards were gathered into the cloth.

"I'm sorry, Lady Asquithe but it looks like two of them have gone." Lady Asquithe looked at the ten glasses on the table and raised an eye-brow in steely surprise.

"Just two of them gone? I thought from the sound of it that I'd lost them all. Such a relief – they were my mother's."

Jeremiah scrutinized the goblets in front of him. They were perfect. Not even a chip. *They must have been lucky enough to have fallen on the rug rather than the floor boards,* he reasoned. Animated with efficiency (or keen to get away from Jeremiah's suspicious looks), Fox bustled out of the dining room and that was the last he saw of her that evening.

Much of the rest of the dinner-party prattle was about the astonishing luck of the glasses, which seemed to release the generally tedious topics of other close shaves the guests had experienced. Jeremiah was polite enough to stay through the port and stilton course (even though he had no idea why the English insisted on waiting to eat their eating perfectly good cheese until it had turned a disgusting shade of green). He didn't pay much attention to the conversation, and his aunt cast him a look that expressed a little disappointment that her usually glittering socialite nephew should not be performing at his best. He couldn't help it; his thoughts were completely distracted by the mysterious girl. Eventually, he stood and made his apologies, explaining that he didn't feel to well and required his bed.

He took the long way back to his room, idly wondering if Fox attended the same college he'd been enrolled at. Going to the local college and not some private boarder, had been the main condition of him going along with the whole ridiculous "reform" plan.

He hated preppy kids and their Hamptons ways, which were partly why he had gone so wildly off the rails; visiting underground clubs and hanging out with a notorious group of street artists. Following along with them, (mainly out of boredom) he'd committed acts of minor political activism against everything his own family stood for in some futile attempt at rebellion. There had been a certain attractive glamour to it – little rich boy raging against his father's capitalist empire. It didn't last. Although he'd made a convincing go of it (even getting arrested several times for petty acts of vandalism) he was too intelligent to convince himself that he really had a cause. It hadn't really been his *scene*, but it was certainly a better scene than the pool parties and polo dinners.

He hoped things would be different here. He knew it was going to be a challenge being an American in a college where almost all of the students came from families that could be traced back to the Doomsday Book, not alone a street-wise, filthy-rich New Yorker, but the thought of going incognito was very appealing. The only hope he had was that the village store didn't sell copies of *Time Magazine* or *Esquire*, both of which had run articles on him in the last twelve months for being one of New York's most eligible bachelors.

A fresh start, he thought. *A chance to become a better person; a chance to be happy.* His thoughts were broken by the sound of a gentle and rhythmic thudding. He stopped on the turn of the stair and listened. It took him a moment to realise it was the sound of something falling step by step down the flight of stairs above him. He anticipated the object coming into view but even after a minute, when the sound had stopped, the object remained hidden. Jeremiah continued his upward journey, only to find his heart lodge in his throat. He was by no means a coward, but the sight of the brightly coloured children's ball sitting brazenly on the stairs made him feel the ice-chill of unfamiliar fear. He stood for several moments just looking it, as if willing it away. When it refused he bent down and went to pick it up for closer inspection. As soon as his fingers touched the smooth painted leather, a jolt of static electricity shot up his arm. He stepped back and almost lost his footing. His heart rate accelerated into a panicked gallop and a cold sweat broke out on his forehead. Using the tip of his shoe, he nudged the ball and it rolled to the step below. He wasn't going to risk receiving another shock, but was worried about leaving it on the stairs in case it would be a danger to Aunt Penelope. Jeremiah stepped down a step and gave the ball another firm nudge, sending it careering down the stairs and down into the hallway, where it would be far more visible. He couldn't explain why exactly, but the presence of the ball made him feel sick to his core.

The thought of having to walk past the creepy nursery (from where he was sure the ball had originated) made him feel even worse.

"But I locked it," he said to the silent stairs. "The key is on my desk." Little shiver-spiders ran over his spine. He knew that he would find the door open. His instincts were not wrong.

Even from the bottom of the long corridor, he could see that the nursery door had been thrown wide open, creating a barrier between him and his room. There was no avoiding it, he would have to not only travel past the open door, but he'd have to face the spider-webbed nursery in order to shut it. With every step, his heart beat a double rhythm, until by the time he was at the door, he felt almost delirious with fear.

He took the handle and resisted the temptation to close his eyes. It was pitch black inside the room. With the shutters continually locked, not even moonlight lit the sad little room. Finding it empty, his nerves began to settle. He strained his ear listening for any tiny movement. It was still. Strangely, he felt a little disappointed not to have been greeted with a glowing pair of red eyes or a ghostly woman in white, as if he had spent all that fear and then been cheated. He let out a little laugh of relief and closed the door, making sure that it was firmly shut.

Just as he started to come down from its adrenalin rush, he saw something move in the corner of his eye and it started all over again. The same little ball was rolling down the corridor towards him.

"So you want to play?" Jeremiah asked the seemingly empty corridor – only he knew with certainty it wasn't as empty as it looked. There was no answer. *Of course there isn't, there's nobody there*, he thought.

All at once the room spun, and Jeremiah had to hold out his hands against the wall to stop himself from falling. Bright lights erupted in his head. Everywhere, he heard the sound of screaming. They were the screams of women and children. Men were shouting. There was chaos and panic and Jeremiah couldn't work out exactly what was going on. He felt himself split into two different existences; the one in his head was full of fire and death, and the one where he was standing in the corridor of Coldstone House as he watched himself having some sort of seizure. Acrid smoke assaulted his nostrils. Savage flames licked his boots. Then as quickly as the vision had come, it faded. Jeremiah was left barely standing.

"What the hell just happened?" he panted.

He stood for a moment, trying to shake away the violence that stained his calm. He looked down at the innocuous little ball. At any other time it would have seemed a sweet relic from a more innocent age but now it was full of sinister and heavy meaning. He sped towards his room, his heart still hammering against his bones. Whatever he'd been witness to, he didn't relish seeing it again. He'd been left feeling dirty, polluted in a way that he couldn't quite express. All he wanted to do was shower. He hoped that as well as cleansing his body it would also cleanse his mind. He headed to his room, collected his towels and travelled back down the haunted little corridor to the shower room. He stripped out of his braces and shirt, exposing his well-defined body (the result of having been on the swim team since his first year in high school). Water had always been his natural element; swimming through the water gave him a sense of freedom he'd never really felt in his daily life. His fingers fumbled over his trouser buttons and he realised with irritation that the events in the hallway had left him shaking.

When he finally managed to wrestle himself out of his clothes, he stood naked looking at his reflection in the mirror. "Jeez, I look like I've just seen a ghost!" he said to the reflection.

"You did!" his reflection replied silently.

He shook the idea away. The tremors had spread from his hand and now his whole body shivered. He tried to convince himself that it was the result of the cold, damp house, and not because for the first time in his life, he genuinely felt afraid. He stepped into the shower. At least the water was hot – almost too hot. Steam filled the bathroom and at last Jeremiah began to calm. He reasoned that he was letting his imagination get the better of him. Coldstone House was creepy at the best of times and it was no wonder that his head had decided to create its own little horror-film montage. *What next? Blood running from the taps? Messages on the mirror?* He'd been attempting to mock himself but as he glanced towards the flash of silver mirror through the steam, he shuddered. He leant his head against the wall and let the hard hot water pummel his tense shoulder blades. “God, I need get out of here!” he muttered.

2

In all times Fox had worked for Lady Asquithe at Coldstone House, she'd never been so relieved to be leaving it as she was tonight. Sitting safely in the warm comfort of Will's car (who'd also been drafted in as a pot-washer) she watched the house recede into the shadowy distance within the frame of the rear-view mirror.

"Do you think the rumours about Coldstone House are true?" Fox asked.

Will, who had been more interested in setting his iPod playlist than concentrating on either the road or his passenger asked, "What rumours?"

"You know, the rumours about the house being haunted?"

"You know I don't believe in all that weirdo clap-trap, Foxy." Fox bristled and Will, realising that he'd been massively insensitive, mumbled, "Sorry, no offence meant."

Fox cracked him a smile and wrinkled her nose. "I know."

Fox's family was well known in Heargton village for their "strange" ways. Fox's mum, Wren, ran the New-Age, alternative lifestyle shop called Moonstone. The shop was the kind that sold crystals, home-made natural beauty products, fairy-charms, and a whole host of other weird and "magical" things. It also had the proud title of the largest independent retailer of books on magic, alternative therapies, and paganism in the county. So it was no surprise that her family secret was a not so secret, secret. Fox had spent all of her life being known as a witch's child – only it had always been said in jest, creating the interesting paradox that it hid who (and what) her family really was.

It was true that her mother and sisters were witches. Not that Fox really understood what that truly meant in the modern age. She knew that others in the witch community respected her family's bloodline because of its ancient blood-flow, and the name Meadowsweet was synonymous with one of the most powerful covens in their kind's history. The Sisters of the Meadow, or the Meadowsweets as they had become known as over time, comprised of not only Fox and her two sisters, Swan and Rabbit (known as Bunny), but also of their cousins Primrose, Violet, and Daisy.

The seven women who made up the Meadowsweets were known in the witch community as a Noble Clan. There had never been a single blemish of dark magic in all the generations of Meadowsweets, and they were revered as one of the purist houses in the British Isles. For Fox, this strange sense of fame within the witch community contrasted greatly with the general contempt that her family had been treated with by the "normal" world.

Despite this, for as long as Fox could remember, the Meadowsweets had shunned the wider witch community. Aside from those of their kind that stumbled into Moonstone, or a few crazy fans who had made a special trip to have their spell-books signed, Fox had met with very few witches – apart from the Ravenhearts who lived in the same village. But even they were really off limits, except for Thalia, the youngest of the Ravenheart sisters who attended the same college.

Their mother had never talked about the reasons why she had turned her back on the witch community, or why she felt the need to abandon her witchcraft. Fox had never seen their mother cast a spell, aside from the brewing of herbal remedies, and making beauty products, which really didn't count in Fox's book. Besides recognizing the traditional festivals, there was very little about their lives that were "witch" – except that was for their emerging gifts.

As cold and mocking as the villagers in Heargton liked to pretend to be of the Meadowsweet family, it was amazing how many of them still kept a willow broom by the front door, sprinkled salt boundaries on their doorsteps, hung corn-dollies in the windows of newlyweds' bedrooms, and would knock on the door of Meadowsweet Cottage after sunset with requests for help with their troubles. Fox was always amazed by her mother's seemingly endless compassion and generosity to the very people who made her family feel like outcasts. When she'd quizzed her mother over the relationship with the villagers, her mother only replied, "It's how it has always been, child."

Will finally managed to pluck a conversation out of the air and break the embarrassing silence that had settled between them. "My great grandfather used to be a gamekeeper at Coldstone House."

"Really? Did he know the Chase family well?"

"More than he cared to. He never said a lot – always clammed up when anything was said about them. Said, 'it weren't his place to talk 'bouts fine folk.'" Will mimicked the strong Lancashire accent of his forefathers. "Granny was much happier to talk about them."

"Oh?" Fox asked with an eagerness to know more about the Chase family that surprised her. *Damn that arrogant boy!* she thought, cross at the way her head was starting to do 'funny' stuff like branding her memories with images of his eyes, and jaw-line and… lips. *Stop it! Right now!* she said silently to herself. Somewhere in her head she heard a little laugh.

"Yeah, Granny said that there'd never been such a divided, warring family as the Chase family. Apparently it went way back. In the end, two of the four brothers emigrated to America just to get away from the other two. The two that stayed behind were linked to all kinds of weird stuff. She'd say, 'Will, you stay away from that there Coldstone House, there be wickedness soaked into its very stones.'"

Fox couldn't help but laugh at Will's granny-impersonation and they spent the last five minutes of their journey taking it in turns to be Granny Wilkins. It was nice to be distracted and before long they were pulling up outside Fox's little thatched cottage.

"Your house always reminds me of the gingerbread house, a proper fairytale house." He smiled teasingly. "Just right for a group of witches to live in."

"A coven: a group of witches is called a coven," Fox said with an air of exasperation that gave too much away. She quickly tried to cover her tracks, "I mean everyone knows that, stupid!" she said, punching his arm.

"If you say so," he replied with a crooked little smile.

Fox was unsettled by the idea that Will was possibly flirting with her, although she couldn't be sure – she wasn't the best at all that boy-stuff. She began to feel hot and worried that she was blushing, giving him the wrong idea. The internal voice went into babbling overload, *I mean Will is alright and all that, but I just don't…*

"Good night then."

She couldn't be sure but she thought his lips were pressing tightly together to prevent them from smiling, or…

I wonder what it would be like to kiss him? She startled at her own thoughts and mentally chastised herself. "Good night then," she replied awkwardly, fumbling with the seatbelt clasp until eventually he had to dive in and help her. Their hands momentarily touched and Fox felt ridiculously uncomfortable. Within moments she'd managed to free herself from the car and half-fallen out onto the pavement.

"Are you okay?" Will asked, full of concern.

"Yep. Fine. Caught my foot in the seat belt." Her voice was clipped with mortification.

"See you Monday."

"Thanks for the lift."

"No, probs, any time."

Then he was gone and Fox was left alone with her impudent internal dialogue.

"Get any more gobby and I'm going to have to give you a name," she muttered.

*

Fox walked into a busy, productive house, despite it being near to midnight. Swan and Bunny were busy at the kitchen table making soap for their mother's shop. The whole house smelt of citrus and lavender. Fox ran her hand along the smooth scrubbed pine of the table. It had been in the family for generations and was worn and shaped with years of activity and feasting. The table was the soul of their home, the place where they gathered to create, counsel, and nourish.

"There you are!" Swan said, handing Fox a tied bunch of dried lavender. "We were beginning to think you'd had a better offer."

Fox blushed. "Lady Asquithe's party went on longer than expected."

"Really?" Bunny teased. "Are you sure it wasn't because you were busy kissing Will's face off?"

"Noo!" Fox squealed. "I don't even fancy him. He's…"

"Very handsome," her mother interjected, laughing. She walked over to Fox and draped her arm over her shoulder protectively. "But he's not Fox's type, is he sweetheart?"

"He's everybody's type," Bunny said, giggling. She was two years younger than Fox and was a fully paid up member of the Will Appreciation Society. Will had a large Year Ten fan-base, and his friends constantly mocked him about it, although in truth it was probably because they were a little jealous of the attention.

Fox really couldn't see it. Well that wasn't exactly true, she could *see* it, she just didn't understand it. Whatever *it* was that he had, *it* didn't do *it* for her.

"So what is your type then?" Swan, the eldest of Wren's daughters, asked.

Fox squirmed and made a show of being busy pulling the lavender heads away from the stem. She shrugged. It was an honest response. She didn't know. She hadn't really put that much thought into it. *Jeremiah?* her internal dialogue teased.

Subconsciously, she shook the thought away. He certainly was *not* her sort; he was arrogant, cocky – totally full of himself. He obviously knew that he was handsome as… which in Fox's eyes, made him quite the opposite.

"Maybe she likes Chip-Shop Paul!" Bunny teased.

Fox picked up a handful of orange peel and threw it at Bunny, who squealed in delight before throwing back a handful of sage. Swan, grabbed each of them by a wrist in a painful twist.

"Pack it in, we've got work to do." Immediately, Swan's calming influence washed over them and their emotions stilled. This was Swan's emerging gift; she was an emotion manipulator, able to influence an individual's feelings and responses with just the touch of her hand. Like their mother, she had been given healing hands. As for Fox, she had been given the gift of a photographic memory, which was good for studying but offered little in the way of party tricks. Bunny's gifts had yet to shine, although knowing her, it was bound to be something dramatic and exciting.

Gathered together at the table and making things for the shop was when Fox was happiest. She couldn't ever imagine a time when she would have to move out and leave her mother and sisters. As Fox was the most artistic of them, it was her job to write the calligraphy labels and finish the bottles with ribbon and dried flowers.

The Moonstone Cosmetics range was famous across the county, and the girls were barely able to make enough to keep up with the demand; especially for the anti-aging Orange Blossom cream, which was made with neroli, palmrosa, and grapefruit-seed as well as a certain sprinkle of magic. Somehow, by complete chance several years ago, an editor at *The Times* had been given a bottle for a Christmas present and she was so impressed that it had made the pages of *The Sunday Times* as a "Must Have". Within an hour of opening the doors on the Monday morning, a long winding queue of women made its way down the village high street. It had been one of the most exciting events to have happened in Heargton for many years.

Their mother had become somewhat of an overnight celebrity, supplying cosmetics and other items to famous people with a more spiritual leaning. Although their mother secretly despised all the attention, the income was undeniably useful in helping to keep the shop open; something that must be done at all costs. In one-way or another the Meadowsweet family had run a potions and lotions shop in Heargton for over six hundred years. Each generation had lived in the same cottage and tended the herbs and fruits of the large garden.

"So Fox, did anything interesting happen?" Wren asked.

"Nope," she replied, trying to sound as natural as possible.

"Did you see the new boy?" Bunny asked.

Fox's mind momentarily swirled with indecision; part of her wanted to say that she hadn't but why? It was a perfectly ordinary question for them to ask. Images of Jeremiah flashed in her photographic memory. There was something about the boy that she couldn't put her finger on. She felt the strongest instinct to keep him as far away from her family as possible. Words were powerful – no one knew this more than a witch, and invocations could happen without intention; talking about him here brought him into their home and for some reason Fox felt that he must not set foot over their threshold. However lying was not in her nature and so reluctantly she said, "Yep!" and then hoped that the matter would be over. In a household of women withholding information about the arrival of a new boy was futile.

"Soooo," asked Bunny, "is he as gorgeous as Freya says he is?"

"Is he as gorgeous as Will?" Swan asked. A blush crept over her cheeks, which elicited a high-pitched response from Bunny who was always keen to interfere in matters of romance. "I didn't know *you* liked Will!"

"Oh, for goodness sake – what is it with the whole Will thing? I know we live in a small village and reasonable looking boys are few and far between but really…"

Bunny turned and flashed Fox a look before sweetening her face, keen for information about the new potential. "So?" she crooned.

Fox picked up the pestle and ground it against the scented lavender heads in the mortar. "Yeah, he's okay – if you like that sort of thing," she said, concentrating intensely on her grinding.

"Oh, intriguing! What sort of *thing* would that be?"

"Arrogant, full of himself… shallow," Fox muttered.

"Oh my! You like him!" Bunny teased.

Wren looked over at Fox, suddenly taking an interest in her daughters' chatter. She cocked her head and tried to get Fox's eye contact. Fox could sense her mother's enquiring look and stubbornly continued to look down into the mortar.

"Not at all. I thought he was… repugnant!"

"What does repugnant mean?" Bunny asked, innocently.

"It means that she loves him!" Swan said through giggles.

Fox sighed. "It means that there is something about him that I really don't like." All three of her companions, including her mother, stopped what they were doing and shot her a look. Fox tried to bluff it out and ignore it, but they weren't having any of it, Fox intuition was legendary in the house.

"In what way?" her mother coaxed.

"I don't know." Fox shrugged again. She was certainly doing a good impression of a surly teenager this evening. "I've just got a feeling."

"A feeling?" Swan asked. Being an emotion manipulator, she held great store in feelings.

"It's nothing," Fox said, waving a dismissive hand as she headed towards the drawer with the pretense of searching for a pen. "He just comes across as a bit of a flirt. You know the sort that likes to go around breaking hearts for sport."

"He sounds more delicious by the moment," Bunny said. Her eyes were already sparkling and she hadn't even set them on Jeremiah yet.

Wren threw her a withering look and sighed before softly chastising her, "Your hormones are all over the place. I think it's about time I started feeding you some Evening Primrose oil to settle them down; either that or I let Swan loose on you. You're fickle as spring sunshine."

Bunny dropped her bottom lip and returned to her job of pouring cream lotion into the bottles. Fox was saved from further interrogation by the sound of the cooker timer.

"That'll be the cookies," Wren said, heading towards the oven, picking up the oven glove as she went. "I thought the workers deserved a treat!"

After cookies, milk, and goodnights, Fox headed upstairs and closed her bedroom door, relieved to be on her own at last. Her head was spinning in a highly irritating way; she wasn't the sort to lose it over a boy, but there was something about Jeremiah that made her skin prickle. She stripped out of her clothes and fell onto the bed, closing her eyes. For the first time in her life she found her photographic memory to be a disadvantage; every time she tried to clear her head, detailed images of the evening flooded in. And all the time, a painful warning siren screamed. *Maybe I'm due on*, she reasoned. She'd suffered with pre-menstrual migraines for the last year and being useless at keeping track of time, a screaming headache was often Mother Nature's calling card. She did a mental calculation and although she wasn't due for another week, it at least offered an explanation; certainly it was a more favourable reason than it being the result of a chemical rush over an arrogant boy.

She leant over and pushed her window wide, relishing the cool air on her naked skin, and switched off the bedside light. She was certainly in no mood to read. The best thing to do was to close her eyes and slip into sleep. Although she didn't need a lot of sleep (she could get by quite happily on five or six hours a day), she slept incredibly deeply, to the point she'd caused several episodes of panic when having sleepovers at friends' they'd been unable to wake her. Fox's ability to sleep through a complete fire-drill on the school away week had earned her a certain amount of notoriety. She'd also never had any trouble getting to sleep; it was as easy as switching off the light, and once out, that was it, nothing but still darkness – not even a dream.

Her sister Swan on the other hand was known for her lucid dreaming, to the point that she would often leave her bed and travel around the house whilst sleeping. She'd been known to conduct baking, painting, and even flower arranging, all under the influence of the Sand Man. Fox was a little jealous of Swan's ability to dream, thinking it must be wonderful to live so many lives and to experience so many surreal worlds.

Within minutes she was asleep.

Morning came in a bright burst of spring sunshine, waking Fox up with an overly cheery blast of light in her face. She groaned and looked at the time on the alarm clock. It was exactly a minute until it was due to ring. She picked it up and flicked the off switch. Her headache had calmed and she didn't want to invite it back. Monday mornings were always a challenge, especially when not naturally blessed with the skill of organisation. It wasn't that Fox wasn't capable, but she preferred to approach life with a spontaneity not really compatible with bus timetables, college bells, and lesson structures. It meant that every Monday morning she was forced into combat with the clock as she sought lost shoes, a misplaced rucksack, scattered belongings, dirty clothes piles, and hidden keys. There was never time for breakfast. She was too busy running around doing an impression of a headless chicken. She'd enter the kitchen to witness Bunny and Swan sat calmly eating their way through sweet, syrupy bowls of porridge, dressed in clothes that had been laid out the night before, and rucksacks all packed according to timetable. Of course they'd choose to be smugly unhelpful, offering no help but the ladling out of infuriating advice.

At last, disheveled and hungry, Fox would follow her two graceful and impeccably dressed sisters down the path and through the rickety gate of the rose-arch to await the school bus. If she'd been together enough to grab a cold piece of toast on the way, she'd spend her few waiting moments stuffing tasteless and soggy bread into her mouth whilst scrabbling through her rucksack to check that she had the essentials; hopeful that her hairbrush was still there so that she could at least drag a brush through her tangles before she got to college.

The school bus, (a small eighteen-seater mini-bus driven by lecherous Peter Smithdon, who also ran the village post office) pulled up outside. Bunny threw back the sliding door and clambered over the seat to where her two best friends, Molly and Evie, waited, eager to catch up on weekend gossip. The sight of Bunny's pert and peachy backside blocked Fox's view so that she had no idea what Bunny was on about when she turned around and mouthed a silent "WOW!" It was only when Fox was bent over double, her hair falling over her face like a wind-torn bird's nest and her mouth still holding onto the remnants of half a slice of limp toast, that she understood what, or rather *who*, had grabbed Bunny's attention.

"Morning, Foxy!" Jeremiah called, offering her a salute and smile that really ought to have been made illegal.

With her mouth full she was in no position to offer an erudite response and so had to settle for a clumsy nod of the head and a half-hearted wave, before Swan gave her a good shove from behind and caused her to fall into her seat.

"All aboard?" Smithdon hollered.

"Does he think he's a ruddy train driver or sumut?" Fred muttered under his breath.

"I said, all aboard?" Smithdon repeated.

A chorus of, "Aye!" rippled flatly through the mini-bus.

What is he wearing? Fox's internal asked. She slid her eyes to the driver's rear view mirror, which offered her a view of Jeremiah. He was sat on the single seat at the very back, one leg up so that his foot rested on the seat and his knee leaned against the window. Fox couldn't say why his body posture irritated her but it did. He had his earphones on and was making a show of looking out of the window, but she caught him glancing towards the front of the bus several times. He was wearing a thick white cotton shirt, the first two buttons undone and the sleeves rolled up (*Ridiculous at this time of year!*) and it was tucked into a pair of neat fitting black jeans. But that wasn't what made his dress stand out amongst the blue denims and hoodies of the other boys, it was the thin black trouser braces. On any other boy in the village they would have made him look like the local scarecrow, but somehow on Jeremiah they looked… Fox refused to finish the sentence. Jeremiah's brown hair was tousled so that it looked beguilingly like he had just got out of bed, although Fox suspected it was a highly polished look. No one could look that chilled and cool without a lot of work. In reality the out of bed look just looked a mess; more like the dragged through a hedge look. She should know, she'd perfected it over the years.

She had the feeling that he knew that she was looking at him and had closed his eyes in order to give her free reign to absorb the details. She didn't need to see his eyes to know what colour they were; she could conjure up the image of them from the first moment they had met. They were grey and blue, like tidal waters. *Stop being so bloody romantic* her internal mocked. *More like the colour of drain water.* Fox smiled in reply and pressed her lips together to stifle the giggle that threatened to escape.

Bunny and her friends were unusually quiet, meaning that they were undoubtedly whispering about Jeremiah. Fox could just see the effect he was going to have on Thornvale's lower sixth girls. It had been bad enough when the trainee art teacher had arrived, all dark and handsome. *Jeez, it had been like a form of weird hysteria. Mind he had been kind of hot,* Fox admitted. High praise from Fox, who was often left underwhelmed by the male species. It wasn't that she didn't like boys, it's just that she didn't really see the point of wasting her time dating when she had too many other things to do.

"Are you okay?" Swan asked, with her usual sense of emotional awareness. "You seem a little…"

Fox shot her a challenging look but Swan was not so easily warned off.

"…pre-occupied." She punctuated her statement with the slightest turn of her head towards Jeremiah.

"I'm fine, I just feel a little…" she began to reply but she didn't finish her sentence. Something was happening inside her head; something violent and terrible. There were flashing lights, like torches in dark fields. Someone was crying but it sounded more like an animal than a human. The heavy feeling of loss and fear washed over her and she though that she might be sick. The white light of the torch flashed onto something pink and twisted on the ground; it was a child's doll, the face of which had been smashed in with the tread of a heavy boot.

Fox tipped her head between her knees with the hope of relieving some of the pressure that was building in the bridge between her eyes. Involuntarily she let out a small groan. Swan reached out her hand and placed it onto the small of Fox's back. Cool calm spread over her. The feeling of dark violence was replaced by the sensation of light. The sickness faded. Fox knew that Swan was breaking an unwritten rule between the sisters and was using her magic on her. Rather than being angry, Fox felt relief. Whatever darkness had come at her, she had been unprepared and it had nearly dragged her under. It took her a moment to realise that Swan was whispering close into her ear,

"Just try and relax. Find your breath and breathe. Ssh. Ssh"

Bunny came scrambling up over the seat. "Hey, what's up with her?" she asked, directing her question at Swan.

"Nothing, she's just dropped her iPod." Swan almost choked on the lie. She hated lies, even white ones, which made her slightly socially awkward.

Fox could feel Bunny's eyes boring into her back and she knew that she didn't buy it. She was rescued from further interrogation by Smithdon throwing open the mini-bus doors. "Alright you rabble, get lost!" he said cheerfully.

Fox stumbled out and gasped in the cold air before righting herself on her feet. She tucked her hair behind her ears in an attempt to tame it and threw her backpack over her shoulder purposefully. Her sixth sense informed her that Jeremiah was watching her and the thought made her skin creep with goosebumps. She wasn't entirely sure if the sensation was unpleasant or not. Swan sidled up to her and leaned in conspiratorially.

"What happened?"

"I really don't know," Fox replied, biting down on her lip and furrowing her brows. "It was like someone was flashing photographs in front of my eyes, but then it felt as if I was actually there too. I think I was… dreaming." She shook her head. "But I don't dream."

"Sounds more like visions to me." Bunny had sprung out of nowhere. "That is so cool; you could be a Saw! Wait until mum hears about this!" Bunny's boundless energy never failed to surprise (or slightly irritate) her sisters.

"A Saw?" Fox asked.

Bunny adopted an overly dramatic voice and swept her hand across the sky. "A woman who sees visions of the future."

"Great!" Fox huffed. "So now I'm a bloody clairvoyant."

"Got to go, we've got some information gathering to do," Bunny said, nodding her head in the direction of Evie, who was already fawning all over Jeremiah. He stood in the middle of the pretty, giggly welcoming committee, flashing his dazzling white teeth in a look of charmed amusement that irritated Fox immensely. Fox rolled her eyes and sighed. *Isn't he just loving it!*

As Bunny skipped over towards them, Jeremiah looked in her direction and clocked sight of Fox watching them. *Damn it, now he probably thinks you fancy him!*

Swan was talking to her, but she'd missed the first part of the conversation having been distracted by Idiot-Boy. "Clairvoyance is a great gift, Fox. Only the most powerful of our kind possess it."

"I don't want to be *powerful*," Fox snapped. "I quite like being a little bit gifted without all the craziness that goes with it. Look at Bunny; her gifts have made her totally daft. All those years of being able to get into mischief and never get caught have sent her wild. Imagine what they will be like when they finally come in properly."

Swan nudged Fox's elbow and smiled before teasing, "My, my, we have got the grumps on this morning, haven't we?"

They set off in the direction of the sixth-form block. Swan was in year twelve, just one year above her, even so once inside college they barely saw one another. Swan moved in a very small, secretive circle of friends and Fox had no idea where they hung out, and neither it seemed did anybody else. She didn't even really know who Swan's friends were apart from Fred, who was possibly more than just a friend, and Dottie, her close girlfriend since nursery school. Swan had always found her witch inheritance difficult to manage in the "normal" world and Fox suspected that the reason her friends were so few and so close were because they knew the truth about her. If that was the case, she was lucky. Fox wasn't close enough to anybody to drop that bombshell into their laps. Even Will, who she was sure had kind of guessed, was hardly someone she could properly share her secret with. If ever there was a least likely couple, it had to be her and Will. He was all sun-tussled hair and sporty and she was… what? A cliché of the girl who will take off her specs to reveal a true Miss World beauty? She snorted a laugh at the thought. No, not quite. She didn't wear glasses and despite not bothering with bronzer or gloss or any other alien face-paint product, she knew that she was quite pretty – just not the Will-would-be-interested kind of pretty.

The closest Fox came to having friends was that she spent her breaks and lunches with Carmen, Dave, and Stewart. They made a funny group, having been thrown together through the fact that they didn't really fit into any other of their year group tribes. Carmen was a gypsy, which meant an immediate rejection by any of the Heargton village children, as their parents had been trying to evict the gypsies from the common-land for the last eight years. Dave was a reject on grounds that he was obese, which it seemed was a criminal offence in Heargton. Of course it wasn't helped by the fact that Dave also had Star Wars obsession, believed in alien communication and had been able to recite the periodic table at the age of seven. Stewart was a reject on grounds that he was too scrawny (yes, the Heargton children had exacting standards) and that he had to wear glasses that looked like the bottom of jam jars. And Fox? Well, she was just Fox. A tomboy who'd always preferred climbing trees to the social popularity ladder. There wasn't anything obvious about Fox on the outside that made her a bit of a loner, but the other children had always intuitively kept their distance as if able to sense the power running through her blood.

When she had been younger, she'd been foolish enough to think it was a good thing to show everybody how clever you were. Her hand was always first up and invariably with the correct answer, which although endearing when you're in primary school, by the time she started secondary being able to answer *every* question correctly was tiresome for both her fellow students and her teachers. Over time, she'd learned it was best to keep quiet; to hide the fact you knew the answer, and your disbelief that nobody else appeared to. It wasn't until she was eight that she understood that not everybody had a photographic memory. Sometimes she wished she could swap her gift with Bunny's; she'd be able to use the gift of invisibility to maximum effect. But no! *And now there's the possibility that I'm a bloody clairvoyant!* she thought angrily. Every witch knew that clairvoyance was a curse. It was bad enough that she could recall everything she'd ever experienced, but now there was the chance that she'd recall everything that was yet to happen! No more surprises.

She was pulled from her grumps by hard physical contact with somebody. "Whoa, steady, Foxy!" Will said.

She blustered with embarrassment. "Sorry, miles away. I'm really sorry."

"Hey no worries, no harm done!" He punctuated his sentence with a wink, causing Fox to smile despite her bad mood.

Will ran his hand through his hair. It reminded Fox of the colour of pheasant feathers; burned chestnut, flecked with black. His green eyes twinkled. She could see what the other girls saw in him; he was certainly handsome, but he wasn't for her.

"I'm glad you bumped into me, I've been meaning to hunt you down." He laughed, amused by his own pun. Fox shot him a quizzical look. "Yes, I think you may have…" he paused whilst he fished around in his pocket, jiggling himself up and down in order to get his hand between the layers of

fitted dark denim. "Here! I think this might belong to you."
He held up the small silver pentagram on a long broken chain. Fox had noticed it missing but assumed it had fallen off somewhere in the garden.

"It must have fallen off when I gave you a lift the other night," he said.

Fox felt the uncomfortable heat of embarrassment. She had never displayed the pentagram openly, letting it nestle down under her clothing, close to her heart. She suddenly felt protective. "What makes you think it's mine? Surely you've had loads of ladies in your car over the weekend," she said teasingly in an attempt to be evasive. She really didn't want Will to know. *But why?*

"Of course," he said, emitting a short laugh, "but I've only given a lift to one witch!"

Fox snatched it out of his hands. "It's a pagan sign for Mother Nature not…"

Fox's defense was cut short by an attack of sound and light. It was so intense that it caused her to reach out and grab Will's arm for fear that she was about to buckle to the floor. He held her fast. It felt hard to breath, as if she had been running, chased down. It was night and she was in the woods, running towards the hill. A crack of lightening slit open the sky. Her ears were full with the sound of a crying child, and she knew intuitively that it was connected to the broken doll.

"Fox! Fox, can you hear me?" Will's concerned voice travelled through the vision and brought her back.

"What's happened?" Carmen asked as she bent down to try and see Fox's face. She pulled back Fox's hair and saw how pale and clammy she was.

"Shall I go and get someone?" Will asked. He was out of his depth and awkward.

"Nah, it's probably just her monthlies," Carmen replied squeezing Fox's hand reassuringly; Carmen rarely demonstrated social grace. Will felt his awkwardness spike.

"I'm fine. Really," Fox managed to croak. "I just need some air."

"Come on then," Carmen said, taking charge and pulling Fox down the corridor towards the door. "Watch out, will you!" she snapped at some poor unfortunate who happened to be walking innocently down the corridor.

Once outside, the cold spring air hit Fox in the face like a slap. She ran her hand through her straggly mop and took in a deep breath.

"That weren't your monthlies, was it? There's somethink up with you!"

"Some *thing*, Carmen. How many times do I have to tell you that?" Fox said snappily.

Carmen shook her head and pouted. "Don't deflect, Fox. I might not speak as posh as you, but I'm not half as stupid as you think. Some*thing* is going on, and I reckon I know what it is. Your third eye is opening."

Well trust a bloody gypsy! Fox stared hard at her and swallowed. *Maybe it is time to trust someone.*

3

The rest of Fox's day was taken up with classes and time in the I.C.T. suite manipulating photographic images for her Art portfolio. She escaped more attacks from the visions, but she wasn't able to completely forget the strange events of the morning and Carmen's words rattled around her head all afternoon. "Your third eye is opening." Fox knew exactly what the third eye was; there was no need for a trip to Wikipedia for that one, although that didn't stop Carmen from going on at length about "gateways of consciousness." Fox had had little choice but to let her rattle on about the various members of her family who had also been *blessed* with the gift, as she was hardly going to turn around and inform her that there were other members of her own *coven* who had "the gift."

Carmen had left college after lunch without any real explanation. She did this a lot; the social convention of eight 'til four didn't really apply to "her kind." Although Fox and Carmen had been friends throughout secondary school, their friendship didn't extend beyond the school gates. Fox had never been one for play-dates, either hosting them or attending them. Not that Carmen had ever invited her over. The camp didn't invite outsiders. Fox had carried, like a lot of people, a developed set of assumptions about Carmen and her gypsy family, many of which had been challenged over the years of getting to know her. It was a shame that others hadn't made the same effort. Carmen was clever but her years of endless moving around during her primary school years had left big holes in basic curriculum so that others were quick to make the (costly) mistake that she wasn't very bright. People didn't understand that the National Curriculum was pretty limiting when it came to learning the stuff that really mattered.

Unlike the representation of gypsies on the reality TV shows, Carmen's father did not sleep on a mattress stuffed full of fifty pound notes, and it was painfully clear to everybody that Carmen came from a very poor background. Throughout her secondary school years, she had worn stout black army surplus boots (the same pair from year seven to eleven, the only difference being the amount of newspaper stuffing in the toe) and her school woolen stockings had been made up more of darning thread than actual wool. Fox had never seen her wear a coat, even through the winters when it had snowed. But despite Carmen's obvious poverty and her slight lack of personal hygiene, she was jaw-droppingly beautiful, and she knew it, wearing it like a magic talisman. Her thick, black curly hair always smelled of rose talc (the means by which she cleaned it) and it was threaded with shells and beads, in the same way as her father's. Her eyes, dark pools that pulled you into their vortex, were lined with heavy khol. Carmen dressed her face in the same way others dressed their bodies. She wore a silver ring in her nose (much to the establishment's disapproval) and a small scattering of tattooed stars danced around her eyebrow. Carmen didn't have a large wardrobe, and her clothes were often a mishmash rainbow effect, which Fox always thought beautiful. But she also knew that they hid the stark reality of living with no electricity or water supplies, and with an overly romantic father who would happily have the world returned to the dark ages.

Fox had only spoken with him once, although she had seen him around the village often; he was hard to miss at six-foot-eight and dressed like a Viking. Carmen had assured her that despite his fierce appearance, he was the gentlest man you could meet. It was whilst she was musing on Carmen's life that Fox heard the familiar voice of Will behind her. She jumped, turning to see not only Will but also Jeremiah.

"Feeling any better?" Jeremiah asked.

Fox mumbled something.

"Good job I was there or else you'd fallen flat on your face, hey?" Will teased.

Jeremiah looked confused, he had no memory of Will being anywhere near Fox that morning.

Will finally got around to telling her what they were doing. "I'm giving Jay the tour. He's taking History too, so we'll be hanging out together a lot."

Great! she thought sarcastically. Fox managed to control the sarcasm of her inner voice and pull together the slightly more sincere response of, "Excellent! What else are you taking?" whilst thinking, *please don't let there be any more of my subjects.*

"French and Literature."

"Same as me then," she said, turning back to the computer screen in order to avoid Jeremiah seeing the roll of her eyes.

Fox tried to ignore them as Will showed Jeremiah around the room, pointing out the location of various supplies and other random, useless stuff. At last, Will had exhausted the excitement (and cupboards) of the I.C.T. suite and they headed towards the door. Just when she thought she was about to be left in peace, Will was back by her side.

"Do you fancy ditching the school bus tonight? I'm happy to give you a lift. I've got some errands to run in Heargton village."

Well that was left-field the internal piped up. Fox was silenced by surprise. An embarrassing tension hung between them. Will was asking a perfectly innocent and friendly question *(yeah, right!)* and Jeremiah watched the event unfold with a strangely intense curiosity. *He's asking you on a date!'* Fox shook that thought away as quick as if she'd just picked up a burning coal.

"I um..." Fox's throat felt thick and she coughed, "I'm sorry, I've got... tutorial after school." Will's face made an unexpected fall. *When did this all this Will weirdness start?* Then she was back-peddling, "But it's only for ten minutes, if you can wait that long?"

Will cracked a smile that looked like an expression of relief. "No problem! I'll meet you at half-past. That should give you plenty of time."

They left and Fox found her head travelling fast towards her waiting palm.

He's going to wait for you for half an hour - that's dedication! Fox heard her inner voice collapse into its own weird little laughter but she wasn't sharing the joke. *I think I've just agreed to a date with Will! What the...*

Fox didn't really have a tutorial after school and now she had to somehow find a way of making it all look authentic. That was the problem with lies, they always came back and bit you on the backside. She'd agreed to meet Will in the common room, hoping that by half-past everybody else would have left. The last thing she needed was the college rumour-mill to start clicking. Fox decided that the best course of action would be to head towards the history rooms and hang out there for ten or fifteen minutes before heading towards their meeting place. That way, she could almost convince herself that she hadn't been lying. She hated liars.

This plan was all going well, until she bumped into Jeremiah. God knows what he was doing *(waiting for you* her internal teased) but he was sat on the staircase newel post, chomping down on a peach. Rather than offer the usual greeting you might expect between acquaintances, he looked at her and continued to eat his peach. *Well this is awkward!* Fox thought, resenting the fact that he was making her now fluster out some form of non-lame greeting, one that showed no hint of attraction or irritation, or…

"What are you doing here?" she blurted in the hostile tone that had become default where Jeremiah was concerned.

Whether it was his general arrogance or that he just wasn't very emotionally intelligent, Jeremiah shook off her hostility and flashed her a smile before cryptically replying, "I was curious."

He returned to his peach and sucked the remaining flesh from the nut.

"Curious?" Fox asked with an involuntary screwing up of her face. "About what, exactly?"

"Curious as to whether you really did have a tutorial or whether you were just trying to brush Will off."

He popped the nut of the fruit into his mouth and then retrieved it with juice-covered fingers. Fox found herself staring at him and she wasn't sure if she was revolted or fascinated by him. Jeremiah continued playfully,

"I don't exactly understand why you'd want to brush him off. I mean he's a handsome guy and clearly from our walk around the school today, he could have his pick of girls — and yet, he seems to have chosen you."

Fox's mouth gaped wide with incredulity. Even the internal had been silenced by Jeremiah's audacious rudeness. She tried to form a stinging, witty retort but words turned to fluttering butterflies in her head and all she could manage to pluck from the chaos was,

"What the hell has any of this got to do with you?" She felt on fire from the chest up and was so seething with anger that she honestly thought she might just go and push the cocky bastard from his post. *Hopefully he might crack his head open!* the internal, finally alert, added for good measure.

She could see him watching this reaction and it wasn't what she had hoped for. He looked completely unaffected. He tipped his head slightly to one side and said, "As I said, I was just curious."

She stormed past him, desperate that she might accidentally on purpose cause him to fall, but he didn't. She heard his voice call up the stairs after her, "By the way, it's Monday so all the staff are in their meeting."

Fox stopped but continued to look towards the top of the stairs. She knew he was about to make the death blow and put her into checkmate. She didn't want to give him the satisfaction of seeing her face as he did.

"So it's strange that your teacher would have arranged a tutorial knowing they wouldn't be able to make it, isn't it?" he asked.

Fox reached for the banister. She'd have to turn down the stairs and walk past him. There was no other way out. *What the hell is this jerk's problem?* the internal asked. Fox had no answer. She had never in her whole life been treated so… viciously… yes, that was the word, Jeremiah was vicious. *But why? Why is he picking on us - I mean you - me? Jeez, now I have a split personality! Let's just thump him and get out of here!*

Fox took in a deep breath, planted a large smile on her face and turned, trying to aim for perfect composure as she walked down the stairs.

"Why, of course," she started to walk down the stairs, her jaw clenched. "It's Monday, my mistake, the tutorial is on Tuesday. How silly of me."

She'd never felt so relieved to feel a door handle in her grasp. She pushed open the door and called out without looking, "See you later," and then dropped her voice to add, "asswipe" as she stormed off across the quad.

She was still fuming when she reached the common room. On seeing her, Will leaped to his feet and almost knocked over his can of coke.

"Everything okay?" he asked.

"Fine!" she replied sharply. Will visibly winced and feeling bad about taking it out on him.

"Sounds like you could do with a cuppa?" he offered.

The internal sprang into life, *So it isn't just a lift then?* "Tea?" he asked. Fox was about to say no, but that would mean somehow Jeremiah was winning (not that she knew quite how). "Yes," she let out a small laugh, "tea would be lovely. Sara's does the best tea and cake in the village." Fox smirked. "Well, to be fair, it is the only teashop in the village."

"Sara's it is then." Will picked up his bag and led the way out towards his car.

They spent the journey from Fallford to Heargton chatting easily about music and their plans to go to The Green Man Festival in the summer. The festival, known by the locals as The Green was the major highlight of the year and it was thanks to the sudden influx of yearly festival-goers that most of Heargton's shops and businesses managed to survive the rest of the year. It had started as a small folk festival in The Green Man pub but it had soon outgrown it and now took place in the clearing of Raven's Wood, in the grounds of the old Asylum, which nestled at the bottom of the Heargton Ancient Burial Mound. As a result, the festival attracted just the right clientele for Moonstone.

The old Asylum (known as the Rookeries Hospital) had been built by the Ravenheart family on their lands purportedly as a charitable act of kindness towards the villagers. It had been a maternity hospital and general medical center when it had first been built, but within a very short time, there was a terrible fire in which tens of people had been killed. When it was rebuilt, it opened as a lunatic asylum. Buried deep in Raven's Wood you'd think that it would not have been possible to hear the howls of the insane, but when the wind blew their cries up over the trees, they travelled deep into the heart of the village. They were dark times for those that lived there. There were those in the village that believed some of patients never left its walls. Ever since she was little, Fox had been told that the wind that rattled through the hightopped pines of Raven's Wood were really the screams of ghostly lunatics. Despite being old enough to disbelieve local fairytales, she could never suppress a shiver when she heard that low mournful sound.

Dark superstitions had cloaked the village of Heargton from its earliest times. The cruciform village had sprouted because of the ancient burial ground to the west of the village. It sat between the river and Raven's Wood. At the center of the village was a communal well, with water that sprang from a deep rock spring. Lay lines ran through the village from northwest to southeast and from northeast to southwest, meaning that the Crossroads and the Heargton Well sat at a crossover point. The whole village vibrated with an ancient and powerful energy. It was no coincidence that Ravenheart Hall, the Church, Coldstone House, and Meadowsweet cottage all sat directly on top of lay lines. Unfortunately, it was no coincidence that the Rookeries had also sat right on top of the lay line transit either.

There were those who believed the Ravenheart family had never intended for the original hospital to survive; rumour was that they'd set the place on fire themselves in order that the lunatic asylum could happen through stealth. There was a strange and dangerous energy that went with lunacy, and that coupled with the natural magnetic energy of the lay-line intersection created a powerful cocktail just waiting to be harnessed.

Heargton was a ghost hunter's paradise. The ancient energies acted like a giant cobweb, ensnaring the souls of poor unfortunates. On the road to Fallford, (the north exit from the village) the ghost of Highway-Man Bob Tassack spent his time causing numerous car accidents every year. He seemed to have a particular axe to grind with red cars. There had been three fatal crashes (each one involving a red car) in the last eighteen months and each had happened at exactly the same spot. A shrine of faded flowers and photos slipped into plastic wallets marked the place as a creepy reminder of the fact that each time the parish council had cleared the memorials, another crash had taken place the very next day. Out of cynical-superstition, the last lot of memorials had been left to decay naturally, and so far, so good.

Then there was Coldstone House, at the far Southern boundary of the village, reputed to be one of the most haunted houses in the county; if you didn't count the Rookeries Hospital, or The Green Man Pub or Ravenheart Hall, of course. Most of the villagers, including Will laughed it all off as hocus-pocus rubbish, but not the Meadowsweet sisters, they knew that all of the myths surrounding the lay lines were true. And so did Carmen and her father.

The winter afternoon was dark but fortunately it was still too early for the ghost of Highway Bob to be out on the Fallford Road, so Will managed to get them safely to Heargton despite his car being red. Fox kept him company as he ran his errands, which involved dropping off a parcel at the vicarage and picking up a jar of honey from the health food store for his grandfather. Then they headed to Sara's. By now it was dark, and the warm yellow light of the tea-shop was softened into a welcoming glow by the condensation fogging the windows. With the setting of the sun, the day had turned bitter cold and the warmth of the tea shop hit Fox like a blast as she tinkled the bell of the door. It was busy. Sara's was a popular meeting point in the village, especially on nights like these when promise of her homemade apple pie and continental hot chocolate made a welcome relief from the winter greys. There was only one table left, right in the back corner, which meant that all of the villagers had a good eye-full of the middle Meadowsweet on a date with a handsome young man! Fox huddled Will into the corner and made her way to the counter to place their order.

She shrugged it off. She'd known when she'd suggested Sara's that it was hardly going to be discreet. Sara was one of mum's closest friends. As the only female business owners in the village they'd become comrades in arms on the Parish Business Forum. Sara was also a regular customer at Moonstone. She believed in angels. Her belief came from a desperate hope. All three of her baby girls had been born sleeping. Their little graves stood in a sad tidy row in the village churchyard. The thought that they'd been carried to heaven in the arms of an angel made the pain a little more bearable for her. Nobody from the village ever mocked her for her belief, nor joked about the hundreds of angels that were scattered all over Sara's Tea Room. Everybody respected the strength it must have taken for her to get up every morning and put a smile on her face – and if it was the strength of the angels then they were welcome to the village.

Sara smiled conspiratorially at Fox as she poured the tea from the giant pot. "So, who's the hunk?" she whispered.

Fox cast an involuntary glance towards Will, who as if on cue was running his hair through his straggly chestnut hair like he was on some posh underpants advert. She blushed and let out a laugh. “Him?” she said with the most dismissive tone she could muster.

“Are you on a date?”

“No!” Fox said a little too passionately, before dropping her voice and mumbling, “I don’t think so.”

Sara laughed. “I think *he* might think you are.”

“Nah, we’re just friends,” Fox said, waving her hand in the air.

“If you say so!” Sara gave a wink and turned her attention to the milk.

Not a date? If it looks like a date, and it sounds like a date then… the internal chimed.

“It’s not a date. I don’t even fancy him!” Fox muttered under her breath.

“Pardon?” Sara asked distractedly.

“Nothing! I was just… talking to myself; do it all the time!”

“Here you go. Want anything else to go with that? How about some warm scones?”

If Satan had been carrying a tray of Sara’s warm scones when he tried to tempt Jesus in the desert, then it would have all turned out very differently. Before Fox could answer, two fat cheese scones were slapped onto a plate and the tray shoved into her direction.

“It’s on the house! I’ll bill your mother later,” she said through a smile.

“Thanks.”

"Enjoy!"

Will had been busying himself rummaging through his satchel looking for his lost phone. He smiled when Fox set down the scones and put the satchel on the floor, offering her his undivided attention. A slightly awkward atmosphere settled between them.

"Well, this is… nice!" Will offered by way of conversation.

Fox wasn't really sure what reply to make. She didn't want it to sound as if this were all more significant than it was. She didn't get the chance to worry for long.

Blinding lights flashed in her eyes and there was the echo-sound of yapping dogs and men shouting; lots of them. They were searching for something. Everything screamed desperation. Fox felt the hard wooden table gripped in her hands but it was no longer that – she now held something else in her hands: a large metal torch. Her foot hit something on the ground, and she knew without looking that it was the wretched doll with her broken face. It was almost the same vision she'd had already that day, only indiscernible things had changed. The voices of the men were now joined by another voice, a woman's, and she was calling out,

"Has anybody seen Martha? Anybody? Please! Please! She still hasn't come home and the police… the police…"

"Fox! Fox can you hear me?" Will's voice travelled through the chaos and pulled her back into the room. Something was terribly wrong. With her back to the door she hadn't seen Martha's mother come into the tearoom, calling out.

" I thought I was... " Fox didn't finish as Martha's mother's pleas came again.

"Please – does anybody know where my little girl is?"

Sara shot around from the counter and swept Mrs. Paisley up in her arms, guiding her to a chair and sitting her down. The whole teashop stopped their chatter to watch the unfolding drama.

"Mrs. Paisley, Annie, slowly now, tell us what's happened?"

Mrs. Paisley was crumpled on her chair, sobbing heavily into one of the napkins, making her words difficult to follow. "She went with that lad, Jack... Saturday. Nobody's seen her since."

Sara wrapped her arms around the woman's shoulders and soothed her. One of the village women, who wore a purple coat and matching hat, left her seat and made her way around the back of the counter to pour a cup of tea from the large tea-pot on the side. She hurried back, placing it into Mrs. Paisley's quivering hands.

"I don't know what to do," Mrs. Paisley said, looking up into Sara's eyes. Sara choked back her own tears as she saw the greatest of a mother's fears – loss. "Please help me," Mrs. Paisley wept.

Sara breathed in deeply. The angels were at her shoulder and they whispered to her; told her things that only she could hear.

"What did the police say?" Sara asked, trying to ignore the message they'd delivered.

"The police found her mobile phone out at the abandoned railway station. What was it doing there? Oh," she whimpered. "Something terrible has happened, I can feel it."

Sara didn't let on that the terrible, gut-wrenching feeling that Mrs. Paisley was experiencing was the angels speaking to her and they weren't offering her good news. The purple-clad lady crouched down and took Mrs. Paisley's hands between her own.

"Now, now, Annie – no such thing. You know what girls are like at that age. Goodness, when I think back to the worry I put my own mother through."

Fox watched in fascination, unable to imagine the lady in purple ever being younger than the smart seventy-year-old lady now offering comfort.

Fox cleared her throat and plucked up the courage to interrupt the mothers' circle to ask the distraught Mrs. Paisley, "Where did they go on Saturday?"

The whole teashop turned towards Fox, surprised by the sound of her voice. Mrs. Paisley took a moment to stare at the pretty girl before recognising her as one of Martha's school friends.

"They went out towards May Hill. There was a party. Did you go?" she asked suddenly lifted by the hope of any connection.

Fox shook her head and Mrs. Paisley dropped her shoulders, turning her attention back to the women who attended her.

"I didn't want her to go. I begged her not to go. We argued. Oh, horrible things were said." Mrs. Paisley collapsed into a heap of sobs.

Several of her neighbours came forward and offered comfort, leaving the rest of the teashop customers redundant and suddenly lacking in appetite.

"I'll go and call Constable Peters. See if he'll come over," Sara said, leaving Mrs. Paisley in capable hands.

Fox and Will returned their attention to their table.

"I thought it was strange that she wasn't at school today!" Will offered in hushed tones. "She's never missed school in all the years I've known her and there was an important assessment."

"Was Jack in?" Fox asked.

"Nope. Didn't think much of it. He's always been a bit of a flake."

"Let's get out of here," Fox offered.

They wrapped their scones in paper napkins and Fox grabbed two of the paper cups from on the counter before waving Sara a silent goodbye. Will led them to the car and flopped in with the clear expectation that she would follow his lead. It would have made more sense at this point to say goodbye and head the short distance home, but it seemed that sense wasn't really playing her part today. Fox got in and balanced her tea precariously on the dashboard.

"So what do you think has happened then?" Will asked.

"I don't know – they've probably decided to play Romeo and Juliet for a couple of days?"

"Really?" Will raised an eyebrow. "The candle girl and the choir boy – sneaking off for some alone time. Hardly likely is it?"

"Well I don't know!" Fox said more snappily than she'd intended.

"Well haven't you got some kind of witch-thing that makes you privy to that kind of information?"

Fox looked at him hard, trying to work out exactly what Will had just said to her, but just like the casualness of his tone, he was busy tucking into his scone as if nothing weird had just gone between them.

"What is it with you and this whole… witch thing?" she asked.

Will appeared surprised by Fox's negative reaction. "What 'witch *thing*'?" he asked innocently.

"Well first the jokes about my house, then the necklace and now – this!" she flustered.

" I don't know why you're getting so upset. It's not like it bothers me or anything."

"Bothers you! Bothers you!" she raged. "Why the hell should it bother you?"

Will held his hands up in submission. "Calm down, Foxy. It's no big deal. I just thought maybe you had some kind of – I don't know – gift for that kind of thing."

Fox was too wired to speak; all she could do was look at Will as if he were an alien from out of space. They were silent as they finished their scones and tea. There wasn't much for them to say. Martha would probably turn up. She wasn't the sort to run away and join a Parisian pole-dancing troupe, but then again, maybe that made it all the more worrying.

When Fox arrived home, she found the house empty except for their mother.

"Where is everybody?" she asked.

"Out doing a leaflet drop for Martha." Her mother turned from the stove and wiped her hands on her pinny. She looked worried but she smiled and said with forced brightness, "I'm sure she'll be home soon. You know what it's like. She's young and in…"

The telephone rang, interrupting her sentence. Fox cursed in her head. She had hoped to take the opportunity to talk to her mother about the visions. She had a horrible feeling that they were connected to Martha's disappearance but she didn't know how.

Her mother returned from the hall with the phone lodged under her chin. It was Sara. Fox rolled her eyes. It would only be a matter of minutes before her mother knew all about her "date" with Will. She wasn't going to sit around and wait for the guaranteed interrogation. Their mother was pretty laid back about their freedoms but for some reason, the boy issue was one area their mother liked to play the role of the over-protective, paranoid parent. That's why Bunny caused so much anxiety; she'd flirt with a pair of trousers hanging on the washing-line given half a chance.

Fox walked by the cooling fairy cakes and grabbed one, hot potato-ing it between her hands as she headed towards the stairs. It was Swan's birthday in a couple of days, and despite Swan now being at college, mum still insisted that she took in a tray of cupcakes for the class, much to Swan's embarrassment and everybody else's delight. Fox always had brownies and Bunny millionaire shortbread. It had always been so. Once in her room, she flicked on some music and picked up her book. It was some American paranormal witch story; always good for a bit of amused eye-rolling. If only it were true that you could conduct lightening out the tips of your fingers or turn people into stone. Unfortunately, her experience of witchcraft so far was all a little less Hollywood and a little bit more barefoot and flowers – or so she thought. Her thoughts returned back to the night at Coldstone House when Amber had dropped the glasses. She had even surprised herself by that little parlor trick. Prior to that, she had only ever managed to get a set of Lego to mysteriously form itself into a small car (when she had been four), and had healed a crack in one of her mother's favourite plates – but nothing on the scale of magically healing ten crystal glasses. *He saw you, you know!* the internal said. *That boy was watching you. You've got to be more careful. There's something wrong.*

Of course there was a dark side to witchcraft. Every witch had to make her choice between the light and the dark, but in the days of science and progress there weren't many who turned to the dark. With the increasing social rejection of God as a quirky superstition, so had the idea of Satan and his minions. *Maybe that is why paranormal books had become so popular,* she mused – *a nostalgic desire for when the world had clearly defined monsters.* Now the monster was the man sitting next to you on the bus, or the woman looking after your children in the nursery. Evil and darkness had become insidious. A sneak-thief, stealing lives from under the very nose of the priest.

The Ravenheart Sisters continued (according to Wren) to play the part of the black coven, but in reality they'd been lacking any power for many generations. They were a parody of themselves, still insisting on wearing dark velvets and overly heavy eye-make up. If the three Ravenheart sisters hadn't been so stunningly beautiful they would certainly have become the laughing stock of the county. Somewhere, far back in their bloodline, there had been Italian blood and even now, many centuries after becoming considered an English Coven, the Ravenheart women had that natural Mediterranean beauty. The youngest Ravenheart, Thalia, was still at college, in the same year as Fox, but the other two sisters spent their days entertaining their posh friends… and … Fox shook her head and shrugged. She couldn't think what the two of them possibly did all day up at that crazy big house.

They lived in a grand Tudor Manor house, spooky as shit, nestled into the bottom of the burial mound, deep in Raven's Wood. They'd never had any desire to keep a low profile; the house was called Ravenheart Hall, the woods Raven's Wood and even the hospital they had founded had been called the Rookeries. Ego was their middle name.

Wren never liked to speak of them, especially in the cottage. Although no longer powerful, the Ravenheart sisters were still cloaked in a shadow that she didn't wish to invite in.

The Meadowsweet and Ravenheart covens had been rivals since the 1600s. They had never been destined to be friends, but then again it was highly unusual for two covens to live in such close proximity; covens were notoriously territorial. Thalia was the nicest of the three, from the little experience Fox had of their company (mum had made a special point of never letting them spend too much time together). Thalia was slim with black wavy hair down past her shoulders, which she always wore up in one of those messy buns that looks effortless and beautiful but whenever you try to replicate it looks like you've been attacked. She had a heavy fringe, which was an effective tool enabling her to peer at people with her huge, black lined eyes. She moved like a slinky, all hips and wiggles. Boys literally drooled when she spoke to them. It didn't help her relationships with the other girls that as well as being beautiful she was sporty and also a talented musician. She'd had the lead in every school production for the last five years. Not that Fox was particularly resentful of that being that her singing voice sounded like a seagull stuck arse-first up a fog-horn. Mind, it didn't half piss off Bunny, who would have easily been the most attractive girl in college if it hadn't been for Thalia.

Are all these rambling thoughts an attempt to put off going to sleep? the internal asked.

Fox looked at the clock. It was eight-thirty, which was ridiculously early for her, but all afternoon she'd felt the pull of bed. She needed to rest. The visions had made her feel like she'd gone a week without sleep. There was also a part of her that wanted to return to them, even though they made her entrails turn icy. She knew there was more to them, something about Martha.

She lay down and handed herself over to the quiet. She was just drifting when her door flew open and Bunny came rushing in.

"Have you heard about Martha?" she asked, flicking on the light switch.

Fox rolled over and groaned at the bright assault of light, "Jeez, haven't you two ever heard of knocking?"

"Well it's not as if you're sleep…" Bunny stopped and looked at her intensely. "So what are you doing in bed at this time of night? Are you sick?"

"No!"

"Oh, sorry - *personal* time!"

Fox reached for the nearest projectile that she could, which was a heavy copy of *Middlemarch*, and hurled it in Bunny's general direction with the aim to miss. It caught her toe causing her to erupt into an impression of a furious foul-mouthed toad.

"You total bitch!"

"Get lost!" Fox replied.

Swan's calm voice cut through the sibling bickering. "She came to tell you about Martha."

"I've heard," Fox said sulkily.

"What? That they've found her dress in the well?"

Fox sat bolt upright in bed. "The well?"

"Yes."

"Oh my God!" Fox's hand flew to her mouth.

Swan came in and took a seat on the end of the bed. "You're in bed early."

Fox rolled her eyes. Who would have thought that having an early night was such a crime. "Yes, I…"

Swan didn't wait for her to finish. "Bunny and I were talking, you know about how strange it was that you should start having visions on the day that Martha goes missing. Have you seen anything?"

Fox thought back over the visions. They were a mish-mash of images and voices. There was nothing substantial; certainly nothing that directly linked to Martha Paisley. She was too old for dolls. Fox shook her head. "No, nothing about Martha – just the woods, the sound of the police dogs yapping, men calling and the bright flashlights."

"Nothing else?" Swan asked.

Fox had hoped to keep the doll to herself. It sounded over dramatic, as if it were a prop from some cliché horror film and yet there was something about that doll. Swan was gazing at her and she suddenly realised that she had been zoning out again. "There is a doll with a broken face."

"A doll? How creepy!" Bunny said.

"Who does the doll belong to? Is it Martha's?"

"No." Fox shook her head. Her answers were coming as if from somebody else. "It isn't Martha they are searching for; it's a child. The doll belongs to one of the children from the village."

"Past, present, or future?" asked Swan.

"I don't know." Fox felt an overwhelming sadness wash over her and she started to cry. The unexpected and out of character emotion prompted Bunny into action.

"Why are you crying? Fox, what's happening? You never cry."

Fox shook her head slowly from side to side. The feeling was alien and uncomfortable. If this was what grief felt like, she hoped she'd never have to feel it close to home.

"I'm going to get mum," Bunny said.

"Leave it, Bunny. Give Fox some time. Let her talk to mum in the morning."

"Mum should know. She'd want to know."

Swan left Fox a crumpled, weeping mess on the bed and walked over to Bunny. She leaned in and whispered something that Fox couldn't quite catch. They had never had secrets; well, not ones that really mattered. All at once if felt as if their safe little world was beginning to crack. Fox could feel the darkness waiting on the outside. Biding its time. Waiting.

"What's happening to me, Swan?" Fox cried.

Swan switched off the light and ushered Bunny out of the room before stopping mid-door close. She whispered across the darkness, "Sssh, try and get some rest. We'll talk in the morning. Mum will know what to do. Mum always knows what to do."

*

Fox floated into sleep with the image of Martha's dress billowing down into the dark, dank of the well. She could see every detail, down to the stitching of the cuffs. Pure white, printed with blue birds in flight. Fox remembered seeing her wear it to The Green Man back in the summer. She had looked so pretty, with her blonde hair all tousled up and decorated with pearls. She'd been up to her wellies in mud; they all had. It had been the wettest festival on record… and one of the best.

Fox and the dress fell into the darkness. The further she fell away from the light, the colder she became. Dread swam through her veins. Wherever they were heading to, there was going to be pain. Fox was sure of it. Somewhere in the distance, out of sight, a dog barked. Fox didn't need to see it to know that it was vicious. The sound of yanking chains told her that she wasn't the only one who thought so.

Her feet were now on solid ground, stood in mud filled craters chipped out of hard-pressed ground. She was surrounded by fields and in the distance the tree line that bordered woodland. The place felt familiar to her, although she couldn't recall where it was or what it was called. She knew before turning that to her left was a dilapidated hay barn. Golden light shone from between the broken planks. There was the sound of many feet moving, then the muffled cry of a girl. Then the screaming began and Fox couldn't decide whether to throw up or to run. Her heart gagged her mouth. The screams were like a terrible song and they belonged to Martha Paisley.

*

"Noooo!" Fox's screams brought her sisters and mother running. When they arrived they found Fox standing in the middle of the room, her hands tearing through her hair and a wild look in her eye. When she saw the concerned faces of her kin she turned to them and uttered, "She's gone. They've killed her!"

Swan's hand flew to her mouth as she surged towards Fox. "No! No! Tell me it isn't true."

Wren turned to Bunny and issued her instructions to go and put the kettle on. They would need sweet tea. They would need to talk. Bunny began to protest, "But… what does she mean? Who are 'they'?"

Wren ushered Bunny towards the stairs. "We'll meet you downstairs. Swan, please help your sister with the tea. I'll bring Fox down in a minute."

Swan squeezed Fox's hand before following after a slightly petulant Bunny. Wren stepped into the room and closed the door behind her. They rarely shut doors. They rarely had secrets. Times were different.

"You saw?"

Fox nodded.

"When did the visions start?"

"This morning."

"And you didn't think to tell me?"

Fox shook her head. "I thought they would pass. I thought it was just my imagination."

"And now?"

"Mum, help me. I don't want to be a Saw. I don't want these things in my head." Fox started to sob once more.

"Ssh, darling. You have to accept the gifts that Mother Nature has bestowed on you, and you are gifted, Fox. I always knew in my heart you would be special."

"Why not Swan? She's so much more…" Fox couldn't find the exact word, but Swan had always been so intuitive, so… otherworldly, not like Fox, who had always prided herself on being the most grounded, and sane, of the Meadowsweets.

Wren came close to her and held her in way that they hadn't done for years. Fox had always been the one least into public displays of affection. She'd squirmed in her mother's arms since the day she had been born - always desperate to escape the constraints of a cuddle in order to get out and do something. Tonight she understood why being held was so important. Sometimes a hug was the only thing physically holding you together, and she was certain that if her mother were to let go, she might just unravel all over the floor.

"Sweetheart, I know that it's hard but I need to ask you what you saw." Wren stroked her daughter's hair affectionately. It felt nice. It felt safe. "Do you think you can tell me?"

Fox began to nod her head. She didn't want to revisit the vision, not that she had seen much. It was the feeling. A feeling that she wasn't sure she'd be able to put into words. How do you convey the feeling of death, the feeling of violence, the sound of a scream?

"I didn't see anything," she said truthfully. "Just fields and trees and a barn." She shook the thought of the barn away. "There was a dog," she said, desperate to please her mother with details when in truth everything was insubstantial.

"That's good, you're doing good. What kind of dog?"

"I don't know. I didn't see it, I only heard it."

"And when you heard it, what did your imagination conjure up?"

"A big black dog. Eyes flashing green. Impossibly big. The size of a… no," Fox stopped and let out a sigh of frustration. "My imagination is running wild. It's clouding the visions."

"Say what came to mind, even if you don't think it can be true."

Fox closed her eyes tight, tried to enter back into the moment she heard the dog bark. She began to tremble. She didn't want to hear the sound of Martha's screams again. Each one had been a blade in her stomach.

"It was as big as a… as a lion!" She opened her eyes and looked apologetically at her mother. "See, I told you. My imagination is all over the place."

"Never mind. Was there anything else?"

"Just the barn. An old hay barn. I had the strangest feeling that we'd been there before but I don't know when."

"Was it in the village? Was it one of the farms out over the railway track?"

"No!" Fox shook her head, "I don't think so. I don't know, I can't be certain."

Swan called to them up the stairs to let them know that the tea was ready. Wren untangled Fox from her arms and walked towards the door. "Put your dressing gown on, you're shivering."

Fox, like an obedient child, did as she was told and followed her mother down the stairs to await the full interrogation of her sisters. Bunny was sure to be merciless, she'd want to know every little detail. Fox wished that she knew more. Swan poured the tea from the pot and Wren grabbed the cookie tin from the cupboard. Flipping the lid, it spun on the table making an uncomfortable racket. She put her hand out to still it.

"You said 'they,' 'they've killed her,' you said."

"Who did you mean?" Swan asked.

Fox thought about it. She didn't know exactly but there was part of her brain that felt sure it did; but it was out of reach, in the same way that sometimes the word is on the tip of your tongue but even a gun at your head won't set it free. It was like snatching at ghosts.

She shook her head. "I'm really sorry, I don't know. I don't even know if it was a 'they.' All I heard was the screaming."

Fox's hand trembled and she grabbed it with the other in order to steady it. She hated to show such weakness in front of her sisters. She'd always prided herself on being strong, unshakeable.

"So what do we do now?" Bunny asked. "Should we go to the police?"

Swan and Wren exchanged looks and sighed. "No, sweetie," Wren said. "They wouldn't welcome our… interference. And to be honest, we don't have anything anyway – just a few vague impressions, which could just as easily have been a nightmare as a vision."

"That's right," Swan said, squeezing Fox's hand. "I'd only just told you about the dress before you fell asleep. It was probably your mind playing tricks on you."

Fox returned a tight smile in recognition of Swan's attempt to make her feel better. "I hope so, because if her screams were real then…"

"Try not to think of it, darling," Wren said, standing and walking over to the sink with the empty teacups. A gesture that was intended to clearly draw a line under the night's discussion.

Fox stood and drew the belt of her dressing gown tightly. She had no desire to sleep. She knew that the screams were waiting for her and there was no doubt in her mind that they had been real.

*

Fox mistakenly thought that if she could fight against sleep, she could fight against the visions, but they weren't discriminating; they were just as happy to attack her in her waking state as when she was sleeping. As Fox lay on her bed looking out of the window and up at the star-sprinkled sky, her body began to move as if walking. When she looked down, it was to find her feet back on that dirt track by the barn. This time there was no screaming, just the sound of a group of voices chanting in unison. They were not words that Fox recognised. They belonged to some other ancient language. A dark energy buzzed all around her and she knew that if she were to be discovered, her soul would be in mortal danger. She crept forward, stilling her breath as best she could. Something in the distance alerted the dog and all at once it erupted into a mass of ferocious barking.

"It's just a rabbit," said one of the voices from within the barn. It was female and strangely melodic, suggesting the owner was young and pretty.

"Yeah, you're probably right."

"Ssh, will you two focus.

"Sorry, it's just…"

"Just. Be. Quiet!"

Silence fell between them. Fox counted three of them, either that or the rest were very silent, but she didn't think so. A slithering feeling worked its way through her belly. One of the voices sounded familiar. Too familiar.

The chanting began again. Fox bent forward and brought her eye to a gap in the wood paneling. No sooner had it focused on the scene in front of her than she threw herself backwards and clasped her hand over her mouth. She fought the overwhelming desire to be sick. It didn't matter how fast she tried to unsee the scene before her, it was branded onto the lens of her eyes. Fox began to run.

What have they done to her eyes? the internal asked.

When Fox shook the ghastly thought away, the internal screamed in her head, *What the hell have they done with Martha's eyes?*

Safely at the boundary of the woods, Fox stopped and leant against a tree, gasping for cool air, hoping it would calm the polluted bile rising in her throat.

"Oh, Mother Goddess!" she cried. "How could you do that to her?"

She was still alive, she was still moving.

She was alive when they had taken her eyes.

And her tongue the internal added out of nowhere.

Fox had tried to blank it out. One horror was enough, but the internal was persistent. *Didn't you see the dried blood around her mouth? Didn't you see her empty scream?*

"No! No! NO!" Fox roared into the night.

"Ssh, my darling. Ssh, my darling." The sound of Fox's mother brought her back into the world, which all at once seemed a lot darker place.

4

Five years of daily routine ensured that somehow Fox arrived at college and made it to her period one class, History. She sat quietly waiting for the rest of the class to arrive. She had a habit of being early.

The teacher, Mr. Saxon (a rather excellent name for a history teacher, Fox had always thought), arrived looking flustered and in rather an eccentric clothes ensemble. With red trousers, a mustard and mulberry striped shirt, and a navy polka-dot tie, the poor man looked like a walking sample swatch. He was unshaven and Fox noticed his wedding ring finger was lacking the essential wedding ring. It was possible that he had just taken it off to shower and had forgotten to put it back on, but he didn't look like he'd brushed his hair, not alone showered.

As he rummaged around in his bag, retrieving a selection of dog-eared pieces of lined paper that served as their coursework drafts, Fox felt an overwhelming sense of sadness on his behalf. Momentary flashes of the man's life flitted before her eyes. Mr. Saxon bouncing his little boy in his arms. Mr. Saxon drinking down a glass of Scotch. Mr. Saxon reaching out a hand to strike his wife and not going through with it – but it was enough. Fox audibly gasped with surprise, eliciting the looks of several of the class that had wandered in. Jeremiah leaned in from behind and whispered into her ear,

"Is everything okay? Are you having another one of those… moments?"

"Mornin'!" Carmen's sing-song greeting saved Fox from having to make a reply, which was just as well because the reply she wanted to give Jeremiah involved a certain level of physical violence.

"Everybody happy?" She flashed a totally oblivious smile and twirled a strand of her hair around her finger.

Fox swore she saw Carmen wink at Jeremiah, but when she whispered this accusation into Carmen's ear, she denied it. The smirk on her face said otherwise. Carmen smelt of soap and heavy rose perfume, she'd clearly felt the need to make an effort, and Fox internally groaned at the thought it might be because of flash-boy behind them. Finally, Mr. Saxon managed to get his act together and he cleared his throat to start the class. Goodness knows how he was going to manage a class of thirty-plus boisterous Year Sevens, Fox thought. Any sympathy she might have had had left with the image of his raised hand. It was a shame because he was a clever and interesting man. People were complicated.

"So today, I am allocating your project partners." An excited ripple ran around the room. "As you know by now, or should know by now, your coursework project is based on an element of local history. The list of possible titles is on the VLE page, so make sure that you check it carefully.

There are also some examples of previous projects to give you a feel of what you need to do. If you want my advice, choose a title close to home and not too ambitious. Researching is always a bigger job than you think."

Carmen leaned in and whispered excitedly, "I'm going to do about the history of the May Hill Horse Fair."

"Cool!" Fox responded quickly, not wanting to miss the project roll-call.

Carmen, mistaking her lack of engagement for not being interested harrumphed in her chair and pouted before muttering, "Well I think it's interesting!"

With one ear on Mr. Saxon, who had started to read out the pairings, and the other tuned into Carmen, Fox said, "Don't get all humpy, it's fascinating. I'm sure it will be great. You know I love hearing about…"

Fox caught Saxon saying her name but it was the tail end of the sentence "….will be with Fox."

"Damn it!" Fox said, searching around to see if she could work out who she had been paired with and having no luck. "Who did you say?" she called out to Mr. Saxon.

"Why, the pleasure's all mine, ma'm!" Jeremiah drawled in his best impression of Rhett Butler.

Great, Jeremiah, bloody, Chase! the internal grumped.

"I've put you with Jeremiah. What with the Meadowsweet family being one of the oldest in the county, I thought it would be good to pair our newest, American import with our eldest English rose."

"How...?" Fox's question remained unfinished as Mr. Saxon was clearly on a mission and had already begun to go over the criteria for the project for the fifth or sixth time.

"So if you can please move yourselves so that you are sitting with your partners, you can make a start on planning your projects."

"Witchcraft!" Carmen whispered low into Fox's ear.

"Pardon?"

"Getting your hands on the handsome American."

"Agreed. A total hex!" Fox screwed her nose up and threw her a look, "Hey, isn't that more your bag?" she said sarcastically.

Carmen flicked her a V sign before moving it to her eyes and back to Fox again. "I'm watching you, witch!" she hissed.

"Get out of here!" Fox said laughing. "Dishy Dave is waiting for you."

Carmen smiled. Fox wasn't being ironic; Dave was quite the hunk and he had quite a soft spot for Carmen.

"Who's a witch?" Jeremiah asked, smiling.

"It's just a joke we share."

He shrugged and flashed another smile. It was clear that he was used to this technique working – it just wasn't going to work on Fox.

"So, local one from ancient blood, what ideas have you got?" he asked.

Fox rolled her eyes. *And he thinks he's funny too – great!* the internal moaned.

Fox flipped through the pages of her exercise book. Being the model student that she was, she had of course already looked up the VLE and jotted down a load of ideas in response to the topic questions. Jeremiah let out a low whistle of appreciation. "I didn't have you down as that type of girl."

Fox bristled. "What *type* of girl?"

Jeremiah flashed that sparkly smile of his again and replied, "You know - the *diligent* kind!"

"Look, if we're going to work together there's one thing you need to do…"

"What's that?"

"Stop grinning at me. It's annoying!"

Jeremiah's laugh bounced around the room.

She tapped her pen furiously on the table, a clear indicator that he had bothered her. She felt herself blushing and it made her angry.

"Let's get on shall we?" she said aggressively. He didn't seem phased that he'd upset her. In fact it seemed to amuse him.

He smirked and waved a hand, inviting her to talk him through her diagrammatic notes. She was sure he wasn't really listening. He had his arms folded up behind his head and his foot over his knee as if he were relaxing against a tree on a sunny spring day. Give him another five minutes and she was sure that he'd actually fall asleep.

"So I thought we could look at how elephant farming in the Heargton area impacted on agricultural crops and settlement patterns."

"Hmm ha!" he agreed, pretending to be engaged. Fox threw her pen down with frustration.

"You're clearly not interested in anything I have to say. If all these ideas are so darned boring, then why don't you come up with one?"

He looked at her intensely and made out he was thinking by tapping his fingers against his cheek. "How about…" he paused in order to lean forward and adjust his body so he had both elbows on his knees and could look directly at her. "How about… we look at the impact of the Ravenheart Family on the village? Aunt Penelope says they're quite the powerhouse; keeps encouraging me to try and set up a supper date with one of them. I think she has ambitions of uniting our two houses – just like in the good old days."

Fox didn't respond at first. She knew that in some way she was being played, she just wasn't sure how. She glanced over her notes, not wanting to return the intensity of his stare. She left a moment before responding,

"Well, if we're thinking of doing local influential families, then how about the Chase family. I've heard that they have quite a chequered and *unpleasant* history!"

She waited for his response. He bit down on his bottom lip and Fox watched as a smile grew. He was trying to predict her next move. Annoyingly, he didn't respond and she was forced to take a lead.

"I'm not sure that we'd like what we unearthed about the Ravenhearts – they're best left alone." She looked over her diagram and traced her pen across the page, tapping it when she got to the idea of the burial ground. "Here. I think this is a much *safer* topic. The burial ground and the early settlement."

Jeremiah yawned and patted his mouth in an overly dramatic way. Fox was quickly losing patience with him.

"Okay," she sighed as her pen started tapping the notepad more furiously. "This one?" She stabbed at another point on her diagram, hoping that she would pick up on the desire to stab the pen into his eye. She recoiled from the thought as it catapulted her back into the vision she had had of Martha last night; those big vacant bloodied spaces where her eyes should have been.

"What about your family?" he offered. "There have been Meadowsweets living in Heargton for hundreds of years and I'd really love to get to know more about you." His eye's flashed and although Fox couldn't be entirely certain (with her very limited experience) she believed that he was flirting with her again.

"Look," she said with a voice raised enough to draw attention, "We're not researching anybody's *family!* It's not… it's not… appropriate."

"Appropriate?"

"Yes, it's not polite to go rummaging through your neighbours' closets – you don't know what skeletons they've got stashed away. Some secrets are best left alone."

"Oo, sounds exciting!" He raised an eyebrow and pressed his lips together cheekily. Fox noticed he had dimples. He leaned forward and whispered, "I love secrets!"

Fox snapped the notebook shut. "How about a compromise. Something linked to the Ravenhearts; let's do the history of the Rookeries."

He shrugged his shoulders, indicating that he had no idea what she was talking about.

"The old lunatic asylum in Raven's Wood."

He smiled appreciatively and nodded his head.

"Yep, that should suit your whole American Gothic thang!" she said affecting an American accent whilst eyeing his braces and the small tattoo of a dripping dagger on the inside of his forearm.

"Awesome!" he mocked.

Blessedly, the bell rang, indicating the end of the lesson and the end of their torturous conversation.

Carmen came bounding back to reclaim her things and to get the opportunity to flirt with Jeremiah some more. Fox stuffed her books into her bag as quickly as she could. She'd had it with Mr. Chase for the day. Anger surged at the thought of having to spend necessary study time together. *Why don't you ask Mr. Saxon to swap your partners?* the internal asked. Fox shook her head in response and let out a heavy sigh. *Oh, so you don't really mind him being your partner then? All that romping around Raven's Wood together, bound for something to happen! I think you'd quite like that.* Evidently, the internal was in as annoying mood as Jeremiah,

"Can you hurry up?" she snapped at Carmen, causing Jeremiah to raise his eyebrows in surprise and for Carmen's mood to shift from all coy and bubbly to Cruella De Vil in a flash.

Fox started to leave, forcing Carmen to issue a hurried goodbye to Jeremiah and chase after her. Fortunately, they had the compulsory physical education lesson between History and lunch, and being as Carmen always took the opportunity to go and have a cigarette, it gave them both the space that they needed.

By the time Fox changed, Swan was already on the netball court, practicing her hoops. She was made to be Goal Shooter, tall and lithe, elegant with an incredible sense of balance. Fox was a defender – slightly shorter, broader and with a tenacious need to stop anybody else winning. It was always most fun when they were placed on opposing sides and Swan and Fox could go at it in the way only sisters can get away with. It always ended up with one of them on the ground and usually blood was spilt. Today they were on the same side, which considering the mood Fox was in, was probably for the best. Swan intuitive as ever, picked up on her sister's sour mood as soon as she saw her.

"Who's stolen *your* bag of sweeties?"

Fox didn't want to talk about it. She was worried that if she started moaning, she might not be able to stop. The lack of rest from the visions was making her cranky and every time she let her mind off its reins for more than a second, it went back to the sight of Martha tied to that chair in the barn and the…

Thalia slinked onto the court, her skirt far shorter than necessary and her t-shirt tighter than it legally ought to be. She was sucking on a lollipop doing her best impression of Lolita. She'd tied her hair back into a high ponytail and her dazzling white ankle socks highlighted the golden glow of her tanned legs. By instinct (or crazy pheromone stuff) the boys doing their practice kick-ups the other side of the fence turned one after the other to take in the sight of her bending down to tighten the laces of her trainers.

"God, I hope she's wearing gym knickers!" Swan said disapprovingly.

"I don't think gym knickers would make a bit of difference to the thoughts running through their pervy little heads," Fox grumped, nodding in the direction of the boys.

Fox looked at Thalia and felt bile rise up in her throat. *How can she act so cool when…?* Fox forced herself to look at her, searching for signs of guilt. Looking for evidence of blood on her hands. She desperately wanted to tell Swan about what she had seen last night; about the Ravenheart sisters abducting Martha and torturing her, but…

"Hi, ladies," Thalia said, smiling sweetly.

Fox felt Swan bristle beside her. After scanning the area, satisfied that nobody could overhear, Swan leant in and whispered sharply,

"Rumour has it in certain circles that your blood has been out stealing eyes."

Fox looked from Swan to Thalia with her mouth wide open. *What the hell! How did Swan know…?*

"I don't know what you're talking about!" Thalia said defensively. Thalia was a practiced deceiver and she eyeballed Swan innocently.

"What…?" Fox began to stutter but was cut short by the nasty little battle of words.

"It's all over the local paper!"

Thalia coughed and cleared her throat. "What is exactly?"

Fox's internal was going bonkers; it started shouting in the high-pitched voice of the hysteric. *What the bloody hell is going on? What is up with Swan?* Fox breathed deeply. It was as if the world had suddenly slid into slow motion. Whoa, she felt sick.

"The horse mutilations that have been taking place at the farms over in the Coppices. Apparently they've found four animals with their eyes taken out and some crazy, satanic stuff branded on their flesh. If it's not you, then someone is jacking your style!"

Fox had no idea why her sister was baiting Thalia so hard. Fox could see Thalia internally combusting and was convinced that if they'd been somewhere more private, a full on fight would have broken out. Instead, Thalia stared hard at Swan as if she could will her dead (maybe she could). Her hand sat firmly on her hip and a cruel, twisted pout sat on her lips. Incredulously, Swan wasn't done and Fox looked at her as if she'd been swapped by aliens.

"Oh, yes, it's just your blood's style."

Fox cleared her throat with a nervous cough and grabbed her sister tightly by the arm. "Excuse me, do you mind if I have a word with you," she said dragging her to the side of the court.

Thalia continued her dagger-stare and called out, "You bitch! I'll see you later!"

"Yeah, whatever!" Swan called out over her shoulder.

"For the love of the Goddess, will you please just shut the freak up!" Fox muttered through clenched teeth. Swan was totally hyped. Fox had rarely, if ever seen her so out of control. "Who are you? I mean you're clearly not my sister, so what's going on? Why are you spoiling for a fight with Thalia? Why are you talking about…" Fox glanced around to check they were not being overheard. "…witch matters!"

"She started it!" Swan said, with uncharacteristic immaturity.

"How? How exactly has Thalia pissed you off so much that you break the secrecy oath?"

"Don't be such a bloody hypocrite, you're always telling people that you're a witch!"

Fox let out a puff of air in an attempt to swallow her quickly rising anger. "Not for real! Nobody really believes that crap! They don't think I fly about on a broomstick with a black hat, do they!"

Swan threw the ball hard to the ground with a thud. "Do you know what? I've had it. I'm going home!"

"You're ditching?"

She stormed off in the direction of the changing room. "I'm phoning mum!" Fox called out lamely.

Swan didn't reply but flicked the V sign. Fox couldn't remember the last time she and Swan had fallen out. That was always saved for Bunny. Swan was the peace-keeper; the diplomat. Whatever Thalia had done, it had clearly cut her sister deep. Of all the times to fall out with her, it couldn't have been worse. She had hoped to talk to her about the visions. Thalia had been watching the whole scene with interest and now that Swan was gone, and she thought she was no longer in danger of being thumped, she slinked over to Fox.

"Whoa, wonder what got her so het up?" Thalia asked.

Fox couldn't tear her eyes away from the glossy-lipped smile on Thalia's face. Her head was hurting from being all knotted up; not just over the fight with her sister but with the images from her visions. *It hasn't happened yet!* the internal said with conviction. *Test the waters. Play it cool!*

Fox cleared her throat and planted a smile on her face. "Hormones! She gets terrible PMT. You shouldn't mind her."

Thalia shrugged. "No offence taken. Us…" she stopped her sentence and mentally readjusted it, "Our *kind* have got to stick together. Especially if what Swan says about the satanic rituals is true, then it won't be long until the villagers are at our doors with their flaming torches and pitchforks." Thalia laughed and it sounded as light and innocent as the sound of a bubbling cauldron.

The thought of being in league with the Ravenhearts didn't appeal to Fox but she smiled sweetly and replied, "Of course."

Fox started to put on her netball vest with the hope that the next topic of conversation would look as natural as any general chit-chat.

"Have you seen Martha Paisley in college today? Her mother came into Sara's last night, she was distraught. Apparently she hasn't been seen since Sunday night." Fox watched Thalia's face for signs of discomfort, but all she saw was a look of concern and natural interest.

"No, she wasn't in registration this morning." Thalia dropped her head to the side and twirled her hair. "Do they think something has happened?"

"They don't know. I think the police think that her and Jack have done a bunk somewhere. They were hoping she'd rock up last night with a love-bite and her tail between her legs."

"That's not really Martha's style is it? She's so… virginal!"

Fox swallowed the gasp that was about to fly out of her throat. *Hear that?* the internal piped up, *"virginal." Weird word choice don't you think? Why...* the internal was cut off by the sound of the gym whistle being blown and Miss Faulkner clapping her hands in order to herd the unruly gaggle of girls into two teams.

"I'm really sorry, Ms Faulkner, I think I'm going to be…" Fox's hand flew to her mouth and she started to run for the changing rooms, "sick!"

Once out of sight, she straightened up and slowed to a walking pace. She needed to change and get home. She needed to speak with Cousin Primrose about the visions. She needed to know if it was the past, present, or future. If it was the future that she was seeing, she had a chance of changing it. Destiny was bendable. It changed on the flap of a butterfly wing, or so she'd been led to believe. Primrose, or Prim, as her family called her, was also a Saw. Her visions had also come in early -- she'd been an Oracle Child; and boy, were they creepy little critters, all glassy-eyed and spooky.

So bright spark, how exactly are you intending on getting to May Hill? the internal asked snarkily. Fox changed out of her gym kit and stuffed her things into her bag. “Will!” she muttered in answer. “He’ll drive me to May Hill.”

She hurried along the corridor, hoping that the Geography class were at base rather than being out in the grounds doing their weirdo geography things like tipexing woodlice or counting daisies. The row of windows looking out onto the corridor made it easy to get Will’s attention – as well as everybody else's, including Mr. Huntley’s. He wasn’t too happy that his fascinating discussion on glacial drifts was being interrupted by a clown at the window and he stomped to the door with a grumpy huff.

“Miss Meadowsweet, can I help you?”

Fox blushed and stammered. She was not used to getting herself into trouble. “S..sorry, sir, I need to get an urgent message to Will.”

“And it can’t wait?”

“No, sir, I’m afraid not.” Fox glanced into the classroom to see fifteen pairs of curious eyes all looking in her direction. Will was blushing coyly. This certainly was not one of Fox’s better ideas. *What are you thinking!*

Huntley sighed heavily. “Okay, as it’s obviously so urgent.” He leaned through the door and called out for William, who made the walk of shame to the soundtrack of his classmates’ whispers and giggles.

Huntley stepped back to let Will pass but was showing no intention of returning to class without knowing what life-threatening missive was being imparted. Fox waited for him to leave, making it clear that she wasn't going to say anything in front of him. Eventually he was forced to return to class, grumbling, "William, two minutes and I want you back in class, please."

"Foxy, what's going on?" Will asked.

"I know this is all a little bit crazy but I really need your help."

He stepped forward, running his hand through his hair in a sign of awkwardness. He glanced into the classroom to see that they were still being watched. He took her by the arm and steered her so they were out of view.

Well that's going to look even more suspicious!

"What's so urgent?" he asked.

"I need you to drive me to May Hill?"

He sighed and looked visibly relieved. "Is that all? Jeez, of course I can give you a lift back."

He thinks you mean at the end of the day, the internal added helpfully. "Not after college - now?" she asked.

"What do you mean, now?" His confusion returned.

"I mean, I need to go to May Hill right now. Can you take me?"

He looked back in the direction of class and shuffled. "I don't know. I don't think I can just walk out of Huntley's class. He's not really that cool with stuff like that!"

Fox's heartbeat started to rise in the first flutters of panic. She knew she had to get to Primrose. She had to know whether there was still a chance to save

Martha – time was running out. *You might already be too late!* the internal said, bleakly.

"Please, I wouldn't ask unless it was…"

Fox felt the warmth of Will's hand on her arm. "Okay, on one condition: on the way, you tell me what is going."

Fox nodded. She wasn't sure exactly what tale she would spin. *You could tell him the truth!*

"Just give me a minute to go grab my stuff," he said, leaving her standing nervously.

"What will you tell Huntley?"

"I'll think of something."

A minute or two later Will returned looking stressed. Huntley had obviously given him a hard time.

"Are you in trouble?" she asked.

"Nothing I can't handle." He slung his satchel over his shoulder and dug into his pocket for his car keys.

"Sorry!" Fox whispered.

"I just hope it's for a good reason."

"It is, I promise."

Will was clearly not very happy about the situation and Fox was surprised to find him so sour. She'd never seen him anything but sweet and smiley. *Maybe you misjudged him.* Fox looked at him. His jaw line was hard and there was a heavy silence that was very uncomfortable. It wasn't until they had left Fallford and were on the long road to May Hill that he finally broke the quiet.

"So what's so urgent that you have to pull me out of class?"

Fox had had time to think over what she would say but she hadn't really come to any solid decisions – now she'd have to wing it.

"I need to go and see my cousin."

"Is she ill?"

"No, but I think maybe… maybe I am."

Will shot her a look full of concern. The weight of it knocked her sideways. *He likes you!* the internal observed. *More than likes you.*

"Is it the fits you are having? Do you think it's something serious?"

Fox nodded. "Yes, but not in the way you think it is. It's not a brain tumour or anything."

"Oh."

"You must know what they say about me and my sisters?"

Will shook his head and looked blank, forcing Fox to continue a conversation that she really wished she hadn't started. "That we're different. A bit weird."

A spontaneous smile teased his lips and he turned with a twinkle in his eye, "That's exactly what I like about you, Foxy!"

See, I told you so. Fox shook the internal away. She could really do with a clear head for this moment and the internal was an increasingly annoying distraction. She knew she was blushing and she wished she weren't. She liked Will a lot but she really didn't want to give him the wrong impression. There was no hope of anything more than friendship between them.

"You know that they say we are witches."

Will burst into laughter. “And what? They’re right? You do know that I was only yanking your chain the other night? I don’t really think that you’re a witch or anything.”

This really wasn’t going the way that she had hoped. She certainly hadn’t expected him to burst into giggles on her as she revealed her big secret.

“My sisters and I have certain talents; gifts, if you like.”

Will stopped laughing and turned to glance at her longer than was safe when driving on a winding country lane. “Talents? Gifts? What like?” he asked cautiously.

“These fits I’ve been having, they’re not medical, they’re… they’re visions.”

Fox saw how Will tightened his grip on the steering wheel. He was uncomfortable with the subject matter.

“Visions?”

Fox sighed. “Are you just going to keep repeating me?”

“Well I’m not quite sure what else you’d like me to say,” he said tersely.

“I know it sounds weird. It’s weird for me to, and I assure you, of all the talents our kind are given, having visions is not the one I wanted.”

“Your *kind*? What exactly do you mean? Bloody hell, Foxy, do you really expect me to believe all that bleedin’ hocus-pocus crap? If I believed in any of that shit I’d heard about you in the village, I wouldn’t have teased you so much about it all would I?”

Fox was startled by his ferocity. She'd expected mocking and a bit of ridicule but not this hostility. She'd been wrong to think that he could help her; foolish to think that he would ride in on his white horse and be her knight in shining armor.

"Forget it," she snapped. "I just thought you might be able to help me. Clearly, I was wrong. Just drop me off at May Hill and I'll go on from there – alone."

A heavy silence fell between them. Fox could see that Will was angry, but she didn't really understand why – well, aside from the usual prejudices, but she thought Will might have been different. She'd hoped that he would be a friend and she had a feeling that she was going to need one of those in the coming days; a terrible sense of dread now followed her like a black dog. After several minutes that felt like hours, Will shuffled in his seat and asked,

"Are the visions anything to do with Martha?"

Fox was surprised by his intuition. Given his earlier responses, she wasn't that keen on telling him any more but it seemed that he had time to think things over a bit and he had become a little more receptive.

"Yes."

"Oh."

There was a natural pause in his response as he stopped at road junction and focused. Fox was in no rush to dive in with details and hoped that might be enough information for him. When they'd safely crossed, he was still silent and she thought she had got away with it until he asked,

"Have you seen what's happened to her?"

Fox looked out of the window. She shrugged and threw him a glance.

"Is it… is it bad?" he asked.

"I don't know yet."

"Well what have you seen? What did your…" he cleared his throat as if embarrassed, "…your *visions* look like."

"It's not really that easy to explain, Will. They're a mixture of sound and light and feelings. They don't really make sense, and I don't know if they tell me what has happened or what's going to happen. That's why I need to see Prim."

"Will she have the answer?"

"I hope so."

"Is she a w… I mean is she *gifted* too?"

Fox nodded. They were nearly at May Hill. She still wasn't sure how much of a friend Will was going to be.

"Turn left. It's at the bottom of the track."

Prim lived with her two sisters, Violet and Rose. The cottage was off the road and up into the fringes of the forest. Fox allowed herself a wry smile at the impression it would give Will. If ever there was your archetypal fairytale witches' cottage then it was Bramble Cottage. With three smoking crooked chimneys, a herb garden, and its original Tudor lattice windows, it could easily have been a prop in Disneyland.

Will smirked and his shoulders dropped. It seemed that the humour of the setting had not been lost on him.

"Nice place. Very…" He laughed and Fox felt a momentary hope that everything might work out okay between them after all.

He pulled the car up behind the sisters' beaten up Land Rover and cut the engine. Fox gathered her bags together and started to get out with the intention of offering her thanks and letting him off the hook, but before she got a chance, he picked up his magazine from the side pocket and said,

"Take as long as you need. I'll give you a lift back when you're done."

She was about to protest when he flashed her a smile that would have been stupid to refuse.

"Thank you."

Prim was in. She was almost always in due to her agoraphobia. It wasn't bad enough that she never went out, but she only went out when she needed to. Violet and Rose were both at work in Lancaster. Violet worked as a librarian and Rose was a college tutor. Prim spent her days growing most of the supplies for Auntie Wren's beauty products. They were not wealthy but they were comfortable. The cottage had been their mother's and hers before that until the day it had been built in 1530. They shared the same name of Meadowsweet and although slightly older than Fox and her sisters, they had always been a close sisterhood. They got together on the full moon for worship, as the family had always done, and in the week, either Rose or Violet would often call in on their way home from Lancaster and have supper with them. Of all the

Meadowsweets, Prim was the one that Fox knew least.

The curse of being an Oracle Child had meant that she'd had a hideous childhood. Unable to control her visions or have any understanding that few others saw the world in the way that she did, she had been bullied without mercy by both the other children at school and the authorities. The school (and then the social services) had pushed her from psychiatrist to psychiatrist, causing her to withdraw further and further into herself until finally they threatened her with placement in a special residential unit. It had been about this time that their mother had fallen ill with a mysterious disease that killed her within six months. Their mother died the day after Violet's twenty-first birthday and a week before Rose's eighteenth. It had been a dark time for Bramble Cottage but at least the older sisters had been old enough to become the guardian to their younger sister. They had withdrawn her from school and finished her education at home, safe from the concern of the school and the taunts of her peers.

Prim had always been happiest in the garden. There was no need for her to know algebra or learn the rules of hockey, so she learned biology and horticulture. She studied ancient medicines of the East, and Astrology. Fox had always known that Prim was incredibly clever in a way few people are, but she wasn't easy to talk to and she wasn't entirely sure how their conversation was going to pan out. Prim had been known to have a complete flip-out when asked about certain things and even now her visions were unpredictable and sometimes volatile.

As to be expected, Fox found Prim in the garden. She was tending the herb beds, cutting back the dead. The sound of Fox's greeting startled her and she nearly dropped her pruning shears. It was hard for Fox to imagine that there were only six years between them. It wasn't that Prim wasn't youthful, she had the kind of looks that would still be youthful when she was in her fifties, but everything else about her shouted 1940s spinster; what with her mustard-coloured wool tights, brown brogues, and Fair-Isle tank top. Her light blond hair sparkled in the weak wintery sun and the cold had blushed her cheeks. Her fine hair had escaped its chignon and was now hanging in wispy tendrils around her face.

"Fox!" she exclaimed. "What a pleasant surprise." Her smile of greeting flickered into concern. "Is there something wrong?"

"No, I was just..." She stopped, knowing that her excuse of "just passing" was hardly going to work. Bramble Cottage was too far off the beaten path. She changed tack. "Mum wanted to know if you had any thyme?"

Prim looked at her suspiciously. It was clear that Fox had no idea about herbalism otherwise she'd have known that thyme wasn't harvested this late into the season. Wren would have known that.

"You're lying," Prim said matter of fact. There was no judgment in her statement but it still made Fox feel bad. Prim turned away from her and started snipping quite furiously at a lavender bush.

"Sorry, Prim. I guess I forgot how… straightforward you are. I was hoping to sort of swing my purpose for visiting into conversation somehow but…"

"I'm not sure how you would have managed that. Your visions coming in are hardly casual conversation."

"You know about them!"

Prim waved the shears in front of her in a manner that could have been seen as threatening if it had been a stranger. "Of course I know about them."

"I guess you saw them coming!" Fox said, attempting to lighten the mood with bit of in-house witch humour. It fell flat.

"Yes,"

"Didn't you think to warn me?"

"Warn you? What a strange choice of words. They are your gift!" she said with a tone heavy with sarcasm.

"It's not one I want!"

A strange contorted sound came from Prim's mouth and it took a moment for Fox to realise that Prim was actually laughing. In all the years they'd known each other, Fox had rarely heard her laugh.

"You don't get a choice!" her laughed words had a bitter edge to them. "It's not like you can just wish them away; goodness knows, I've tried." She returned to her lavender. "You are already beginning to understand the responsibility that comes with them, aren't you?"

The question was more of a statement. Fox mused on what it must have been like to have always known what the future held. No wonder people thought that Prim was a little bit crazy.

"I don't understand them," Fox said, "I can't work out if what I am seeing is past, present, or future. I don't understand how something in the future can form so substantially and be so real, so it must be past but if it's the past then..."

Prim turned to her and raised an eyebrow, clearly impressed by the existentialist nature of her question. "You need to start undoing all you understand about time."

Fox sighed and leaned back against the wooden rose arch. She'd never been scientifically minded, especially not when it came to physics. Too much of it was invisible; intangible, like most mathematics. She suspected that she was about to be subjected to a lengthy and confusing lecture on quantum physics that would leave her none the wiser. Prim found the abstract notion of time so straightforward that she was able to continue multi-tasking.

"The way we measure out time is purely a clumsy way of organising something that doesn't really want to be organised. Man likes to keep things structured, under control. He devised measurements in order to establish the "passing" of time, as if time were on a single straight line out into infinity. He called them centuries, decades, days, minutes, seconds, and so on, and he put them on a nice, sensible linear approach that was helped by the clockwork motions of the orbiting planets. But time doesn't really *work* like that. Time doesn't *pass or move,* it just *is*!"

Fox shook her head. She was only holding onto her understanding of all of this by a thread and the thread was rapidly fraying. "What do you mean by time *is*?"

"I mean, it isn't a machine. Time isn't a clock. If it helps, think of it as being more of a living, pulsing energy source. Imagine a giant, universe-sized jellyfish, with all her tentacles reaching out into space. They ebb, they flow, they connect, they part. Sometimes they extend or retract. This is what time looks like."

"A jellyfish?" Fox asked cynically.

"Yes."

"And the visions, are they really in the future?"

Prim sighed with a mild frustration. Fox's use of the word "future" told her that Fox was struggling to understand that there wasn't such a thing. She returned to her overly pruned lavender. "Because you are a witch you have the ability to see all ways, and all times."

"And can non-witches get the *gift*?"

"Yes, sort of. The easiest way to define their gift would be to call them psychic. They can connect with the past, pick up on trace memories and energies, and from those a vision forms, but they can't see forward in quite the same way; all they can do is predict."

Fox feared that if Prim kept snipping at that poor lavender any more then there would be nothing left. Fox adjusted the question, "Can I stop what I've seen?"

Prim snapped her full attention onto Fox. She'd paled and her previous confidence slipped. "W... why would you need to?" she stammered.

Fox didn't want to give Prim too many details; her reactions were quickly becoming unstable, but she needed to press Prim for more information. "Let's say hypothetically I'd seen someone die from an accident, is there anything to stop me from stopping it?"

Prim flustered and stood up. She started to head to the cottage. Fox's question had unsettled Prim a lot and instinct told her she asked an unaskable question.

"Yes!" she called over her shoulder. "Everything should stop you. You can't go meddling with fate. It's not my... I mean *your* place. Fate changing belongs to the darkness, to the dark arts. You must trust in the ways of the Goddess." Prim was literally running towards the door. "You have to go now, I'm terribly busy. It was lovely to see you!"

"But what if ..." Fox called after her.

"There are *no* buts. And it doesn't matter how much we love them - we can't save them!" The slamming of the cottage door punctuated her statement and cut short any hope of more conversation.

Realisation hit Fox so hard that it winded her. She stopped in her tracks, staring after the closed door ahead of her. *Prim's seen one of our loved ones die!* the internal gasped. *Why haven't you seen that?*

"Who?" Fox called out to the closed door. "Who have you seen die, Prim?"

Silence replied.

Fox took a few deep breaths and swallowed down the anger at Prim's weird and unhelpful behaviour. *Maybe she is mad as a box of frogs after all,* the internal suggested. Fox had come here hoping for some sensible, straightforward answers but instead all she'd ended up with was the answer that time was a jellyfish and that somebody they loved was going to die.

"Bloody hell, Prim!" Fox fumed.

She marched back to the car full of rage. *Let's hope that Will isn't annoying – for his sake!* the internal quipped.

Fox threw open the car door and fell into the seat. "Well that was a bloody waste of time!"

"Want to talk about it?" Will asked sweetly.

"Not really!"

"Apple pie at Sara's make it any better?"

Fox nodded and then shook her head. "No, it will get back to mum that I'm bunking. I can do without that hassle."

"Want to go somewhere else?"

Fox turned to Will and smiled. It felt good to have him here with her. Sitting beside him, everything in her bat-shit-crazy life felt a little more sane. Will put the car into gear and threw his arm around the back of her seat in order to reverse up the lane. It felt strangely intimate and despite Fox's anger and frustrations, she felt herself smile.

Fox bent double and let out a cry of anguish at the sensory assault of the vision. Will slammed on the breaks. He placed his hand on her back and waited for her fit to pass. Fox still had not got used to the feeling of violence that a vision brought with it. It was as if an invisible giant picked her up in the palm of his hand and tossed her through space. The sensation was painfully physical; to the point Fox feared that her heart might burst out of her chest.

She was back at the barn but this time it was daylight and the whole place looked far less sinister. In fact it almost looked charming. There was a sense that she was seeing something far back in time. There wasn't anything specific that she could put her finger on to help orientate her but everything looked more… simple, more pure. The colours of the paintwork, the lack of mechanical machinery, the basic willow fencing where now there was electric wire. Chickens pottered around, and the fields were full of golden corn. In her vision Fox was standing tall, inhaling the golden light of summer. Then something caught her eye. It was a small wooden doll, handmade with love and dressed in thin white cotton, including a strip of white cotton across the dolls face, forming a blindfold. *Strange,* the internal mused. As Fox held the doll, two little red dots started to form on the blindfold, creating little bloodied eyes. Fox dropped the doll in horror and stepped back from it. Across the dress, small bloody fingerprints emerged as if the doll had been clasped by a child's bloodied hand. Fox started to scream and the screams pulled her out of her vision into the warmth and safety of Will's car. He was holding her firmly, bundled up in his arms as if protecting her from wild elements. Fox was sobbing, consumed by an overwhelming and confusing grief.

"It's happened before," Fox sobbed.

"What has?"

She shook her head. "I don't know – something bad. Something connected to that place."

"What place?"

She shook her head again. When she was there she had the strongest feeling that the place was familiar to her, but she didn't have a definite memory of having ever been there.

"We've got to do something about these visions, Foxy. You can't go on like this. They'll send you mad."

"I think it's already too late!"

Will squeezed her reassuringly and then Fox felt the lightest of kisses land on her head.

5

"Where do you want to go?" Will asked as he pulled the car out onto the main road.

Fox was staring out the window, preoccupied by the images of her visions. Her mind refused to focus. "I don't mind."

They travelled on in silence until they got to the junction when Will declared that he was starving hungry and that he could murder a burger.

"I'm vegetarian," Fox replied, still not really engaging with their day plans.

"Oh, perhaps Macky D's isn't such a good idea then!" he said, laughing. He fell quiet, thinking of where he could take a vegetable eater. "I guess it's Pizza then!"

"That would be good."

They drove back through Heargton village and to the small market town of Lewit. There were only two reasons to visit the run down town; one was for bank and the other was for Tony's Pizza shop. Tony's wood-oven meant he made the best pizzas in the whole of the county. He refused to do delivery, so his little, dark wood restaurant was always packed. It hadn't changed since the day he had opened its doors back in the late seventies. The tables were dressed in red and white gingham table clothes and red, drippy candles were stuffed into rattan wrapped Chianti bottles. The restaurant was dominated by a large dark bar, at which several locals sat drinking draft continental beer. The back mirror plate was covered in postcards. Tony's was hardly chic but it had its own charms. The Meadowsweet girls had spent many childhood birthday meals within its walls.

Will ordered the house special (in a clear attempt to consume the most amount of meat possible) and Fox went for the spinach and goat cheese, her personal favourite. It wasn't until after they had ordered and suddenly found themselves sitting opposite each other in a restaurant "having lunch" that Fox realised how much this was turning out to be like a date. Maybe Will had the same thought because he flushed and looked slightly awkward.

Twice in one week, Foxy! This is getting serious, the internal teased.

Fox found something of interest on the far wall and attempted a convincing impression of being relaxed. It didn't work. Fortunately, just before the whole situation became unbearable, Tony delivered the pizzas with a flourish. Just when Fox thought she was safe and that things were turning out pleasant, Will plucked up the courage to ask her the question she'd been dreading.

"Will you tell me what you've seen in your…" he cleared his throat and lowered his voice as if the next word was something almost dirty, "…visions?"

Fox stopped chewing. The food turned unpalatable. *You could easily lie,* the internal offered. Fox was a useless liar and she knew that she'd tie herself in knots. She looked at him, wishing she could truly know what he was thinking. He seemed to like her for who she was, but it was clear that her whole way of life was far out of his comfort zone. Anyway, why did he *want* to like her? What was he hoping to get out of their friendship? She was hardly his girlfriend type; she couldn't see herself draped on his arm like Sophie had been, or Caitlin before her, or… *Do you want to be?'*The internal's question floored her. It wasn't that she hadn't thought about what it might be like to let him kiss her, or to hold his hand or… Her head was already short-circuiting all over the place and the last thing she really needed was to flood it with loony-love hormones.

Tell him! the internal directed. *What have you got to lose?*

If laughing at your inner conscious wouldn't lead to the general impression you were a complete fruitcake, she would have laughed. All the time Fox ran through these rambling thoughts, Will waited patiently. His blue eyes watched her intensely. He was opening himself up to her in a way she knew he did with few other people. It was beginning to feel like a responsibility.

"You'll think I'm crazy."

"I already think that," he said, flashing a wry smile.

She breathed in deeply, put down her knife and fork, and plunged her hands between her thighs in a brace position.

"Okay." She closed her eyes and thought back to the visions. "There are definitely two different visions, maybe three, but they're all kind of the same. They're all connected. In two of them I'm standing in a field and there is a barn to my right. In front of me is a cornfield that leads onto woods. They are both in the same place but I think the time is different."

"How do you know?"

"I don't, not really, but it just feels different. The one that is now, in our times, is at dusk. There is a horrible feeling all around me, like a dark energy." Fox opened her eyes and took a glimpse at Will to see how he was doing. He looked calm, interested. Most of all he didn't look like he thought she was raving mad – yet.

"I know something terrible is happening in the barn. Something so violent and awful that it roots me to the spot. Then somehow I'm looking through a gap in the wooden siding and I can see…" Fox pauses and gulps. She knows that this is the bit that will throw Will into a tailspin. "I see… I see Martha."

"Oh my God! Is she hurt?" he asks urgently. "Is he hurting her?"

Fox nods. "Yes, she's hurt."

"What has he done to her?"

The image of the bloodied bandage across Martha's eyes and the painting of blood on her chin flashes hard in Fox's memory.

"It's not a he," she says, hoping to distract him from his question.

"A woman! Do you see who it is?"

"No." The lie shoots out of Fox's mouth before she can stop it.

"So how do you…"

"I just do!"

Will physically backed away from her answer, knowing that he'd been too pushy. Fox took a sip of her water and decided to change focus. She told him the other vision was mainly made of sounds and light, where the air is full of mens' voices calling out across the fields.

"I think they might be looking for a child but I'm not certain. I'm running alongside them but I'm not sure why I'm there. Then I stop because my foot makes contact with something. It's a doll, just a normal doll; the kind that any little girl might have, but it's all battered up and spattered in mud. There is a bandage around its eyes."

"Woah, that is freaky!"

"Yeah, well what is freakier is that in the vision that is older, the one that is set in the daytime, there is also a doll."

"No way!"

"It's an old fashioned doll; wooden. The kind a father might make for his daughter. It's got a simple white cotton dress and around its eyes is also a bandage, only this time, as I'm holding it blood starts to seep through the bandage where…"

You've done it now! You've let slip about the eyes. He's not stupid, he'll easily connect the dots, the internal says snappily.

Will waited patiently for Fox to finish. She became aware of her mouth hanging open rather unattractively and snapped it shut. Thankfully Tony came to the table and cleared the plates whilst having a lengthy exchange with Will about their meal. Fox used the time to work out a verbal escape plan but the best she came up with was the hope that by the time Tony stopped chattering on, Will might have forgotten exactly what they were talking about it. Fox cursed internally when she heard Will agree to coffees. That was a lot of time for them to fill with conversation. As soon as Tony turned his back, Will leaned forward ready to listen to her ending.

"Dolls freak me out! I've never understood what girls see in them," he said reaching for the sugar sachet and giving it a shake. "Do you think we should go to the police?"

Fox startled. That was the last thing she expected him to say. "The police! What? Tell them that your friend has had a dream about Martha Paisley. She hasn't got any idea where she is, or what has happened or who…" She stopped and breathed. She was over-reacting to his suggestion and it was making her sound skittish, as if maybe she had something to hide, which she did. She *did* know who was involved.

No, you think you know, she thought. *A policeman would laugh you out the station if you walked in and said you've got a hunch the Ravenheart sisters are marauding around the countryside ritualistically murdering virgins.*

"Well… what if we took a drive around to see if we could see the place your visions are set and then we could…" Will shrugged. "I don't know – maybe leave an anonymous letter at the station."

"Look, I know that all seems really simple but I'm not sure."

Tony placed the coffee down and was about to start up his friendly, jolly banter when he realised he was interrupting. He threw his hands up with apology and returned to his regulars at the bar.

"Come on, it could be an adventure!" Will said.

"No, Will, this isn't a TV drama. Martha has really gone missing and its quite possible she'll turn up murdered, which means we're living with monsters. I think it is best if we leave well alone and let the police do their thing."

"But what if your visions are…?"

"What? True!" Fox snapped.

Will fidgeted in his seat. "Sorry, I didn't mean to upset you."

"No, I understand, you were just being thoughtless!"

Silence settled between them but Fox could sense that there was something else Will wanted to say. She waited, and then waited some more. *Well this relationship is certainly volatile!* the internal teased. *Sexual tension or what?*

"What if your visions could help the police save Martha?" Will asked as he poured the sugar into his coffee.

Fox stared at him. She felt an inexplicable rising anger. Despite the internal telling her that it wasn't Will's fault that he'd asked the obvious, Fox still felt the urge to slap him across the face. Her grip tightened on her coffee cup. *He's only asked what you've been thinking yourself,* the internal reasoned.

"If I have any more visions, and I learn something definite, I promise I will think of a way to go to the police. At the minute I'm more likely to confuse matters." Fox didn't think Will was convinced, so she dealt the killer blow, "Maybe they're on to it and if I rock up with my hocus-pocus it might throw them off the scent." She paused and eyeballed Will into submission. "Imagine how terrible it would be if our meddling caused them to go off on the wrong track!"

By the time they'd finished lunch and made it back to Heargton, it was the same time that Fox would have returned from college. In order to keep up the pretense that everything was normal, she waved goodbye to Will at the road junction and walked the rest of the way to the family shop. Swan was already behind the counter wrapping a set of tarot cards for a customer. Swan was as surprised to see Fox as she was of Swan (they'd both hoped that the shop would be safe ground away from each other). They greeted each other with a challenging stare, not yet over the incident earlier that day on the netball court. Fox was keen to know what had set her off with Thalia. She wanted to warn Swan to be careful. If her visions were right Thalia was a lot more dangerous than your average school bitch.

Fox watched Swan work her magic with the customer and by the time the lady had left, she had not only purchased the tarot set, but an expensive crystal threaded dream catcher and a pot of their mother's famous anti-aging night cream. Swan's gift was certainly a lot more profitable than her own she thought grumpily.

When the shop doorbell stopped jingling and the coast was clear, Fox pounced. "And where did you go?"

"Me!" Swan snapped. "What about you?"

"What do you mean?" Fox replied defensively.

"Jeez, Fox. You've got no idea the scandal you've caused, breaking William Harrington out from Geography and driving off together into the sunset!"

Fox felt warm heat flush over her. The internal was corpsed with laughter. "How…?"

"Don't be so naive Fox! You didn't honestly think that you could hook up with Will and keep it a secret. Every one of those short-skirted-nail-polished-Barbie-dolls has got their talons out for you!"

Fox stood desperately wanting to retaliate but her mouth had gone on strike. Swan hadn't finished. "You've made a total idiot of yourself!" she sealed her diatribe with a tut and a roll of the eyes.

Fox let out a low whistle and raised her eyebrow. "Wow, Swan, tell it like it is, why don't you!"

"Just thought you should know before you head into college tomorrow - that is if you're going in tomorrow and not bunking off to spend your day getting your rocks off with Will Harrington."

"Jeez, Thalia really did switch on your bitch button, didn't she?"

Swan flashed a look that sent a clear warning signal. It was a look that Fox could not remember ever seeing in her usually placid and loving sister.

Whatever had happened between Swan and Thalia it had caused a complete personality transplant.

"That's none of your business!"

"Oh, and I suppose what I'm up to with Will Harrington is yours?"

Swan shuffled the tissue paper on the sales counter. "Touché!" she snapped, pressing her mouth together in a hard line.

The anger was palpable between them, to the extent that several of the lotion bottles on the counter started to vibrate under the force of their energy. Wren came in carrying three cups of tea.

"I sensed you were here, Fox," she said by way of explanation, then stopped in her tracks, looking from one daughter to the other. "I think I might take mine and drink it out back if you two can manage the shop for five minutes. I've got a stock order to process." She placed the cups on the counter and made a hasty retreat from the bad vibes flooding the place.

"So?" Fox asked.

"So what?"

"What has Thalia done to upset you so much?"

Fox could see that Swan was reluctant to talk about it, and normally Fox would have respected her privacy but not today, and not when it involved her sister making enemies with a Ravenheart.

"It's nothing," she said, shaking her head. "Just a misunderstanding."

"About what?"

"It doesn't matter."

Swan's mobile phone beeped and keen to escape her sister's interrogation, she answered it. It was Fred and he was also on the end of her bad mood. Fox tried not to listen – tidying the books on the shelf by the counter in a bid to distract herself from the conversation. However, her nature won out and as the conversation went on, Fox saw images of Fred and Thalia in a dark room. Fox shook her head, either to clarify the image or to shake it away. Music played in the background – it was a party and Thalia was driving Fred into a wall, her eyes full of promise. *Thalia's made a play for Fred!* the internal concluded.

"… that's not the point! No, I don't want to talk about it. No, don't come over. Maybe. Yep!" Swan switched off her phone.

Fox waited for Swan to explain but Swan had always been secretive about boys. Fox wasn't even sure if Swan and Fred were more than friends; well, she hadn't been until today. There was only one approach and that was to ask her directly; it wasn't as if she wasn't already in a bad mood.

"Did something happen between Fred and …?"

"What's it to do with you?" Swan cut in before Fox could finish her sentence.

"Well if you want to know about me and Will Harrington, then it's only fair to share!"

Swan looked at her over the edge of her teacup. She was assessing the odds of this sharing being weighted in her favour. Unable to be entirely in a bad mood for long, Swan smirked and wrinkled her nose. "So there *is* a you and Will?"

Fox shrugged. "We're just friends. He's a nice guy. I think he likes me."

"Will Harrington! Mr. look-at-my-sparkly-white-teeth-and-my-rippling-six-pack-Harrington!" Swan said, collapsing into a breathless giggle.

Fox felt herself blushing.

"I'm sure it's nothing; he's just being friendly – I think." Fox's forehead crumpled in confusion.

"I've seen the way he looks at you when he thinks you're not looking!" Swan said softly. "I think he more than likes you, Fox."

Fox heard the undertone of hurt in her sister's voice. Fox had never understood the thing between Swan and Fred. They'd been close since primary school and he was loyal to a point of fault when it came to her. In the summer he'd taken a total beating when fought one of the Year twelve boys for calling her a freak. He'd gained a broken nose and a suspension for it. If Swan and Fred were just friends then it was a very intense and complicated friendship. Fox understood that when it came to Fred it wasn't something to idly gossip about. She was about to leave it when Swan blurted out,

"Fred screwed Thalia at Maria's party."

Fox shook her head, her worst fears confirmed. "No! That can't… it's got to be just playground gossip. Fred wouldn't…" Her protests sounded hollow – she'd seen exactly what went on between Fred and Thalia.

Swan's eyes were full of tears but she was too proud to let them free. "It was Fred who told me." She twiddled the ends of her hair, a gesture she did when she wanted to fade away.

"Are you and Fred …?" Fox didn't know how to finish.

Swan nodded her head. “I thought so. We’ve never actually said we were. We’ve never tried to define who we are to one another but I didn’t think…” she sighed heavily and her whole fae-like frame shuddered. “I never thought he’d betray me – especially not with a Ravenheart witch.”

“Does he know about the covens?” Fox asked, surprised. It was an unwritten rule that they never spoke of their witch lives with outsiders.

“He’s known for years. Since we were children. He’s the only one who truly knows me. I thought…” she stopped, unable to hold her tears back any longer, they slid down her cheek. “I hoped I was the only one who would *know* him … but I’m not, and it can never be undone. He’s given himself to a Ravenheart and now it means we can never be together.”

Fox screwed up her forehead. She got the whole betrayal thing but she didn’t understand what it was exactly Swan was saying; why could they never be together? Surely it could be worked out over time.

Swan saw her confusion and realised that Fox had no idea about the curse of her particular gift. “You don’t know about the…?” she stopped, not sure if she was breaking some code or other.

“What? What don’t I know?”

“My gifts suggest that I’m a Vestal. I can only ever be with someone who is pure. Vestals…” she paused, searching for the right phrase. She was blushing. “Vestals mate for life.”

Fox managed to swallow down the laugh erupting from her chest. “I’m sorry, pardon, what?”

Swan’s blush deepened.

"I'm really sorry. I'm having a hard time understanding what you are talking about," Fox offered by way of an apology.

"My emerging ability to control the elements probably means that my powers are Vestal powers and if they aren't kept pure then things can get … dark."

This was the first that Fox had heard about her sister's elemental powers and she wondered what other secrets were floating around their family. "How long have you had these… gifts?"

"They started a couple of months back. There was a downpour of rain and I'd forgotten my coat. I wished it to stop raining – and it did – instantly, just as if someone had turned the tap off. After that there were several other things – like when I was angry at Bunny and a strike of lightening suddenly forked out of the sky and hit the ground right next to her."

Fox let out a low whistle. "Cooool! Shame you didn't strike Thalia down," Fox said smiling.

"Yeah, well it's not funny. The elemental powers take a lot of controlling – it's quite exhausting really.

"And Fred, do you think he was the one – you know, who you were going to …"

Swan nodded and she bit down hard on her lip. "Now, that's out of the question."

"Does Fred know what he's done?"

She laughed bitterly, "No, of course not. I've not told him any of what I've just told you. There's only so much freak I like to reveal at a time."

"Do you think Thalia knew?"

Swan studied Fox hard. "I don't know. I don't see how she possibly could know about me being a Vestal, but I wouldn't rule it out."

"Do you think maybe she bewitched him?" Fox asked.

"I don't know. It's possible that she did," she said wiping her eyes, "but it doesn't matter, he should have been strong enough; his feelings for me should have been his shield."

"You know it's not as easy as that. The Ravenheart's bewitchment powers have been notorious for generations. It wasn't a failing in him if he came under a spell, Swan. Surely you can't be that hard on him."

"Why? Why did she do it?" Swan asked, sadly.

Fox mulled the question over in her head. *They want to weaken you!* she thought, but she said, "I don't know. Who knows what makes the Ravenhearts tick!"

Sex, kidnapping, murder, and torture for a start, the internal offered.

Swan let out a tight smile indicating that the conversation was no longer open. Fox drained the rest of her tea and went to the kitchen, passing mum on the way. She was on the phone. Fox made the unusual effort to wash her cup but it was only in order to listen in on mum, not something she'd normally do but it sounded like she was talking to one of the nieces at Bramble Cottage.

"I'm really sorry, Violet. I'll talk to her about it. Yes, I understand. I've been so snowed under that I've probably taken my eye off them a bit. Okay.

Yes. Pass on my love to Rose and … and to Prim. See you tomorrow. Be blessed."

Fox let out a curse under her breath. *You're in for it now!* the internal warned. *You've sent Prim on a loopy-loop!* Fox considered her options, she could play it innocent and walk right by as if she'd heard nothing and then spend the evening avoiding her mother (probably impossible) or she could hover about and look all meek and apologetic. She decided on option one. Waiting for exactly the opportune moment, when her mother was rifling through a pile of papers at the back of her desk, Fox picked up speed and dashed by with a cheery, "See you later - got loads of homework on!" By the time her mother had realised her daughter was there, Fox was gone.

"Fox by name, Fox by nature!" Wren said, sighing.

Back home in the relative safety of her room, Fox flicked on her laptop and waited for her e-mail to upload. She'd given Jeremiah her e-mail address so that they could start their project remotely – which was exactly how Fox would prefer to do the entire thing. She didn't think that was going to be the case. Jeremiah was playing the part of the diligent student – not that his facade fooled Fox. He was clearly out to impress – or fool. She suspected that all Jeremiah was really doing was biding his time until he could find some trouble. *A boy that handsome doesn't need to abide by the rules!* the internal said wisely. *So why would he?* Fox let her mind wander over her knowledge of Jeremiah

Chase, from his silly (but weirdly attractive) dress sense, to his stubble (clearly more man than boy), to the wicked sparkle in his eyes (obviously knows how it all works). There was something about Jeremiah that made Fox's skin do weird things. She wasn't sure if it was creeping or tingling. The confusion was irritating. Swan would know him immediately; she had the knack of being reading a person's soul. There was no hiding with Swan. *Which is why Fred had to tell her about Thalia – he knew she'd find out anyway.*

"What's your story, Mr. Chase?" Fox asked the empty air.

Suddenly her fingers were tapping out, "The Chase Family, Heargton, Lancashire" into the Google bar. "Just a little curiosity. Knowledge is power!" she said, pre-empting the internal's predictable backlash.

"Wow, impressive!" she said as she saw the very long list of links. She started with the Wikipedia page, which was surprisingly lengthy, "Boy, you're almost famous!"

She scanned through the page, taking a mental note of the various pieces of "useful information." The Chase family had settled in the village in 1510 - earlier than even the Ravenhearts or the Meadowsweets. Connected to King Henry, they were a powerful and wealthy family. The house passed down from father to son throughout the fifteen and early sixteen hundreds until a serious scandal in the family meant that the true heir of Coldstone House emigrated to America, settling in the small but important town of Boston,

Massachusetts in 1660 where he became a minister at the Church of Mathers.

So that's the American link. Jeremiah must be a descendent of James Chase, the internal noted.

Fox scanned over the rest of the document. It didn't contain much of interest. Petty political squabbles and other boring historical engagements until the estate of Coldstone House passed to Lady Asquithe in 1979. She was about to press the back button when she saw an interesting link at the bottom of the page, "Chase Enterprises, New York City."

Chase Enterprises! Sounds like something out of Batman! the internal said through snorting laughter. Fox clicked on it out of idle curiosity, not really expecting to find anything of interest. When she saw Jeremiah's flashy white smile on the front of *Time Magazine* with the caption "New York's most eligible bachelor comes of age," Fox let out a groan.

"Oh, you have got to be kidding!" Fox flitted over the page and took in the briefest of details about the bio-technology firm that was Chase Enterprise. The one detail that jumped out at her was that it was worth over ten billion dollars.

Fox opened a new tab and punched in the name Jeremiah Chase. Pages and pages of links appeared. Image after image of his suited, wealthy, and eligible self with beautiful women draped all over his arm like a Hollywood celebrity. *He is a celebrity, Fox, and he's your study partner – lucky you!*

"So, what the hell is he doing here?" Fox asked.

As she flicked through the pages of links to newspaper articles, magazine shoots, and TV interviews, the recurring phrases, "New York's number one party boy" and "scandal rocks…" proved hard to ignore. She clicked onto several of the links. Not all the newspaper articles were complimentary. Clearly Mr. Jeremiah Chase had been a very naughty boy. As Fox read the lurid details of Jeremiah's relationship with his school teacher and the numerous incidences of drunk and disorderly behaviour, Fox began to feel a deep sense of satisfaction. *He's here as punishment; they've banished him to his crazy old aunt in order to clip his wings.* She couldn't help but laugh when the most recent link read, "Where is NY Party Boy Jay Chase? Come back; all is forgiven!"

"He's right here in Heargton Village!" she said to the screen.

The Facetime application on her Mac buzzed into life and Jeremiah's e-mail address flashed across the screen. "Great!" she said, rolling her eyes. "I can't even escape him in the privacy of my own room." She pressed the reject button. He could write her an e-mail like any other normal person – *and besides, you look a mess!*

Perhaps if she hadn't been so keen to chase down the gossip on Jeremiah, she would have noted the link at the end of the Wikipedia article that led to Professor Daniel Chase, the world's leading expert in the occult and witchcraft, but she didn't.

*

Jeremiah watched the "Call Ended" button flash red and guessed Fox must not be home. It never occurred to him that maybe she had rejected his call. Rejection was something alien to him. He stretched out his legs on his desk and tipped back his chair, flicking through webpages on his iPad. He had resisted Googling himself since his arrival in England. He'd grown tired of it all. He'd spent the last three years of his life not being able to move without a camera bulb flashing. It had been blinding. It was no surprise that he had lost his way. His original anger at his parents' decision to send him to some sleepy backwater in the middle of The Green and Pleasant Land had waned. It had been refreshing to walk about unnoticed. Here, nobody knew how much he was worth, or who is father was having dinner with (it had been the President last night), or what designer underpants he favoured. Okay, so to be fair, he had courted it when it all started, agreeing to every photo-shoot and interview that was offered, but then he had fallen in love with Rachel and he'd realised what a fickle friend the press could be.

When every morning you wake to see the woman you love branded a whore and a child molester, the press becomes an inescapable horror. It didn't matter to them that Jeremiah was seventeen (nearly eighteen) and perfectly capable of making his own choices, or that in the state of New York, seventeen was actually the legal age of consent. Rachel was only four and a half years his senior (half years were important in this ethical debate) but the fact that she had been his teacher made her a monster. The kind of monster that the press likes to destroy until there is nothing beautiful or good left. His father refused to understand. He reduced the whole scandal down to an over-active sex drive and a general lack of respect for the family name, which really meant the business.

He had been told in no uncertain terms that should his father discover that there had been any contact between Jeremiah and that "Scarlet woman!" (a pun his father had found particularly fruitful throughout the whole ordeal) then Jeremiah would be cut loose without a penny to his name. Jeremiah had then undertaken a whole series of ridiculous Romeo-style actions, believing his love for Rachel was totally worth the ten billion dollars he would inherit one day. But then he had seen her in the arms of another man - a "grown up" who had swept in and rescued her from the misery of the press-intrusive months. A man who would show the world that Ms. Scarlet was capable of being reformed, that she was turning her back on her debauched, inappropriate sexual affair with one of her students, and was going to settle down into a perfectly respectable life. The large diamond ring on her finger was a symbol of her taming.

That was the night that Jeremiah had "stolen" his father's Maserati and driven it at over a hundred miles an hour through several speed clocks and past a patrol car. The sensible thing would have been to stop but Jeremiah had never been very good at being sensible. In the end he rather un-dramatically fell low on fuel and was forced to pull over, where he was immediately arrested. His police mug-shots made the second page of the *New York Times* the very next day. As Luce quipped, "Clearly your popularity is waning bro – you're becoming old news!"

God, how he missed Luce! Crazy Aunt Penelope was hardly a substitute. When Jeremiah had first arrived he thought that he had been mistakenly dropped off at some historical amusement attraction. The traditionally dressed staff (all two of them in these times of fading aristocracy) had been waiting for him on the steps of Coldstone House and then he'd been ushered through to the parlour, where his aunt was sitting on some uncomfortable looking antique sofa with a wolfhound resting on her lap and a bone china tea cup and saucer in her hands. She still wore a high necked collar with the customary cameo broach pinned precariously near to her throat and spoke with an accent that Jeremiah thought had ended with the War. He smiled at the recollection. Pearson (the butler at the Chase's Hamptons mansion) had sagely offered the advice,

"There are three things that you shouldn't speak about over there, sir; money, religion, and most importantly, don't mention the War!"

Jeremiah missed Pearson. He was a funny and kind man. He tried Fox on Facetime again. When he didn't get a reply, he gave up the idea for the evening. He didn't want to appear too keen. With little else to do, he flicked aimlessly through the Google search engine for any information on Heargton village and the Rookeries Hospital. He was surprised to find quite so many hits. He'd assumed that Heargton was an innocuous little village with a boring, quiet history. What he was surprised to see was the name Heargton connected with several hundred paranormal blogs, websites, and articles. He reached out and retrieved the apple from his desk. He took a big bite and said with a stuffed mouth, "Ooh, things have got interesting!"

Jeremiah hopped between blogs and articles. Most of them were about the ghosts reputed to haunt the Green Man Public House and the ghost of the grieving widow in the Churchyard of St. Ursula's. There were several posts about paranormal investigations that had taken place at the Rookeries, finding pretty much what he expected – nothing except for a few draughts and banging doors. He was just about to put it aside for the evening when he caught sight of mention of Coldstone House. Memories of Saturday came back to him. He had done a really good job of blocking the impossible things out since then; the way that the little red leather ball had rolled along the gallery hall, or the way that the door of a locked room could suddenly be found open. He shook his head, trying to convince himself that those events had happened in a dream and not in his rational world. He scanned over the page, learning that the Georgian manor house was built on the site of the original Tudor house and that when they had pulled the old house down, they had found the body of a young woman in the wall, which was apparently the way they staved off evil spirits back in the middle ages. "Shame it didn't protect young girls against murdering aristocrats," Jeremiah mused. A cold shiver ran up his spine and he shuddered, cursing the draughts from the old windows. All attempts by paranormal investigators to visit Coldstone House had been rejected. Jeremiah smiled at the thought of Aunt Penelope replying to them in no uncertain terms.

Finishing his apple, he switched the iPad off and stripped off his clothes down to his boxers and stood in front of the window, the moon and the woods beyond. He closed his eyes and stretched out his arms, breathing deep from within his diaphragm. Yoga was Jeremiah's salvation – at least there was one thing he could thank his father for: the month in the Swiss retreat, which his father had sent him to in an attempt to calm down his party-crazed son. It had had limited success.

From the next room, the sound of a wind-up music box floated down the corridor and through the gap under his door. If Jeremiah hadn't been lost in the throws of a violent vision of flames and smoke he would have heard it and understood that he was far from being alone.

6

Thalia Ravenheart had arranged to meet her sisters at the barn on the farm at dusk. She had been given a list of errands to run after college and she had completed them dutifully. At first she had been unsure whether her sisters' plans would work or if they had lost their minds entirely. Of the three of them, Thalia felt that she was the most streetwise, the most connected to the real world. She was the one who truly understood they no longer lived in the "glorious" days of the past, and that they had to adapt for a smaller modern world. It was increasingly difficult to do anything these days without somebody watching. The whole world seemed recorded through the lens of a CCTV camera or posted on Facebook.

Abducting a girl from their own village community had been risky, but Nigella had been confident that to snatch a girl from their own ground would be less suspicious; nobody would search for a beast amongst their own. The police would be searching for an outsider, a faceless and unfamiliar threat. People didn't like to think of an enemy in camp. Although the village had always kept the Ravenhearts at arms' length, Nigella knew that they were an accepted eccentricity. Their long bloodline, attached to the very stones that built the village, afforded them a certain respect – like a relative that you're not particularly keen on but you tolerate because blood is thicker than water. Much to Thalia's surprise, this approach appeared to be working. She'd been surprised by the general sense of disinterest surrounding Martha's disappearance. Everyone at college seemed to think she would turn up in a few days. It helped that Jack wasn't at college either, adding to the whole Romeo and Juliet story circulating the corridors. It had been a shame about Jack; he was a nice boy, but needs must. Somebody was sure to find him soon, lying in that warehouse at the edge of Lancaster, coming down off the high that Lilith had skillfully administered. Physically he would be fine but there was no telling about his mind; Lilith had a nasty little habit of lacing her concoctions with a good dose of psychotic horror that left her victims scared in a way no medication could heal.

Martha Paisley had been specially selected based on Thalia's inside knowledge of the Heargton community. If there was a moment of guilt over selecting Martha over anybody else, it was fleeting. Thalia had no time for saps. Martha was the perfect archetypal virgin. Blonde, blue eyed, sweet, and innocent. She had played the Virgin Mary in St. Ursula's church nativity for most of her childhood – of course Jack had been Joseph. It had been during the Saturday Church Youth Club that their young love had blossomed. In these promiscuous times the selecting of virgins was a bit of a gamble, but unfortunately for Martha, her wearing of a chastity ring and her constant bleeting on about how her and Jack were going to wait until they were married before having "relations," as she quaintly used to refer to them, had been her undoing.

At the time of her abduction, Martha had no idea who her captors were. They had come at her like shadows in the night. Masked and hooded, they had sacked both Jack and Martha and thrown Martha into the back of the Land Rover and Jack into the boot of his own car. Thalia had been surprised that abducting another human being had been so easy and was curious that more people didn't do it. Lilith had dealt with Jack first, driving him out of Heargton, to the abandoned warehouse on the industrial estate. She'd applied the tourniquet and injected him with her potion swiftly and expertly into his vein. It had only taken a matter of minutes for the toxins to take root in his system. He'd have no recollection of what happened to him whilst under the influence, meaning that he was never going to be in a position to honestly deny any involvement in his girlfriend's murder. His drug misuse would come as a terrible shock to the community, but it would offer them an explanation that they'd be eager to hang on to.

Martha had shown an amazing amount of spirit once they'd actually got her back to the barn. Thalia was surprised to discover her physical strength, even if she was disgustingly emotionally weak. During the first night of Martha's captivity, Thalia had been driven almost to violence with Martha's cries for her beloved. It took her a whole twelve hours (and a gag) before she finally accepted the fact that he had abandoned her to fate. Despite the barn being locked and Nigella and Lilith keeping watch, Nigella had a perverse taste for suffering and had strung Martha by the arms to one of the wooden beams of the barn, ensuring that the rope was just the perfect length for making her stand on her tip-toes. Thalia had been sent away at the first light of day. It was important that a sense of normality continued. She was directed to go to college as usual (a challenge that Thalia took a surprising amount of delight in) and then to go and retrieve some specific tools from a range of different DIY stores around the county. It would not do to buy them all from one store, as it would make them more traceable.

The sisters were waiting for the full moon, which would be in one day's time. Being a blood moon, it was a particularly powerful night and had been selected specifically as the night they would conduct the resurrection ritual. Thalia was still not sure what the ritual involved; Lilith and Nigella had an annoying habit of still treating her like a child and excluding her from the more "grown-up" details of things; she still had no idea why they had set about abducting Martha before they actually needed her – aside from opportunity.

It had been quite a wild party and Thalia could understand why two frigid little bible criers would want to make an early exit, but she had been taken off guard by just how early they'd made moves to leave. Thalia had been on a mission of her own that night – the snagging of Freddie Simons. Sensing that Martha and Jack were getting antsy about the way the party was turning out (fun!) it meant that Thalia had had to use a surprisingly concentrated amount of power on bewitching Fred into bed. There had been little time for hearts and flowers but then again, it hadn't been romance that she was looking for; she had simply wanted to break Swan Meadowsweet's heart. Breaking the heart of your opponent (even before the game began) was a sure-fire way of winning, especially when that heart was as sweet and good as Swan Meadowsweet's.

This little twist on their whole endeavour had of course been Nigella's idea. Always a merciless chess player, her idea was to break the opposition before they were even aware they were involved. Thalia had been issued with instructions to break the Meadowsweet sisters one by one. She had jumped at the chance of a little bit of old-school wickedness, but had known from the start that the real challenge was always going to be Fox. That was until Thalia had gleefully learned the unlikely fact that Fox Meadowsweet was in love - and with none other than Will Harrington, Fallford Comprehensive's very own calendar boy. He was so far out of her league that it was pathetic. She'd already made a complete laughing stock of herself when she threw herself at him in front of the whole Geography class. Mind Thalia (and quite a few others) had been surprised to see him go off with her. "Perhaps love really is blind," she mused. In a way, Thalia was disappointed that Fox was making it so easy for her. She'd had a little more respect for her. Now the simple "love breaks your heart" tactic was probably going to suffice for her too. Disappointingly predictable but effective. At least seducing Will would be more pleasurable than the fumbling, virginal Fred.

"Hey ho!" she said to herself, 'There's always Bunny left to play with!"

*

It was Wednesday. Fox hated Wednesdays. She had lessons back to back and all over the school. Wednesdays always felt like she spent the whole day dashing about. It didn't help that she'd forgotten her watch and had to assume that she was running late for everything.

Jeremiah chased after her down the corridor, weaving in and out of the other students. Totally mortified by the unmistakable American-accented shouts of, "Hey, Foxy! Foxy, wait up!" she kept her head low and hoped she might get away with pretending that she couldn't hear him. There was only one person she didn't mind calling her Foxy and that was Will. Hearing Jeremiah use it felt uncomfortably intimate and clearly other people thought so too. Fox could hear the whispered and pointed comments of some of the girls. She became conscious of blushing. It wasn't because of Jeremiah's *very* public attention, but because she was angry: angry that they should think her unworthy of having the attention of a boy like Jeremiah and in turn, of a boy like Will.

She'd spent a self-surprising amount of time thinking about what it would be like to be Will's girlfriend, and how the school-bitches would react. She guessed it wouldn't go down well. She had no *real* interest in being his girlfriend. After all, what on Earth would a school rugby jock and a white witch really have in common? She couldn't imagine filling their time with shared conversation. *Which would leave a lot of time for...* the internal piped up. By the time that she reached the door of the English classroom, it didn't stand a chance against her rising irritation. It flew back with a crack and a bang, causing her teacher, Miss Pearson to jump from her skin. She scanned Fox, reading her student. She had an unnerving habit of this – almost to the point that Fox had idly wondered if she wasn't one of her kind.

"Is everything okay, Fox?" she asked in her lyrical voice.

Fox didn't get a chance to answer before Jeremiah came bounding in behind her and sent her flying.

"Jeez, what is it with you?" she snapped at him.

He was bent over, with his hand on his stomach, acting out that he was exhausted from the chase. He was laughing, which by this point Fox found intensely irritating.

"What's with *me*? I've been chasing *you* down that corridor for miles! Are you hard of hearing?"

Out of the corner of her eye Fox could see Miss Pearson watching the interaction between her and Jeremiah with bemused curiosity. *Even she thinks that you're batting way out of your league!* the internal said snarkily.

"What do you want? I've got class!" she said, turning her back on him and heading over to her desk.

"Me too!" he said in a ridiculously cheery voice. He walked up to Miss Pearson and extended a hand before turning on the Chase Charm.

"Nicc to meet you, M'am. I'm Jeremiah Chase, the new boy!" He flashed her a smile and Fox saw Miss Pearson's impeccable professionalism slip as she blushed and faltered.

I guess his effect on female teachers is universal, Fox thought, remembering what she had read about the New York scandal of Jeremiah and his pretty teacher of Philosophy.

"Nice to meet you, Mr. Chase. Please take a seat. The one next to Fox is free!"

He turned and flashed Fox a look of triumph and Fox dived into her rucksack, rolling her eyes. *What is your problem with him?* the internal asked innocently. Fox was surprised by the question. She looked over her bag at him as he headed towards her desk, smiling. *He's been nothing but polite and charming.*

He sat down and dropped his battered leather school-satchel onto the desk. Clearly he thought native accessories were ironic and cool. Thankfully he seemed at last to have got the idea that Fox didn't want to make small chat and he busily set about pulling out his note books and pens. Now that Fox knew just how wealthy he was, she became conscious of how everything about him was expensive, including his trendy-rustic-alternative-Amish look. She noted the iPad case in his bag and for one scornful moment thought he might be a flashy enough prat to pull it out and use it to make his class notes. He flipped the lid down, leaving it in the bag. She watched him out of the corner of her eye and tried to reason what it was about him that affected her so negatively. He really hadn't given her any reason to be so cold. She pulled out her Dairy Milk and snapped off a square. Chocolate always offered some form of answer. Impulsively she handed out the chocolate to him and offered him a piece. It was a small token but one which he noted. He dropped his shoulders and smiled at her.

"Thank you!"

" I guess we'd better arrange a time to start this history project," she said with little enthusiasm.

"How about after school today? I'm getting the school bus back so we could do coffee at that place in the village."

"Sara's?" Fox asked, taking a deep breath. It was bad enough having been witnessed on one non-date that week let alone two

"Is that a problem?" he asked.

"No, I suppose not!" she said with resignation.

"Cool. I've got loads of material from the tourist office."

"Cool," she repeated raising her eyebrows and nodding. *See he's not such a jerk after all!* the internal concluded.

At lunch Bunny came skittering over with a big lip-glossed smile. "Hey, big sis!"

"Hi, Bunny. Are you having lunch with me?"

"Nope, just a swing by, I've got choir."

"Can I help you?"

Bunny was almost bubbling over with excitement. Her hazel eyes were dazzling. "Is it true? Oh, tell me it's true! I mean, obviously I'll hate you, but it would still be cool and anyway he's not the only…"

Fox raised her hand in the air instructing her to halt the ridiculous babble that was coming out her mouth. "What are you on about?"

"You and Will Harrington! It's all over the school that you and him got a 'thang going on,'" she sidled her shoulders in a move she'd learned from watching far too much American import TV.

Fox put her sandwich down, suddenly losing her appetite and rolled her eyes. It had been an eye-rolling kind of day. "Bunny, listen and listen carefully – there is nothing, I repeat, *nothing*, going on between Will Harrington and me. We have a project to do together and so we are hanging out. That is all!"

"I thought it was Jeremiah Chase that you had a '*project*' with?" She eyeballed Fox letting her know that she wasn't going to be fobbed off. "I have to say, I didn't have you down as the two '*project*' kind of girl." She laughed loudly at her own genius.

"Well, that is how it is. Let's just say I lucked out on the project partner front!" she replied snappily. "Hadn't you better go to choir?"

"I heard that you and Will bunked lessons yesterday afternoon."

Fox didn't dignify the statement with a response. Frustrated that Fox wasn't letting her in on what she clearly believed to be the hot new romance of the school year, Bunny struck the low and vicious blow. "I can't imagine how much trouble you'd be in if Mum found out."

Fox stared her down. She loved Bunny dearly but there were times the Fox could quite happily smack her one. "Don't try and be clever, Bunny, it isn't your strong point!"

Bunny's hand flew to her chest in mock pain. Then turning on her heels she clicked her fingers in the air causing the bottle of water on the table to lift into the air and fall over, pouring water all over the table and narrowly missing Fox's jeans. "Bitch!" Fox muttered under her breath, but she was too busy mopping up to retaliate.

Swan appeared seemingly out of nowhere. "Did I just see Bunny…" she dropped her voice, "use magic in the school canteen!" It was clear from her tone that this breach in protocol was so going to get back to Mum. As much as Fox relished the idea of Bunny being for it when they got home, she knew that Bunny was always keen to pull whoever she could into the hot water with her for company. She could really do without that being her. She was already in mum's bad books for the incident with Prim.

"No, I think I must have jogged the table."

Swan shot her a look and said, "I don't believe you for one second but I'm going to let it pass." She smiled. "Are you okay? I guess you're having a tough day being the daily news!"

Fox sighed heavily. "Why doesn't anybody have anything better to think about then who's going out with – or *not* in my case? It does my head in!"

Swan laughed. "You should be flattered they think that you have your claws into both of them! "

"Not you too?"

"What?" Swan asked.

"Thinking that I couldn't get a boy like Harrington or Chase if I wanted to."

Swan was taken aback by the sudden twist in conversation and couldn't organise a response before Fox continued to vent, "I mean, what if Will and I were going out? Why would that be such big news? Why would everybody feel the need to comment on it? Is it because I'm so unattractive that for a slightly handsome boy to fancy me it's worthy of a national news broadcast?"

Swan raised both of her hands. "Whoa, Fox, take it easy. You know that's not how I think."

"No, but others do!"

"This isn't really about Will or Jeremiah, is it? There's something else eating you up. This is just a convenient annoyance to hang your hat on. What is it?" Swan sat down, indicating that whatever plans she'd had, she'd changed.

Fox looked at her and bit down on her lip. "Not here! I can't talk about it here."

"Where then? Shall we meet after school?"

"No, I've got a study date with Mr. Chase."

Swan couldn't help but slip a smile and Fox shot her a warning glance. "Okay, so I'll see you afterwards. Mum wants some nettle nectar and you know how particular she is about it being gathered on the waxing. We can go together. It'll give us a chance to talk."

Fox nodded, but she didn't much relish the idea of a moonlit walk through the woods with a crazy abductor on the loose. She mangled the last few bites of her sandwich. It tasted like cardboard but deep down she knew that she should start building her strength. She was coming to terms with the visions but they hinted that a greater darkness was rising. There was a reason the Goddess had sent her them – and she guessed that she was expected to act on them. Only she had no idea what course of action she was meant to be taking. She'd been hoping for the mysterious and convenient appearance of a Vision's Manual, but nothing had turned up – and Prim had been as much use as a chocolate tea-pot. All that the visit to Prim had achieved was to draw attention to her newly established insanity. Martha had been missing for too long and there really wasn't much more time to get her shit together – that was if it wasn't already too late. She refused to believe that it was, surely the visions would have stopped if Martha was … *You've not had a vision in nearly twelve hours!* the internal offered.

As if on cue, Fox felt her body rushing through a tunnel of blackness and was vaguely aware of her body hitting the ground. Her last conscious thought was the absurd idea that she could summon the visions when she wanted.

*

It's the kind of darkness that hides your hands from your own eyes. There is the crunching of gravel underneath foot. The night is screaming. Speeding, navy clouds mostly block the light of the full moon. She can smell the rich metallic tang of blood and wishes she could see her hands because she wants to check that they are clean. Part of her fears they are not. The terrible sound of invocations travel on the cool eddies of air. The words shake her bones and cool her blood. They are calling the Ancient Ones: those who move without substance or soul. Fox looks to the moon and the tears of the Goddess fall to Earth like salted rain. It is the beginning of the end.

Way out in the grey and swirling distance of the sky, Fox hears the voice of her sister, Swan. It is soft and beautiful. She becomes aware of his sister's touch and it feels like the touch of an angel. Warmth and light spreads through her, replacing the dark stain of the vision.

"Fox? Are you okay? Take it steady. You fainted."

Fox feels her body lifted up into the air but it feels like her spirit is still pinned down to the floor. When her eyes finally come into focus, it is to find herself surrounded by a cast of actors that all look like somebody she knows from her real life, but in that moment, she can't be entirely sure that they are who they say they are. Everything looks different. Whatever knowledge she has brought back from the vision, it has skewed the way she sees her world, and she isn't sure that it will ever look straight again.

"I need to speak to Will!" she muttered. "Please, somebody find Will!"

*

By the time Will made it to the canteen, Fox felt incredibly foolish. She had no idea what she wanted with him now he'd actually arrived. The afternoon lesson bell had gone and the canteen was at least empty of spectators, which was good because he looked about as awkward about his summoning as she felt.

"They said that you had a turn and that you…" he cleared his throat and blushed "…asked for me," he said, flashing a look at Swan. He seemed to have difficulty looking Fox in the eye. "Are you alright?" he asked, stuffing his hands deep into his pockets.

Fox stared at Swan, urging her to leave them alone but Swan was purposefully refusing to read her sister's demand. Instead she compromised by shuffling off to the water cooler on the pretense of getting Fox a drink but they all knew that she was listening in, trying to get to grips with all the weirdness. Will pushed back the plaid cotton of his sleeves and bent down on his haunches. He lowered his voice and asked,

"Was it another vision, Foxy?"

She looked at him and for the first time she saw something in him that she'd never seen before – she saw the man he would become. This shift in her perspective was disturbing and yet at the same time strangely reassuring. Fox bit down on her lip and nodded before croaking,

"Yes!" She felt the threat of tears and forced them away. "What am I going to do?"

His eyes flicked to the floor as he thought for a moment and then back to her face.

“I think we should try and find the place where your visions are set.”

“Really?” Fox gasped. The thought had of course passed through her mind but she’d filed it in the Insane Ideas file. “And what if we…” Fox paused to let her mind cope with the tens of different scenarios.

“I guess we’ll have to cross that bridge when we get to it.” He stood up and looked back over his shoulder at Swan who was still fiddling with the water cooler. “Look, I’ve got some stuff I’ve got to do straight after school but shall I pick you up about seven?”

Fox nodded, relived that at last that something seemed to be happening. Swan, approached with her eyebrows knitted together and her lips pressed tightly. Clearly she’d managed to hear, despite the distance. “What exactly do you have in mind? Driving around the countryside in the dark, looking for a murder house and then what? Breaking in, saving Martha and…?” Fox shrugged. “Don’t you think that all qualifies as being a little bit stupid?” She stopped to take a breath, but it wasn’t an invitation to respond.

She’d already formed her own answer. “The whole idea is ridiculous. You two aren’t Thelma and Scooby Doo; you have no idea what you could be getting yourselves into – and besides it’s all a waste of time. Everybody, including the police, is quite convinced that Martha and Jack have eloped. If that’s a good enough explanation for everybody else then, visions or no visions, why isn’t it…” Swan stopped and pressed her hand to her mouth,

"Oh, my – you've seen something more haven't you? Something that you haven't told us?"

"Sssh, keep it down will you!" Fox warned.

Swan turned her attention to Will. "And you knew about this?" She looked at Fox with a look of vicious accusation. "You told *him* rather than your own sisters!"

Sensing an oncoming argument between the two of them, Will made a mumbled farewell and left.

"I didn't think it was…" Fox shifted uncomfortably in her seat. She didn't really know why she hadn't told her sisters the whole truth about the visions. "I thought you would think I was crazy – or imagining it all."

I wanted to protect you. I wanted to keep you safe. I didn't want you stained by the darkness, said the internal.

"And what…? You thought that Will Harrington would *understand* you more than your own sisterhood!" She dropped her voice but it sounded less like a whisper and more like the hiss of a serpent, "Does he know what you are?"

"*Who!*" Fox mumbled, correcting her sister. "Who I am. Not *what* I am!"

Swan shook her head and turned on her heel, running her hand through her hair with frustration. "I get it! This is some whacky rebellion. You don't think we understand you; you feel different from us? You've seen Bunny and me gaining in powers and gifts and it's making you feel…" Her voice pitched hysterically for the second time in two days.

Fox genuinely hadn't had any of those thoughts, but now that Swan had put such ideas into words, there was something that rang true about them. She was thrown into confusion with a whole set of new things to angst about. She shrugged. Swan hadn't finished. "So what is it? An identity crisis? Hormones?" she paused and eyeballed Fox. "Don't tell me that it's *love*?"

Fox couldn't help but burst out a laugh even though she knew that it was probably the worst thing she could do at that moment. "For Harrington? Give me a break!" She rolled her eyes and snorted.

Swan was running out of steam. The events of the week had made her exhausted and out of balance. Fox felt sorry for her and wanted desperately to offer her an answer, an apology to make things right between them, but she didn't know the answers herself and she really wasn't sure what she was meant to be apologising for. She started the sentence and hoped that the Goddess would somehow end it for her.

"It's not that I don't love you all, or that I don't feel I belong. I'm not rebelling. I have nothing to rebel against. I am loved and I am known. The visions – they've done something to me, Swan, and I really don't know what it is..." she stopped, finding herself washed over with emotions she'd not previously acknowledged. Something Prim said flew back into her memory: *They come with a responsibility.* Seeing Fox upset, Swan softened and crouched down next to her, putting her arm around her shoulders. Fox snuffled, "They make me feel... polluted."

"Polluted?"

"Yes. I know it sounds a funny kind of word, but the things I see in the visions are…" Fox trailed off. She didn't want to relive them. "And it's not just what I see, it's what I hear and smell… and feel. That's why I went to Prim. I thought she would help me understand and tell me how to deal with them."

"And did she?"

"No," Fox cracked a smile, "she just managed to freak me out more!"

Swan laughed, "Yep, she's a little…" Swan twirled her finger alongside her forehead.

"I'd say, quite a lot …" Fox echoed her sister's hand gesture and they laughed.

"But seriously, Fox, you've got to go to the police with what you've seen. Do you know for certain if she is dead?"

Fox shook her head. "Not yet, but I have a feeling it is going to be soon. The moon is waxing and tomorrow she will be at her most powerful."

"Then whatever you tell the police has got to help."

"How about I tell them who's taken her?"

Swan's eyes rounded with surprise. "You know that?"

"Yes, but when I tell you, you really will think I'm crazy!"

"Who is it? Do we know him? Oh, my, I don't think I want to know." Swan breathed in deeply. "Okay, tell me."

"It's not a him, she's been taken by the Ravenheart sisters."

"No!" Swan shook her head. "I know they're a bit out there, but… really?"

Fox nodded her head. "Really. They're planning on using her as part of a ritual to call forth the Ancient Ones."

Swan didn't respond at first. The atmosphere had turned so heavy that it compressed the lungs making it hard to breathe. She fixed Fox's eye and something ran between them, some elemental bond of understanding. Until that moment, Fox had never realised that she and her sister could communicate telepathically; she'd always assumed that Swan had been astute, sensitive. She never knew that all this time, her sister had been able to dance around her thoughts and steal every secret. It hadn't been highly sensitive hearing, it had been thought reaping. Now Swan's voice spoke loud and clear in Fox's head despite no sound coming from her mouth.

"Don't ever mention the Ancient Ones in voice. Do not speak of this with anybody, especially our mother. I am with you. Share your vision with me."

Fox's mouth hung open, her eyes wide with new knowledge. Swan's thought-voice was stronger than Fox could ever have imagined. It resonated strength and courage and was in complete contrast to Swan's exterior delicacy.

Fox shook her head and began to speak from her mouth but Swan placed her finger over Fox's lips and commanded her through thoughts, "Think-speak. If we are overheard we're in mortal danger. The Ancient Ones have ears everywhere."

Fox focused hard, hearing her own voice in her head, forming the words carefully, watching Swan's face for a reaction that showed she was receiving. "Can you hear me?"

Swan nodded.

"I can't call forth the vision. I feel so weak."

"You must. Close your two eyes and open up you third. Feel the eye taking in the light so that it can see."

Fox felt strangely submissive under this new awesome voice of her sister and she did as she was bid. It was hard; she didn't really want to open her eye. The sense of horror still felt like a dark stain. She felt her heart beat rise and a dull ache settle in her chest.

"Don't forget to breathe, Fox!"

Fox gasped for air and found herself hurled back through her consciousness into the realm of visions. Her visions pounded past her, as if they were running away from something terrifying. The overall effect was that of a film on fast forward and they added to her sense of disorientation. She felt sick. Sounds layered upon sounds. Screams and chants, hollers and weeping all rolled together boisterously. Bright white lights flashed like Morse-code signalling so that she was forced to back away squinting. There was no clarity to any of it. There was no hope that she could work out from all the psychic mess where Martha was. There was no saving her.

"It's no good!" Fox cried. "Everything is such a jumble. There's more than just Martha. It's like there is a whole history trying to be heard."

"Don't be too hard on yourself, Fox. It takes time to cultivate your gifts. I have something else we can try when we go nettle picking later."

Fox looked at her sister in a new and strange light. Until now Swan had always appeared mostly normal, apart from her slightly whimsical ability to entice small woodland creatures into her hand or the way she sang to the four winds, but now Fox understood that her sister had much stronger powers than she'd yet displayed, and Fox wasn't entirely sure as to how she felt about this; part of her felt slightly afraid - after all, the mind talking stuff was pretty crazy shit.

Fox stood and gathered her stuff together. Her sister seemed surprised that Fox should be about to continue her usual Wednesday routine and cocked her head in question.

"I'm fine!" Fox said defiantly. "I just want to try and go on as normal as I can."

Swan flicked her golden hair and a waft of rose perfume erupted from her. "Okay!" she sighed. "I'll catch up with you later."

Fox smiled. "Laters!" As she walked out of the door, she heard Swan's voice loud and clear in her head.

"Be safe, sister."

A chill ran up Fox's spine.

7

Fox reluctantly took the last seat on the school bus next to Jeremiah, which considering they had at least a two-hour study date ahead of them, shouldn't have bothered Fox as much as it did. He, on the other hand, seemed really pleased that fate had worked to bring them more time together. As the engine started, sealing Fox's fate, Bunny couldn't resist turning around and flashing Fox a big, cheesy grin. If Jeremiah hadn't been attempting to engage her in an intensely energetic conversation about the Heargton lay-lines, she would have replied with the highly mature response of sticking out her tongue.

"So, what I've discovered is that Heargton rests exactly on the intersection between two lines."

"You discovered that did you?" Fox couldn't help the mocking tone.

"Well, I *read* it." He rolled his eyes in minor exasperation. "Do you know what the consequence of that is?"

Fox shook her head. "Why don't you tell me?"

"It means that Heargton is the perfect portal for paranormal activity!"

"Really?" Fox replied in her most bored tone.

"What, like those bloody animals that 'av been taking out the eyes of Bartly's mares?" Smithdon asked from the driver's seat.

"My mam says it's the work of satanists," said Jimmy, a rather loud-mouthed Year eight who had the unfortunate look of a far too closely mixed gene pool.

"Satanists?" Jeremiah asked, practically leaping out of his seat with excitement before leaning forward between the front seats. "Hey, Smithdon, is it true what Jimmy says, that they think there are satanists in the area?"

Fox was somewhat surprised by the sudden excitement that the idea created in Jeremiah.

"Put your belt on!" Smithdon snapped. "You elder ones are meant to be settin' a ruddy example."

Fox smirked at Jeremiah being put so unceremoniously back in his place.

Jeremiah fell back into his seat and clipped his belt, muttering something inaudible under his voice before pulling out as much belt as possible and swinging around in his seat.

"Hey, Jimmy," Jeremiah called, but Jimmy had stuck his earphones in and was blasting himself to premature deafness. With no one else to turn to, he turned his attention to Fox. "So, Satanists? Well it wouldn't surprise me. These transecting lay lines are like honey to a bee for those weirdos."

"Pollen."

"Pardon?"

"Bee's *make* honey, they're not attracted to it – they're attracted to pollen!"

Jeremiah stared at her, his mental cogs whirling. His brows knitted together and then he dipped his head into her personal space and whispered, "Where do you get off being such a bitch?"

Fox recoiled, surprised by his quickly changing mood. "I…I…" she stammered.

"No, I've had to put up with your shit all day. You've been rude, cold, and condescending. What exactly is your problem, Foxy?"

"It's not me that has the problem!" she snapped, bringing the fleeting attention of those sitting around her.

Expecting Jeremiah to retreat, she was surprised to feel him close in, his lips brushing her ear and his breath hot on her neck. "Is it because you want me to kiss you and you just don't know how to ask?"

Fox's heart thumped. Adrenalin coursed through her body. She felt a great swell of anger and she wasn't sure that she had the strength to contain it. Before she could fully register what she was doing, the sound of a crack startled her. Jeremiah clutched his cheek, rearranged his jaw, and smiled.

Fox felt the eyes of the whole bus stare at her.

"Wow, lady - you sure know how to burn a slap!"

If it had been anybody else, she would have collapsed into an apologetic heap. She'd never hit anybody in her life, and yet she couldn't get over the fact that Jeremiah had totally deserved it.

"Everything all right back there?" Smithdon asked, clearly amused that the cocky Yank had got his come-uppance.

Fox caught Swan staring at her in the rear view mirror but she had decided to stay well out of it – not even a crazy mind message. Bunny was grinning from ear to ear, soaking up the drama.

Fox glanced at Jeremiah sideways. He was still rubbing his grinning jaw, playing on the drama of it but Fox also saw that when he thought that she wasn't looking, he winced with genuine discomfort. The thought of it made her feel good.

He spent the rest of the bus journey sulking. Fox left him to it and retrieved her headphones from her pocket. Two could play at the no-speaking game, and she certainly wasn't going to apologise. *He was being a complete ass - the only thing you need to apologise for is not hitting him harder,* the internal said in her haughtiest voice.

When Smithdon pulled up outside The Green Man (the stop for most of his passengers) Jeremiah bundled out of the bus after Fox.

"So you're still on for a study date, then?" Fox asked him.

He flashed her a tight smile and rubbed at his jaw. "I thought I'd brave it out." He laughed and Fox's smile betrayed her head.

Fox hadn't really put much thought into where they should go to study. All she did know was that she didn't want Jeremiah in their home. It wasn't that the small cottage embarrassed her, more that she felt protective over it, which was silly, as Jeremiah posed no threat.

With typically awkward timing, Wren was watering the flower baskets either side of Moonstone's door. Seeing her daughter she raised a hand and waved, then she saw Jeremiah and an emotion passed over her face, but it was so fleeting that Fox couldn't rightly interpret it. She half raised a hand back and smiled.

"Is that your mum?" Jeremiah asked casually enough.

"Yeah."

"Does she work there?"

"It's our shop."

Fox knew that he was looking at the shop sign with its golden pentagram and at the crystals that made up most of the shop window display.

"Very… new age!" he said distractedly. Fox blushed. The way he said it made it all seem slightly silly. "There are loads of shops like that down in the Village. My sister, Lucia, is quite into all that…" his sentence trailed off, unwilling to define exactly what it was.

"Anyway," Fox sighed, "I guess the library is a good place to start. They close at five so we've only got an hour and a half."

She turned and walked off in the direction of the library but Jeremiah continued to look at the shop with a fascinated curiosity, before shaking his head and following after her.

The library was empty except for the lady that Fox recognised as the crazy bat that spent a lot of her days sat on the well at the center of the village, feeding the pigeons. When their mother had caught Fox and Bunny saying cruel things about her, she had sent them both to bed without their supper; a surprising display of hard discipline from their otherwise soft and gentle mother. In the morning Wren had told them that "that crazy old bat" was called Mrs. Higgins, and she had once been young and beautiful, just as they were now. She went on to say that something terrible had happened to her, which had sent her into a great sadness from which she had never returned. She told them that they should think on that next time they were tempted to mock her. Wren had refused to tell the girls what had happened to Mrs. Higgins and so in retaliation Fox had continued to think of the old woman as the crazy old bat. But for the first time today, when she looked on the sad wretched figure of a woman that had once been, Fox felt a pang of remorse. Fox had spent the last ten minutes staring at her, lost in her thoughts whilst Jeremiah had been flicking through the pages of a local history book.

"Did you know that Heargton is reputed to be one of the most haunted villages in the world?"

"Um ha!" she offered, still focused on Mrs. Higgins, who was now nibbling on a sandwich, which she was attempting to hide in her handkerchief. Fox hoped it was clean.

"And that the village has long been associated with witchcraft! That is very interesting – especially in light of…" He trailed off, noting that Fox was not paying him hardly any attention. "You're not listening to a word I'm saying, are you?"

Fox pulled her attention back to him. He was sat with his hands laced, his fingers tapping against his lips.

"Are you still upset with me for what I said on the bus? You know that I was only teasing, don't you? I wouldn't have said it if I thought you weren't going to find it funny."

Fox looked at him. She really didn't believe that he'd meant it to be funny. He hadn't been in a joking kind of mood. She wasn't sure what kind of mood he'd been in.

Fox nodded. "Of course!"

"Then why did you slap me?"

"You deserved it!"

"What for? Because you thought I was flirting with you?"

"Yes!"

"I thought you'd be flattered!"

Fox almost choked on her cough.

"What's so funny?" he asked, genuinely surprised by her reaction.

"You are!" she managed to cough out.

"You're really not in the mood for this are you?" he said.

Fox screwed her eyes together and wrinkled her nose. She was trying her best to focus on the project, but her thoughts were all over the place. It seemed totally wrong, sitting here working on schoolwork when poor Martha was suffering unimaginable terrors. She was also increasingly disturbed by Jeremiah's interest in Heargton's more paranormal past. She had hoped that it would be at least a few weeks before he discovered the darker aspects of the village history – a history far too closely connected to her own. She shook her head and sighed heavily.

"I'm really sorry. I've got a hideous headache," she offered.

"Are you unwell?"

Fox screwed her face back up in question.

Jeremiah continued, "It's just that you've been having those fits and now you have a headache; perhaps you should get checked out."

She was about to offer a snappy response telling him to mind his own, but then she saw that he seemed genuinely concerned about her welfare.

"I'm fine. I think I just want to go and have an early night. Can we reschedule?"

"Of course. Why don't you come to mine Sunday afternoon?"

Fox stood and packed her bag. She nodded and offered him a smile.

"I'll see you tomorrow," he said, returning to his book. Fox was surprised that he wasn't going to head off himself. She didn't really have him down as the library-mole kind.

She headed out into the village and saw that the parish council had been busy preparing for the New Light Festival - a strange local tradition that had been revived with increasing enthusiasm (and opportune commercialism) in recent years. The New Light Festival involved a quaint craft market, a bonfire, the Rotary Club running a mulled wine stall that seemed to have a bit of an extra kick in its mull, and late night openings for the handful of stores in the village. There was also a procession headed by one specially selected village girl who would visit each house of the village on the night of the first full winter moon. She would be dressed in the ceremonial robes of the Queen of the Flame (which also served as the Angel Gabriel's costume at the annual St. Ursula's Nativity service.) In procession, she would carry a lit taper to each house and light the "receiving candle," which occupants left on the doorstep.

Traditionally, when all the houses had had real fires, the owner would light the fire from the receiving candle, which served to bless the house for the coming year. Now most of the house owners just took the candle (often placed inside a jam jar) into the home and put it on the dining table. Wren used it to light Meadowsweet Cottage's yule log, combining the two ancient rituals into one powerful blessing spell.

Fox was hit by a sense of sadness as she recalled that this year it had been Martha Paisley that had been selected to be the Queen of the Flame. She watched the parish committee continue their preparations regardless of Martha's disappearance and battled with the conscience that it all seemed a little inappropriate. Fox recalled how grumpy Bunny had been that she'd been overlooked for another year. She was desperately aware that if she didn't get selected next year, she would miss her chance. The Queen of The Flame had to be under seventeen years old. Swan had been chosen when she was just nine years old but Fox had (thankfully) avoided the humiliating spectacle of being dressed in a white dress and ivy headdress.

The small ceremonial fire from which the taper would be lit (with great ceremony and usually to the soundtrack of dodgy microphone feedback,) had been set on the elevated stone in the middle of the well trough. Heargton Well wasn't the wishing-well type, but was a large structure consisting of four sturdy stone pillars and a red-clay tile roof. A rectangular stone basin took up most of the floor space, into which natural spring water pooled. One side of the basin had a channel cut into the side, allowing the water to run down and overflow into a round metal grid inserted into the stone floor. The grid denoted the well. A reputedly endless stone chamber that led straight to Hell itself, or so the children's tale went.

It had originally been built as a place for the animals to drink and for the women to wash their clothes and gather drinking water (they weren't particularly bothered by the notion of hygiene and it was preferable to the lanolin polluted stream that ran to the side of the village.) Now it had become the center of village life and was often decorated with flowers, bunting and small ceremonial fires. People had almost forgotten that the well had once also been used for far more macabre rituals; that way back in Heargton's history, the large oak beams that supported the roof had once been used as gallows and that several infamous locals had lost their lives there, including the highwayman Bob Tussock and the Heathmoor witches.

Fox shuddered, a reaction to the unnerving feeling that somebody was watching her.

"Are you alright, Miss Meadowsweet?"

She startled, surprised to hear somebody speaking to her.

"You look miles away."

She scanned the structure of the well, finally finding the source of the voice. Reverend Stewart was up a ladder, pinning white and green bunting. He scrabbled down and crossed over to where she was standing, looking proudly at a tricky job well done.

"I was just thinking about tomorrow night and… Martha," she said in a fading sentence.

"Ah!" he said, nodding his head. "Her mother is so worried. It's been quite a shock to all of us – them running off like that."

Fox turned to him, "Is that the official line then?"

He sighed. "It would seem so. We knew they were very fond of each other but we had no idea how serious it had all become. I'm sure God will return them to us soon."

"What if it isn't like that?"

"Pardon?" He'd been distracted by something.

"What if them running away together is just a terrible assumption? They could be in danger."

Reverend Stewart walked away from her, fiddling with one of the electrical wires. He turned and flashed her a smile. "You mustn't worry yourself. Things like you see on those terrible crime shows don't happen to children from Heargton!"

Fox shook her head in frustration. She knew he was trying to be reassuring but he was being totally blind to any other possibility; and if this was his standpoint, she guessed it was the same with the police too.

"Who's going to be Queen of the Flame now?" Fox asked, not really that interested but unwilling to give up the conversation quite yet.

"I guess you've not been home yet?" he laughed. "We've asked your sister, Bunny. She's very excited!"

Fox rolled her eyes and sighed. “Yeah, I bet she is.”

“Anyway, lots to do. Nice chatting with you Miss Meadowsweet. It would be nice to see you at service once in a while if you can make the time.”

She raised a hand in farewell and offered him a smile that quite clearly told him that it wouldn’t be happening any time soon.

*

Jeremiah finished the chapter he was reading and then packed his bag. He was just about to leave when he saw Fox talking with the Vicar. In light of their mother’s shop, Jeremiah found it strange that Fox should know him; they hardly struck him as the most likely Christians; in fact there was something about the Meadowsweet sisters that was decidedly… pagan. He smiled to himself. He was beginning to see witches everywhere, just like his Uncle Daniel.

He hadn’t heard from Daniel in a couple of days, which wasn’t a particular surprise being he was still somewhere in South America on “business.” Jeremiah had a deep affection for Daniel, who would turn up at the family office in his “Indiana Jones kit” (as his father would call it). Daniel had a battered leather knapsack, which as far as Jeremiah could tell was the only thing he ever carried on his travels. However, the bag was like the one from Mary Poppins - endless treasures and spoils came out of that bag, which always included chocolate as well as a small battered bible and a crucifix. Daniel wasn't an overtly a religious man - he certainly wasn't the kind that would stand on a street corner and preach, but he had a deep faith, which meant that a meal never passed without him saying a private grace or that every move he made he believed was done with the knowledge and blessing of God.

Jeremiah's father found his brother's belief in God a thing to mock; his only God was the god of capitalism. But it was no surprise that at least some of the family bloodline should follow in their ancestor's footsteps. Jeremiah had no real leanings either way – he'd been having far too much fun to consider it. He sure wasn't a puritan in any of his tastes, but being brought up in the lap of luxury surrounded by excess, he could hardly be blamed.

There was much about Daniel that Jeremiah didn't know; he'd got what little knowledge he did have through random snippets of information picked up over the years. In this way Daniel was much like a collage; a picture of composite parts that when you got too close dissolved into randomness. Jeremiah knew that Daniel was a witch slayer. A totally surreal job for anyone in the twenty-first century, not alone for a man who, as first born son, had been destined to inherit a multi-billion dollar business.

Jeremiah had refused to believe this could be true for a while, thinking that witches were something that only existed in the pages of children's books. He had changed his mind when he'd come face to face (well, it was more body to body) with a witch after a particularly wild party in downtown New York City. At first he thought that it might have been the drugs - he'd gone through a stupid experimental phase which lasted all of a year before his father found out and had sent him on some intensive screwy rehab session where he was forced to live with addicts for a month and see first hand the damage that drugs did. It worked. However, on this particular coke-filled evening, it went from sexy to crazy in the space of an hour when he found himself unwittingly tied up in the woman's basement, which was clearly some from of temple dedicated to the gods of darkness. Thankfully - but not entirely by coincidence - Daniel had been in town and happened to be passing. (Well it wasn't quite like that, but Daniel would never reveal the reasons why or how he had magically turned up.) It had all ended weirdly - to the point that it had all seemed like some crazy trip that the mind refused to accept as a proper memory. Jeremiah had woken up on Daniel's battered Chesterfield sofa to an empty flat and a note that told him to get his act together by the next time his uncle was in town.

Jeremiah watched Fox with curiosity. He couldn't figure out what it was about her that was so… He shrugged and sighed, resting his head against the frame of the library door. He was having difficulty ordering his thoughts around her. He didn't think he fancied her – not in the way that he'd been attracted to other women, but there was something elemental when he was with her that he didn't quite understand. He had an overwhelming desire to kiss her but then a barrier came up when his thoughts began to stray anywhere past that. His heartbeat skipped about when he was with her and he found himself flirting with her even though he knew it was a totally pointless exercise. He continued to watch her as she said goodbye to the vicar and walked through the village towards the family shop. Swan was coming out of the door and the sisters exchanged a brief conversation in which Swan seemed to be offering Fox some kind of comfort before they shared a joke and walked off down the road. They were a pretty family, he gave them that; they reminded him of the bewitching women from Waterhouse's 'Hylas and the nymphs; it was a purity of prettiness, far removed from the constructed looks of the New York girls – even those who sought (too hard) to defy convention.

He continued to watch the vicar busying around the well, hanging up the bunting. The light was fading. Jeremiah had already ensured that the last leg of his walk through Chase Woods would be in the dark – something he didn't particularly relish, not since the weird events that had started at Coldstone House. He smiled and let out a little laugh at his own silliness. He shuffled his satchel onto his shoulder and headed down the south road from the village.

Within minutes it was raining; not heavily, but enough to get him soaked on the mile-long walk. He stepped a little way into the woodland that flanked the roadside, seeking some protection from the rain and hurried his step. Several cars passed as the commuters from Lancaster returned to the village.

They were a welcome connection with civilisation. The contrast between his life in New York just one month ago and here in Heargton was enough to derail anybody.

He was nearly home when the sound of laughing children stopped him in his tracks. He turned to the source of the noise, expecting to see them running through the trees, playing. There was no one there and it was certainly too late for young children to be out on their own. He stood for a minute, listening hard, but there was nothing more. He forced his heartbeat to calm and tossed the idea away, putting it down to a trick of the time and environment. All at once he felt very alone. He made a silent prayer for the reassuring headlights of a car to come past, but the road was empty and dark. He picked his pace up into a run and was flooded with relief when ten minutes later the trees ended and he hit the manicured lawns of Coldstone House.

He continued his jogging pace up the oak stairs, avoiding the attention of Aunt Penelope, who was fiddling with the flower arrangement on the hall table, with a shout of, "I'm off for a shower, I'll see you at dinner, Aunt!"

He could hear her muttering to herself. It was pretty evident that his youthful presence was a bit of an imposition in the quiet world of Coldstone House, although Jeremiah had to admit that he was beginning to quite like the old dear. He was still spooked enough by the weird sounds in the woods that he wasn't fully looking where he was going and with his over-hyped sensitivity, he emitted a yelp as he knocked into Paulina. She was coming out of the bathroom and was evidently not expecting to come across anybody, judging by the use of a towel that barely covered her essentials. It took him a moment of flustered apology before he realised that she was far from embarrassed. In fact, she was looking at him directly in the eye with a certain look of wicked playfulness. Then her towel was on the floor around her ankles and she leaned her head coquettishly to one side before offering a belated, "Woops!"

Jeremiah was used to bold women; he certainly wasn't the flustering virgin type and now that Paulina had drawn a clear battle line between them, he breathed in deeply and relaxed, flashing her a charming and flirtatious smile.

"Oh, dear, how..." he leaned in and traced his finger down the side of her stomach, "unfortunate."

"Would you mind being a gent?"

Jeremiah ran his thumb over her blood-thickened lips. They were impossibly soft, almost as if they weren't there at all. He had to admit that these events were taking him to a place beyond surprised, and there was something very intoxicating about that.

She let out a small moan.

It would be easy to take complete advantage of the fortuitous situation, but he understood enough about desire and pleasure to know that the promise was often sweeter than the offering. This moment, left now as it was, would fuel his appetite for much longer than it would should he push her back into the bathroom and accept her invitation.

He cupped her naked hip in the palm of his hand and turned her sideways, allowing space for him to pass by. He stopped momentarily as their bodies pressed together in the doorway. She had her head tilted upwards, her lips parted. She was full top to toe with desire. He moved his lips onto hers in a brief, chaste kiss and whispered,

"What a beautiful and sweetly surprising invitation, Paulina. Thank you, but not today!"

Her face wrinkled with confusion; she'd clearly assumed that things were going to end differently. Hurt flashed in her eyes, followed by a brief look of humiliation. He ran his hand up over her throat and kissed her full on the lips, offering her enough of him for her to know that her advances were not rejected but they were a future possibility. She wrinkled her nose and pouted her lips, but he had nothing more to give her at that point. He shut the door and fell back against it trying to steady himself. His mind refused to ignore the image of Paulina's pale and athletic body bending over to retrieve her towel. A part of him considered opening the door on the scene, but he knew that would leave him in a trickier situation than he'd already gracefully navigated.

He flicked the shower to hot and let the room warm from the steam before stripping off his wet clothes and leaving them in a dishevelled pile on the floor. How he missed the walk-in power-shower of the New York apartment, all nozzles and blue LED lights. The dribble that came from Coldstone's ancient wood-fuelled heating system was a poor relation (as it seemed was everything at Coldstone

House). Thoughts of Paulina swam lazily through his imagination but every time they started to get interesting, thoughts of Fox cut them off. They were images of her running through a meadow, the sunlight streaming through her hair making it look like spun copper. The cottons of her skirt swished through the grass. He was chasing after her - but something was wrong; he had thought that when she turned to him, she would be smiling or laughing, but instead, she looked full of fear. He understood that he wasn't chasing her, he was hunting her.

The water switched to freezing cold and Jeremiah leaped out of the bath, forgetting his disturbing thoughts. He held his hand under the shower, hoping it was just someone running the kitchen tap, but after a minute or so, it became evident that that the storage boiler had been emptied.

"Great!" he grumbled.

He gathered the towel from the radiator and wrapping it around his waist, made his way to the sink. He shivered violently, caught by the sight of writing in the steam of the mirror that read, "SAVE ME." Fear gave way to uncomfortable laughter as he came to the conclusion that Paulina had played a skillful practical joke. What other explanation could there be? He wiped the writing and the steam away from the mirror, part expecting the sight of some Halloween freak standing behind him, and sighed with relief when aside from his own spooked face, the reflection remained empty. His heart hammered and his body went from ice-cold to burning hot in one swift flush. He ran the cold tap and splashed the water over his face. He chastised himself for being such a city boy and letting the spooky old house get to him. It was old and there were perfectly rational reasons for all of the events that had happened – although at that moment, he couldn't quite fathom what they were.

Once back in the safety of his bedroom, he dressed and settled at his desk, opening the lid of his Mac. He wasn't entirely sure what he was about to look up but there was something niggling him and he hoped that some random surfing might enable fate to offer him an answer. His mailbox pinged. It was Daniel. He was nearly finished in South America and would be travelling to London for a conference later that month; he hoped that he could fit in a visit to Coldstone House. For the first time that day, Jeremiah found himself feeling genuinely happy. He replied with a simple emoticon, knowing that Daniel was very rarely in a position to sustain a conversation.

He continued to flick through sites pulled up from the search engine. There was little of interest, except for the rather lurid history of the Heathmoor witches, which once you knew the story of the Salem Witch Trials through first-hand family legends, offered little more than curiosity.

Just like Salem, the witches had hanged for their crimes. Rather ritualistically, the villagers had bypassed the legal system and done it themselves, hanging them over the Heargton Well. What made the case of the Heathmoors slightly more interesting was that unlike the infamous Salem trial (at which his forefather had undertaken a lead role), the Heathmoor's trial had been by rather more arcane methods. The witches had been tried in the old way, through torture rather than through a court. Documentation about the case was prolific; clearly the town clerics had been proud of their duties. Jeremiah read the translations of the Middle English in detail. The three sisters had been accused of attempting to raise the Devil through the ritualistic murder of several innocent village girls. They were further accused of the failing harvest, of some random cases of sick livestock, and a whole list of other minor village mishaps. They'd been taken from their farmhouse during the dark hours and held for questioning. When these intimidation tactics had failed, they were paraded at dawn into the village, where an audience had gathered in anticipation of a coming spectacle. They were not disappointed. Each woman was stripped naked, ducked, and slashed to check the colour of her blood. She was then force-fed a poisonous herb to bring about a bodily evacuation, and when that failed, she was whipped to bring out the demons. One rather more artistic cleric had provided a series of small black and white sketches of the events. The women were portrayed as young and slim with pretty features. *It was no wonder that the wives of the village were so keen to see them get their comeuppance*, Jeremiah thought skeptically. At last, when the women confessed their crimes, they were hanged from the rafters of the well, where it is reputed they hanged all day by the neck until sundown, when their bodies mysteriously disappeared. The belief was that the Devil had come to claim his own, which added a nice melodramatic twist to the tale and vindicated the villagers' torture of three young and beautiful women.

As well as many hits to the documentation of the "trial" there were thousands of pages of paranormal sites that had links to Heargton and the surrounding area, which made looking for details about the old lunatic asylum, the Rookeries, rather difficult to find. After several challenging attempts at the advanced search option, he finally found a couple of hits that promised to actually be of some use; strange in itself that such a prominent socially historical building should have so little web presence - almost to the point that it was suspicious. He sat up and leaned forward, suddenly finding something that truly captured his attention.

The Horrors of the Asylum. Rookeries The.
www.SamstheMan/heargton/The
Rookeries/34gZ/blogspot.com

....a history of terrible abuses and tortures at the hand of doctors and orderlies. The authorities were forced to investigate the ***Rookeries*** *Hospital after local vicar raised concern about Satanic practices taking place in the Rookeries Hospital,* ***Heargton****...*

He clicked the link, not expecting much from 'SamtheMan,' and was surprised to find a very detailed and serious looking post. Sam, whoever he was, had clearly done his research, including having taken some rather spooky looking photographs of the asylum. The flaking, crumbling walls were plastered with freaky (and slightly witty) graffiti; a series of red, bloodied hand prints had been placed "walking" along the wall, pentagrams and demonic third eyes covered wall after wall. Scratchy looking writing spelled out words from horror films. Then Jermiah stopped smiling wryly to himself and peered closely into the screen – there in the background of one of the pictures was a fireplace with a mirror, covered in a film of dust. Written into the dust were the two simple words, exactly as he had seen them written on the bathroom mirror: "SAVE ME!" Jeremiah snapped down the lid of the Mac and inhaled deeply. He knew that it was just as clichéd as the rest of the decorations, but something in his gut had turned sour and a certain knowledge refused to be ignored – the same person who had written that, had written the words in the bathroom at Coldstone House. Just then, the sound of a children's musical box floated under his door. Jeremiah walked over to the door, angry at his own nervous reaction. He opened the door and the music stopped. He peered left and right into the gloom of the hallway. There was nobody there. Then he looked down and saw the little push-mechanical merry-go-round sat neatly at his feet. It was still spinning.

8

"Come on, slowcoach," Swan called out behind her.

Fox was picking her way through the winter debris of the woodland, cursing that she'd worn her impractical converse pumps rather than having, like Swan, opted for a sturdy pair of wellies. At this time of year the forest was pretty bare, and what fruits it did still bear long after the damp autumn were tired and insect nibbled.

"I don't see the point of this; it's the wrong time of year for nettles, what was mum thinking?"

"She said that she saw some the other day."

"Still, it's hardly likely."

Swan shrugged. "Stranger things have happened. Maybe she cast a growth spell."

"Hmm," Fox grunted. The nettle gathering exercise wasn't the only pointless thing they were about to undertake. Swan had attempted to convince Fox that they would find success scrying at the pool. Scrying was an old parlour trick and far too much like magic for Fox's comfort.

Swan continued to march on slightly ahead with purpose. She always had loved a project and Fox guessed that she was now just that. Both of them purposely stayed off the subject of boys, filling their walk with sporadic observations about the woods.

Despite the growing darkness, neither Swan nor Fox felt any fear being in the Abundance Wood. They had known it since birth as a safe and bountiful place. In the summer they pretty much lived off salads gathered from the treeline, nettle soup, acorn bread, and elderflower press. The woods were scattered with ancient English trees, hazels, cobnuts, walnuts, and chestnuts. In the summer it was a magical place filled with the green filtered sun but tonight, in the strange winter light, it reminded Fox of a silent army of skeletons.

They approached the pool where Wren had told Swan the nettles were, and although snuggled right against the rock in their own little shelter, there they were. Fox sighed and rolled her eyes in defeat. "Well, what would you know."

Swan took a handkerchief from her basket and used it to pluck the spikey, nipping leaves.

"Look!" Swan commanded, pointing to a little group of mushrooms nestled deep under the rock in a warm bed of moss.

"It's far too late for them," Fox said, trying to muster some kind of interest.

"I'll take them back for mother – they'll be powerful if they've survived the season change.

"What would mother want with Cortinarius Ruebellus?"

"She can dry them and put them by."

"What for? Poisoning somebody?" Fox giggled.

"Well you never know; it's good to have some things in stock. You never know when they might come in handy."

"Well if Cortinarius Ruebellus suddenly becomes handy, I guess we'll have bigger problems."

Swan cast her sister a glance before returning to harvesting the precious and deadly mushrooms. "Mum asked me to keep an eye out."

Fox's interest prickled. Now that was curious. Why would her mother ask that? What were the chances of them actually finding any?

When Swan had plucked the last one and laid it into its cotton cradle, Fox asked, "Seriously, what does mum want them for? Do you know?"

Swan fixed Fox with a stare. "Some things are best left unasked."

Not convinced that leaving the subject was best at all, she muttered, "Boarding a bit towards the dark, don't you think?"

"Not everything can be defined as dark or light, Fox. You really need to try and work that out before that kind of thinking brings you to harm. In nature there isn't just day or night, there are times between; highly magical times, when the world is softly lit with either a birthing or dying light. Dawn and twilight are times of promise, and sometimes a promise is more powerful than a certainty."

Fox twisted her lips, "Have you been reading those dippy-hippy books in the shop again?"

Swan laughed. "Don't mock what you don't understand. Sometimes you are such an arrogant ass."

Fox raised her eyebrows, "Sssh! What would The Mother think of you swearing in one of her sacred spaces?"

"She'd know that you were being an ass!"

Swan flipped the cotton cloth over the mushrooms, stabilised the basket, and knelt down beside the pool.

"We haven't got much time; the night is coming and the water will start to be effected by the shadows. Here, kneel beside me."

Fox reluctantly did as her sister bid, feeling the hard, uncomfortable rock pressing against her knees. She looked down into the depths of the pool. It looked endless.

"Breathe deeply and free your mind." Swan commanded before muttering under her breath, "Which in your case shouldn't be too hard."

"If you're going to keep poking me then how am I meant to concentrate."

Swan wrinkled her nose and inhaled deeply, her usual patience and serenity felt sorely pushed with the day's events. She reached over and grasped Fox's hair in her hand, pulling it back off her face for her. "Don't look into the pool – look across the surface of it and watch the light. Be patient. It takes time for the image to come. You need to coax it from the surface."

Fox fleetingly wondered how often Swan undertook the practice. There was nothing, just a few dead leaves floating on the surface and other woodland debris. Then Fox caught sight of a pale patch of light, sitting on the surface. It was shapeless and formless but there was no denying that it was spreading. She focused all of her vision onto it and grounded her breathing deep at the bottom of her diaphragm. Her head started to swim and she began to feel the increasingly familiar feeling of a vision coming on. Part of her wanted to shy away, but somehow the presence of the water surface made her feel safer, more removed.

She returned back to the farm and the barn. She heard the sounds of the chant and the screams. She looked up towards the moon, in all her pale majesty. She was full-ripe. It was the night of tomorrow. There was still time. She walked up to the barn and entered brazenly – there was nothing to fear, they could not see her because she wasn't really there. Or so she thought, until Lilith suddenly broke from chanting over Martha's bound and supine body and looked to the space where Fox was standing. Lilith's eyes looked right through her as though aware of a presence but unable to identify it. Her sisters, sensing their sister's alertness, all stopped and turned to look in the same direction. Nigella's face registered with surprise at the sight of a familiar although unwelcome face. Fox pulled away out of the vision quickly, escaping the Ravenheart sisters and their bloody ritual. She fell backwards off the rock and landing painfully on a branch.

"Shit! They saw me!"

Swan leaped to her sister, failing to catch her in time before part of the branch skewered her skin. Despite the physical pain, Fox was too preoccupied to worry about it.

"Nigella saw me watching them!"

She shook her head, "That's impossible! You're just being paranoid."

"She bloody saw me! Nigella looked right at me and she recognised me."

Swan made soothing noises. "Ssh, ssh. You're hurt, sit still." Swan examined the wound and snapped the small penetrating branch away from the larger stump.

"Are you going to leave it in there?" Fox asked incredulously.

"You really shouldn't..." Swan trailed off as Fox grabbed ahold of the stick and gave it a good yank accompanied by a loud echoing expletive. Blood seeped quickly.

"That was really stupid!" Swan shouted.

"It's alright, it wasn't that deep."

"Deep enough to get infected. Deep enough to bleed – a lot!"

Fox fought back the tears in her eyes. It hurt like hell. "We've got to get to Heathmoor Farm – that's where Martha is. I can't believe I didn't recognise it earlier."

"Why should you? You've never been, have you?" Swan's question was loaded with accusation. The Meadowsweet girls had been raised with knowledge of the Heathmoor witches and the terrible events that took place at the farm and in the village. Unlike many who now believed them to have been persecuted innocents, Wren was in no doubt about their dark magical practices, and although a peaceful person by nature, she felt no sadness for their execution. The girls had been told in no uncertain terms that should they ever set foot near to Heathmoor Farm they would feel Wren's parental force at full blast. She had told them it was a place stained with misery and fear; a place where true evil resided. Her warning extended to most of the North Eastern quarter of the village; the quarter dominated by Ravenheart Hall and the Rookeries.

Fox didn't have the time for a sibling spat. She stood, wincing, and pressed her hand tight against her checked shirt and into the wound to try and stem the bleeding.

"Here let me help you." Swan rummaged in the basket and pulled out a clean cloth, which she folded into a compress. "We need to get you home and let mum take a look at it."

"No, we need to go to Heathmoor Farm!" Fox said, already heading off through the woods.

"Of course we do," Swan muttered. "Totally, sensible idea for just the two of us to take on another coven with no preparation." She sighed and followed after her sister. She knew that when Fox was in this frame of mind, the only thing that was to be done was to follow her and hope that she would be able to catch her when she fell.

Twilight had already slipped into the inky darkness of evening. Within the hour it would be too dark to see anything. Swan took out her wand and channelled her energy through the oak of the shaft and out the end as light. Fox turned to her and grinned with genuine admiration. "Soooo, you're carrying a wand now?"

Swan nodded.

"Someone has been watching far too much Harry Potter!" Fox teased, despite wincing after almost every word.

"Give it up!" Swan said, pretending to be offended but unable to hide the proud smile on her lips.

"Cool!" Fox nodded her head. "I didn't realise your magical skills had become so developed."

"Violet has been tutoring me," Swan replied. "But you mustn't let onto mother. You know she doesn't really approve."

"Oh!"

Swan had always had a secretive side but Fox had assumed that her secrecy only extended to the way she handled her emotions; to discover that she had been going out behind their mother's back felt more hurtful than Fox would have thought. It was a feeling mixed with a little jealousy. She had been asking mother if she could start her magical arts studies for the last eighteen months, but Wren had continually found excuses. A surge of anger rose in her. Now she had been cursed with her gift but had no weapons to use alongside it. She hadn't even had her wand ceremony yet, despite turning sixteen almost a year ago. Swan was still meant to be waiting for hers, but evidently she'd gone ahead without her mother's blessing, which was a surprising act of subversion for Swan.

Fox was so wrapped up in her grumpy jealously that she arrived at the roadside with some surprise. The wound on her back felt like it was literally killing her, and her shoulder had started to ache with the awkward angle and pressure of holding the makeshift compress. Every instinct told her that this was a fool's mission; that she should wait until tomorrow. *But what if they take out her eyes tonight, in preparation?* the internal asked.

Fox continued across the road with no real plan except for a vague notion that somehow she would manage to stop the horrendous events that she had foretold. As if reading her mind, Swan said, "We have time, Fox. We should go home and gather the others. We need strength in numbers." She paused and said with a heavy weight of authority, "We need Violet."

Since when had Violet become so damned important? the internal snarked. It was the second time that Swan had mentioned her in as many minutes and both times her name had been said in a way that almost sounded like a talisman.

"Why?"

Swan shook her head, not fully understanding the question. "Why specifically do we need Violet?" Fox asked.

Swan's face flickered as she quickly pulled together an answer that might satisfy. "No other reason than that she's the eldest."

"What other reason might there be?"

"Pardon?" Swan asked playing innocent.

Fox continued to needle the point, "Saying 'no other reason' suggests that there *is* exactly another reason, which you are keen to conceal."

Swan crumpled her forehead. She was far from stupid but her sister had always been impossible to outwit. Fox had a way of taking words and tying thoughts into knots so that you were left feeling completely defeated. The best way to try and hold out against her was to go silent, which is exactly what she did.

Fox waited for the car to pass and crossed the road into Ravenheart territory. The woods here were very different, being planted a couple of hundred years ago with Norwegian spruce and Nordic pines. The ground was mostly bare, made acidic and poisonous by the dropped needles. Fox thought it was a fitting woodland for the Ravenhearts. Tall, proud, and poisonous. The woods were a natural labyrinth of crisscrossing pathways. A low mist hung around the ankles of the trees.

With no soft ferns, mosses, or nettles to cushion the woodland noises, the sounds of the crows echoed around the hollow chamber of the woods. Fox shivered. It was amazing how uneasy she felt amongst these woods compared to Abundance Wood. She couldn't imagine what those poor lunatics must have thought when they looked through their bars; no hope in and no hope out. The ground was spongy underneath her feet making their journey soundless. The light from Swan's wand was just enough to make the whole place look more eerie.

"Do you actually know where you are going?" Swan asked Fox with irritation. Their twenty-minute stride through the forest should have taken them to the foot of Heathmoor Hill, on top of which sat the nasty little cottage and its barn of horrors. They had been travelling for twice that time and still the trees showed no sign of thinning or the ground no sign of incline.

"I reckon we're going around in circles," Swan complained.

Fox stopped and turned full circle, scanning the woods. "Something isn't right. We're travelling straight but we're not going forward."

Swan's face screwed up in confusion, "I don't get what you mean."

"I mean, I think you might be right – sort of. Wait here a minute. I'm going to stand in front of you and put one foot in front of the other in a straight line. Watch what happens."

Fox looked carefully at her feet, placing one tightly in front of the other, sure to travel a straight line. After about thirty footsteps, she stopped and turned to seek out Swan. As she had predicted, her sister was not stood directly in front of her but at a twenty-degree angle.

"Magic!" Swan's whispered word floated over to Fox, who walked back towards her sister. Swan continued, "It looks like a shield spell. We could walk all night and not arrive at Heathmoor Farm."

"How far are we away from the road?"

"It can't be far. The chimneys of the Rookeries are just over there," Fox said pointing her hand in their direction. "If we head towards it, there is a path straight out towards the road. It should only be ten minutes or so from there." Fox winced and pulled her hand from her back. It was stained with blood and tiny rivulets of blood flowed down over her wrist.

"It's not stopping." Her statement was directed more at herself than Swan.

Swan swept the light up over the wound and saw that her sister's shirt was soaked with a dark and spreading blood stain. It was serious and Fox needed to get home before she lost any more blood. The stick really hadn't looked as if it had gone in deep enough to do any real damage and yet…

Fox had already set off in the direction of the Rookeries and Swan fell back into her sullen mood. She really couldn't think of a more ridiculous idea than traipsing through the Ravenheart Woods, heading towards a derelict asylum but she didn't put up an argument as it was probably the quickest way home and that was what really mattered.

The Rookeries Asylum for the Insane and Morally Degenerate (another name for any woman out of wedlock and found to be with child) loomed large in front of them. The scrappy metal fence surrounding the crumbling building served less as a barrier and more as somewhere merely to hang the requisite yellow health and safety signs. Where some of the local village kids had taken a fancy to creeping themselves out, sections of fencing lay scattered on the floor.

"Have you ever been inside?" Swan asked Fox, knowing it was exactly the kind of temptation her wild and insubordinate sister would relish.

Fox shook her head. "No. Even I'm not that stupid."

They laughed and the sound of it echoed around the woods eerily. A large clattering sound of metal caused both of them to jump and reach out for each others' hand.

"What the hell was that?" Fox whispered.

"I don't know but I'm not going to wait to find out." The flash of sisterly solidarity soon faded as Swan snapped, "I knew this was a stupid idea. We need to get you home NOW!"

Fox froze, she wasn't sure that moving was necessarily the right thing to do. Sometimes the trick of escaping was to stay exactly where you were. "It's all right for you - you've got that weirdy magic thing going on," she hissed. "You can probably teleport or something. If I start moving about, I suddenly become prime prey."

"Suit yourself but I'm heading home." Swan turned on her heels, her light scanning back across the back of Fox's shirt. She gasped. Saturated, Fox's shirt had started to drip blood onto her jeans. "Fox, please we really need to get you home."

"Stop stressing. It's only a scratch," she replied, more to convince herself than her sister.

"You are totally impossible," Swan said through clenched teeth. "I'm calling rank. We're going home right now."

The sound of movement to their left and the sweep of a flashlight made them startle once more. Fox felt her stomach tighten into a deep cramp and she cursed herself for being so pathetic.

"Reckon it might be too late for that," she whispered low enough for only her sister to hear. Swan snuffed out the light and tucked her wand into the sleeve of her jumper. They were now completely at the mercy of the nighttime wanderer.

Fox held her breath, hoping that whoever it was would pass by them.

"Evening!"

The shadowy, ominous form gave way to one far more familiar.

"Jeremiah – what the b-jeez are you doing here?!" Fox asked, surprised as if she had just come across and axe murderer and only slightly less relieved that it wasn't

"Could ask you the same question."

"Well, I asked first."

"Fair."

"So?"

"I thought I'd start our research project by doing a bit of a recky."

"In the dark?"

"Why not? Thought I'd like to see it at it's most… alluring. I find lots of things look better in the dark – even you, Foxy!" He laughed at his non-funny quip.

Swan watched the two of them play out their little exchange with bemused curiosity whilst saying nothing. It was almost as if Jeremiah had not even noticed her.

"Find anything good?" Fox asked, clenching her teeth against the pulsing pain that was upping its tempo.

"What's wrong?"

"Why?"

"You've got your teeth all clenched, or is it that you're just pleased to see me? Steady on, it almost looks like a smile."

"She's injured; quite badly." Swan helpfully informed him. He jumped at the sound of her voice and stared at her momentarily before looking back to Fox.

"What's happened?"

"It's nothing – just a … " her sentence was stopped by a sharp gasp.

Jeremiah moved around her and shone the torch on her. He let out a low whistle, "Jeez, Foxy, that's not a scratch! We need to get you …" his sentence morphed into a, "Whoa there!" as he dropped the torch and used both of his arms to catch her.

"Told you it was serious!" Swan said, in the way that only sisters can totally underplay a serious incident for the sake of scoring a point.

Jeremiah fixed Swan with a look of serious concern. "We really need to get her home fast – better still, to a hospital."

Swan let out a tight, distressed laugh, "You'll be lucky, the nearest hospital is nearly an hour drive."

"Great, got to love the countryside!"

Jeremiah placed one arm under Fox's knees and scooped her into his arms. "Are you able to take my torch. Two will be better than…" his sentence trailed off as he saw the noticeable absence of a torch in Swan's hands. "Or one will be better than… none!" His head gave an involuntary shake.

"It's okay, our mum will be able to fix her up," Swan said,

Jeremiah raised an eyebrow at her. "Is she a doctor? I thought she ran that new-age shop?"

Swan let the question slide. She didn't have time to get into that kind of conversation. She led them back through the forest. Every now and then she looked back at Jeremiah and he'd flash her a reassuring smile. She was bemused by the effect it had on her; she wasn't one to usually be affected by a handsome face, but there was something about Mr. Chase that was different and she was surprised to feel her heartbeat quicken and her stomach fluttering. She smiled to herself, thinking how her sister's animosity towards Jeremiah was obviously an attempt to deal with similar strange feelings.

Swan's pace through the forest was swift. Every now and then, Fox would come around and fight against the arms that held her. It was a good sign; there was clearly still a lot of life left in her.

The night had settled thick like a blanket and the west road out of town was empty. Jeremiah, seeing Meadowsweet Cottage within sprinting distance, picked up his speed. Fox had become heavier as she'd slipped further into unconsciousness and he wasn't sure how much longer he could carry her.

He hadn't the time to knock and politely wait on the doorstep and so the result was a chaotic, noisy crashing into the house, where he dumped Fox on the first available surface he could find, which happened to be the kitchen table. Holding her like a rag doll over his one arm, he swept the table contents to the far end, sending some utensils scattering to the floor and laid her down. Wren scuttled across.

"What's happened?" she asked, pulling her hand away sharply with the feel of sticky blood.

Jeremiah roughly rolled Fox onto her side, knowing that tenderness was not really a priority. Fox moaned in protest. "She's been…" his sentence was cut short by Swan, who seeing the state of her sister under the bright electric light, started to cry.

"She fell and landed on a stick. I didn't think it was that bad."

"Pass me those scissors!" her mother commanded Jeremiah, pointing him in the direction of the kitchen worktop. He slipped off his jacket, letting it fall to the floor. He was efficient and calm, which could not be said about Swan. Bunny must have sensed the high drama unfolding and came bounding in from upstairs.

"What's happened?"

"There's been an accident. Fox is hurt."

"Should I call for an ambulance?" Bunny asked her mother, whilst moving around the table to take a closer look.

Wren was snipping at Fox's shirt, exposing her blood stained skin.

"No, she should be okay once I put a stitch or two in. She's fainted from the drop in blood pressure but she'll soon be okay." Wren pulled one side of the shirt away as Jeremiah pulled the other. He was proving to be a calm and useful addition. Bunny looked at him, trying to fathom what his role could possibly be in all of it.

"There's a lot of blood," Jeremiah said with concern.

"It looks worse than it is. Back wounds always bleed a lot. She's lucky, it's missed her spinal chord and it's not deep enough to have damaged any organs."

Wren turned her attention away from Fox for a moment and asked Bunny to gather her medicine bag from the sanctuary; Wren's barely-used study at the back of the house. Jeremiah flicked a look at Bunny and then over to Wren, who was once again absorbed in her study of Fox's wound. The words "medicine bag" and "sanctuary" niggled his brain. He was beginning to get the distinct impression that the Meadowsweet family was not what it seemed on first appearance.

Bunny returned quickly, carrying an antique leather doctor's bag. She put it on the table next to Wren and flicked it open and instructed Bunny to get the honey from the cupboard and to fill up one of the large plastic syringes with water.

"Honey?" Jeremiah asked.

"Yes, it's the most effective antiseptic for an open wound."

"Surely antiseptic lotion from the chemist would be more…" His reply was cut short by a sharp look from Wren.

Bunny handed the syringe to Wren, who used it to wash out the wound. Then she took a large finger full of honey and smeared it into the wound, where it mixed with the blood to make a sticky congealing mess.

"It's going to need some stitches. Swan, could you please boil the kettle and make a sterile dish for the needle, and whilst you're there make us all a cup of sweet tea. I think we could all do with a cup."

The rest of the procedure was carried out in silence as Wren and her daughters worked together in well-practiced unity.

Fox whimpered as the needle threaded in and out of her flesh, but Wren was swift and the stitching was over in a matter of minutes. It was clearly something she had done many times and Jeremiah's curiosity was stirred. Wren unwound a piece of cotton muslin from her bag and placed a cotton pad over the wound. It created a deep satisfaction in Jeremiah to see the wound tidily hidden behind the dressing and for it to begin its healing. Swan brought Fox's dressing gown in and between them they maneuvered her to the saggy patchwork sofa at the far end of the kitchen. Wren instructed Jeremiah to sit and for Bunny to finish the tea off whilst she scrubbed down the table with disinfectant. Whilst the girls were busy, Jeremiah's eyes roamed around the large room that was part kitchen, part snug, and part study. It couldn't have been further from the sleek, sanitised granite and steel kitchen of his New York home.

Movement flickered at the corner of his eye, and Jeremiah turned to see the grey tabby cat, which, sitting on an old tapestry cushion stretched out its limbs and yawned. Fox yawned, a natural response to her body needing more oxygen. Her eyelids fluttered open and she looked at him, her forehead wrinkling as she tried to orientate herself.

"Here drink this. It'll restore your strength," Swan said handing him the tea. He sniffed it. It wasn't the usual English tea but it smelt sweet and syrupy. Swan watched him assessing the drink. "It's oatstraw and lavender."

"Unusual!" he said, smiling tightly.

"It's nice, I promise."

He took a sip and nodded his head. Swan crouched beside Fox and stroked her cheek, encouraging her to come back to them. Fox stirred.

"Try and take some tea," she said, helping her sister to sip from the delicate china cup.

"You have a charming home, ma'm," Jeremiah called out to Wren, who was still scrubbing the table hard with a bristle brush.

"Thank you." She smiled. "I'm sorry, I don't think we got around to introductions. You can call me Wren."

"I'm Jeremiah, ma'm. Jeremiah Chase."

The rhythmic sound of Wren's scrubbing fell silent and she fixed the young man with a look. "Chase?"

"Yes, ma'm."

"As in the Chases of Coldstone House?"

"The very same."

Swan looked at her mother, alerted by her off-chord behaviour. Her mother paused a moment, before taking up her scrubbing once more.

"Well Jeremiah, it's getting late. I'm sure Lady Asquithe will be starting to get concerned over your safety."

Jeremiah stood and drank down his tea before smiling at Wren politely. "Yes, she probably will be. I had better be going."

Swan was confused by her mother's coldness towards the boy who had saved her daughter's life. If Jeremiah was offended by their mother's obvious desire for him to leave, then he was being too much of a gentleman to make a point of it. Embarrassed, Swan picked up Jeremiah's jacket from the floor and held it out politely, smiling.

"Thank you so much for your help this evening. You have been a true friend."

He flashed her a smile and slid his arms into his jacket. "No problem. Anytime."

"Good evening, m'am," he said, walking towards the door.

"Jeremiah!" Wren called after him. "Thank you."

"No problem. I just happened to be passing. Anybody would have done the same."

As soon as the door clicked back in its lock, Swan came to her mother's side. "Care to share?"

Her mother picked up the cloth and rubbed the table, avoiding a response. Swan wasn't to be deterred that easily.

"I can't believe how rude you were to the boy! He's just carried Fox half way across the village and helped you stitch her back together and you treat him like he has just come in and tried to rob you.

Her mother shrugged. "I'm just not fond of the Chase family."

"But you don't know him."

"Leave it!" Wren warned. She swiped away a stray strand of hair. "There are things you do not need to know."

Swan sighed. That was exactly the sort of statement to raise her curiosity, but she saw that her mother was in no mood for breaking. Sensing her daughter hovering, Wren instructed her to take Fox up to bed.

Although pale and still woozy, Fox was looking much better than she had just half an hour ago. When Swan approached her she managed a weak smile and asked croakily, "Jeremiah?"

Swan smiled and nodded her head, "Yes, quite the Sir Lancelot!"

Fox rolled her eyes. She was not unwell enough not to still be completely irritated and Jeremiah's act of chivalry made him all the more annoying because now she was in the position of owing him one.

Once they were both out of the hearing of their mother Fox quietly asked, “Don’t you think it strange that he happened to be there at that very moment?”

Swan shook her head. “I think it was just lucky.”

“I don’t know – it’s seems a bit… odd.”

“Aren’t you two doing a project on the Rookeries?”

Fox considered for a moment whether it was plausible that he had gone to do a bit of research, but the internal was quite opinionated, *What fool would head out to an abandoned asylum at nightfall?*

“Yes but I don’t reckon that was the reason he was there.”

“Why not?”

“It’s just a feeling. I don’t trust him. Everything about him is a lie.”

“What do you mean?”

“Go Google ‘Jeremiah Chase’ and get back to me.”

Swan raised an eyebrow. “Google him? Is he famous?”

“Just go and do it. I don’t want to spoil the surprise.”

Swan guided Fox down into her bed and tucked the duvet up around her.

"Rest. You're going to need your strength for tomorrow. I'm going to contact Violet and ask how we can get around the Shield Spell."

"I think you should tell her everything," Fox said, surprising herself by this statement as much as her sister.

"Are you sure? I mean, I think you should. Violet has studied the Dark Arts, I think she'll be able to help us."

"I didn't know that Violet…"

Swan cut her short, "Well it's not common knowledge. Even mother doesn't know. You know how she is about all of that, she wouldn't understand; she'd assume the worse. Violet has studied them so that she can defeat them, there is no other reason."

"And you?"

Fox's piercing question caused Swan to falter. "I…I…yes, Violet is tutoring me."

"Why?"

Swan shrugged. "It's late and I'm really tired. I need to rest up for tomorrow. We can talk about this another time."

Fox sat up, wincing with each movement. "No. I want us to talk about it now."

"Well you can want it all you like, but I'm not talking with you now." She stood up and made towards the door. "Until tomorrow, sister. Heal well." She blew a kiss and left, closing the door behind her.

Fox stared at the space her sister had occupied for many minutes after she had left. She had thought that Swan had always been straightforward; nothing but light and sweetness and now…

9

The Meadowsweet sisters were woken by the sound of screaming sirens; a sound that was alien and terrifying in the quiet village of Heargton. As Fox woke she let out a low groan of discomfort at the pain in her back. She dragged herself out of bed and pulled back the curtains of her bedroom window. Several police cars streamed past, not slowing for the junction. Dread filled her stomach; something terrible had happened and her instinct told her it had to do with Martha Paisley.

She threw on her jeans and jumper and limped painfully down the stairs and out of the cottage. Swan must have followed a similar pattern as shortly after, she heard her sister's footsteps sound swiftly behind her. They travelled towards the commotion, which centered on the well. A large policeman dressed in full anti-stab uniform formed an almost successful wall, yet his arms were not large enough to stop Fox from seeing the horror.

Propped up against the small bonfire set in the tray of the well was the body of Martha Paisley. She looked like a Victorian rag doll, dressed in a flowing white gown that was spattered with rubies of blood. A tight white bandage had been wrapped around her head, and in the place of her eyes, were two red blooms of blood. A garland of ivy had been placed on her head in mockery of the Fire Queen. Around her neck, hung by a piece of coarse rope, was a piece of ripped fencing that had been used to fashion a sign. There was no writing on it, just the glyph of an inverted pentagram, drawn on with chalk.

Bright flashes of the forensic photographer's camera broke the morning gloom, giving the surreal impression of a lightening storm taking place under the cover of the well.

Fox heard her own voice screaming, "No!" and felt the thin, iron arms of Swan holding her tightly.

"Please return to your homes, ladies. The police are dealing with this. You shouldn't distress yourself further." The policeman moved on swiftly, trying to approach a group of other residents who were swiftly making their way towards the well.

"We're too late. We're too late," Fox repeated the mantra over and over until fearful that the busy police officer should hear what Fox was saying and find it to be of interest, Swan placed her hand over her sister's mouth and ssshed in her ear like a mother to a distressed baby.

"Let's go home. There's nothing more we can do."

"I don't understand…I …"

Swan squeezed her sister's hand as she led her back towards the cottage. "We'll talk about it when we get home."

As Swan and Fox headed back towards the cottage, Bunny came bounding towards them, desperate to see what all the activity was about.

"What's going on? Is it Martha?" she asked, peering over the top of Swan's shoulder, who had purposely turned herself into a human barricade.

Swan nodded and took hold of Bunny's elbow with the intention of steering her back to the house.

"Come home with us," she commanded.

"No way," she said, shaking her arm free from Swan's grip, "I want to go and see what's happening."

"Trust us, you really don't."

Bunny put her hand on her hip and pouted. "You've seen!"

Fox snapped, "Yeah, well I wish I hadn't."

"It's not fair," Bunny whined.

"You are exactly right, Bunny, it's not fair. None of it. I should think that is exactly what Mrs. Paisley will be thinking when the police explain that her beautiful daughter has been murdered and then put out on show for the world to see the horrors she endured."

Bunny's hard lips softened with the realisation of her behaviour. Her voice dropped, "Is it truly horrible?"

Swan's voice response came out cracked, "Yes."

"What did he do to her?"

"Come on, I'll tell you the gory details back at home. I'm sure mum will want to know."

Wren was standing on the doorstep waiting for them to come home. She looked gripped by a shared sorrow and Fox knew that her mother was thinking how lucky she was to have her own three daughters alive and walking towards her. She smiled weakly at them and held out her arms, waiting to sweep them up in them.

“Come on in. We’ll have tea and talk about it.”

Fox leaned into Swan and whispered, “Should we tell her about the scrying – how it’s our fault she’s dead?”

Swan shook her head, “It will raise too many questions about the Ravenhearts. We need to be careful.”

There wasn’t time to come up with a specific plan, but Fox guessed that their meeting with Violet would still go ahead – not that there was much point to it now that the Ravenhearts had already killed Martha. Goodness only knows what the results of their perverted ritual had brought about. Fox had underestimated the Ravenhearts; everybody had. They’d been cunning, Fox gave them that. Signing off their work so blatantly was perfect for throwing everybody off the scent and sending the police off on the wrong track of chasing down a “Satanic” cult that didn’t exist. For all the village suspicions and tales, there was no way that anybody was going to believe that three such young, beautiful, and accomplished women as the Ravenhearts would ever be capable of the horrific torture of Martha Paisley.

Fox fleetingly wondered if Thalia would have the nerve to attend college. She almost laughed aloud at the thought of Thalia raising the Ancient Ones during the evening and heading off to do her Music and Drama A-level the next morning as if nothing had happened. It wasn’t that she found it funny, but that the whole situation was so absurd that she could hardly get her head around it.

Wren poured them all tea and placed a plate of buttered toast in the middle of the table, not that any of them felt much like eating. Swan gave their mother a quick and factual description of what they had seen, leaving out none of the details. It was better to tell her now about the witchcraft related details rather than her find out later and wonder why her daughter had felt it necessary to omit them. Wren sat sipping her tea, listening carefully.

"So Martha was murdered as part of a ritual?" she said when Swan had finished.

"It looks that way."

"A black magic ritual?" Bunny asked, drinking in every aspect of the account.

Fox nodded. "Well, someone *trying* to make it look like the result of a black magic ritual."

Wren looked sideways at Fox, her mouth twisted in question, "What do you mean? You don't think it's… authentic?"

Fox shrugged. "I don't know. It all looked a little… dramatic; the white dress, the headdress, the bandaging, the sign around the neck. It was all too flamboyant. And why, if they murdered Martha as part of a black magic ritual, would they want to make such a public display of what they were up to?"

"They?"

The internal cursed at Fox's slip and she quickly garbled out, "Well it's most likely *them* if it's a cult or something…"

Wren nodded her head, satisfied with Fox's reasoning.

"It's a terrible shame. She seemed such a sweet girl." She stopped to pour out another cup of tea. "And, Jack, her boyfriend… do you think it's possible he might be involved with some kind of cult?"

"Well he's always been heavily involved in St. Ursula's!" Bunny quipped. Wren threw her a warning glance and Bunny picked up a slice of toast in order to deflect.

Fox's chair made a horrible noise as it scraped across the flagstone floor. Swan looked at her, surprised that she should have anywhere else to be going.

"Surely you're not going into college? Not after what you've seen this morning. Not with your back all stitched up. You should take some time to …" she shrugged, not really sure what advice she should be offering.

"Why not?" Bunny offered, "It's not like Martha and Fox were really good friends; she barely knew her." Bunny smiled sweetly, "And I'm sure that the healing effect of Will Harrington's warm hands will be much better for Fox than laying around in bed all day."

Swan turned to look at her sister with her mouth ajar. "Bunny…" she shook her head. "Words fail me; I can't believe what a total…"

"She's right," Wren offered, to the surprise of both Fox and Swan. "It's not our grief to steal. It's terribly sad, but Martha wasn't ours. You should all go to college as normal. We will light candles for her tonight."

Bunny grabbed another slice of toast as she stood and headed off towards the stairs, whilst Swan sat stubbornly at the table.

"It doesn't feel right, to be going off and living our lives, when Martha is out there like that!"

"What would you do?" Wren asked, stroking Swan's arm. "Your tears will not bring her back and the further we remove ourselves from this whole business, the better."

The Meadowsweets were not used to their mother being quite so pragmatic or cold-hearted. She had brought them up to feel the pain and sorrow of other people, to be sympathetic and open-hearted. Her response to Martha's death seemed the exact opposite, but she knew it was for the best. Her sweet, innocent daughters had no idea how the community's spotlight would soon come shining down on them, how every tiny suspicion and ill feeling going back generations would rear its ugly head. When the villagers came with their pitchforks and burning torches, they were never much in the mood for a discussion on the difference between white and black witchcraft. A witch was a witch and when one of the villager's own had fallen at the hands of one, then any witch hanging in the gallows was seen as a victory against Satan. Hard times were coming and Wren feared that the death of Martha Paisley was just the beginning of many more to come.

When all of her daughters had left, she poured the last of the tea into the saucer, leaving just the leaves. She swirled them, letting them settle and read their message.

"Just as I feared," she muttered to herself.

Wren walked over to the sink, flushed out the tea leaves with water and headed towards the sanctuary. Here she took a large leather-bound tome from the shelf and dusted the cover with her sleeve. It was too heavy to open up in her arms and she dropped the book on the oak table with a thud heavy enough to cause the collection of glass bottles to rattle. The title read *The Occult Histories of Heargton.* It had been a long time since the book had been opened and some of the pages were worryingly brittle under her fingers. The covens of Heargton had been settled for at least two generations and even the once powerful Ravenheart family had withered into a genteel existence… until now.

Wren flicked through the pages, scanning the various coven signals until she came across the image of a black raven with a heart held in its talons. A long sprawling family tree occupied the first couple of pages before the lengthy written history. It was a proud, violent, and murderous history, with connections to royalty and other high-born aristocrats woven throughout. Ravenheart Hall had suffered two devastating fires during its time, each the result of vengeful villagers in response to dastardly deeds on the part of the family. One had been after the bodies of several slaves were discovered butchered like animal carcasses in the ice house, and the other time when several young children had gone missing from the village over the course of one long, hot summer; although there had been no evidence to prove that the Ravenhearts had been responsible, the discovery of a black ritual room by one loose-tongued servant had been enough to cause a village riot and a ritual burning.

Wren's fingers traced down the page until she hit upon the passage she had been looking for. It concerned the discovery of five female bodies hanging in Ravenheart Woods in the late winter of the year 1799. Each girl had been discovered dressed in a white robe with a strip of white cloth covering the wounds where her eyes had once been. The eldest son of the family, Gaston Ravenheart, had been arrested and tried for murder, although many of the villagers believed it was the hand of the eldest daughter, Felicia, who had murdered the girls; she had a reputation for violence after one of her maids had been beaten so badly with a horsewhip that her flesh had been cut down to her spine. She lived but she never walked again. The murdered girls became known in local folklore as the Angels of the Woods and it was generally believed that they had been killed as part of a satanic ritual.

Time had caused the legend to fade and now the only legacy of their tale were five tall stone columns that had been placed in the forest as a memorial, but even these had weathered until the inscriptions had disappeared and now there was a general assumption by the villagers that they were ancient standing stones connected to the iron age burial ground that lay on the far west of the village, and after which the village was named.

The Ravenheart history was cut short at 1890, the year that the book had been published. Since then, apart from the occasional rumour of violence, a couple of unfortunate suicides, and some rather convenient accidents, the Ravenheart Hall had been quietly biding its time.

Of course all of this was an outsider's interpretation of the Ravenheart family history. Horrid as it was, Wren carried the true tales of the various covens that had been passed down through the generations, and they were far darker than even the superstitious imaginations of the village gossips. There were many crimes against nature and their God that had gone unrecorded in *The Occult Histories of Heargton*, most notable was their continual attempt to call up the Ancient Ones, a desire that seemed to run like a plague through the Ravenheart bloodline. Each time it had been up to the Guadians to stop them from achieving their goal. The services of the Guardians had not been required for over a hundred years, but now, Wren thought with a feeling of nausea, she would have to sit her daughters down and tell them that it was time to fulfill their role.

*

"What a total waste of time!" Nigella snapped. "I can't believe that you could get something so simple, so totally wrong. Are you a complete idiot?"

Thalia backed up against the wall under the strength of her sister's anger. She stuttered,

"H…how was I to know?" Thalia asked. "I mean she always acted so… pure and…"

Nigella grabbed hold of Thalia's arm and twisted it hard, "Well clearly she wasn't! Clearly she was a little more Jezebel and a little less Virgin Mary."

"I'm… I'm sorry," Thalia pleaded, cowering with the expectation of her sister's hot hand striking hard against her cheek.

"Back off," Lilith commanded. "There was no way she could have known. That little Martha-whore was even wearing a chastity ring, pious as you like. Hell, I can't stand hypocrites! She deserved exactly what she got."

Lilith swept past them with a swish of her black silks. She was preparing to meet with one of the high priestesses of a coven from the North and had decided to go full-on with the Ravenheart look. Her neck, from nape to chin, was covered in row after row of dripping rubies and her hair was pinned up so that tendrils fell like coiling snakes. She looked nothing short of an Empress. Thalia, still under the grip of her sister, hoped that the priestess that was visiting didn't make the same fashion faux pas as the last one, who had turned up in a rather unfortunate sackcloth robe affair. For some reason it had angered Lilith for weeks as she lamented the slipping of standards.

"It's really very simple," Lilith said as she rummaged through the drawer looking for her athame. "We need to make another sacrifice. A younger, purer offering. Damn it, where did I put it?"

"What have you lost?" Nigella asked.

"My blade. I was sure … Ah, here it is." Lilith recovered the soft leather sheath from the drawer and withdrew the glinting knife blade. She looked at it lovingly before slipping it back in its cover.

"Why are you meeting with her?"

"Because she requested an audience."

"Don't you think your time would be more wisely spent, given the circumstances?" Nigella asked.

Lilith headed towards the door and raised her hand before letting it fall dismissively, "Our subjects remain loyal. They, unlike my sisters, have faith in my powers!"

Nigella sighed and pulled away from Thalia, giving her the slightest nudge as she did so that she cracked her elbow painfully against the wainscoting.

"What does she mean, a younger sacrifice?" Thalia asked.

Nigella rolled her eyes, "You really are very dumb aren't you!"

Thalia blushed, rubbing her elbow with her hand. "Do you always have to be so… mean?"

"Really?" Nigella smiled, "you ask a Ravenheart *that* question. Sometimes I genuinely wonder whether we share the same blood."

Thalia chose to ignore the bait and responded, "I get the whole 'younger' thing, obviously. I was just wondering how young she meant."

Nigella headed over to the mantle piece and clicked her fingers at the hearth. Immediately a roaring, green flamed fire erupted.

"I guess she means a child, one who we can be sure is pure as the winter snows, one whose blood is filled with life energy."

"From the village?" Thalia asked, knowing that there were only a handful of younger children who lived in the village. (Strange, now she thought on it. With a population of six hundred people, there really should be more young children.)

"Of course! The village still owes its debt. It's long over due."

"And Fox Meadowsweet?"

Nigella turned to look at the flames. "Leave her to me. She won't be playing her little games for much longer."

10

Fox beckoned Will across the sixth-form common room. He had obviously not heard about the fate of Martha Paisley as he came bounding across the room with his usual goofy grin. Fox used the time that it took him to navigate his way across the busy common room to try and work out how exactly she was going to break the news to him. By the time he reached her, she still hadn't quite come to a conclusion.

"Hey," she said.

"Howdy! Are you up for …" he stopped and gave her a second glance, registering that something wasn't right, "Are you okay?"

"No, not really."

"Oh. Want to talk about it?"

Fox looked around the busy room and nodded her head, "Yes, but not here. Can we go somewhere else – somewhere quiet?"

"Sure," he replied, reaching out to touch her on the arm in a strangely familiar way. Fox recoiled from his touch and Will flushed with embarrassment. "How about we head over to the library?"

"Okay," Fox said, heading off in its direction.

They didn't speak on the way. Fox found herself battling a swell of grief that she had not expected to feel over the girl; after all she had barely known her. Nevertheless, Martha had been part of the backdrop to her personal history right from when they'd been toddlers at playgroup, and now Fox was facing a lifetime of possibility in front of her whilst Martha… her thoughts trailed off, too sad to carry on.

Will held the library door open for her and she dipped her head under his arm. Increasingly she noted how the two of them moved around each other in some weird form of synchronicity; they had even started finishing each other's sentences. These things confused her; she didn't know what it meant. She was quite sure that she didn't have feelings for Will other than friendship, but why did she even seek that from him? They were hardly the most obviously compatible friends.

When she was sure that they were alone, she dipped her voice and told him of the morning's events. He stared wide-eyed at her as she explained how Martha's body had been propped up in the well, a bandage around her wounded eyes, dressed in white with a pentagram hanging around her neck.

"I was too late, Will. It's my fault that she's dead."

He shook his head, "No, Foxy, you're not the one who did that to her."

"But I saw it before it happened; I could have stopped it."

"How exactly?"

It was a simple question but it was one that she hadn't asked herself. The moment she'd seen Martha that morning she had decided to carry the guilt for her death but now, in that one simple question, Will had made her understand that there was little she could have done. She couldn't be held accountable for the evil of another. Yet, even though she had been given this lifeline, she couldn't help but feel that she'd failed.

She shrugged. "I don't know. I just think that things could have been different."

"Well, you'll never know that, so you can't torture yourself over it. All I know is that bad things happen to good people and sometimes good doesn't triumph over evil. You can't take this all on yourself and if you continue to believe that somehow you are responsible, then that means you must think I am too, because you confided in me. You told me as much as you knew."

Fox looked at him, amazed by the clarity of his thinking. It wasn't that she thought Will to be stupid, far from it, but she had never really had him down as… wise.

"But what if…"

Fox was unable to finish because she was suddenly held between solid arms and pressed against Will's warm chest. He held her unashamedly for far longer than she felt comfortable with, and yet she didn't try and break free. She closed her eyes and rested her head against him. She heard his strong, beating heart and tried to calm her own from racing towards destruction. She knew that she was blushing and she hoped that she could calm it down before they parted.

"It isn't your fault," he whispered. His breath was warm against her skin. "Whatever is happening to you, you need to know that you're not alone, Foxy."

Fox took the words in and breathed deeply and then she patted him on the chest as a sign to let her go. "Thank you. I have a feeling I'm really going to need a friend." She could feel tears prickling at her eyes and she desperately didn't want to cry in front of him; she'd already shown far too much vulnerability. They'd both been so wrapped up in their exchange that they hadn't heard Jeremiah come up beside them. "Hey, fancy finding my two favourite people in one place!" he said cheerily, with a smug, knowing smile on his lips that told them he'd witnessed their *moment*.

"Hi, Jay," Will said without any trace of embarrassment, "alright?"

He flashed a smile, "Yep, just dandy, and you?"

Fox looked hard at Jeremiah's face, trying to read him. Jeremiah hadn't been on the bus that morning, meaning he probably hadn't heard the gossip about Martha's body. Will glanced at Fox and shuffled his feet uncomfortably.

"They found Martha Paisley this morning," Fox said, irritated that Jeremiah should be walking around so untouched by the events. She knew her irritation was unfair but she felt like venting on someone, and the jerk deserved it more than any other, even if she didn't quite know why.

At first the statement didn't register with him. Why should it, he had been in the village for less than a month. Then he understood, "Oh, the girl that went missing. Oh, that's great news!"

Fox stepped back from him and was just about to lay into him when she realised he had mistaken her words. "When I say 'they found her,' I meant they found her body," she corrected.

"Oh!" he said blushing. He ran his hands through his hair with embarrassment. "Shucks, I'm…" he fidgeted with the strap of his satchel, "I'm sorry. Was she a close friend?"

Fox sighed and pulled the weight of her bag onto her shoulder before setting off towards the door. "Forget it! It's got nothing to do with you anyway."

When Fox had left the two of them standing awkward at her sudden shift in attitude, Jeremiah turned to Will and exclaimed with a raised eyebrow, "That's one quirky chick!"

*

As soon as Fox entered the common room she could tell that news about Martha had got out. She headed over towards Swan, who was sat with Fred in the farthest corner. When she saw her sister coming, she smiled weakly, causing Fred to turn. On seeing Fox, he muttered something to Swan and stood to leave. He nodded a shy greeting at Fox as he walked by her.

"Something I said?" Fox asked Swan as she slumped into the chair opposite.

"You know Fred." She shrugged. "I guess he's worried that I told you about him and Thalia."

"You did."

She twitched her nose in response. "I shouldn't have. It was personal business between the two of us."

Fox snorted and it had a slight edge of cruelty to it. "I think he gave up on it being between the two of you when he shagged Thalia."

Swan winced at Fox's indelicate use of language and Fox guessed that she had misfired her sisterly solidarity bullet.

"Yeah, well..." Swan said, drawing a close to the topic. "So have you heard that they've found Jack?"

"No. He's not..."

"No. There isn't much news but it's said that he's in intensive care at the Royal."

"Do they think that he was..." Fox's question trailed off. There had been no sign of Jack in her visions. She was sure that he had not been there.

Swan shrugged. "Someone said that they found him in some crack den and that he'd taken a drug overdose."

Fox shook her head, "No, I'm not buying that. This is Bible Jack we're talking about. Hell would freeze over before he took drugs."

"Well, you'd have thought that about the whole girlfriend thing too, but you never know what's going on behind someone's eyes."

Someone caught Swan's attention and fixed it. Fox could tell by the fall in Swan's face exactly who had walked in but she couldn't quite believe it. Her stomach gave a flip and she steeled herself to turn around. She knew that when she did, she would come face to face with Thalia Ravenheart. Although just how close up she'd approached took her by surprise and she couldn't stop herself physically pulling back.

"Ladies," she greeted.

Fox urged her response to come out and to sound as natural as possible but her head was having a serious issue believing the audacity of her turning up to college the day her victim's body had been discovered.

"Thalia," Swan replied. Fox let out a breath at having been relieved of a response.

Thalia continued to stand there, looking at each of them in turn, her eyes lingering long enough on Fox for her to feel her heart starting to burn, in the same way a leaf smoulders when sunlight channels through a magnifying glass. The silence was heavy between them and Fox felt that at any moment the laws of physics would cave in, sending them free falling into a chaotic darkness. Just when Fox felt she might start screaming, Swan asked, "Was there something we can do for you, Thalia?"

Fox watched as Thalia was strangely confused by Swan's question. She raised an eyebrow and glanced towards the window, as if expecting to find a witness.

"No. I was just wondering if Fox had the coursework sheet for history. I seem to have misplaced mine. Things have been a little… busy."

Fox's heart hammered as she rummaged around in her bag, searching for the spare copy she had picked up for Jeremiah. She held it out, urging her hand to be steady. Thalia reached forward to collect it and their skin connected. Fox winced with the onslaught of a vision. Her internal screamed, *Not now!* Her body went rigid and the last thing she heard was Swan shouting out, "Oh, shit. The window!"

When Fox came around from her vision she was sitting completely alone, the rest of the students were all piled at the other end of the common room standing around in a circle looking at something on the floor. A freezing cold blast of air travelled in through the smashed window. Fox staggered to join her sister, who was positioned with Thalia right at the heart of the commotion. She followed the track of their gaze to see a large black raven lying dead and bloodied on the carpet, surrounded by shards of glass.

"What the hell?" Thalia asked.

Swan looked up to see Fox staring at the mess of blood and feathers on the floor. When Fox looked up to meet her sister's stare, Fox heard Swan's voice clear in her head even though her lips were still, "It was me. Look what I can do."

Noise was coming from her right and she turned to see Thalia having a girlie fit, her hand held dramatically to her chest and her lips quivering with hyperventilation,

"Oh, shit, it's an omen. It's an omen!"

Fox grabbed her by the shoulders and looked hard at her.

"It's just a bird, Thalia, get a grip. Ravens are proud and stupid. They fly into glass all the time and they… die!" The heavy emphasis on the last word caused Thalia to look up at Fox from under her heavily mascaraed eyelashes. Fox hammered the point home, lowering her voice into a husky whisper, "…they die. It's the natural way of things."

Thalia gave a strange little squeak before breaking free of Fox's grip and scampering from the common room. A few minutes later the caretaker arrived to clean up the mess and the students dispersed, chattering about the weirdness of such a thing happening on the same day that Martha had been found murdered.

Swan came up beside Fox and took her firmly by the elbow, steering her back to the quiet spot in the corner.

"Care to tell me what all the Mafia-like theatricals were about."

Fox shook her head, trying to wriggle out of her sister's chastisement. "I don't know what you mean."

"Yes you do, Fox Meadowsweet. Do you think that your pathetic threat went unnoticed?"

"Yeah well I'm not the one who murdered a raven just to score a point."

Swan shifted uncomfortably and continued on with her rant, ignoring Fox's point, "She's probably on her phone right now with her twisted, murderous sisters telling them exactly what has just happened, and do you know what their response will be…?" she paused as if she was inviting a response, but Fox knew better than to interject in her sister's outpouring. "First they'll piss themselves with laughter and when that stops they'll just be… pissed, and the Goddess help you, Fox Meadowsweet – and come to that, let her help me too because I am the one that caused that bloody piece of theatre in order to stop Thalia seeing you have a complete freak out."

At last she stopped to breathe. She shook with rage. Fox had nothing to say. Swan inhaled deeply and held out her hands flatly trying to regain her balance. "Care to tell me what happened?" she asked.

Fox replied contritely, "When she touched me, I saw something."

"What?"

"A child. A blond-haired child." Fox's face crumpled and tears threatened, "And she was so tiny, Swan, just a baby."

"Are you sure?"

Fox nodded.

"Do you know the child?"

"No."

"Could you identify her if we went looking?"

Fox shook her head, "I don't think so. I only saw the back of her head."

"Nothing else?"

"No."

"There was nothing else in the vision?"

"No," Fox lied.

The unmistakable voice of Jeremiah Chase cut into their conversation from across the room, "Well, the drama never ends in this place!" He flopped himself down in the chair at Fox's side and she responded sharply,

"You really are an insensitive bastard aren't you!"

“He faltered and flashed her a smile, “Sorry, you’ve lost me.”

“Fox is a little upset at having seen Martha’s body this morning. Perhaps a little more mindfulness would be appreciated,” Swan said in her most soothing voice.

“Oh, yeah, sorry. I only meant the bird through the window. I wasn’t thinking about…”

“Well, perhaps you could do us all a favour and turn down the happiness dial a bit,” Swan continued to advise.

“Noted and acted on, ma’m” he said, offering a salute.

Fox rolled her eyes. Clearly Jeremiah was too busy at the front of the charm line to be bothered about picking up any grace.

Swan reached out a hand and placed it on Fox’s arm; a sign that she had been forgiven for stirring it up with Thalia. Swan’s flashes of frustration went as quickly as they arrived.

“I’ve got to run. I’m already late for class. I’ll see you later. We’ll talk more then.”

Fox turned to watch Swan leave and then realised that she had been left alone with Jeremiah and sighed before sitting down.

“So, I thought we could go and do a bit of a field trip after school – out to the Rookeries?” he asked.

“Today?”

“Sure, unless you’ve got anything else on.”

Fox desperately tried to find an excuse but her brain wouldn’t think quickly enough. Sensing her reluctance, Jeremiah offered, “Of course we could leave it until the weekend, but I'd rather go today if you think you're up for it."

"What's the rush?"

Jeremiah stiffened at her question as if she had just tapped a nerve.

"There's no rush, I just thought, well, the weather is good and I've brought the car and the camera equipment, so it would be a good opportunity."

Jeremiah's rambling and poorly delivered response immediately alerted Fox to something not being right.

She stared at him and pouted. "Nah, I'm not buying this, there's something up. Why are you so keen to go back to the Rookeries today? Especially when there's psychotic killers on the loose, and come to it, what the crap were you doing there the other evening; in the pitch black?"

"It's just a really cool place, don't you think? All that… history. It's bound to have its ghosts."

Fox cocked an eyebrow. "Well I know you Yanks have a thing about historical buildings, being as you've got no history of your own."

Jeremiah laughed scornfully. "Yeah, your racism dressed as sarcasm is so not cute!"

"And ghosts?" she asked, her face full of challenge. "Don't tell me *you* believe in all that?"

"Why did you say '*you*' like that?

"Like what?"

"Like I was incapable of having an open mind or something?"

"Do I really have to answer that?"

Jeremiah leaned forward with his elbows propped on his knees and his hands knitted together. The white cotton of his shirtsleeves were rolled back and held by two small pearl buttons. On his right arm he wore the cluttered combination of a leather strap watch, that looked like an old airman's watch, a thick leather cuff, and a tattered red thread with a silver charm tangled into it. The remains of a cotton gig wrap poked out from under the cuff. He wore a simple silver ring on his thumb. She saw that on the inner wrist of his left arm he had a small black tattoo of an Egyptian eye. It looked homemade. The rest of him, apart from the dagger on his arm, was squeaky clean, although pale violet shadows sat beneath his eyes, as if he hadn't slept properly. He smelled of expensive cologne and despite the apparent, "rustic" look, everything he wore was beautifully made and cut, accentuating his swim-gym physique. Jeremiah shot her a look that hinted at a hardness matched only by his jaw line. Instinct told her that Jeremiah was a breaker of hearts. He was a boy used to getting exactly what he wanted and had never had to ask the price of it, including girls.

He leaned forward until his knitted hands propped his chin. "Do you believe in ghosts?" he asked. His blue eyes, the colour of tanzanite, flashed with light.

Is this a trick? Fox's internal asked. *Is he trying to suss out just how weird you are?* Fox looked at him and twiddled her fingers, stalling her answer. He continued, "I mean I know you have these… fits and things, and your family owns that New Age shop in the village, and… well you know how village gossip travels, especially into the ears of a newbie, so I guessed I thought I'd come right out and ask."

"But you haven't, have you, because I'm still not sure what it is that you're asking me," Fox replied, playing innocent.

"You know… is it true what they say?"

"Well if I knew what it was *they* were saying then I might be able to answer you," she said snappily. The slight bedazzlement of his handsome good looks began to wear off with his annoying game-playing.

"I do."

"You do, what?" she asked, tired of the conversation already.

"Believe in ghosts."

Fox tried to suppress a smile. "Do you now?"

"That's why I was at the Rookeries the other night, in the dark, all alone."

"Really?" she asked sarcastically. She laughed. "Okay, wannabe ghost-hunter, lets head out there this afternoon and you can show me your open mind."

*

Jeremiah flashed her a smile. He had hoped that Fox might have taken him a little more seriously, to find someone who not only might offer some understanding about his situation but who might be able to offer some form of explanation. Okay, so he'd hit a bad day and the whole conversation could have gone a lot better, but at least she was now smiling at him, and maybe when they got to the Rookeries and she began to see some of the stuff for herself, she might be more willing to engage in a proper conversation about it all, whatever *it* was.

After the message had appeared in the mirror he had been unable to sleep for hours. It was only when his tired body won the battle over his imagination that sleep had claimed him, but even then it was so that he could be tossed on a wild sea of nightmares. "It wouldn't have been so bad if I'd had the high beforehand," he quipped silently. He was seriously beginning to miss the concrete certainty of New York City with all its manmade solidity and synthetic fun easily bargained for with the flash of a black plastic card.

Not here; here everything felt insubstantial, like the painted flat-boards of some Hollywood film set or the decaying surface of some pastoral idyll by Constable. The English countryside was beginning to get to him, not to mention the iron-grey weather. At least in New York the weather got up in the morning and made an assertive decision to either snow or be sunny. Here it took several hours of gloomy contemplation, shed a few tears, and then settled on whatever seemed to be the least effort.

The creepy house wasn't helping; it was full of drafts that felt like whispers at the ear and which caused the slamming of heavy oak doors like intermittent gunshots. The smell of damp clung to the swollen wooden panelling, impregnating everything with the faint smell of death, exacerbated by the heady smell of lilies and wood polish that hung to every molecule of air. He sighed heavily, wondering how long his father's punishment would go on. Surely he'd made his point. Jeremiah mused on how he could ring home and beg forgiveness with the hope that his father, feeling triumphant in his own brilliant parenting skills, might arrange for his son to be put on a weekend flight home.

Jeremiah slapped his thigh in an attempt to bring about some determination. He had a free period and then it was History, which meant it would be easy for him and Fox to slip away together afterwards. He was about to start an internal monologue, thinking over his unfathomable attraction towards her, but he didn't have the strength to work that one out. All he knew was that for the first time in his life he had met someone completely unimpressed by the Chase name and charm. It was a novelty, and sometimes that was enough to get the heart missing a beat and the temperature to rise a little; something that hadn't happened since the forbidden fruit that had been Rachel. When every other girl you knew threw themselves at you with their simpering puppy-dog eyes and the artfully crafted caricature of a silver-screen siren, the whole boy-girl game quickly became stale.

His mind tracked back to the event at the house when Paulina had made it very clear that she'd happily jump his bones at the click of his finger. The whole incident had been weird. Paulina was weird; cute, but way too kooky. And the spooky house-of-horrors shit that had come after had almost made him file the whole event under "dream." He hadn't seen her since. In fact, he barely saw her at all. In the several weeks that they'd shared a house, he could count on one hand the times he had seen her. She didn't dine with them and his Aunt Penelope seemed happy enough to pretend that she wasn't even there. (Clearly she was another act of family sufferance.) *Maybe, she'd rather I was slightly less present*, he thought.

Eventually, Jeremiah stood and headed off towards the netball courts, which were a poor substitute for a proper basketball court. He put his ear buds in and headed out into the dank English weather. *God, how this place is beginning to get me down*, he thought.

Fox watched Jeremiah from the window of the second-story classroom. He hadn't been out on the court for long before he'd been joined by a couple of other students and now they were playing competitively, rushing at each other and speeding all over the court. Fox turned her attention back to her book. She was meant to be silently reading a chapter of the Art History book on the Surrealist Movement so that she could present her "area of expertise" to the rest of the class in twenty minutes time. She'd been lucky, having visited a surrealist exhibition on their last holiday in France. It might have been better, though, for her to be given another topic, as then she wouldn't have had time to be daydreaming out the window and looking at Mr. Chase. She challenged herself to stay focused. It didn't last for long.

When her attention wandered back out towards the court, she was surprised to see that events had taken a turn and that the friendly game had turned into a full-on altercation. Clearly whatever had happened in her absence had not made David Shoreditch, a giant bully of a boy, very happy, and he was now squaring up to Jeremiah in classic ape-man fashion. Fox knew she should alert Mr. Brentford to what was happening, but part of her was curious to see how Jeremiah would handle himself. The worst that could happen was that he might get lumped, *And that might be slightly amusing,* the internal said with a wicked a smile.

Jeremiah started by deflecting. He bent down to pick up the ball as if David's challenge was slightly insignificant, but David saw it purely as a chance to get in an early point; he nudged Jeremiah with his foot, so that he was thrown slightly off balance. It was clear that Jeremiah would rather avoid a confrontation but that the time to let things go had passed. Fox leaned closer into the window and gave it her full attention. Jeremiah stood and seemed to laugh. As he walked up to David, he stroked his jaw as if weighing up some big decision. David greeted him with arms spread wide and his chest puffed out. *Do they know how totally ridiculous they look when they do that?* the internal asked.

Jeremiah said something that Fox couldn't lip-read. Whatever it was, David flooded with aggressive energy. Fox watched how his aura flashed deep purple to red. The boy bounced up and down on the spot and his neck craned forward as he started shouting. The other two guys that were with

David came up beside him and tried to reason with him, but he was way beyond that. The Shoreditch rage had descended and there was only one way this was likely to turn out. Shoreditch was notorious for his temper tantrums and had spent almost as many days of his school life excluded as he had in attendance.

On his very first day of school he'd managed to break Joe Lion's nose and it had set a pattern of violence that had dogged their school year. As Fox expected, Jeremiah began to back away. *As I thought; all talk and no walk,* the internal snarked. When Jeremiah thought he was far enough away, he foolishly turned his back on Shoreditch and headed off in the direction of the gate. Shoreditch broke free of his friends' arms and thundered after Jeremiah like a bull on charge. Fox leaped from her seat, regretting her decision not to alert Mr. Brentford earlier. She'd misjudged the situation as a scrap but it was about to get dangerously out of control.

"Mr. Brentford!" she yelled across the classroom, "There's a fight!" With that battle-cry the whole class scrambled across chairs and tables to crush behind her, pushing her up against the glass so that she had to press her hands to the glass to steady herself.

"Someone go to the office!" Mr. Brentford's command was pretty pointless as all of the class were in their gladiatorial spectator mode. Nobody was shifting until blood was spilled.

Shoreditch came within striking distance of Jeremiah and extended his arm in order to make his catch. Jeremiah had heard the sound of the charge but had continued on with his course of action. It had been a bluff. As Shoreditch's fist went to make a grab for him, he turned at lightening speed, took hold of Shoreditch's arm, and twisted it hard so that Shoreditch's body turned with it and was completely thrown off balance. He landed with a humiliating thud onto the floor. He fought against his captor but Jeremiah stood firm as Shoreditch flopped around. When his rage caused a sudden burst of energy, Jeremiah got the heel of his boot and pushed it down onto Shoreditch's neck so that he was forced into the ground.

"'s alright, sir. Looks like Chase has got it covered."

The whole of the class whooped at Chase's triumphant victory. Some of the boys had opened the window and were hanging out of it, cheering. The sound caused Jeremiah to turn and look up, where he clocked Fox looking at him. Shoreditch, a natural-born fighter, saw a golden opportunity with his opponent's lack of attention and took his chance, bringing his foot up and kicking Jeremiah in the chest. The blow was hard enough for him to lose his grip and reel backwards. Jeremiah clutched at his chest and the crowd booed.

Fox felt her anger surge. If the bloody idiots hadn't been acting so stupid then Jeremiah wouldn't have been distracted.

"Shut up! Shut up! It's your fault that he's hurt," she shouted.

Her classmates fell silent more with surprise at Fox's overreaction than out of respect. Their silence was only momentary. Shoreditch was going in for a right hook but Jeremiah managed to get his breath back just in time and danced sideways away from it.

Fox butted her way through the mob and sped at breakneck speed down the half-turn stairs and through the heavy double doors out onto the playground. She ran over to the court, adrenalin allowing her to carry the pain of her burning lungs and the excruciating pain from the wound in her back, which re-opened as she ran. She heard the jangle of keys from the teachers' lanyards, who followed behind her and hoped that they'd all get there before Shoreditch knocked Jeremiah out. Fox crashed through the gate and towards the scrapping boys. She had no idea what she was going to do when she got there. From a distance she could hear the chants of her classmates,

"Go Foxy! Go Foxy!"

Jeremiah turned to see her running towards her and he shouted, "Don't Fox, get back! I've got this…" Shoreditch landed a blow to the side of Jeremiah's head, grazing his ear with a stinger.

The sound of a male staff member bellowed across the court. "Stop it! That's enough!"

Jeremiah wrapped his leg around the back of Shoreditch's kneecaps forcing him to the ground. Fox took the chance to run head-down towards him, shoving into the side of him and sending him sprawling onto the floor. He fell hard on his hip, and the pain caused him to rock backwards and forwards.

"I said that's enough!" The booming voice of the Deputy Head drew both Fox and Jeremiah to a standstill.

Jeremiah was bent double, catching his breath, but he looked up from under his mop of hair and flashed Fox a smile that was a mixture of bemusement and impressed surprise. Sensing that everything was over, the Deputy Head turned up to the cheering crowd at the window and bellowed,

"Close that window!" which they did, just after they shouted one last, "Go, Foxy!"

Throughout her entire schooling, Fox had never been reprimanded by a senior member of staff, and now her heart pounded and she felt sick. She was also completely confused as to what she was doing in the situation. The last time she remembered having had a sensible thought was back in the classroom. Several more male members of staff jogged over to support and two of them went over to Shoreditch, helping him to stand and then guiding him back towards the main building.

"Miss Meadowsweet, would you care to explain yourself?"

Jeremiah began to speak, "She was just…" but he was cut off by the deputy's raised hand. "I don't recall asking you, Mr. Chase."

Fox shifted her weight between her feet and dipped her head before croaking out, "I was just trying to help."

"By involving yourself in a fight. On today of all days."

Fox mumbled an apology but clearly the deputy was having a really bad day.

“I’ve had to leave a meeting with the team of grief counsellors to come and sort this out. I’ve got students weeping all over the place, I’ve had the police interviewing members of my staff, I’ve had to deal with crazy hysteria about some black bird that smashed through a window, and now I have a full on fight involving students who really should know better.” He took a deep breath and turned to Jeremiah, “And I’m sure your father is going to be absolutely delighted by the news that his son has managed to make such a good impression during his first week here.”

“I’m truly sorry, sir.”

“Yes, well I’m sure, being that it involved our good friend Mr. Shoreditch, you’ve probably already been taught a lesson. You have to understand that I can’t let either of you go unpunished.”

“That’s not fair!” Fox complained.

“Sorry, but at the end of the day, the two of you have been involved in a serious physical fight. One in which, Miss Meadowsweet, you clearly took a decision to attack a boy who was already down.”

“B…but,” her response trailed off. He was right, although she couldn’t have believed just a couple of hours ago that she would ever be guilty of physically attacking somebody.

“Given the circumstances, I’m going to be lenient; you must have had a terrible shock this morning what with the news about Martha. As for you Mr. Chase, I’d like to see you in my office at the end of the day. Can I trust that until then you can keep yourself out of trouble?”

"Yes, sir!"

The deputy and his staff headed back towards the warmth of the school building. Once they were out of earshot Jeremiah let out a low whistle. "Well, I guess a thank you is in order," he said, smiling.

"Yeah, well, I do that all the time; it's part of the job."

Jeremiah looked at her with a cocked eyebrow and asked, "What job?"

"Being Superwoman," she laughed, and he joined in.

As the adrenalin began to subside, the pain in her back flared, and she winced. Jeremiah looked at her hard, but she turned her grimace into a less than convincing smile.

"You're hurt – is it your back? Did you damage it?

She waved her hand dismissively. "It's nothing. Really. It's just a little sore."

"Fancy going and getting a coffee? My nerves are completely shot," he asked.

"I guess. I don't really want to go back to class, not after…"

"Yep, you made a pretty spectacular job of saving me. They'll be crowning you with laurels and throwing rose petals at you next time they see you."

"It's not funny. I'm not going to live this down for like… forever!" she groaned.

"Imagine what it's going to be like for me; I had a girl save my ass."

"You were doing alright until the mob got involved."

"I can hold my own," he said with a tinge of pride. "I've done marital arts since the moment I could stand."

Fox nodded and gave a sideways glance in the opposite direction. If he'd been expecting some kind of swoon, he was mistaken. Once at the canteen, they ordered their coffees and took a seat. Now that all the drama had died down, Fox felt a little ridiculous. She hoped that the twenty minutes they had until next lesson would pass quickly - and mainly quietly. She sipped at her coffee and looked out of the window, trying to look as unapproachable as possible. Jeremiah was busy attending to his war wounds so didn't notice her sulky behaviour. She was still trying to process why on earth she had run into the situation like a kamikaze. Fox looked over at him and watched as he drank his coffee. The bruise on his cheek was beginning to show and a flash of sympathy flared in her.

"What did you say to him?" she asked.

"What do you mean?"

"To set Shoreditch off on one."

"Oh, that." Jeremiah did a quick scan of the room and leaned in, "I told him that his ball skills sucked." He smiled conspiratorially.

Fox wrinkled her forehead, "Really, was that all you said?"

"Pretty much."

She nodded and took a sip from her coffee repeating his words in a whisper, "Pretty much! Yeah, sure."

The bell rang. They picked up their coffee cups and ditched them in the bin before heading off in the direction of the humanities block for their History lesson.

"It's started to rain," Fox said, grumpily.

"It's always raining," Jeremiah replied.

"Still want to go up to the Rookeries this evening?" she asked, hoping that the dismal weather had put him off.

"Sure; we'll be indoors anyway."

"Great!" she muttered. "Can't wait."

11

"Master Chase, you need to understand that your father has made this move for your own good. You were out of control in New York and this is meant to be a chance for you to get your act together and start thinking about the man that you will be required to be when you come of age," Mr. Hound, the Headteacher, said as he flexed his folded knuckles. He paused, expecting a form of grovelling apology. It didn't come. "I'm sure he's going to be very disappointed that you found yourself embroiled in a fight today, and as for Miss Meadowsweet's uncharacteristic involvement, I think you need to go home and do some serious reflection on your responsibility for her dramatic change of character."

Jeremiah crossed his leg across his knee and leant back in the chair. The thought of Fox rushing to his side because of some charismatic wizardry made him smile. It was a move that irritated Mr. Hound; he wasn't used to his students being so dismissive of his authority.

"I think that Miss Meadowsweet is perfectly capable of changing her character without my interference," Jeremiah said as he stared coolly at the man across the desk.

"Your arrogance may be seen as a strength in New York City but it is not viewed as a strength here; do you understand? I will not tolerate the Chase Empire settling its court in *my* school."

"Understood, sir," Jeremiah said, unfolding his legs and leaning his elbows on the desk. "It really isn't the impression that I wanted to put forward."

"Quite," Mr. Hound replied, slightly taken off guard by Jeremiah's sudden switch to humility. "So I think you should prove to me just how serious you are about becoming part of this community and you should show off your talents in a more positive way rather than flashing your karate skills."

"Juditso, sir."

"The particulars are irrelevant, Mr. Chase," Mr. Hound said, irritated.

"Yes, of course, sir. Sorry."

"So as a gesture of your reform, you are going to do two things. Firstly, you are to take a post on the school newspaper, and secondly, you are going to do one after school club a week coaching the Year seven basketball team."

Jeremiah ran through the deal in his head. Working on the school newspaper might be fun, but coaching the Year seven's basketball didn't hold quite the same charms. He began to protest, "But sir I haven't any experience in coaching and…"

Mr. Hound raised a hand and steadied his gaze, "Practice is on Tuesday, three o'clock sharp. They have their first county match at the beginning of next month."

Jeremiah sighed and stood. As his hand touched the doorknob, Mr. Hound offered his parting shot,

"Of course if we win, I'm sure we can make this little incident disappear before your father hears about it."

Jeremiah turned and smiled. He had to hand it to the man; Hound wasn't half as spineless as he'd first appeared.

Jeremiah had arranged to meet Fox in the carpark. She'd arrived early and was leant against his car with her earbuds in.

"Hi!" he said, startling her. A look of puzzlement passed over his face. "How did you know this was my car?"

Fox cocked an eyebrow. "Really, do you have to ask?"

The key fob of the red Porsche Boxter beeped. "Am I that much of a cliché?" He smiled but part of him felt uneasy that Fox should have worked him out so easily.

She slung her bag down into the well and fell into the seat laughing. He followed, disconcerted by the idea that for the first time in his life he was fooling nobody. All at once, the red sports car he'd been unable to resist buying felt like a shameful toy that he should have given up a long time ago, along with his other toys. It wasn't quite the image he'd envisaged when he'd driven it off the forecourt last weekend.

The feeling didn't last for long; especially when he saw Fox wiggle back into the leather seat and smile. She may have seemed unimpressed but deep down he knew that the little red car was working its charm. He flicked on the stereo and the sounds of classic Americana filled the car, deepening Fox's knowing smile.

"Do you miss home?" she asked. Her eyes were closed against the winter sun streaming in through the window.

He hesitated before answering. A hundred different responses offered their services. In the end he settled for a quiet and honest, "Yes."

She glanced at him before returning to her cat-like basking. "Why are you here?"

The question might have seemed like a piece of general friendly enquiry from anybody else, but the way Fox asked it was like it was punctuated with the cocking of a gun.

He flexed his knuckles on the steering wheel before saying deliberately, "I think you know why I'm here."

He glanced over at her but her head was turned towards the window so he couldn't read her.

"I think you know exactly who I am."

She smiled and was about to reply with some pithy comment when she was plunged deep into a vision. It took a moment to orientate herself, having expected to find herself in the familiar territory of the Ravenheart sisters, but she wasn't.

Sunlight bounced off the glass in shards. Fox shielded her eyes with her hands and looked up and up towards the sky. The skyscraper was monolithic in its size and presence. All around it were other tall office blocks - but none so tall as the one she stood at the foot of. She glanced back down to the large revolving entrance and watched as tens of people scurried in and out of the building. She turned around, trying to work out exactly where she was. Several canary yellow taxis sat in the traffic and she understood that she was connecting with Jeremiah; that she was in New York.

She turned back towards the skyscraper and now the flashes of sunlight had faded so that she could read the sign above the door. It read "Chase Enterprises." There was the sensation of being yanked and she found herself standing in a classic oak-panelled office. The sound of angry men bounced around the room. She recognised Jeremiah's voice and searched him out. He was standing by the window with his back to her. His whole body was wired and he ran his hand through his hair with frustration. An older man, handsome, silver-haired and blue-eyed sat behind the large desk. There was no mistaking the family resemblance and Fox deduced that this man was Jeremiah's father. He was angry – very angry, although experience had taught him how to deliver his wrath without losing control. Fox couldn't make out the exact words but she could tell that whatever was being said, it was causing a deep wound between the two men.

Fox felt a warm stickiness on her hands and when she looked down her heart skipped a beat at the sight of blood. So much blood that a small rivulet trickled from her palm in a gloopy string and headed towards the floor. When she looked up from her hands, she saw a body lying on the floor, but it was no longer the carpeted floor of the New York office and neither Jeremiah nor his father was anywhere to be seen. The body on the floor was a woman. Fox tentatively stepped forward. She didn't recognise her, and even closer inspection didn't lead to any more understanding. Her dark tresses of hair fanned out across the wooden floor and her scarlet red dress did its best to hide the horror of all the blood. There was a stab wound above her hips on the left. It had been this wound that had killed her. The utilitarian kitchen knife lay by her side. Her chocolate brown eyes stared wide at the ceiling. She had been beautiful; very beautiful.

Fox gasped and came rushing back into reality.

"You okay?" Jeremiah asked.

He'd slowed the car right down so that it was barely crawling along the country lane. His face was full of concern but it lacked surprise. She had been making quite a habit of this kind of weirdo behaviour over the last few days.

"Another… urm, thing?" he asked, uncertain about what word he should use.

She nodded and pressed her lips tightly together for fear that a hundred invasive questions might fly from it. She couldn't let him know that the vision had been about him – not yet. She had to be sure what it meant. She had to know who the dead woman was, even though she had a pretty certain suspicion that she already did. *Rachel,* the internal whispered. *The Philosophy teacher he had an affair with. So beautiful.*

"Yes," Fox whispered in reply.

Jeremiah mistook her reply as intended for him and he offered her a weak smile.

"I'm sure they'll pass soon enough." He stared at her for a minute before returning his attention back to the road and picking up the speed of the car. They spent the rest of their journey to Heargton in silence; Fox was too lost in Jeremiah's world and so was he.

He couldn't fully explain the effect Fox had on him, as it was like none other. Whenever she was with him, he felt naked, stripped of all the masks and carefully constructed costumes that made up Master Chase; a title that would change to that of his father's in less than a few months. "Mr. Chase." The thought brought an unreasonable sense of loathing with it. He shook his head and let out a sigh. He was a hypocrite and he despised hypocrites. His father was the biggest one of all; kicking off about his relationship with Rachel and cutting him with blades of shame and fear. Even now, his father's words refused to leave his head: "It's making us a laughing stock," "It's a freak show!" "She's nothing but a whore, Jeremiah," "What would a woman like that possibly want with a boy? You're fooling yourself if you think it's love – and it certainly isn't lust – unless she's very easily satisfied. You're nothing but a pretty cheque book."

They had rowed. His father's cruel laughter had chorused with a thumping fist and a deep, low warning growl. He hadn't even bothered to stand, as if even the effort of the "discussion" was something of a distraction to his otherwise busy schedule. He had sat down and shook Jeremiah's world from the roots and it was done without even a shred of remorse; not a care for the pain his son was feeling. Jeremiah had stood at the window, looking down on the New York streets that teemed with little lives and in that moment he truly understood that his father was a god.

"I've decided that you're going to England. I have a distant cousin who is willing to host you," his father had said as way of wrapping up their talk.

Jeremiah momentarily lost the capacity to speak. He had expected punishment; the withdrawal of his credit card, the garaging of his beloved Ferrari, maybe even curfew – but he hadn't expected to be sent away half way across the world. "B…but…"

His father's raised hand and firmly pressed lips stopped him from going any further.

"You are not yet eighteen, Jeremiah. I am your father. I will decide where and with whom you should live. We all need some time out from your behaviour."

His father was losing attention with this "petty" trifle and had started to scroll through his e-mails on his desktop.

"And if I refuse?" Jeremiah asked.

His father's head flipped up and shot Jeremiah a curious look, as if he was genuinely surprised by his son's attempt at defiance. His eyes closed slowly, like a reptile considering its next move. His words came out slow and deliberate so that they resonated around the room, "Then you would give me little choice but to get rid of *all* your pretty little trinkets, Jeremiah."

Jeremiah heard his father's threat on Rachel's life loud and clear and where there had been a small seed of contempt for the man in front of him, a poisonous hatred bloomed.

"You wouldn't…" Jeremiah protested, knowing full well that his father's empire ran as deep underground amongst the criminals and gangs as it did sideways through the most powerful houses of New York City.

"Don't test me. You'll regret it." His father returned to his messages on the laptop, typing out a response and making it very clear that he had nothing more to say about the matter.

Jeremiah turned and left with his head reeling. He'd always known his father was secretly a complete and utter bastard, he'd even had fleeting moments of suspicion about the lengths to which his father had stooped to keep Chase Enterprise the powerhouse it was, but until this afternoon, his father had always at least had the decency to hide it all behind a perfectly veneered mask; the charity dinners, the patronage of the arts, the weekly mass attendance, the apprenticeship schemes, the school library builds, the sports sponsorships, the college scholarship program – the all-around, good, honest, American-made good. Everything was a lie. Even Rachel. That had been the worst of it; most of what his father had said about her was more than likely true, but it didn't stop him loving her. She had this kind of power over him – a temptation he just couldn't resist.

Jeremiah pinched the bridge of his nose and wrinkled his forehead. He needed to forget Rachel. To accept that she had been as transient as the summer, and now she was gone, filed away in his personal history as a fun and roguish phase. *It's already over.* The thought hit him at the same time he realised that it had been at least a week since he'd last had contact with her.

During his first few weeks of exile there had been daily texts, tortured declarations of conflict about her engagement, regrets that things had not turned out differently. There had been flirtatious photos with drunken sentiments of love, but now days had passed and he had heard nothing from her. He shook the immediate fear of his father's threat away. He had kept his end of the bargain, coming to England as instructed so that there was no reason for his father to… Jeremiah shied away from ending his thought.

"The turning is coming up on your left. It's hidden by the bend." Fox broke the silence of the car and Jeremiah was surprised to find that they were already driving alongside Raven's Wood. He slowed the car and looked for the turning. The light was already fading, giving the woods a pleasantly spooky atmosphere. He knew from his previous explorations that they would only be able to drive so far before the old driveway became too overgrown for the car to handle. Jeremiah let out a wry smile at the thought of a more practical four-by-four.

"Have you ever been into the Rookeries?" he asked.

Fox laughed, “You’re kidding right – only a complete nutter…” her sentence trailed off as she realised the multiple ironies in her statement. “As kids, we were told in no uncertain terms that if we were ever caught going into the Rookeries then we’d be grounded for life, and when my mother makes a statement like that, she isn’t talking figuratively.”

He pulled the car up and cut the engine. “Ready, Thelma?”

“Hey,” she said nudging his elbow. “What’s with the Thelma label, surely I’m more Daphne?” she said, flicking her hair.

He snorted a laugh. “Well I guess that would make me Fred, then.”

His response had come out spontaneous and natural but it had raised alarm in Fox. *Why should that make him Fred?* the internal quizzed. Fox tried to rid herself of the ridiculous thoughts. He hadn’t meant anything by it, it had been a quick-fire quip and no real reflection of a relationship growing between him, but nevertheless, something about the comment niggled her.

“Come on, Scooby Doo!” she said, taking the lead towards the foreboding relic of the Rookeries. “If you insist on following through with this stupid idea then let’s get it done before darkness falls.”

She heard the beep of the remote locking system and the sound of Jeremiah’s footsteps behind her. The vision she’d had about him continued to bite at the edges of her consciousness, but she knew that she’d get no further with it until she had time to actually sit quietly and fully process what she’d seen. Since she'd had the vision she felt she saw Jeremiah with new eyes; eyes that had seen the inner workings of him. But rather than it making her feel that she understood him more, it made her realise just what a complex machine he was. She'd had him down as shallow; a plastic mannequin with good dress sense and a well-recorded banter, but seeing him under the full force of his father, she now understood he was more. As he approached her, he instinctively reached out a hand and placed it on the small of her back. It was a fleeting gesture but one that made Fox involuntarily smile.

"Are you sure that you're okay about all of this?" he asked. "You seem a little on edge."

Jeremiah asked the question because, in truth, he felt a little on edge about the whole thing himself. On the last visit to the Rookeries he had searched out the room with the mirror writing, but he'd had no luck. He had, however, stumbled across a whole load of other freaky-looking rooms, which ever since his visit he had found himself revisiting in his dreams. For the past few nights he'd wake to the sound of screaming, which he knew for certain came from within the labyrinthine walls of the asylum, and last night the wretched toy carousel had decided to go all shlock horror film and start spinning wildly around as soon as he startled from his sleep. He'd taken the insidious little thing and stuffed it deep into the dark shadows of his wardrobe.

Whatever had decided to make its presence known certainly knew how to go about creeping him out to the max. He'd selfishly used the History project as an excuse to have Fox for company. If he was going to come face to face with the crazed souls of the undead, then the thought of having Fox with him somehow made him feel a little more protected – not that he knew why. Maybe it was something to do with her mother running the New Age shop and the whole spooky-girl vision thing.

The main door of the Rookeries was boarded fast, so they were forced to stumble through the weeds and building debris to the side of the old hospital. Jeremiah had scouted out a loose board that had been put over a smashed-in window. There was definitely going to be no elegant way of entering, so Fox allowed Jeremiah to take the lead, subconsciously holding back from entering the gloomy looking place.

There was very little light left in the sky and this was lessened to a half-light shadow by the boardings over the windows. After a minute to adjust her eyes to the light, Fox saw that they were standing in the middle of a once beautiful room, complete with a half-disintegrated chandelier.

"Wow! I hadn't expected this," she said in a half whisper.

"I guess the doctors had a taste for the finer things in life. I mean, imagine spending all your days working amongst the squalor and horror of the hospital wards. I guess when you finished for the day, you'd want to come somewhere more beautiful."

Fox shrugged and made her way across the floor to the far wall, which was painted with images of woodland nymphs in diaphanous robes. The damp had done their beauty no favours and they were sadly not destined to become the immortals they had once promised. Pale pink flakes of paint peeled away, giving the unnerving impression that their skin was shedding. Fox moved away, shivering with the cool air as she did. Despite the images being beautiful there was something about them that made her feel uneasy. They were out of place, and although she couldn't exactly put a finger on it, there was something about them that felt really inappropriate; and it wasn't just the fact that the lightness of their fabrics did nothing to hide their modesty, but something in the way the seated male figures looked at them with eyes that burned through to their very soul. It made Fox think of the doctors sat here looking on them in very much the same way.

Jeremiah lacked any interest in the mural and was already heading out of the room and into the first of the many corridors that they'd travel that evening. Fox attempted to strike up a conversation, but the sound of her voice sounded so loud in the eerie silence of the cavernous rooms that she gave up and fell silent. Jeremiah had recovered his torch and his camera from his rucksack and was busily snapping photos of anything spooky he could find - he certainly wasn't short of material; rusty wheelchairs and weird medical equipment littered the rooms with no sense of order or sense. Fox guessed that they weren't the first trespassers to enter the Rookeries. A thought that made her feel even more like she was about to become a cast member of some dodgy horror film.

"Remind me again about why we're actually here."

"Urgh… for our History project!" Jeremiah attempted to pull off sarcastic but failed and just sounded silly.

"You do know that history is about studying the past, don't you? So there isn't actually a need for us to be here today."

"Sounds like someone is getting a little spooked! Want to go home back to mommy?" Jeremiah continued to snap photo after photo as he spoke to her.

Fox had noticed how Jeremiah had travelled ahead, ducking his head into rooms and giving a quick sweep of them before assessing their merit or not; it had given Fox the distinct impression that Jeremiah was looking for something. A feeling made all the more strong by the fact that Swan and her had caught him sneaking around the place all alone the other night.

"What are you looking for?" Fox asked, surprised at her own surety.

"Pardon?" he said flustering, "What makes you say that?"

"The way you're looking over every room as if you're on some kind of slightly crazy treasure hunt."

He let his camera fall to his side and looked at Fox square in the eye. He stalled before sighing. She could see that he was building to say something – something big and then she saw how he changed his mind and was trying to now find something to say that would justify the build up but divert her from the truth. Before he got a chance to lie, she jumped in with, "You might as well tell me. It was you who pushed for us to do our project on the Rookeries, and then there was the small matter of us catching you sneaking about the place in the dark on your own, and now," she shrugged, "call it instinct if you like, but I know there is something up with you and this place and it isn't a love of history."

Jeremiah seriously considered just blurting out about the weird shit that had been happening at Chase House and the freakin' creepy House of Horrors mirror trick, but he didn't. Internally he edited the whole thing down to, "I've just got a feeling about this place. I don't know, there's something about it."

"A feeling?" Fox teased. "Now who's gone all spooky?"

She continued teasing him as they left the corridor and headed into one of the rooms. Jeremiah went in first, the camera flashing – and then the flashes stopped.

"No way!" he said, almost dropping his camera.

"What is it?" Fox asked pushing past him.

"Yeah, that is… creepy!" Fox agreed looking up at the large over mantel mirror, across which was scrawled the words, "SAVE ME!"

Jeremiah brought the camera to his eye and fiddled with the exposure, trying to capture the writing on the glass.

"Those kids sure have a sick sense of humour!" Fox offered by way of explanation.

"Kids?" Jeremiah asked distractedly.

"Well, yeah, everybody knows that the place is used as a weekend drug den."

Jeremiah didn't respond, just sort of made a "urgh huh" sound, but Fox didn't get time to be pissed that he wasn't listening to her, because as he pressed the button of his camera, the sound of screaming travelled down the rotting, empty corridors. It headed towards them like a barrelling bullet.

"Go!" Jeremiah shouted, grabbing her hand and leading her through the gloom at break-neck speed.

They fled the house with a devil at their backs, scrambled through the window, and burst out into the fresh air of the woods. Darkness had settled, making their flight towards the car a challenge more of instinct than of skill.

"What the…" Fox asked as she threw herself into the passenger door.

The sound of slamming doors and the panicked roar of the engine barely drowned out their hyperventilation. It wasn't until the wheels of the car reassuringly hit the sound of tarmac that either of them dared speak, and then they both began at once.

"What was that?"

"Bloody hell!"

The fear turned to hysterical giggles and Jeremiah said, "I can't believe we ran out of there like a pair of girls." He glanced at Fox, "Well that I ran out of there like a girl."

The rest of the ride into town wasn't far but Jeremiah didn't seem ready to be alone and he continued on through the village and out towards

Coldstone House. Seeing Fox fidget, he told her he'd drop her home later. Normally she would have told him not to bother but she didn't fancy walking along the wooded lanes on her own any longer; even if they were the familiar and kindly territory of the Abundance Woods. She settled back and enjoyed the luxury of the leather seats and the amazing quality of the stereo.

"Do you think we could go for a drive?"

Jeremiah looked at her with a puzzled smile. "Yeah, sure. Anywhere you want to go in particular?"

Fox shook her head. "Not really – just somewhere that isn't here for a while."

"Okay." He pressed his foot to the accelerator and they cruised past the grand gated entrance to Coldstone House and left Heargton behind.

There was something about the screaming that had infected Fox's soul. If she'd heard the story recounted by any of her friends, she would instantly have dismissed it as some prankster, or some trip-wired security system, but she knew what they had heard was neither of those things. And, even though the writing on the mirror had looked as if it had been scrawled by a drunken teen, she couldn't help but connect the two things, or the unshakeable belief that the voice had screamed out Jeremiah's name.

She looked at him. He was concentrating on the road because he knew that he was pushing the speed boundaries and that the bends in the road often liked to slip away from you and then jump back out at you when you were least suspecting it. His jaw was clenched tightly together so that she could see the muscle solid under the skin. She wondered if he'd also heard his name within the body of the scream. He hadn't mentioned it, but like with her, the scream had obviously unsettled something at his core. She turned back to look at the speeding shadows of the woods and then they broke into the vast expanses of agricultural lands. The landscape undulated gently as if the Goddess were flapping out her sheets.

It was a good while before either of them spoke and when they did, it was about something that would drown out the events back at the Rookeries.

"Have you heard any more about Martha?" Jeremiah asked, not taking his eyes from the road.

Fox shook her head. "No. But I got a text from Swan to say the local police had paid my mum a visit this morning."

Fox's surprising response fully snapped his attention towards her.

"Really?"

Fox fidgeted uncomfortably in the seat, wishing she hadn't brought it up. "Because of the whole…"

"Pagan thing? So are you …" he coughed uncomfortably. Fox braced herself for an uncomfortable moment. "Are you and your family pagan then?"

She wrinkled her nose. "I guess that's how you might define us."

"Oh."

He returned his attention to the road. "Being a pagan isn't exactly much of an option when you're the son of a corporate leviathan. The only nature you witness in New York is the human variety; most of that isn't worthy of divine worship."

It was the first time that Jeremiah had alluded to his life back home. It would have been the perfect moment for Fox to ask him about his statement and to have the great unveiling of the "real" Jeremiah Chase, but she let it pass. She wasn't sure that she wanted the real Jeremiah unveiling. She'd learned enough about him via the internet and gossip magazines to know that the Jeremiah Chase, next in line to the throne of Chase Enterprises, was a character she could never like. This Jeremiah, the one sitting next to her now (albeit in a car that was a totally crass display of capitalist ego) was a far more loveable boy.

He seemed puzzled that she did not jump on the chance to unpick him; he was so used to that with other people who always wanted to know exactly what his value and his social currency was. Strangely, he felt a bit niggled about her apparent disinterest, because he wanted Fox to be interested in him, and it wasn't until this moment that he understood exactly how much he wanted it.

"Did the police say anything?"

Fox furrowed her forehead and she resisted the urge to snap that of course they had said some*thing;* that they hadn't conducted their investigation in mime, but instead she waved her hand dismissively before saying, "Nothing much. They just wanted to know about the significance of all the pagan paraphernalia."

"Don't they have a profiler to do all that?"

Fox laughed. "In Heargton?"

"Yeah, I guess that was a pretty stupid question."

"We're in the country now, boy, and you're a long way from the safety of the city."

Jeremiah laughed nervously. She had meant it to be an ironic quip but he had never felt so vulnerable as he did here in all the years he lived in the metropolis. Things here didn't appear to follow reason or human psychology. Nature seemed to have her own rules and they weren't prepared to be nailed down. The sound of his name being screamed out in anguish by whatever-the-hell-it-was in the belly of the Rookeries still reverberated around his stomach, unsettling him. At last he broached the taboo, "So what do you think happened back at the Rookeries?"

Fox took a moment and looked out over the grey gloom of the moorland and watched how the headlights picked up the purple splashes of colour from the heather.

"I think," she paused, "I think our imaginations got the better of us."

It wasn't the answer he had hoped she would give but he had no choice but to nod his head in agreement and with a dropped voice said, "Me too."

12

Jeremiah dropped Fox off back at Meadowsweet Cottage and then headed back to Coldstone House, envious that he didn't live in a similarly cozy home. It had turned gloomy and the rain had flooded the gravel driveway, ensuring that his shiny red sports car would be a nice shade of splatter-brown. *This is a sign that I should definitely trade it for a four-wheeler*, he thought as he pulled it into the garage. The grounds of Coldstone House were poorly lit. Except for the large coach lamps swaying either side of the great doors, the rest of the grounds were dark. He slammed the door and ducked his head down into the collar of his coat, breaking into a half run across the drive towards the side door - the one that had once been reserved for the servants. It wasn't locked. His aunt stuck to the tradition of the basement floor never being locked, allowing for the staff to come and go as they needed.

He was just about to head into the dry sanctuary of the house when something caught his attention. A white shape hovered at the corner of his eye. He stopped, turned around, and looked out onto the formal lawns. It took him a moment to realise that the white blurry shape was Paulina. She was spinning in a circle, with her arms extended to the falling rain. Her cotton tea-dress clung to every curve and her hair dripped with raindrops. She stopped, sensing that her joy was being witnessed. She looked directly at Jeremiah and smiled before stretching out her arms and throwing her head back.

Jeremiah found himself captivated. There was something entirely bewitching, and quite a bit sexy about the way she was handing herself over to the elements. Jeremiah had always been seduced by the idea of the wild-child. He shook his head and let out a laugh, deciding that it might just be worth getting a drenching to share a moment with Paulina. He jogged across the grounds towards her. She was laughing.

"What are you doing?" he asked, also laughing. Her joy was contagious.

"Dancing. Want to join me?" She asked with lips bright red. Her eyeliner had run slightly in the rain causing her eyes to look smoky and dramatic – maybe a little tragic too.

"You're insane!" he joked.

"Well of course; so would you be if you were kept cooped up in that place!"

The soaking was chilling him down to the bone and he began to understand that moments like these were more full of discomfort than romance. Even so, he found his eyes caressing the curves of Paulina's body. Since she had stood in front of him stark naked the other evening, it didn't take much work on the part of his imagination to strip the saturated cottons from her frame.

The clock on the stable wall struck the hour, spreading a hollow chime across the grounds. The effect on Paulina was extraordinary. As soon as she heard the sound of the bell, she became agitated. Her dancing turned to a nervous hop. She dropped her arms and looked towards the house. Her body shivered with the cold.

"I've… I've got to get back now," she stuttered.

Jeremiah frowned, confused by her transformation. She folded her arms tightly around herself.

"God, it's cold," she said through chattering teeth.

Jeremiah pulled of his coat and was just about to drape it around her shoulders when he was attacked by the sound of screaming coming from the woods. He turned to discover its source. Eerily, it mirrored the scream he had heard earlier at the Rookeries. He forced his eyes wide open to try see into the shadows of the trees. He hadn't realised how long he had been distracted, but when he went to complete his chivalrous act, Paulina had already gone. Although the house was not that far away, she had still moved at an impressive speed.

Jeremiah was left bewildered and feeling uneasy. He waited a moment, scanning the grounds before jogging back to the house. Soaking wet, he decided against greeting his aunt and headed straight up to his room where he stripped down to his boxers before slinging on a pair of comfy grey sweats and a white t-shirt. He patted his soppy wet jacket down, looking for his camera, and then flipped open the bottom, removing the SD card. He stuck it into his Mac to start the upload and whilst waiting, made the trip down to the kitchen for a hot chocolate. That was another thing he really hated about the house, even going for a simple mug of hot drink felt like an expedition. He took the servants' stairs, a quicker and unfortunately colder route. The stone steps felt like gravestones under his feet and there was the definite smell of ancient stone-grown damp. Servants were clearly not considered important enough to warrant aesthetic pleasures – the walls were bare except for a couple of trophy animal heads and a few ceremonial swords that somebody had clearly thought too special to be relegated to the store houses but didn't want on public display.

As he neared the bottom of the winding stairs, he heard the sound of a woman singing. Thinking it must be Paulina, he straightened his t-shirt and ran a hand through his hair. He had always been a vain bastard, he thought smiling to himself. It wasn't that he thought that Paulina was conventionally attractive but he sensed the familiar uneasiness that came with being attracted to a woman that promised him something extraordinary – because "*extraordinary*" was the word that sprang to mind when he looked at Paulina.

She reminded him of one of those 1940s pin-ups, what with her hair all rolled into soft waves and her bright red lipstick. In his mind, he envisioned her sat on the worktop, a cigarette in her hand as his hand ran up the length of her thigh to reveal stocking tops and suspenders. In this way, she was a dream, regardless of whether she was a distant relative or not. He put on his most charming smile as he prepared his duck under the low doorframe. The swollen wood scraped across the flagstone tiles and the singing stopped. Behind him, one of the little servant bells jingled, distracting him momentarily from making his grand entrance.

By the time he half-fell into the kitchen, it was empty. He silently cursed at a possible opportunity missed.

The kettle took forever to boil and he made a mental note to purchase a thermos flask from the hardware store tomorrow so that he could make batches of supplies to sustain him through the evening. He hopped from foot to foot against the cold stone, wishing that he'd had the foresight to wear socks. The kettle sat on the gas ring with a sense of nonchalance and a general attitude of being uncooperative. Eventually, the water began to boil and the kettle let out its high-pitched scream. Grabbing the oven glove, Jeremiah picked up the heavy metal kettle and flicked the whistle lid in a bid to silence its hideous complaint.

However, the scream didn't stop, and he became all too aware that it wasn't the kettle. The sound was so eerie that he nearly dropped the steaming water (which would have been a definite trip to the emergency room). Fortunately, it fell back onto the hob with a clatter as he spun around trying to discover the source of the sound. His blood turned cold. The screaming went on until not being able to stand it any longer. Jeremiah clapped his hands over his ears and prayed for it to stop. At last the room fell silent and he removed his hands. With shaking hands, he poured the water from the kettle, but he didn't stop around to make his hot chocolate properly, happy to put up with clumps of floating powder rather than stay the extra several minutes in the kitchen. He dashed towards the main staircase, unwilling to make his way through the gloomy, beast-headed route he had come.

It felt an age until he eventually made it to his room and it took even longer for the hammering of his heart to steady and for him to get his breath back. He sat at his desk, desperately stirring his chocolate round and round in the hope that if he lost himself in some minor task, he might just reclaim his sanity. The message notification function pinged on his laptop, pulling him from his state of fear.

With half a mind, he flicked his hand over the mousepad and pulled up the latest message. It was from Uncle Daniel. As soon as he saw the subject line, "Witchcraft in Heargton?" the message gained his full attention. He dropped the teaspoon onto the desk and scan-read the rest of the message at break-neck pace. Key words jumped out from the missive: "*Vatican. Heargton. Withcraft. Ancient rivals. Covens. Ritual killing. Know anything? Get close. Not too close!!!! Report. Will be there as soon as commitments allow*." But the one phrase that grabbed him by the jugular and refused to leave was, "*The Meadowsweet Sisters.*"

"Oh my, God!" Jeremiah whispered aloud into the darkness. For the second time that evening he felt his heart burst into a fearful flapping. An overwhelming and completely inexplicable sense of loyalty filled him. Fox. "No!" he knew exactly what his uncle's involvement would entail; he'd heard the stories, hanging on to every gruesome and mystic detail his Uncle had spun.

Jeremiah's hand hovered over the keyboard and he noted how it trembled. His nerves were shot. His mind was completely frayed. He tried to formulate a response but the responsibility of it felt overwhelming. If he dived straight in and offered a gushing character witness of the Meadowsweets then it was sure to raise his uncle's suspicion, and yet if he failed to let his uncle know that he was close to the middle daughter, then when his uncle found out, which of course he would, things would be even worse.

Just as he was about to press the first of the keys, still undecided as to what he should do for the best, a low soft and seductive whisper filled his ear, "Save me! Please, save me!"

Cold shivers scaled his body as if his nerves were the keys of a piano. He slammed shut the lid of the laptop and breathed in hard, trying to force the voice from his head.

His jaw clenched.

"Leave me alone!"

His fist hit the desk as he pushed his chair back and stood, ready to face his invisible stalker. Aggression, he realised, was pointless. How could you fight a voice in the dark?

"Please, just leave me alone," he pleaded.

"Only you," the voice replied. "Only you…" she continued to repeatedly whisper in a fading retreat.

Jeremiah walked towards the window. A flurry of snow was falling, laying an intricate lace carpet over the grounds of Coldstone House. He shivered. The house lived up to its name; it felt as if he could never quite get warm. He watched the snowflakes fall as he re-read his uncle's e-mail over and over in his mind. He was surprised and not a little impressed that the murder of an ordinary schoolgirl in a sleepy English village should attract the attention of the Vatican, and in turn, his uncle. But then again, nothing had quite been ordinary about Martha Paisley's death or the other weird happenings that he'd experienced since arriving in this damned village. He increasingly feared he was losing his mind; that he was now paying the price for his "experimental" years. He'd known it happen to others – the voices in the head, the paranoia, the long-lasting harm.

A frail knock fell on his door, making him jump. His aunt's clipped voice came through the oak,

"Jeremiah, are you joining us for supper?"

He cursed silently, "Damn it!" He had completely forgotten that his aunt expected him to join her at her weekly supper evening. *Strange*, he thought, *that she should call on him herself rather than send the staff.* He dismissed the thought, he had enough to worry about.

"Yes, Aunt Penelope. Sorry, I lost track of time. I'll be down shortly," he said, continuing to conduct the conversation through the heavy door. He let out a sigh, hoping that the sound of impending boredom couldn't penetrate the door.

He ran his hand through his hair as means of grooming and threw open the doors of the wardrobe, rifling through his collection of hand-tailored suits, slacks, and shirts. At last he settled on a petrol blue suit with a crisp white shirt and a thin navy tie. It was smart enough to honour his aunt without being too stuffy. He wondered briefly if he might not get away with abandoning his shoes and heading down to supper in just his socks; he was in his own home, sort of, after all. The thought of his aunt's horrified face amused him and added to the temptation, but then he remembered how the floors were a bloody nightmare for conducting the chill, damp ground up through the feet and into your bones. He rummaged around, eventually finding his tan suede ankle boots, which were the nearest thing to slippers he owned. After a splash of cologne, he headed downstairs with the charming smile he saved especially for such occasions.

By the time he arrived at the library for the pre-supper drinks, the guests were already downing the last mouthfuls of their champagne. He grabbed a glass from one of the waiters doing the rounds with a silver tray and tipped most of the cold, crisp champagne down his throat in one go. At least his aunt had good taste when it came to such things. He scanned the room, knowing before he even looked that there would be absolutely no one in the room who would be in the least bit interesting – unless of course you had an interest in parish politics, gardening, or classical music. Which is why when he blindly reached out for another glass of champagne from a passing tray carried by one of the staff, he found himself taken pleasantly and completely surprised to come face to face with Fox.

“Hello!” he said, unable to contain his grin. “Wh… What are you doing here? You didn’t say…”

Fox blushed. She’d known when she’d agreed to Lady Asquithe’s panicked phone-call requesting help due to one of her regular girls calling in sick that she would more than likely be seeing Jeremiah, but she had assumed that he would have found a way of getting out of such a tedious event. She would normally have made up an excuse, but the offer of a hundred quid for an evening of work was hardly something she could turn down. Now she realised that a hundred pounds was not worth the feeling of weird humiliation she felt standing in front of Jeremiah in a maid’s uniform; not that it was the first time.

“Shouldn’t you be resting your back?”

“It’s fine. Mum took a look at it when I got back; it’s already healing. She put a couple more stitches in, bandaged me up and gave me some aspirin.”

He looked at her not entirely convinced. She smiled tightly and headed off in the direction of the other guests. Feeling Jeremiah’s eyes roam over her as she left him sent a thrill of pleasure through her and she couldn’t help but smile.

Jeremiah was completely bewitched by Fox as she made her rounds around the room. She was purposely avoiding him and she didn’t look at him once, or so he thought. The champagne went to his head fast, making the room pleasantly glittering and turning the sound of the village chit-chat into a gentle babble. He took a seat in one of the overstuffed armchairs, hoping that nobody would attempt to make small chat and ruin the pleasant fantasy running through his head. The information that had come from Uncle Daniel had piqued his curiosity over Fox Meadowsweet and had given him a desire to take apart her life. He wanted to understand everything about her; it wasn't everyday you happened to run into a girl on the Vatican's most wanted list.

His mind wandered back to the events of Martha Paisley. There was no way that the Meadowsweet sisters had been involved in her murder, of that he was certain, but it was clear that their quaint little New Age shop was not quite as innocent as its first impression and neither, it would seem, was Fox.

The gong summoning them to dinner clanged and he purposely fell to the back of the line as the guests made their way through to the dining room. Fox was clearing glasses and still doing her best at pretending that he had turned invisible.

"Ignoring me?" he asked, teasingly. He knew that a bold confrontation was the best way to needle her into an honest response.

She carried on walking through the room, picking up glasses. "No, I'm just busy. Some of us are working."

"You seem angry at me. Have I done something wrong?"

She sighed and put the glass abruptly down on the tray. She *was* angry at him, but not for anything that he had done as such; just being here, like this – dressed like that, all… the exact words escaped her and she didn't want to acknowledge the internal's suggestion of *'Hot as hell!'* Her eyebrows knitted together in irritation.

"It's not always about you, you know!" she snapped, revealing more of her mood than she had intended. He looked genuinely wounded at her retort and she felt bad. He hadn't done anything wrong at all; in fact, he had been completely charming and humble all evening. He certainly hadn't rubbed her nose in the fact that she was only there as paid staff. She took a deep breath and smiled by way of apology.

"Sorry, it just feels a little awkward, me being paid to serve you – and my back is killing."

He laughed generously. "To serve my aunt, you mean? And as for your back," he shrugged. "I told you, you should have been resting. We over did it going to the Rookeries today – I was thoughtless."

Fox looked him directly in the eye and unwilling to let the whole servant conversation go quite yet said snappily, "So me serving your aunt – you're going to get your own dinner are you?"

Jeremiah coughed uncomfortably, "Well, no, not exactly, but if it makes you feel any better, I won't insist on you calling me 'sir' for the rest of the evening." His teeth bit down into his teeth and he flashed her a disarming smile.

"Good. Then I won't insist that I punch you on the nose," she replied, picking up her tray and sweeping out of the room with the pretense of being highly offended.

*

Downstairs in the kitchen, Will was battling with a battalion of wine glasses at the kitchen sink. This evening he was on pot duty, having drawn the short straw, although sometimes it was better to be down in the kitchens with the radio playing and not having to worry about being the perfect servant. With the first course served, there was a chance to have a break. Fox went to the fridge and grabbed two cans of coke, flipping the tab of them both and placing one down by the side of Will. He smiled and it was infectious. Fox felt her mood lift.

"Anything exciting happening up there?" he grinned, flashing his straight white teeth.

Fox rolled her eyes. As if anything ever exciting happened at one of Lady Asquithe's supper parties. "You know, just the usual; one jewel theft and a murder, for which I'm holding Colonel Mustard accountable for both."

"Quiet night then?"

"Yep." She took a swig of her coke and asked, "Do you mind giving me a lift home after the shift?"

He looked at her with his eyebrows raised, "Of course I don't mind. I kind of guessed I'd be dropping you back anyway."

"Oh," she replied, feeling that somehow she'd just overcomplicated their friendship.

"We've got loads of catching up to do. You've been really…" he paused, searching for a phrase that wouldn't sound too accusatory, or jealous, "preoccupied today."

Fox felt her nerves bristle. Will had failed on not sounding too jealous and his feelings about her spending time with Jeremiah were confusing; it wasn't as if he had any claims over her, and they were still fairly new into their whole unlikely friendship thing – unless she'd misread all the signals and the "thing" between them wasn't just a friendship thing. She never had been very good when it came to understanding boys.

The servants' bell tinkled just in time to stop her thoughts colliding into a smashup and although it was a relief to escape the tricky conversation with Will, it meant that she had to now go and face Jeremiah.

Fox spent the evening desperately fighting the urge not to throw something over Jeremiah's lap. Ironically, Jeremiah had a vague hope that something just like that might happen and allow him to escape thc total tedium of the evening. At last the cheese and port was served, meaning it would be at least another hour before Fox would be called on again. She made her way back down towards the kitchens, pleased at the thought of being able to sit down for a while.

She was surprised to find the kitchen empty and wondered where Will had gone. There was still a mountain of washing up to do so there was no fear that he wouldn't be returning soon. She took a seat on one of the old pine chairs and rummaged around in her bag, cursing when she realised that she'd left her book on the kitchen table back home. Sitting with nothing to do, the sound of the large kitchen clock was ridiculously loud and irritating to the point that she knew there was no way that she could stay in the room alone. She looked over at the washing up and fleetingly thought that she could make a start on it to help Will out but then selfishness and pain won over and she decided that with the Chase family tied up it might be the perfect opportunity to go and explore the house and walk the ache off.

She eyed up the door to the old servants' stairs (no longer required to be used, as Lady Asquithe liked to show her staff off). Although Fox had been to Coldstone House many times, she'd never really had the opportunity to have a sneak around – in fact, the thought of it had never occurred to her until tonight. Despite the internal offering the unwelcome suggestion that this new found curiosity might be the result of stumbling across Jeremiah's room, Fox refused to make any such connection. She waited another minute or two, waiting to see if Will might return and rescue her from such a stupid idea, but when he didn't arrive, she took it as a cue from fate that it was all a very good idea.

It wasn't long before she began to think otherwise. The gloomy, oppressive staircase promised a rather spooky escapade and the steady flow of adrenalin from doing something "naughty" started to make her a little jittery; a sensation that was heightened with the sound of a slamming door deep within the house.

"Too late now!" she whispered to herself, daring herself to move on. At the top of the stairs she took a left down the Persian-rugged gallery. Her foot falls were silent thanks to the plush wool. The house was lit with the minimal light, and she could only guess at what the cost of the electric bill must be, or what types of room lay beyond the closed, heavy oak doors. At last she found a room with a door open but it didn't offer much of interest. Just another sitting room, or morning room, or whatever else you called the fourth spare lounge. It was decorated prettily in powder blue and a small desk sat in the bay window overlooking the rose gardens. Instinct told Fox that it was a woman's room. A pretty porcelain vase of Narcissi sat whimsically on the desk, although Fox could hardly imagine the iron Lady Asquithe indulging in such a fanciful act as sitting daintily at the table and penning a few lines of poetry. A heavy waft of perfume travelled under Fox's nose and she shivered. There was the unmistakable feeling that she wasn't alone in the room and that whoever was with her was irritated by her presence. Before Fox realised exactly what she was doing, she whispered an apology and left.

It was at this point that she knew she should return back to the kitchens. No one had invited her to snoop around the house and it was clear that it wasn't just the privacy of the current Chases that she was invading. However, this thought in itself was curious and she wondered just who else was still lurking within the rooms of the house.

She continued down the corridor, the noise of the supper party fading the further she travelled. She was not going to go as far as to start opening doors, or heading up stairs (her parental conditioning was too strong for that), but she reasoned that if a room had an open door, it was fair game to steal a look. As she headed towards the light pouring from one of the open doors, it suddenly slammed shut. Fox couldn't shake the feeling that somehow the house was alive and shutting itself away. Whatever secrets Coldstone House held, it wished for them to remain secret.

As if her heart wasn't beating fast enough, the sight of a small children's ball rolling down the corridor towards her, sped it up. The feeling was irrational; she'd been brought up to not fear the dead or the spirits that still clung to the Earthly realm. She knew that most of them meant no harm and even those that did would have little chance of success; she'd been taught from a young age how to protect herself against them.

She bent down and watched as the ball rolled slowly closer and then stopped in front of her. Once it stopped turning, she saw that it was covered in pixies and rabbits; something from an age before Disney dominated every toy. She reached out a hand tentatively, almost in trepidation that the ball might do something else, like disappear or burn her or… Her thoughts were broken by the sound of Jeremiah's voice behind her,

"Thank goodness. I thought it was me going mad."

She turned and looked up at him. He was stood looking curiously at the ball. She wondered how long he had been there. The carpet had silenced his footsteps too.

"This happens a lot?" she asked, still crouching down with the temptation of touching it to ensure it was real.

Jeremiah shrugged. "It's this house – there's something here."

"Some*things*," Fox corrected. She saw how his face flickered in confusion and continued, "There are a lot of different presences here."

"Are you psychic?" he asked.

The answer should have been simple but she didn't really know. Until a couple of weeks ago she'd not shown any real special gifts, but then the prophetic visions had started happening and now it seemed that the past wanted to speak to her too. She wasn't sure that she was ready for this three-way living; past, present, and future.

"Have you seen the ball before?" she asked, deflecting the question.

"Not this one, but a ball – a red one."

"Did you touch it?"

"No," he lied. He didn't want to talk about the strange episode that had happened when he'd made contact with it. He laughed awkwardly and said, "I was chicken shit!"

It was nice to hear Jeremiah being less cocky. Fox turned her attention back to the ball and let her fingers trace its surface. It was ice-cold and the surprise of it caused her to gasp. "Do you think I should roll it back?"

"I don't know. What do you think?"

"I think I'd like to know who is at the other end of the hallway."

"Haha! That's not exactly my thoughts."

Fox rolled the ball back down the hallway and waited.

The sound of children's laughter danced back towards them, but they were clearly not in the mood to play any more. Their laughter trailed off and the hallway fell silent.

"Who are they?" Fox asked.

"I was kind of hoping you might be able to answer that."

Fox stood and faced him. "Sorry," she shrugged. She looked past him down the corridor. "I'd better get back. They've probably finished and want the table clearing."

"Do you want to come up afterwards to look at the photos we took?"

"Hmm," she paused, "that almost sounds like a chat up line." She was surprised by her own flirtatious behaviour. She shuffled. The invite was innocent enough and they'd need to look at the photos together at some point. "I don't know, I… I've arranged a lift back with Will."

"Oh, sorry, that was why I came to find you; Will had to leave about an hour ago. He got an urgent call. Sorry, I was asked to pass on a message. He said he'd catch up with you tomorrow and that he'd shout you a cab. I told him not to worry, that we'd stick one on the account."

Fox bristled with annoyance. She couldn't believe Will would bail on her without telling her. Then a hundred different and dreadful reasons as to why he'd have to leave so urgently assaulted her head.

"Did he tell you what the emergency was?"

Jeremiah shrugged, "Nope. Just said he had to go home urgently and that he'd come back tomorrow to finish off the washing up."

"Okay then. Just for a bit though; it's late and mum will worry."

"Head on up when my aunt's finished with you."

She smiled as she thought on how he'd made it sound as simple as finding him in a small, regular house; it would probably take her an hour to find his room, if she could ever find it at all.

The guests had retired to the library to wait for their taxis to arrive, leaving the dining room empty. There wasn't too much to do and Fox had the room tidied in under ten minutes. All the time the internal mocked her new-found efficiency being the result of an impending visit to Jeremiah's bedroom. She shooed the thoughts away. She didn't fancy Jeremiah; she wasn't even sure that she even liked him very much, and yet here she was speeding through her jobs so that she could go to him.

She removed her white pinny and stuffed it into her bag, then made her way up the staircase. When she reached the top, she had the debilitating decision of whether to head down the left or the right corridor. Looking down the seemingly endless corridors, there was little clue as to which direction she should head to reach Jeremiah's room. In the end, she opted for the right hand corridor, mainly because the left one, as she had discovered earlier, was haunted; in her book that was a good enough reason to avoid it.

She made her way down the corridor eventually picking up the sound of some unfamiliar American band, which being an unlikely music choice for Lady Asquithe, told her that she was heading in the right direction for Jeremiah. At last she reached his room. The music was loud enough to conceal her approach, giving her a chance to secretly observe him; he was sat at his desk, one leg up on his chair, his elbow resting on his knee. He was concentrating on his computer screen intensely. Dressed in grey sports and a white t-shirt, he looked unusually casual, almost as if he had changed for bed. The thought made her blush and she had to admit to the mocking internal that maybe Jeremiah was just a little bit handsome after all. The only light on in his room was the desk lamp and it threw his face into a warm golden light, sharpening his features. *Okay, I admit it, he's a lot handsome!* A smile danced across her lips. She extended her hand and rapped lightly on the door. Her knock was lost on the heavy wood of the door and she was forced to give out an awkward cough to try and gain his attention.

He jumped and turned towards her, cracking a warm smile at his own foolishness, and at the sight of Fox leaning against his door. She looked tired. The thought of it made him feel strangely nurturing. She'd freed her hair from the tight bun she'd worn earlier and now her hair fell slightly wild around her shoulders; the effect was startling, causing her usually defiant face to look delicate, almost doll-like. Desire unfurled in his stomach and he was surprised to feel the force of the effect she had on him.

"Hello!" he said, his voice cracking.

"Hello!" she whispered back. "Can I come in?"

Jeremiah smiled and waved his hand beckoning her in. "Of course, take a seat," he said pointing to the large four-poster bed.

Fox couldn't restrain her curiosity and allowed her eyes free roam around Jeremiah's room. It was clear that he was a visitor. The antique striped paper and coordinated bedding were hardly Jeremiah's style, however, he'd managed to carve out a space in the corner of the room where he'd put his desk. Above which, he had tacked a whole load of family photos, post cards and other curious items that she couldn't quite read.

He closed down his e-mail page and swivelled around in his chair to face her.

"I've uploaded the photos from the Rookeries, but I've not had a chance to look at them properly yet; I thought we could do that together. I think they're going to be awesome."

"Cool," Fox replied, moving awkwardly off the bed and over to the desk. Jeremiah turned back to the desk and pulled up the folder. Fox's eyes roamed over the back of Jeremiah's neck and over his slender shoulders. He smelt good. A mixture of light cologne and sweat. In her mind the image erupted of her leaning forward and kissing him; the warmth of his skin under her lips, the faint taste of salt on her tongue. She gasped with surprise at the intensity of the image and the sensation of goosebumps running over her skin.

He turned to look at her, an eyebrow cocked in concern,

"You okay?"

Fox nodded and let out a funny little noise, not trusting words to come out steady enough. He didn't look convinced and Fox feared he could see her thoughts. He waited for her to explain but she wasn't sure herself what had just happened. In the end he returned to the screen and the first image of the Rookeries.

Fox leaned in over his shoulder, fascinated by the play of shadows and the spookiness of the derelict hospital. It looked even more haunted when captured through the lens of a camera. She felt the warmth of Jeremiah's body on her cheek but even this distraction wasn't enough to pull her away from the beautiful and eerie images in front of her.

The closeness of Fox's face to Jeremiah's made his heart skip at a playful pace and his skin warmed under the surge of blood to his cheeks. He was glad Fox was so transfixed because he knew that he was blushing and he didn't want her to know the strange power she held over him. Her hair had fallen over her shoulder creating a veil between them and he could smell the scent of her shampoo, herbal and rich. He let his eyes slide to the side to look on her. She swept her hair back over her shoulder, exposing her face, removing the barrier. The automatic slide show on the screen shunted the picture on and he glanced at it before returning his eyes to Fox.

She turned, sensing him watching her but rather than turning away, he continued to look directly at her. Their faces were less than a handspan away and Fox wondered if Jeremiah could see her tremble. The slightest movement forward by either of them would cause their lips to connect. The space between them felt both small and vast all at the same time. She felt her breath deepen. She'd never kissed a boy before, and the thought that it could be so easy was almost as terrifying as it was thrilling. She watched the muscle of Jeremiah's eye twitch and saw how his lips parted slightly but she still wasn't sure if he was going to kiss her or not – and she didn't want to make a fool of herself. She'd been taken by surprise by the emerging events of the evening and she hadn't had time to consider what might happen if they kissed; would she somehow be signing some unwritten contract between them, would she…? The air shifted slightly and she felt his breath fall on her skin. Through instinct her eyelids began to drop as she anticipated their lips meeting. She braced herself for the warmth and rush of sensation but nothing came.

"Holy shit!"

Disorientated by Jeremiah's cry, her eyes snapped open to see him sat stiffly forward in his chair staring at the screen with a hand clamped over his mouth.

"Do you see it? Tell me you see it!" he asked desperately.

Fox saw it but she didn't believe it. Stood in the middle of the shot, in the photograph of the room with the large mirror, was a woman, and she had been looking right into the eye of the camera.

"That's not possible! It's Paulina!" Jeremiah whispered.

"Paulina?" Fox repeated confused.

"Yes, Paulina. Paulina who lives here with us."

Unable to bear looking at the image any longer, Jeremiah pushed back his chair and stood. Running his hand through his hair, he paced up and down the room, turning intermittently to look back at the screen as if testing his own sense of reality.

Fox took his seat and reached out a hand towards the screen touching the image of the woman trapped inside the picture. Her hair was loose and wild and her arms open wide in offer of an embrace. Her lipstick had smudged and her cheeks were stained with mascara-tears. She had once been beautiful but madness had turned her ugly and sinister.

"But there was nobody else there, Jay!" Fox said with the lilt of hysteria in her voice.

Jeremiah stood by the window and looked out across the shadowy grounds of Coldstone House. Thoughts travelled towards him like bullets intent on shattering his sanity; memories of Paulina, naked in the bathroom, then her dancing in the rain, the sound of screaming in the kitchen, and Paulina's impossible disappearance on the striking of the clock-chimes. He returned to the computer screen to check that he hadn't been hallucinating. Leaning over Fox, he placed his hand on her shoulder to steady himself, but whereas the slightest touch from him a couple of minutes ago would have set her nerves alight, now she didn't feel a thing because she had transported her thoughts to Paulina, and she was lost in her past; living the days and sorrows of Paulina in one streaming narrative – and Fox thought that her heart might break; just as the fragile skull of the baby boy had broken when

Paulina had cast him from one of the attic windows of Coldstone House before leaping to her own death.

13

Fox had barely slept. The couple hours of dreamtime she'd managed caused her to surface exhausted and with her thoughts frayed. She'd arrived home from Coldstone House in the early hours of the morning. Her mother had been sat at the kitchen table waiting for her. The look of worry on her face had told Fox all that she needed to know – her mother had seen something coming and feared it had already happened. Death was stalking the Meadowsweets; Fox knew it. When a witch saw a ghost it was a terrible omen, and despite Jeremiah's reassurances that it must have been some form of trickery done by Paulina whilst he was down at dinner, Fox knew that on this night they had both looked Death straight in the eyes.

Fox hadn't told him about the vision she'd had about Paulina and the baby boy. She wasn't sure he could cope with any more trauma in one day. Then on top of it all, before everything had gone bat-shit-crazy (well even more bat-shit-crazy than children's toys moving around all by themselves) there had been a moment between her and Jeremiah when something passed between them and shifted the sands beneath their feet. The way he had looked at her had disarmed her completely; she had never felt so momentarily beautiful. She knew that he had been about to kiss her; a thought that she might have dismissed as ridiculous only a day ago, but now there was no denying it. Now she had to formulate a battle plan, because love was a game and she knew that if she wasn't careful she could easily end up losing.

Groggily, she made her way to her drawers and pulled out a navy jumper and then recovered her skinnies from the floor. The college bus would be pulling up in less than twenty minutes. *Thank goodness it's Friday!* she thought as she combed her hair with her fingers and pulled it up into a messy knot. Her mobile beeped with an incoming message from Will. It informed her that he wouldn't be at college as he'd had to go and see his grandfather, who'd been taken ill. She let out a heavy sigh knowing how precious Will's grandfather was to him. With Will's absence, it left her little distraction from the whole Jeremiah situation, nor much help with the ongoing Martha Paisley situation. She thought back to a month ago when everything had been quiet and ordered; now it was like her life had been turned into a storm-circus; death, ghosts, ancient surfacing rivalries and… boys! She shrugged her shoulders in defeat and gave herself over to fate. She heard Swan head towards the kitchen and Fox followed, meeting her at the kitchen table where she already had a cup of chamomile tea on the go.

"Morning!" she said.

"Have you seen my English folder anywhere?" Fox asked.

"Nope. Where did you leave it?"

"Yeah, thanks, if I knew that…" Fox offered a tight sarcastic smile.

"What time did you get back from work last night?"

"What's it to do with you?"

"I was waiting for you."

Fox flashed her a look of curiosity.

"Yes," she continued, "We have some *things* to talk about, don't you think?"

Fox shifted on her feet, still scanning the room with the pretense of looking for her folder. "I guess. How about I meet you fourth period in the library?"

"I know what you're doing," Swan said.

"What?"

"You're trying to walk away from this whole Ravenheart thing."

Fox let out a snort of laughter, "Really, do you think? My thinking is it's all a little bit too late for that!"

"You seem…" Swan paused, dramatically searching for a word, "unfocused!" She punctuated her analysis with an accusing eye.

Fox glared back at her and knew that her over defensive response had just confirmed Swan's suspicions. *So what? What if she thinks there is something going on between you and Jeremiah? Because there so is!* interjected the internal.

Fox twisted her mouth in frustration and checked the room to be sure they were alone.

"The thing with the Ravenheart sisters is under control," she said as firmly as she could. "We have some time; nothing is going to happen until the waxing of the new moon, which isn't for another two weeks."

Swan sipped her tea, looking over the edge of the cup and humouring her with the impression she was accepting what she was saying. Fox continued, but she couldn't keep the tone of conviction in her voice,

"It's best to take a step back and observe for a few days. They know we're on to them and it's going to make them volatile. Thalia was in class yesterday, so I know they're laying low. It's a good plan. I suggest we do the same."

"Do you?" Swan asked. "What if they are sending Thalia out to make it look as if everything is normal whilst in the meantime, her two ugly sisters have some poor innocent girl locked up in that barn? What if they have already taken her eyes from her? Or carved out the Devil's sign into her flesh?"

Fox shook her head. Her sister had a way of really hitting a conscience where it hurt. "I'd have seen it, wouldn't I?" she said with a voice now totally devoid of her earlier confidence.

"So you have your visions under control now, do you?"

Fox winced. "Why are you being like this, Swan? What is your problem?"

Swan stood and drained her teacup before taking it to the sink. "My problem is, Fox Meadowsweet, that we are about to possibly go into battle with a very powerful rival coven and rather than spending your time honing your gifts and strengthening your powers, you're busy falling in love with Jeremiah Chase!"

"Love? Jeremiah Chase! Are you mad?"

"No," Swan replied picking up her bag and passing by her on transit to the front door. "But I think maybe you are."

As if on cue, the school bus rounded the corner and pulled up outside the cottage. Jeremiah's face was framed in the back window. He had his earphones on and his eyes closed. Clearly he hadn't got much sleep after Fox had left.

"Why doesn't he ride his car?" Swan asked, pointedly looking at Jeremiah asleep, "rather than roughing it with the locals."

Fox looked at her sister with surprise. It was unlike Swan to take such a dislike to someone and she just didn't seem to want to let off Jeremiah. *Maybe she's jealous!* the internal offered. Fox considered the thought for a moment. It didn't seem likely; Jeremiah was hardly Swan's type, although it would explain her constant sniping at him. Jeremiah opened his eyes and seeing Fox, flashed her a smile and a wave of the hand, at which Swan turned and stared at her sister to examine her response. Fox busied herself with the business of getting onto the bus and when she was happy that Swan couldn't see, she flashed him a smile in return.

The ride to college seemed impossibly long. Fox had sat next to Swan just to make a point. It was a decision she instantly regretted. The thought of Jeremiah sat at the back of the bus on his own felt like a missed opportunity, and after their near kiss, she'd really wanted to get their awkward meeting out of the way. *Now he must think you're avoiding him.* She could feel him looking at her. She rummaged in her bag, pulled out her iPod and plugged herself in. She closed her eyes and tipped back her head. She felt tired. Her back was still sore and her period was coming, making her feel heavy and agitated. Despite their mother's usual insistence on only using herbal remedies to cure their ills, Wren had given Fox a stash of aspirin, reasoning that as aspirin came from the Willow tree, it counted as herbal enough. Fox planned on taking one as soon as she was away from Swan's prying interest.

With her eyes closed and the music calming her thoughts, Fox let the dreams in. They, unlike the visions, were nothing to fear. They were just a way of her brain ordering the chaos of her existence; destiny finding a voice. They were pleasant enough, full of sunlight and meadows. She felt the golden grasses under her fingers and the sun on her face. Above her head, in the cloudless blue summer skies, the swallows danced. Clearly it was a quiet day in Dreamland. The shuffle mode of her iPod flicked to another song, and pulled her momentarily half-way between dream and reality. When she slipped back into her consciousness, the wind had picked up and the clouds gathered quickly. A storm was coming. Fox tried to leave and return to the real world before she had to face whatever the storm was bringing with it. The music was heavy in her head; the deep cuts of the cello were joined by the haunting voice of a woman singing. She didn't recognise it as something she had downloaded and there was something about it that made her feel ice-cold. The internal screamed at her to open her eyes, but no matter how hard she tried to force them open, they stubbornly refused. A vision was coming thick and fast.

The grasses withered under her touch, falling to the ground and rotting into the dark winter soils. Frost laced the furrows of the tilled earth. Above her, the sky was leaden with the threat of snow. She let out a little whimper as she turned to face the barn. Faint in the distance, she heard the internal call out to her, *Run!* But she couldn't. She was rooted to the spot with the only possible movement being forward, towards the barn and the horrors it contained. As she walked, the snow fell. Then feathers. Then blood, until the sky was raining crimson droplets. Flames leapt up around the foot of the barn turning the whole landscape into a vision of Hell. From within the barn, inhuman voices cried out in victory. Despite the flames, Fox continued to walk forward into the mouth of the inferno. She was bathed in cold light that shielded her from the hungry fires. Inside the barn, the Ancient Ones danced in an out of the flames, celebrating their release from the sealed pit.

At the center of their dance lay a small bundle of bloodstained white cottons that covering the unmistakable form of a child. Fox walked on, heading towards the lifeless body. She'd never felt such sorrow and it threatened to reduce her at any minute but somehow within the sorrow there was a strength that kept her moving. She avoided looking onto the faces of the Ancient Ones, because she knew that if she did, she'd never reach her goal. Stooping down, she picked up the child in her arms and carried her out of the barn and into the fields beyond. The flames died down, the crimson rain ceased, replaced by pure white snows. Everything fell silent.

Fox gasped and opened her eyes. The bus had stopped at the gates of the college and the rest of the students were fidgeting about, getting ready to leave. Out of herding instinct, she gathered her bag and moved off the bus. Her legs were weak beneath her and despite having left the vision behind, she still hadn't fully returned to the here and now, causing everything around her to feel insubstantial and not fully real. She took a few paces and the world shuddered like the flats of a theatre stage. She held out a hand to steady herself, but it only grasped air and she felt herself falling towards the hard ground. Arms circled her but it was too late and her knees smacked into the concrete with a hot searing pain that faded into black.

Jeremiah eased the rest of Fox's body down to the ground. Swan cupped her head in her hands and stroked her cheek, calling her name.

"We should get somebody," Jeremiah said.

"She'll be alright, she just needs a minute or two," Swan replied.

"It isn't right that she keeps doing this. There might be something seriously wrong."

"There's nothing wrong with her," Swan snapped back. "You don't understand, that's all."

"What don't I understand?"

Swan shrugged and shook her head. "Leave it. This has nothing to do with you."

Jeremiah was cut by Swan's sharpness. "She's my friend and I'm worried about her."

"Well don't be. She doesn't need you."

Fox was still not responding. A crowd had gathered around the scene, as much interested in the exchange between Swan and Jeremiah as by the drama of Fox passing out. After a couple of minutes, the crowd parted and Ms. Sky, the school first aider, came busying in whilst commanding the rest of the students to head in for tutor period. The crowd slowly dispersed with the arrival of one of the senior teachers. Eventually, the playground was empty except for Jeremiah, Swan, the teachers, and Thalia Ravenheart, who, seemingly invisible to the staff, stood watching the scene with a cold disinterest. Swan felt her gaze fall on her and turned to Thalia. Their eyes met across the distance. An energy flowed between the two girls and sensing it, Jeremiah turned his gaze in the direction of Swan's.

"What is it?" he asked.

"Just one of the Ravenhearts getting a sick kick out of somebody else's misfortune."

Jeremiah looked again but he couldn't see anybody. To him the playground looked completely empty. "Where?"

Before she had to invent some kind of plausible answer, their attention was drawn to Fox, who was at last joining the land of the living.

"Hello!" Jeremiah crooned, flashing her a smile.

"Hi!" she croaked.

"Come on, you," Ms. Sky said, helping Fox up into a sitting position. "You," she ordered Jeremiah, "sit behind her and take her weight. I don't want her going again and smacking her head on the concrete; she's daft enough already." Ms. Sky continued to ask Fox a hundred different health checklist questions, the answer to all of which was, "No."

"This has become a bit of a habit in the last few weeks, Miss Meadowsweet," Ms. Sky said in the clipped voice of someone who feels that they have been inconvenienced and has no desire to hide the fact. "Has your mother taken you to the doctors about it?"

"No, not yet, we don't really *do* doctors."

Ms. Sky rolled her eyes. She knew that the Meadowsweet family had a reputation for being a little alternative but the thought they wouldn't use modern medicine was a frustration too far and her tone became increasingly abrupt,

"Well I really think that she should *do* doctors in this case. I want to see you tomorrow and hear that you've been tonight, otherwise the next time this happens, and there will be a next time, I'm going to phone straight for an ambulance and I'm sure that isn't what anybody wants."

She unscrewed the cap of a water bottle and shoved it into Fox's hand. "Drink that and we'll see how you're doing. If you're still feeling woozy then we'll get the office to call your mother and she can come and collect you."

"I'm fine. Really, I'm fine," Fox said as she tried to get up.

"Sit down," Swan commanded. "I'll wait with you." She turned to Jeremiah and said tersely, "Thank you for your help, you can go to class now, I've got it covered."

Jeremiah faltered. "It's okay, I have a free period first thing and you might want some help."

"I'm sure we'll be fine, won't we, Fox?"

Fox looked at her sister and saw the no-argument face. It was always useless to try and fight against that. She turned to Jeremiah and agreed, "It's fine. I'll catch up with you later."

Ms. Sky packed up the last bits of her emergency medical bag and stood. "Come on Mr. Chase, I'm sure there are plenty more damsels in the common room waiting for you to step in and rescue them."

When they were on their own, Swan leaned in and took Fox's hand in hers. "Are you really alright?"

Fox nodded out of habit and then shook her head, fighting back the tears. "No!" She tried to smile through it but the vision had been too horrid.

"Do you want to tell me about it?"

Fox shook her head. "No, not yet. Later when I've got my strength back. I need tea!"

Swan helped Fox to her unsteady feet and led her off in the direction of the canteen. "You know, we really should tell mum about what's happening," Swan said.

"There's no need. I think she already knows."

Swan looked at her with a cocked eyebrow, "What do you mean, she already knows?"

"I think sometimes you forget that the reason we are witches is because Mum is one."

Swan laughed. "I guess you're right. It's just hard thinking about her in that way. It's even harder thinking of Bunny that way what with her One Direction fetish and her bubble-gum existence. Really, sometimes I think that our baby sister was actually a changeling."

"Let her enjoy her innocence," Fox said heavily.

"Innocence!" Swan screeched, "you should have seen the state of her school uniform this morning, it looked like something from a Gentleman's Japanese Sake bar. Any shorter and her skirt would have been her blouse."

The sisters laughed.

"Yeah, I guess she could probably teach us both a thing or two about dealing with boys," Swan said, casting a look at Fox that dared her to spill but Fox wasn't going to play. Clearly Swan had already had enough fun rummaging through her sister's thoughts. *You're going to have to put a stop to that,* the internal instructed.

The process of buying tea offered a welcome break in the conversation and it wasn't until they'd almost finished their cup that Swan brought their talk back to the morning's events. Fox told Swan about her vision, moment by moment, not wanting to leave out any detail in case it might be relevant. When she had finished, Swan sat silent for a while before proclaiming,

"I think we need to go and visit Violet tonight. You need to tell her everything that has happened today and maybe she can help with planning what we should do next."

Fox nodded. It would be good not to have to deal with all of this on their own. Knowing that Will was away for the week had made her feel surprisingly alone; he was the only other one who really knew what she was going through, and although an unlikely battle partner, she didn't relish having to move forward without him.

"You know that they are holding a memorial service for Martha on Monday?" Swan asked.

Fox shook her head. She'd tried to avoid the college gossip surrounding Martha's death. The well at the center of the village had become a shrine, with at least a couple of church members holding vigil all through the day and night. Even when she'd driven past in the taxi in the early hours of yesterday morning, the well was lit with candles, casting light onto hundreds of luminous white flowers and ribbons. There were terrible fears that Martha had been murdered by a serial killer who would be waiting to torture the village with yet another gruesome sacrifice.

During the first few days, the village had been inundated with media vans and reporters. Fortunately and rather sadly, Fox thought, Martha Paisley was already becoming yesterday's news, and almost all of them had moved on to the next human tragedy. There wasn't going to be a funeral for the time being; Martha's body was still required by the police. A memorial had been planned, mainly as a way of everyone getting together to purge themselves of their fears.

Nobody thought her boyfriend Jack would be there. The story was that he'd been admitted to a psychiatric unit after trying to throw himself off the hospital roof; a reaction to being told what had happened to his "fiancée." Only his closest college friends had been to see him in hospital or had had any contact with his family. Despite having been found in a terrible state, and clearly the victim of some awful crime, there were still those in the village who refused to believe that he hadn't somehow been involved in the murder of the "Angel Martha." Even his choirboy status refused to save his reputation. Fox felt sorry for him; she knew that he was as much a victim at the hands of the Ravenhearts as Martha.

"Are we going?" Fox asked.

"Mum and Bunny are going. You know what Bunny is like." Swan rolled her eyes. "The Year Tens are making it into some sort of forum theatre trip. I even overheard one group of girls in the corridor discussing which brand of waterproof mascara they thought would be best."

They finished their tea and Swan stood up. "I've got to go and meet Fred. We're meant to have prepared a presentation for French this afternoon."

This news took Fox by surprise, especially as Swan's aura flickered to a pale melancholy blue whenever she mentioned Fred. She would have thought that her sister would have been keeping Fred at arm's length, but then again, old habits were hard to give up.

Fox smiled. "No probs, I've got class in about ten minutes anyway."

"I'll catch you later then."

Fox watched Swan walk out of the door and then scrabbled for her mobile at the bottom of her bag. She tapped in messages and fired one off to Will.

Hope you are okay. Sorry to hear about your granddad. Sending thoughts.

She considered adding more, like, "miss you" or, "phone me," but then she thought better of it. She didn't want him to read too much into it and get the wrong impression. Will was far too used to girls throwing themselves at him and she couldn't bear to think that he thought she was like the rest of them. There was another reason, one that she was reluctant to accept, and that was she felt she had somehow betrayed him with Jeremiah. She pressed the send button and headed off towards History. She was almost at the stairs when she heard her name called.

She turned to see Thalia standing behind her. She quickly scanned the rest of the corridor but it was empty.

"Thalia," she replied, forcing a smile onto her face.

"Are you recovered?" Thalia asked.

"Recovered?" Fox asked, feigning innocence.

"From your vision this morning."

Thalia's words came at Fox with force and she stumbled over her reply, "I d… don't know what you mean."

Thalia sidled up to Fox until she was in whispering distance, "Of course you do. We both know what you are. What *we* are," she corrected. "See anything interesting?" Thalia's words slid out like the hissing of a snake.

Fox wasn't sure what to say for the best. She knew that the Ravenhearts had seen her when she'd been scrying for Martha. They hadn't done anything about it yet for a couple of reasons. Firstly, the Meadowsweets had played it cool and given them no suggestion that they were aware of the Ravenheart's involvement in Martha's death and secondly, because they knew that as soon as they made the move, the whole of the Meadowsweet coven would strike back.

Fox decided that the best thing to do was to lie, "I'm having fainting fits because of my periods. I don't have any… gifts."

Thalia was surprised by Fox's reluctance to reveal her powers. Denying your powers was a novelty to a Ravenheart, who believed it was best to let the whole world know exactly what you were capable of with the idea that they'd be impressed enough to fall at your feet.

"Not visions then?" Thalia asked suspiciously, forcing Fox further into her lie.

"Nope."

"Nothing? Not even a few little flashes?" Thalia asked.

"My gifts haven't come in yet. I'm not sure they even will." A silence fell between them, forcing Fox to fill the space. "I guess we've all grown weak over the years. Not been much cause for…"

Thalia sucked her lips in and put her hands on her hips, looking Fox up and down before declaring,

"You're lying." A nerve twitched in Thalia's cheek and she hissed, "I know you're lying! The question is, why?"

Before Fox had chance to really consider the consequences of her response she replied,

"How do you know that I'm lying? Are you a mindreader?"

The question wrong-footed Thalia and the power shift was palpable. Just then the bell rang and the corridors filled with the noisy throng of students for changeover. Fox heard Jeremiah call her name and when she had returned her attention, Thalia had been swept along with the others.

Jeremiah made his way through the body of year sevens and eights with his hand raised in the air and his body weaving as if he were undertaking some extreme sports activity. Fox couldn't suppress the smile as she caught sight of a gaggle of disgruntled girls watch his smiley path towards Fox.

"Feeling better?" he asked, finally stopping.

"Yes, thanks."

"Heading to History?"

"Thought I'd better. Didn't want to let my handsome History partner down."

Jeremiah was just about to bask in the glory of her admitting that she thought he were handsome when Fox undercut him with, "You do know that I've changed partners, don't you?"

For a moment, Jeremiah's face crumpled in confusion. *Aw, bless him, he almost looks hurt,* the internal teased. He studied her face and on seeing her crooked smile, sighed. "Yeah – funny! Really funny!"

They laughed and it felt good.

"Want to go back to the Rookeries this afternoon?" he asked.

Fox looked at him incredulously.

"The Rookeries! After what we saw last night, you want to go back to that freak house?"

"*Because* of what we saw! I need to go and see what the hell that was all about."

Fox thought back to the vision she'd had at Coldstone House and of Paulina and the child falling from the window. She knew that she really ought to tell Jeremiah about it but she feared that he might not take it well. After all, who would want to know that someone had died so horribly so close to where you slept at night?

"You know, the more you talk, the more I think the Rookeries Asylum for the Insane, is a perfectly fitting location for you," Fox joked.

"You sure do have a case of the funnies today, don't 'cha!"

They headed towards the history room and being the first there, took a seat towards the back. The teaching would be minimal today as they were being given time to work "independently" on their projects. Fox guessed that half of the class wouldn't even bother coming, choosing to fool themselves with the belief that they'd work better in Starbucks.

"I've got to pop into town this afternoon during Enrichment," Jeremiah said. "I've got to do a bit of shopping, but I can swing by and pick you up at half three if that's good with you?"

"You got the bus in?" Fox asked confused as to how he would get to town and back to college all before three.

"Like I said, I've got a bit of shopping to do."

"What have you got to get?"

"It's a surprise!" He cracked a cheeky grin and tapped his finger against his nose.

With Jeremiah, it could be anything from a roll of cello-tape to a harrier jet, so it was absolutely no point wasting any time guessing.

"Oh, I'm really sorry but I can't, I've got to go and visit family. There's kind of an… emergency."

The mention of family piqued his curiosity, especially in light of Uncle Daniel's e-mail.

"Oh, you have family that live locally?"

"Yes," she answered innocently. "My cousins Primrose, Rose, and Violet live out in the next village: Mayhill."

"I guess all of your family have a name-theme thing going on." He laughed but there was something else hidden in the laugh, as if the cogs of some great mechanical puzzle were whirring and things were slowly clicking into place.

"Never really thought about it," Fox said lightly.

"Well your sisters are called Swan and Bunny and you're obviously Fox. What's your mother's name?"

"Okay, what is it with you? Are you secretly some kind of crazy stalker?"

"No," he shook his head. "I'm just curious; your family are hardly nor…" he let his sentence trail off. Fox looked at him with a mixture of being potentially offended and bursting into laughter.

"And I suppose your family are totes normal," she said, her eyebrow raised in challenge.

He snorted.

"Nowhere near. My family are a really bad stereotype of the typical Hamptons family. My mother has had so much work done she's barely recognisable, my father is a classic wealthy capitalist with a smart suit and a traded soul, and my sister is a beautiful but tortured prima donna. Literally. She's just made it into the New York Ballet Corps. Dad spends his time divided between the boardroom, the golf course, the yacht club, and his secretary's bedroom. Mum spends her day shopping, lunching, and going to the salon. My sister, Lucia, is the only one I have any real time for."

Fox was surprised by Jeremiah's sudden outpouring of personal stuff and she didn't really know what to say. Mistaking her silence for disapproval Jeremiah continued,

"Yeah, I guess it's all a bit of the poor-little-rich-boy cliché, you know the one that also includes an overbearing father who thinks of his son as a constant disappointment and a mommy who never knew how to love anything other than her diamonds and toy poodles."

Fox smiled and pouted her lips. "That's not quite what I was thinking. I was surprised, that was all."

"By what?"

"By the way you feel about it all."

Fox couldn't take her eyes off him. She tried to imagine what he'd be like without his money and status, if he'd stayed forever the boy she'd known in her very first impression; funny, too handsome to be good, charming, clever, and not afraid to stand out from the crowd. Was that a boy she could fall for? *Of course it is.* Then she had discovered Jeremiah's true identity and that had somehow eclipsed the rest of him. Now she understood that she had been unnecessarily hard on him. It had also made her step away from seizing the chance to kiss him last night.

He stopped talking and was watching her think. The compulsion to lean forward and kiss him right now came over her, but even though she guessed he would be pleasantly surprised, the fact that he would still be surprised might backfire horribly. She was saved by the flustered arrival of Carmen, who came bundling in and plonked herself down next to Fox already half way through a conversation that she naturally expected Fox to catch up with.

"So it's hardly fair is it?" Carmen asked.

"What isn't?"

"Compulsory bloody Enrichment! As if my life is really going to be enriched by playing tennis with Jock Strap Joe and that bitch, Thalia!

Sara, a student who Fox and Carmen had very little to do with, leaned in from the desk behind, "Thalia's not in today."

It took a moment to register what Sara had said and even then it didn't sink in until Fox asked, "Did you say that Thalia isn't in school today?"

"Yep, something on with her family. She's going to be away for the next fortnight. She's got a family wedding abroad or something." Having imparted her information and not really being keen on either “Freaky Fox” or “Crazy Carmen,” she returned to her conversation with her friend.

“That’s strange,” Fox muttered.

“Yeah, that *is* strange. I could have sworn I saw her this morning,” Carmen said, wrinkling her nose up. “Must have been seeing things. So anyway, great, that leaves me solo with Jock Strap Joe! I’ve a premonition that I might have to have an emergency doctor’s appointment this afternoon. What do you think? Think I’ll get away with ditching?”

Fox laughed. “You’d be a fool; Joe is pretty hot in his tennis shorts.”

Jeremiah raised a curious eyebrow at Fox, as if genuinely surprised that she should find another boy attractive. Fox noted his reaction and filed it away for later as ammunition. She was pleasantly surprised to see that he was bothered by it.

Carmen sighed. “Yeah, maybe you’re right. Just as long as he doesn’t try and talk to me; jeez he’s a total airhead!”

Jeremiah coughed down his laugh and pretended to write something important in his folder. Fox slid him a conspiratorial smile.

“So, bestie, when are we going to get to hang out together? Ever since he’s arrived on the scene, I’ve not had a look in,” Carmen said, nodding over at Jeremiah.

Jeremiah continued to bury himself in his project work but Fox knew he was listening. She flustered, embarrassed again by Carmen’s lack of social grace.

"If you haven't noticed, Carmen, we're meant to be working hard, with our *project partners* on our History coursework; Jeremiah is my *project partner* and that's why we're spending so much time together!" Fox's repetition was intended to deliver a message to Carmen, but it failed.

"Ohhh," Carmen replied over-dramatically, "I suppose that makes sense! Well, I was a bit confused because I thought you and Wi…"

Carmen didn't get chance to finish her brilliant display of social stupidity as Fox kicked her hard under the table causing her to break off her sentence and replace them with outraged cries. The effect wasn't exactly what Fox had hoped for, being that it made more of a thing of it then it already was.

At last Fox was saved by the arrival of Mr. Saxon, who, true to form, arrived late with a mug of coffee swinging perilously in his hand. He made some general effort to get the class into order by basically informing them to carry on as they already were. He explained that he'd be checking in with each partnership in the next couple of weeks and that in the meantime, "Have fun exploring, guys!" Once this required speech was complete, he sat down and began marking a mountain of lower school exercise books.

Carmen sulked off to the back of the room and reluctantly pulled out her folder and pencil case. Fox watched her and flashed her a smile of encouragement. Fox had always been Carmen's own personal coach, pushing her to do better. The formal institution of school was not really considered a positive thing by her father or the small community that lived on the back meadow. Carmen's family (which was a term that extended to all ten members of their camp, blood relative or not) had settled in Heargton over ten years ago and had slowly proven their harmlessness to the village over the years. Now they were almost accepted as "upstanding members" of the community, even having representation on the village council. Carmen's father made a modest living cleaning windows and her brothers did all right out of doing the gardens of some of the residents. The men drank in The Green Man as regulars and were quite a force to be reckoned with on quiz night. The women took it in turns to help out at the local primary school, running workshops in sewing and music. It might have been a very different story of prejudice if they had rocked up in their large shiny caravans and quad bikes, but most Heargton people admitted that the traditional gypsy caravans dotted over the far meadow added a certain romance to the village; adding to its chocolate-box aesthetics. None of this held any sway at school though, where kids from the other satellite villages chose not to get past the media stereotype. As a result, Carmen had always been an outsider and increasingly, as she chose the more conventional life of college and possibly university, she was becoming an outsider from her own community too. Fox understood more than most what if felt like to feel a disconnect with those around you.

"What you thinking about?" Jeremiah asked, pulling Fox from her thoughts.

She shook her head and smiled, "Nothing much."

He returned his head to the photos, peering at every one to see if he could find more evidence of Paulina.

"Do we need to talk about last night?" Fox asked.

Jeremiah flashed her a look from under his eyelashes and returned back to the photos. "What about it?"

Fox fidgeted in her seat. She wasn't entirely which part of last night she was asking the question about – the kiss that never was, or the crazy ghost lady in the photograph.

Jeremiah saved her making a choice. "You know that when I tried to print *that* photo off, it came out just a blurry mess."

"Really?"

"Yep." He shuffled through his papers and recovered a mess of black and white streaks. "Here, see!"

Fox took the picture between her fingers. He was right, there wasn't a trace of a figure.

"Do you think we imagined it?" he asked.

She turned the question over in her head. She knew they hadn't and she knew exactly who the woman had been. Jeremiah had stopped scrutinising the photos and had turned his attention to Fox, who had her forehead screwed up in concentration. Fox felt her phone vibrate. She slipped it from her pocket and read the text under the table out of the sight of Mr. Saxon. It was a message from Will saying that things weren't good and that he would be staying until things settled. Fox read between the lines and knew Will was really saying he'd be staying until his grandfather died. The thought made her feel sad.

"Will," she gave as means of explanation.

Jeremiah mouthed, "Oh," but didn't expand. "So the Ravenhearts," he said by way of moving on, "owned the Rookeries asylum and that whopping big house. They seem to be quite a dynasty in the area?"

"You could say that."

"I think we need to do a little digging around about their family past, don't you?"

There was something in the way that he said it that made Fox's skin prickle. All at once, the image of a game of poker flashed in her head and she saw Jeremiah with a handful of cards, but they weren't the ordinary playing cards, but old tarot cards – he was holding them tightly to his chest. She shook her head to clear her thoughts, not sure if what she had seen was a momentary vision or just her over-active imagination.

There was no way that she could tell him what a stupid idea rummaging around the Ravenheart's family closet was without giving the whole game away and so she had to settle for a slightly strangulated noise and a nod of the head. All she could hope for was that the Ravenhearts had been clever enough to hide their skeletons well.

14

Jeremiah sat down and logged onto his e-mails. He was expecting a message from Daniel about the investigation. Jeremiah had been making a very determined effort to get Fox to trust him and he was pleased with the moves forward he'd made. He knew he needed to keep her close if he was to offer her any form of protection; he also knew that he was courting dangerous ground. Daniel had no tolerance for witches in any form, or so Daniel had said over the years. His regular quip had been, "Even the good ones are bad for you, my boy!" It was only as Jeremiah had got older that he was able to read the sense of regret that was woven between those jesting words.

Instead of a message from Daniel, there was a message from his sister, Lucia. Usually this would have made Jeremiah smile but there was something about the subject line that made Jeremiah falter.

URGENT. PLEASE OPEN A.S.A.P. I LOVE YOU.

Lucia was by nature a slightly over dramatic girl, but she'd never been the hysterical type. A little paperclip icon sat ominously next to the subject line. Instinctively Jeremiah braced himself for the contents. Lucia's message was brief but made the attachment all the more sinister.

Jay,

I tried to phone you but your phone has been off all day? Where are you????

I wanted you to see this before it hits the papers tomorrow.

I'm so sorry, Jay. I really didn't want to be the one who you connect in your mind with this news.

Know that I love you and I'm thinking of you with all of my heart.

Lucia x

P.S. Please don't tell daddy where you got the news - a courier delivered this tonight and I trespassed his office to get a hold of it. He'll be furious with me if he finds out. xxx

Jeremiah's hand quivered as he scrolled over the attachment. The time it took for the little blue download bar to fill felt endless. He had a terrible feeling he knew what the news was. It had only been a matter of time before his father tied up *all* the lose ends. The PDF document unfurled on screen. It had been badly scanned, done in a hurry.

Jeremiah let his eyes roam freely over the page, trying to close down his mind as he did. He really didn't want to read it.

CALL REPORT

NYPD

INCIDENT: *HOME INVASION AND HOMICIDE*
ATTENDING OFFICERS: *BROWN 3432 and PETERS 9802*
DATE: *October 20th 2013*
TIME OF CALL: *20.03*
ADDRESS: *4, Hilton Avenue, The Hamptons.*
VICTIM: *Mrs. Rachel Garison (aka Miss Rachel Scarlet)*

PROFILE:
Female. *24.*
Caucasian. *Brunette.*
Stats: *1.64m*
Marital status: *Married.*
Profession: *Lecturer at St. Sebastian's College. New York City.*

INITIAL OBSERVATION FROM ATTENDING OFFICERS:

Forced entry to rear side door. Home invasion. Female vic. found in Kitchen. Had been phoning for assistance at time of death. Jewelry removed. House disturbed. Initial motive, robbery. No initial signs of sexual assault. Initial MOD, extensive knife wounds to lower abdomen and chest. Defensive wounds evident. No other casualties.

ACTIONS:
House swept. All clear. CSI called. Officers remained until relieved.

Too many emotions hit Jeremiah at once. She had married? Throughout Coldstone House the phones rang. The sound of them screwed deep into his head. He could hardly breathe. Sobs caught drily in his throat. A raging anger swelled. At last the phones fell silent. He stood, despite his legs feeling weak and insubstantial beneath him.

"I know it was you!" he said, pounding his fist against his forehead. "I know it was you, you bastard!"

Jeremiah's anger was full and fierce. In place of his father's face, he picked up the bedside chair and threw it hard against the panelling where it crashed and splintered into a pathetic heap, mirrored by Jeremiah's own crumpling frame. He lay on the bed, curling his knees up under his chin. He rocked himself backwards and forwards, trying not to let the screams escape. He had not heard the turn of the doorknob nor his aunt push the door open.

She stood, with her willowy and formidable six-foot frame held straight as a rod, and said in a voice that could have lead men into battle, "Now, that is quite enough of that, young man. Pull yourself together. Your father has phoned and informed me of the news. It is unfortunate, as is the waste of all young life, but we do not need to conduct ourselves in such an unnecessary manner."

The shock at his aunt's cold commands startled him out of his hysteria and he lay staring at the wall. His breathing eased and his sobs calmed.

"I shall see you in the library in five minutes when you have composed yourself. I don't expect to have to come and get you," she concluded before leaving and closing the door.

With no real idea how he should respond to such hard-hitting grief, the rigid, clipped instructions of his aunt offered him structure to which he could cling. He swung his legs off the bed and wiped his face with the back of his hand. His breath snagged and his frame shuddered, but he felt himself solidifying back into flesh once more. He swept his hands through his hair and straightened his shirt before heading down to the library. He knew he was in shock. Reality felt like a thin veil, billowing in and out on a light breeze. Carefully, he made his way down the stairs, not trusting his legs not to buckle underneath him at any minute. Voices whispered all around him, "It wasn't love, Jeremiah." "Let her go, Jeremiah." "She was nothing to you, Jeremiah."

His aunt was waiting for him in the library and pouring out two large tumblers of golden spirit, which could have been Scotch or brandy. Jeremiah didn't really care which as long as it numbed the pain in his chest.

She met him with a steady eye and handed him one of the tumblers. He took it and watched with confusion as she raised her glass in salute to him before tipping back most of the spirit in one gulp. Jeremiah brought the heavy crystal tumbler to his lips and filled his mouth with the burning liquid. Flames licked his throat.

Aunt Penelope pulled herself up tall and breathed in heavily, preparing herself for the speech she was about to make.

"I'm going to make a few things clear to you, before your head has the opportunity to conjure up all kind of fanciful ideas. You will *not* be going back to New York at present. You will *not* be involving yourself in any of this circus. You will be staying here and moving onwards with your life. You will lock this away in your memory as a bittersweet experience; the kind that defines who we are and what we become. The death of Rachel Scarlet is a tragic and unfortunate accident that has happened to a person you once knew but who is not part of your present life."

Jeremiah listened to her intensely with a curious and disbelieving surprise. The coldness that penetrated her words was almost inhuman and yet they were strangely comforting.

"You are going to feel out of sorts for a while; that will be the effect of the shock, but don't for one minute start to fantasise that you are grieving for any kind of love between the two of you. If you think what you had with Miss Scarlet was love, then clearly you have no understanding of the word."

She paused to top up her tumbler. She drank and Jeremiah mirrored her. "But…" he began to stammer. She raised a hand and cut off his words.

"I'm sure it was all very romantic and exciting, and I'm certain that in some of those moments you had together you believed you were as happy as you could ever be, but it wasn't real, Jeremiah and your insistence on following the dream caused damage, not only to you, but to the family too."

"It had nothing to do with the family," he blurted out.

"Not initially, but things were getting… complicated."

"Complicated?" he repeated. "In what way?"

She waved her hand dismissively. "That does not concern you. There is a duty within any family for the elders to ensure the family is protected and that shame and embarrassment do not stain the good name of that family. The Chase bloodline is hundreds of years old and is one of the powerhouse families of the world. I don't quite think you really understand how far reaching our blood flows; it runs through global governments, the Vatican, world banks, all major global industries, from diamonds, to oil, to pharmaceuticals. The Chase family have financial stakes in most of the large media corporations and their altruistic charity contributions to health care and police systems across the world ensure that the Chase family maintain their power."

Jeremiah downed the rest of the brandy. Too much information was hitting him at once. His father had spoken of their family in terms of Chase Enterprises; he had been raised knowing that he was part of something bigger than his own mother and father, but it wasn't until Aunt Penelope laid it so bluntly in front of him that he really began to understand. The feeling wasn't one of being impressed, rather that he was standing on a desolate beach watching an incoming tsunami and there was nowhere to run.

"This is all too much," he said, rubbing his hand fiercely over his face.

"You need time to absorb it," she replied. "But I think we really should sit down and have a proper conversation about your family history at some point, Jeremiah. Clearly your father has been remiss in fully educating you." She sat down in one of the high wingback chairs and picked up her silver cigarette case from the side table, flicked it open and had it lit in a couple of deft movements. She handed the open case in offering to Jeremiah, who declined with a shake of the head.

"You may go now. You should have some time to meditate on the events of this evening." She inhaled deeply and let out a slow winding plume of smoke. "Feel free to take the rest of the decanter with you; it might help you sleep."

Jeremiah was about to dismiss the idea and then thought better of it. It was surprisingly heavy in his hand.

When he returned to his room, he sat down in one of the two nursing chairs either side of the fireplace. He wished it was lit so that he could lose himself in the flames. He poured himself a large tumbler of brandy, convincing himself that it was for medicinal purposes. It was in this way that he sat, drinking and staring blankly at the empty chair opposite him until the clock headed towards the midnight hour. He allowed the film of his romance with Rachel to play out in his head. She had been so beautiful, so full of life, with a mind so artfully constructed that you couldn't help but fall in love with her. But he realized, as the internal film played out, that the love he felt for her was not a shared love; it was the same way that one might fall in love with a painting or a song. It was something that moved your soul in the most intimate and private way, but never really belonged to you.

His eyelids were heavy with the alcohol. Finally, he stopped fighting and let his eyes close, only to wake a moment later and find the fire lit and Paulina sat in the chair opposite him.

"You're not real," he managed to slur.

She smiled and reached forward to take his empty tumbler from him before topping it up from the almost empty decanter. She curled her legs up under her, giving him a momentary flash of stocking underneath her olive green wiggle skirt. Her hair burned amber in the firelight.

"Real? Not real?" she shrugged, "There's not that much between it – not really."

"Who are you?" he asked.

"You know who I am, silly!" she laughed flirtatiously.

He rubbed his eyes, hoping that the dream would dispel, but she stubbornly sat there smiling at him.

"Okay," he paused, "are you alive?"

She let out a laugh. "Oh, this is such fun. It's like one of those silly parlour games Eddie used to like us to play." She straightened her face, trying to make it serious but only achieving a pouting, sultry look. "No, I'm not alive. Next question," she said, leaning forward coquettishly.

"What were you doing in the photograph that we took at the Rookeries?"

Jeremiah watched as a shadow flitted over her face and he knew that she wasn't enjoying the game any more. She ran her hand subconsciously through her ringlets and wrinkled her nose.

"I don't want to talk about it."

"Well I do."

She tipped back the tumbler.

"They sent me away because I was..." she faltered, "I was unwell."

"Unwell? What was wrong with you?"

"I'm not meant to talk about it."

"Who says?"

"Penelope."

"Aunt Penelope? What has she got to do with it?"

"Everything." Her voice whimpered and her eyes filled with tears. "I brought shame to the family and she dealt with it. It's what Aunt Penelope does – that's her role – she deals with family shame."

Jeremiah thought back to the conversation he'd had with her in the library. Everything about that conversation had been so polished to the point he had thought she had rehearsed it, but it wasn't that after all, it was a speech that she had given many times before to many different errant Chase family members.

He reached forward and took the glass, thinking that he was in no danger of getting any drunker than he obviously already was. Paulina wiped a tear from her cheek.

"Tell me about it. I need to know. Maybe I can help," he said.

Paulina shook her head.

"It's got something to do with the Rookeries, hasn't it?" he pressed.

"The Asylum for the Insane and Morally Dissolute." Paulina nodded. "I guess I fell into the later category."

"Me and you both," Jeremiah said raising his glass, to which she raised a sad, tight smile.

"That's why you are here?" she asked.

Jeremiah nodded his head. "And you? Why did your family send you to Aunt Penelope's Correctional Institute?"

Paulina glanced down at her belly and her hand subconsciously swept it.

"Oh," Jeremiah sighed. "You were with child?"

"No," she let out a bitter snort of laughter. "I was with shame."

"I'm sorry," he said.

"Don't be. We are together now, me and my baby boy."

Jeremiah's cocked eyebrow invited her to tell her story; something later he wished he had not done. On top of all the sadness he already felt, Paulina's story stretched his heart to breaking point.

"My parents delivered me to Aunt Penelope to get me away from the boy I'd fallen in love with. He was the stable hand – a completely unsuitable match." She smiled wryly. "They didn't know at that point that I was carrying his child. When the baby began to show, and the servants began to whisper, Aunt Penelope packed my case and walked me to the Rookeries, reassuring me that it had once all been a maternity hospital.

"The labour was fierce and it was only the thought of holding my little baby in my arms that pulled me through. But when I woke, the baby was gone.

"They moved me downstairs from the maternity ward to the lunatic cells using drugs and other… procedures to "*fix*" me. I was apparently an interesting case worthy of special note."

She stopped to stifle a sob.

"Eventually, Aunt Penelope, hearing what brutal techniques they were using, stepped in and rescued me, bringing me back to Coldstone House. Then one of the kitchen girls let slip that a young couple from the village had been given my baby."

Jeremiah sighed heavily. "I'm sorry, Paulina. I'm really sorry."

She drank deeply and looked at him for a long time before whispering, "Me too."

A heavy silence settled between them. She was lost for a moment in her grief.

"I killed us both. I stole him from his pram, and when the police came to take him away, I jumped from the nursery window. We both died instantly."

Jeremiah stifled his response. There was nothing – absolutely nothing – he could say.

"I thought the angels would save us, but the angels never came," she said wistfully.

"And now you're stuck here on Earth?" he whispered.

She nodded. "I guess it's better than being in Hell."

"And it was you we saw you at the Rookeries?"

"Yes, sometimes I find myself back there, I don't know how. It's never for long, but it feels like a lifetime. It was a bad place, Jeremiah. A terrible place."

"I can only imagine."

She shook her head, "No you can't; it's beyond imagination. It wasn't just the whole medical brutality thing – there were other evils."

"Other evils?"

"Evils to do with the Ravenheart family," she whispered. "True evils."

Jeremiah sat forward, imploring her to say more, but she was fading before his very eyes.

"Stay away from there, Jeremiah, it's full of witchcraft," she warned. Then she was gone and with her, the fire faded too.

*

Jeremiah woke the next day with a pounding headache, still slumped in the chair. It took him a while for his groggy head to reboot the events of the previous night, and even then it was hard for him to truly understand which of them were real and which were a dream.

He stretched out his limbs and felt the knots in his muscles protest under such rough treatment. He could tell from the flat-white light that it was already late into the morning. He was surprised that his sergeant major aunt had not come and rudely woken him and sent him packing off to college. Obviously he was being allowed at least one day to come to terms with the death of his ex.

He stood, yawning and regretting hitting the brandy as hard as he had. He gathered up his towel and headed towards the cold white sterility of the bathroom down the hall.

"For such a bloody wealthy family, you'd have thought they could install some en-suites," he grumbled. *But then, I suppose that kind of luxury might spoil us*. He thought back to what Paulina had said about Aunt Penelope, "She deals with family shame." And that was what he had become – a family shame.

With little choice other than ice-cold or scalding hot, he flicked the shower to cold and braced himself for the punishment. The water hit his skin like needles, giving him precious inability to think. After several gasps for air and a quick rub down, he hopped out and headed back towards his room, which at least was warm thanks to the over-efficient central heating system on the first floor. Paulina's visit last night had given him a purpose with which to fill his day and he was grateful. He couldn't bear to spend the day thinking over his times with Rachel, nor the manner in which she had died – or by whose instruction.

He shook his head, loosening wet droplets from his hair, and slid into a pair of grey sports and a black t-shirt. He had no intention of going anywhere; he had too much to do. There was checking out Paulina's story for starters, and then the rather murkier world of the Ravenheart family. What with his uncle's Vatican interest and the comments from Paulina last night, he knew that there was much more to their family than a large fancy house and a bloodline.

He flicked open the lid of the Mac and then phoned down to the kitchen in the hope that Aunt Penelope's butler, Vincent, might be lurking down there and would be able to make him a cafétiere of coffee. Calling on the staff wasn't something he'd normally do but he didn't relish roaming around the house and possibly bumping into his aunt, especially not with his self-inflicted booming headache. He'd made a resolution to avoid her at all costs today; he really did not want a trip down family lane, not when he was so busy researching other peoples' lives.

After a quick conversation in which Vincent insisted he bring breakfast as well as coffee, Jeremiah settled down to his day of work. Firstly, he searched for the story of Paulina Chase in the archives of the national papers, guessing from her appearance that the whole sad affair took place sometime in the early fifties. There appeared no media mention of the event, which was surprising given the notoriety of the family and the scandal that the event must have created at the time; then Jeremiah remembered his aunt's words about the family infiltrating every aspect of life including the media and he wondered if it were possible that the family had paid to have the whole scandal covered up.

At last, after much clicking into dead ends, he found record of it in the local *Heargton Times*. The website was hard to navigate and he guessed that some poor work-experience boy had been given the joyful task of scanning and uploading the archived articles. Eventually he found it; a small, sorry article that offered very little information other than that there had been the death of a female and a child at Coldstone House. Police did not seek anybody else in connection with the death and the rest of the article comprised of the funeral arrangements, which were to take place in the family chapel with a strict family only rule.

Jeremiah sighed heavily and thought back to the image of Paulina sat opposite him. She too had been so beautiful and full of life and just like Rachel, her only crime had been to fall in love. “You and us all,” he whispered into the air. A knock at the door caused him to jump from his thoughts. It was Vincent, carrying in a tray of boiled eggs, toast, and coffee. The old sod looked even more miserable than usual but Jeremiah had enough woes to carry without asking what was up with the butler, so he flashed him an appreciative smile and remained silent until Vincent shuffled out. The events of the last twenty-four hours had left Jeremiah with very little appetite and so he passed over the eggs, pouring out the thick tar-like coffee and spooning in three spoonfuls of sugar.

He sat back down in front of the screen and sipped at his coffee. The bitter sweetness of it provided a momentary distraction until thoughts of Rachel crept up on him. Before he could stop himself, his vision blurred with tears. Jeremiah rarely cried; in fact the last time he remembered crying was when he had been eight and he had fallen out of the old peach tree in his grandfather's garden and had broken his wrist.

Time passed, the coffee cooled. The day turned from white to grey as the heavy snow clouds gathered. Jeremiah shivered and he noted how the heating must have clicked off. He got up, picked up the sweater from the chair and stood in front of the ceiling to floor window that looked out over the grounds, watching the first snowflakes fall. He closed his eyes and breathed in deeply. He was searching for some sense, for some reason why Rachel had died but there wasn't any – other than the terrifying thought that it had been his father. As he stood there meditating, his attention was pulled to a figure moving near the tree line. He leaned in further and focused. It was a woman with a child held on her hip with one arm and the other extended out into the snow. Even from this distance, Jeremiah could see that she was laughing. Then she twirled around, catching the snowflakes in her hand. As if sensing Jeremiah watching, she stopped and looked over in the direction of the house before raising a hand and waving. Jeremiah shook his head and pressed his eyes together firmly, refusing to believe that the dead Paulina conjured up by his alcohol-fuelled brain was now standing in the garden waving at him. When he opened them, she had gone.

"I'm going mad!" he said to himself as he ran his hands firmly over his face checking that he was still awake.

Impulsively he grabbed his keys from his desk and swept out of the room and down the stairs in a half-jog, escaping the house and its ghosts. The front door banged heavily behind him. He headed towards the garage where he jumped up into his newly traded Range Rover. The gravel slipped beneath the tyres as he pulled hastily away from the house. The further he moved away from Coldstone House, the calmer he felt. He had no real idea where he was going; all he knew was that he needed to leave the whole goddamned Chase institute behind him.

The snow fell steadily. The fields were quickly powdered in a fine coating of snow. He spent an hour driving around the snaking lanes of the surrounding countryside until the snow began to fall too heavily for the windscreen wipers to work effectively. With most of the landscape whited out, it wasn't long before Jeremiah found himself completely lost and regretting not having loaded the updates onto the inbuilt Sat Nav system. It was now stubbornly refusing to come to his rescue.

"Great!" he said, slamming his fist into the steering wheel.

The wind had picked up and the snow was now driving to the sides of the road where it was beginning to build up rapidly. He slowed the four-by-four down and crept along, peering out through the snow in the hope of seeing some lights or buildings in the distance. The whole landscape was nothing but a white billowing sheet. He continued creeping forward until, with relief, he saw a large pair of wrought iron gates on his left. They were held open by a choker of ivy, giving a sense of elegant decay. He stopped the car and wound down the window, hoping to be able to see what they might be guarding. Far in the distance, at the end of a very long driveway flanked by skeleton Cyprus trees, he could just about make out the blue shadow of a large country house. He wound up the window and turned the car slowly into the driveway. As he passed through the gates, he smiled at the sight of a large black raven shaking the snow from her wings.

"Great, as if this couldn't get any more Edgar Allen Poe!" he said through nervous laughter.

He crept up the drive, hoping that someone might be home, and then hoping that whoever it was didn't also own a dungeon and have a taste for young American flesh.

Eventually, he arrived at the turning circle, which was made from an ornate fountain covered in icicles and topped by some poor naked stone cherub blowing a trumpet. He killed the engine and stepped out into the blizzard, peering up at the imposing gothic frontage. He pulled the bell ring, hopping from one foot to another as he waited for a reply. Just as he was about to give up, the sound of deep barking and a female voice commanding the beast to "Be quiet!" came from the other side of the heavily carved door.

The door swung open to reveal a very beautiful young woman dressed in a heavy, floor-length crimson skirt and black polo neck. She was draped in a heavy paisley shawl and her black tresses fell to her waist. Jeremiah was rendered completely spellbound by the girl's appearance, finding himself unusually lost for charm and words.

"Yes?" she asked in a haughty voice. It was the kind of voice that could turn a lion into a mouse.

Jeremiah stumbled over his thoughts and wrapped his arms tighter around his body.

"Sorry to disturb you, it's just that I've been caught out by the weather and I was wondering if I could use your telephone. I know it's a complete imposition but…" Jeremiah's words were cut short by the low menacing growl of the giant black Doberman by her hip.

The girl looked bemused by Jeremiah's whole situation and broke into a smile. "Come in," she said, waving him in and stepping back to let him through.

Jeremiah, fearful that he might loose a limb, hesitated. Seeing him nervous, she reached out a hand and patted the dog on the head, "Now, Shadow, be nice to our guest." She turned to face Jeremiah, looking him up and down in a way that made Jeremiah feel suddenly naked. "Sorry about Shadow, he's not used to guests. He's completely harmless. Don't be afraid."

Jeremiah stepped in and shook the snow from his body.

"If you go on through, the fire is lit. I'll make us some tea," she said, already walking away from him down the dark wood-panelled hallway. "Make yourself at home," she threw out over her shoulder.

Jeremiah stood for a while gawping. He was no stranger to wealth and Coldstone House was impressive enough, but he'd never seen anything quite like the house he was now standing in. *You were right about Poe!* he thought. Everywhere he looked he saw wealth and history. The hallway, larger than most apartments, was mainly home to a sweeping staircase, its banisters intricately carved with beasts and flowers. All up the stairs hung heavy oil portraits, dating right back to the Tudor period, all of them relatives of the woman who had opened the door. There was no mistaking the bloodline with the thick black hair, the green almond eyes, and the delicate features.

He walked through the hall, his head tipped back to look at the painted ceiling, not sure where he was meant to be heading. A movement in the corner of his eye caused him to drop his focus to the floor, where he saw that the center table, hosting a large ornate display of blood red roses, was sat on top of a marble inlaid pentagram. A black cat wound its way around the pedestal leg.

"Oh crap!" he muttered under his breath.

Suspicions gathered and he searched out clues to confirm them. It wasn't long before he began to see the motifs of ravens and hearts everywhere; in the carved wood panelling, in the painted ceiling, on the crest of each heavy, dark oak door. *You're at Ravenheart Hall!* he finally admitted. He couldn't believe that he had not known that the instant he had met the woman at the door; she was of course one of Thalia's sisters.

He glanced back towards the door but he knew it was pointless to try and set out in the blizzard. He'd only make it five minutes down the road before he got snowed in and probably perished from hyperthermia. He continued onwards, with the intention of playing innocent and getting out as quickly as he could without causing any harm. He headed in the direction of the open door and saw that it lead to a comfortable, if not gloomy drawing room, where two large wood fires blazed. He walked in and took a turn around the room, curious as much as he was nervous. Every table was heavy under the strain of large leather bound books, including the coffee table between the two sofas. He stepped over to the fire and warmed his ice-cold hands before turning to try and dry off his uncomfortably soggy jog-pants.

The sound of the woman's voice startled him and he turned. Despite carrying a large tray of cups, saucers, and a cake stand, she had entered silently, without even a rattle of the china. She flashed him a smile and it was completely captivating.

"It's Earl Grey, is that okay?" Jeremiah nodded but didn't get time to verbalise a reply before she continued. "We blend it with dried orange blossom from the grounds. It reminds us of the summer." She leant over and poured the tea over the silver tea strainer before handing out the cup and saucer in offering. Jeremiah took the delicate china in his hand. As it rattled in his shivering hand, he hoped she mistook it for the effects of the cold rather than his nerves that jangled under her eyes.

He took a sip and smiled appreciatively. "It's lovely, thank you. Just like summer."

The heavy chime of a clock tolled, cutting short their introduction. Jeremiah waited for the seemingly endless chimes to cease and convinced himself that he must have miscounted when he heard the thirteenth chime. He took another sip of his tea in the hope that it would give him time to get his wits together.

She poured out her tea and took a seat on the sofa, scanning Jeremiah's pleasing form up and down from under her heavy, sultry eyelashes.

"So stranger, do you have a name?"

Jeremiah coughed on his tea and hurriedly extended a hand, "Oh, I'm so sorry, how rude of me, my name is Jeremiah Chase, I'm…"

"There's no need to explain. I know Jeremiah Chase." She punctuated her comment by tipping her head coquettishly and smiling through pouting lips. "You look a little… incognito. You've probably worked out by now that I'm one of the Ravenheart sisters."

Jeremiah nodded. There was no need to pretend that he didn't know.

"I'm the eldest sister, Lilth."

"Pleasure to meet you," Jeremiah charmed.

"Likewise."

The two of them drank the rest of their tea in a heavy, uncomfortable silence until she invited him to have a refill of tea and directed him to take a cake from the silver stand.

Jeremiah bent down, spoilt for choice. The last time he had seen a collection of patisseries as pretty and delicate had been when he was having tea with Lucia at the Laudree tearooms in the Upper East Side. After much deliberation he choose a small violet fondant fancy topped with a crystallised rose petal.

"I'm afraid they're a little bit girlie," she smiled, "but that's what you get in a house full of women."

"You live here with your mother?" The question slipped out before he had chance to reign it in. Jeremiah had intended on asking as few questions as possible.

Lilith shook her head. "Sadly not. Both our parents are dead. The three of us live here alone."

"Oh," he said, hiding behind his teacup.

Uncomfortable at the personal nature of his question, Lilith turned the conversation, "So I guess you'll be needing refuge until the snow passes."

Jeremiah glanced towards to the window where he saw the snow was still falling heavily. Reluctantly he nodded his head and said, "I guess so, that is if it isn't too much of an imposition."

"You're welcome to stay, just don't expect too much from the hospitality. I'm not used to having visitors and I'm quite hopeless at small chat. I'll show you around and then I'm going to leave you to your own devices if that is okay?"

"Sure," he replied, hoping he could be trusted to be left alone to his own devices in Ravenheart Hall.

She led him out of the room and towards the kitchen, which the Ravenhearts had the sense, unlike his aunt, to have moved from the basement and put into one of the many large ground floor parlour rooms. With its slick, modern gloss cabinets and granite worktops, it was a stark contrast to the rest of the house. Jeremiah smiled at the heart attack the heritage nuts would have had about such a travesty. Lilith gave him a tour of the kitchen, pointing out the kettle, tea, and coffee and inviting him to help himself to anything from the fridge, informing him that cook kept them stocked up with roast meats and soups ready for quick meals. Then she showed him the workbench, which was home to a PC that she put at his disposal.

"We tend to spend time in here because it's the warmest room in the house, what with the underfloor heating."

Jeremiah scanned the rest of the room and saw that it was almost like a self-contained apartment with a large saggy sofa and flatscreen mounted on the wall.

"I'll show you to the guest quarters should you need to stay overnight," she said, leaving the room and causing him to trot behind her like a puppy. At six-foot, Lilith was a striking figure as she ascended the stairs. *All she needs is a three branch candelabra to complete the effect*, Jeremiah thought, still not really relishing the idea of having to spend the night at Ravenheart Hall.

He distracted himself from the very pleasing vision of Lilith's bottom swaying seductively in front of him by taking a closer look at the paintings, each of which had been done by a very skilled hand.

"All of these are your relatives?" he said, genuinely impressed.

"They have all lived here at Ravenheart Hall at some point or another."

It took Jeremiah a moment to notice that out of the hundred or so portraits, only a handful were of a man. He was just about to express his surprise when a voice in his head told him in no uncertain terms to shut his mouth.

At last they made it to the guest quarters and Jeremiah wished he had been less distracted because he wasn't entirely sure how they arrived. Lilith pushed open the door to reveal a room not too dissimilar to his room at Coldstone House, only this was slightly older and rather than the muted tasteful Georgian blues of his room at Aunt Penelope's, this room was decorated red, almost to the point of silliness. The whole effect was disconcertedly like walking into a heart.

"There's an en-suite shower room at the far left. We had the dressing room converted. There's towels and toiletries. I'm afraid we don't have a change of clothes, although you can put your sweater through the tumble drier downstairs if you wish."

Jeremiah nodded, unsure of what to say.

"You may make use of the sitting room and the library as well, but I'd ask you to limit your wanderings to these rooms. The rest of the house is not fit for guests; it's mostly covered in dust-sheets." She started towards the door. "I'll see you in the dining room at eight for dinner. There's no need to dress," she giggled girlishly at her own flirtatious double entendre.

Jeremiah was left surprisingly unsettled. Mixtures of grief and desire blended into an intoxicating cocktail. He listened for the door clicking shut before stripping off and placing his sweat pants and t-shirt onto the radiator. It was blasting out so much heat that his clothes would be dry by the time he had finished his shower. The en-suite was another pleasant surprise of modernity - all sandstone tiles and spa-like lighting. *I really aught to bring Aunt Penelope round for some interior design tips*, he thought with a wry smile.

The shower, being the first power shower with a regulated temperature that he'd had in over a month, was a moment of pure heaven. He poured out the shower gel, noting that it was a Moonstone product made by Fox and her sisters. The heady smell of rosemary and lavender and another that he wasn't so familiar with, filled the small steam-filled shower room, instantly relaxing him. As he stood, with the hot waters washing over him and the scent of herbs cleansing his mind, he felt the effects of the traumatic news of Rachel's death shift and re-settle into a deep and quiet sadness. The feeling, although a heavy weight to carry was manageable and over time, he knew that it would get lighter. He flicked off the shower and took the towel from the heated rail, wrapping himself up in the luxury of warmth.

Having dressed, he headed back down towards the kitchen to make a cup of tea and attempt to log in to the PC. He walked through the windowless corridors, knowing that he could have travelled back in time and not be any the wiser. The house was eerily quiet and felt strangely empty. He wondered where Lilith was and what she was doing. A pleasant fantasy of finding her started to play in his mind until it ended abruptly with the memory of Paulina's conversation.

It seemed strange that with the weather so bad, the other sisters were not home, but then again it had come down so quickly that maybe, like him, they had been stranded whilst out on their daily business. He was just about to make his way down the staircase, towards the modern sanctuary of the kitchen, when a large crack-bang sounded from one of the rooms. Unable to resist a mystery, and having become quite used to ghosts, he turned and snuck back along the corridor, convincing himself that Lilith's instruction not to go wandering didn't quite mean not investigating a strange noise happening in a room you were standing close to.

Every one of his senses was tensed, waiting for a repeat of the noise. There wasn't one but the sound of a loud shriek told him that something odd was definitely going on in the room to his left. The door was pushed to but not fully shut. Jeremiah placed his hand flat against the wood, preparing himself for whatever lay behind. A mixture of fear and a sense that he was trespassing caused him to hesitate. The sound of shrieking erupted again and he guessed that a bird had fallen in through the chimney. He pushed open the door, with the thought that he would simply open the casement window and let the creature out. But as soon as he saw what lay behind the door, he immediately wished he'd left well alone.

The room was like something out of a fairytale – a dark fairytale. Lined from floor to ceiling with heavy wooden shelves that housed bottles and potions and goodness knows what else, the room was dark and busy looking. At the center was a large scrubbed table, so well used that it bowed in the middle. Test tube racks, bowls, phials, and all manner of apparatus lay scattered over the worktable. Several wooden bookstands held ancient books, open at pages of interest. Dried herbs and flowers hung from the ceiling, causing Jeremiah to duck as he made his way further into the room.

Turn around and close the door behind you, the voice in his head warned. *Pretend you haven't seen this*. But rather than taking his own advice, Jeremiah walked around the table, trying to decipher the sight in front of him. A dramatic crash from the corner of the room caused his heart to jump. A great black bird hopped from shelf to shelf, knocking things off as he went and cackling loudly at the mess he was causing. Jeremiah went over to the window and threw it wide open, hoping the bird would smell the cold scent of freedom, but it just turned in the direction of the window and continued on its path of destruction.

"Get out you stupid bird," he shouted, flapping his hands in the air.

"Get out! Get out! Get out!" the bird mimicked.

Jeremiah stopped dead in his tracks. He knew that ravens made good mimics but he'd never heard one speak so clearly.

"Get out! Get out! Get out!" The Raven's speech morphed from the cawing mimic of a bird to the voice of a male human being, "Get out whilst you still can, boy!"

Jeremiah scrambled back towards the door, relieved to feel the cool brass doorknob under his touch. He continued backing out until he was safely in the warm light of the corridor. He pulled the door shut and made sure that the latch was firmly caught. Then, running down the stairs two at a time, he headed towards the front door with the intention of doing exactly as the raven had advised. No sooner had he stepped outside then he was forced by the strength of the wind and snow to retreat back inside with the heavy understanding that he was trapped.

He made his way to the kitchen, hoping that a cup of coffee and a sit down in a more familiar world might calm his jangling nerves. He also wanted to send Fox and e-mail, letting her know where he was as an insurance policy. He made coffee and logged in to the thankfully efficient wi-fi system. He loaded his Hotmail account and fired off a message to Fox, letting her know that he was stranded at Ravenheart Hall and it looked like he'd be spending the night. He desperately hoped that by the morning the snow might have cleared enough for him to try and make it home. He didn't mention the news about Rachel; she belonged to a different world and one that was now well and truly in the past.

With Fox messaged, he clicked on his inbox to see a message from Uncle Daniel. He was due at Heathrow that evening and was planning to make his way to Coldstone House tomorrow; although his plans were now a little dependent on the snowfall. Jeremiah hit the reply button and checked behind him to make sure that he was completely alone;

Daniel.

You'll never guess where I am; I'm at Ravenheart Hall! Long story but got stuck in snow and have had to take refuge - most likely having to stay the night. Have met the eldest of the three sisters, Lilith. Very strange (also very beautiful!). House is like something from a Poe story!

Thought you might like some inside info on the place. Lots of small details; ancestral paintings everywhere but almost all of them women?? (All very beautiful) Black cat roaming around the place = cliché! Pentagram on hallway floor (bit obvious!) Lots and lots of antiquarian books and lot of stuffed animals etc. Some very pleasant surprises; they're definitely blending their heritage with twenty first century comforts - best shower in over a month.

No parents. Just the three of them live here, although only Lilith seems to be home at moment???

Weird discovery - hoping I'm not rumbled but seem to have stumbled across a laboratory / study room (I've never seen anything like it before) looks very witchy!! Potions and crazy occult stuff everywhere. Big scary bird that I swear tried to warn me off in some form of possessed voice (think I let imagination get better of me) Going to try and find out some more details to feedback to you tomorrow. (Hoping snow clears) Wish me luck and hope that I survive the night LOL!

Never more, Jay x

In less than a minute, Jeremiah's in-box pinged back with a reply from Daniel.

Jay,

Get out of there! You don't know what you're meddling with. This isn't a game. Leave Ravenheart Hall before it's too late!

Daniel.

A shiver ran the length of Jeremiah's spine. Despite the distance, Jeremiah could hear the desperation in his Uncle's voice. This wasn't some paranoid warning, Daniel knew something about the Ravenhearts that he didn't. He closed down his Hotmail account and shut down the lid on the PC, hoping that some solution as to how he was going to leave Ravenheart Hall during a blizzard might suddenly leap into his mind. He looked out of the window. The storm still raged outside. It brought with it a premature nightfall.

A voice close behind him startled him. "Find everything you need?"

He turned to see Lilith with a steaming cup of tea in her hand. Jeremiah forced a smile onto his face, despite the understanding that Lilith must have been in the room making herself a cup of tea for at least several minutes: all the time he had been communicating with Daniel. He read her face to see if she had seen. It was difficult to tell. She was smiling and looked unfazed, but for a girl that appeared to be able to walk around and make a cup of tea without making a sound, that meant nothing.

"Yes, thank you," he grinned goofishly. "Best shower I've had in ages!" he said by way of making light conversation. "Coldstone House is a bit trapped in the dark ages."

She nodded, happy to let him ramble.

"Did you manage to get the internet working? It's sometimes a little unpredictable; the rats gnaw through the cables, making it a bit hit and miss."

It took him a moment to understand what she had said and then he nodded his head enthusiastically. "Yes, fine thank you."

He told himself to calm down; he was acting like a spooked child caught with his hand in the cookie jar.

"Looks like you're definitely going to be here for the night; the snow shows no sign of letting up."

"Will your sisters be okay?"

Lilith glanced towards the window. "Oh, they'll be fine. They know how to survive the elements." A crooked little smile lit up the corners of her mouth. "I'll expect that they'll probably make it back in time for dinner."

"Really?" Jeremiah couldn't contain his surprise. "But the roads are blocked?"

Lilith turned and headed towards the door. "Don't worry about them, they won't be taking the roads."

Before he could ask her exactly how they might be travelling home through a blizzard, she'd gone out of his hearing, leaving him sat alone and slightly afraid.

He flipped open the PC once more, desperate with the hope that Daniel might have some advice on surviving a night's stay in a nest of witches.

Daniel.

There's no way out. I'm trapped. Tell me what to do. I think she suspects me.

Jay.

The e-mail pinged back almost instantly as if Daniel had been waiting.

Sit tight. Play innocent. Don't give them ANY cause to further suspicion. Do exactly as you are told. You're not much use to them so they will probably not be interested in you. Lock your door and place a cross beside your bed whilst you sleep. I'm on my way. I'll try to be there by morning latest. Cursed weather!

Dx

Jeremiah heard the sound of the front door bang and the laughter of the two sisters tinkle through the house.

"Lilith!" Thalia called. "Lilith, are you home?"

Jeremiah closed the PC and made his way out into the hallway. His game plan was to play it as naturally as possible; ask no questions, get no lies – hopefully not get into trouble.

"Hi, Thalia!" Jeremiah said as cheerfully as he could.

She flashed him a confused look before recovering her social grace. "Hey, Jeremiah, what are you doing here?"

"Caught in the snow storm. I'm afraid I've gatecrashed your hospitality."

She bounced over to him, flashing him a grin. "Oh, what fun – so I guess you're here until the morning?"

Jeremiah hesitated, resisting the temptation to ask them how they had managed to travel through such weather but he knew that he wouldn't like the answer. He glanced over at the middle sister who was eying him appreciatively.

Time to use your Chase charm, Jay old boy! he thought. He walked over with his hand extended and introduced himself. "Jeremiah Chase. It's a pleasure to meet you…"

She smiled and returned her hand. It was slim and cool under his touch, reminding him of a bird. "Nigella."

"Nigella! What a pretty name."

He turned his attention back to Thalia, conscious of keeping both ladies happy.

"Well Thalia, it's going to be so nice to spend some time getting to know you properly; we just don't seem to have had the opportunity since I arrived."

Thalia twirled her hair between her fingers and tipped her head, "No, well you're always with that Meadowsweet girl; she seems to have quite monopolised your attentions." She turned to throw a look at Nigella, who was listening with a keen interest at the mention of a Meadowsweet. "More's the pity, hey?"

"Well," Jeremiah cleared his throat, "quite an oversight on my part."

"Quite. You don't know what you've been missing!" Thalia crooned, placing a hand onto his shoulder. She smelt of snow and perfume and the effect was enchanting to the point he almost forgot he was meant to be defending himself against possible impending sacrifice.

“If you give me a minute to go and get out of these damp clothes,” she paused to give Jeremiah time to fully appreciate the dramatic effect of her already undoing the buttons of her blouse. He let out a small, embarrassed laugh and turned his face away in an attempt to hide his blushes. He knew that he was being played with but far from minding, he was quite enjoying it. “Then I’ll come back down and entertain you.”

“Okay,” he laughed, flashing her a smile designed to melt hearts.

He watched the sisters head up the stairs arm in arm, whispering about their visitor in a voice loud enough for him to hear. Reaching the top of the stairs, they both turned before collapsing onto one another in a pile of giggles. Jeremiah heard Lilith’s voice travel crisply along the corridor.

“Get a grip!”

Jeremiah didn’t hear the obviously comical reply that set them all off giggling again. He turned back towards the kitchen but not before glancing up, where he saw Lilith staring down at him curiously.

15

"Have you seen Jeremiah today?" Fox asked her sisters.

Both of them shook their heads and returned to their canteen hot chocolate.

"Nope, not seen him all day. Maybe he's ill?"

"Maybe he read the weather forecast and made a smarter move than we did," Swan said with irritation. "Do you think we've still got time to make it home?"

Fox looked out of the window. It had started with a light flurry about an hour ago but the wind was picking up and the snowflakes had turned from powder to small cotton wool balls.

"I think if we're going to make it, we need to leave now."

"Do you think they'll send out the school bus?" Bunny asked, flushed with the excitement of a possible afternoon of snowballing and sledging with the village boys.

"I doubt it. I think we need to think about making our own way home."

"Shall I ring Mum?"

"I don't think she's about; she said she had something on."

Their conversation was interrupted by the sound of Swan's mobile ringing. She checked the name before clicking the answer button and mouthed the name "Violet" at her sisters.

After a brief exchange, Swan clicked off and smiled. "Good news! Cousin Violet is going to swing by and take us home. She's about to leave the library now and will collect us from the gate in about twenty minutes."

"Great. Time enough to grab a refill," Bunny said, placing the three mugs onto a tray and heading off in the direction of the counter.

"I could really do with talking with Primrose about the visions. Something's going on; something bad. I've a horrible feeling that Martha Paisley was just the beginning," Fox said.

Swan, more cautious than her sisters, instinctively glanced around to make sure no one could overhear them. "What do you mean?"

"I mean, I think Martha was the first attempt and as that clearly failed, it's just a matter of time before they try and do it again."

"How soon?" Swan asked anxiously.

"Very." Fox picked at the label of her water bottle. "Like soon as in the next couple of days."

"We should have started planning."

"Planning what exactly? You make out that this is something we can solve with a bit of careful planning but we don't even know what it is that we are up against. All we've got is my stupid, unhelpful visions and a suspicion that somehow the Ravenheart sisters are involved."

"It's not exactly a suspicion, is it? You've seen them. You saw exactly what they did to Martha Paisley."

"What if I just dreamed all of that because I was mad with Thalia for what she did to you and Fred?"

"Don't kid yourself, Fox. You know that your vision was just as good as being there yourself. More than that, you know that Thalia knows you know, and she isn't happy about it. That's why she's been so keen to keep a track of you."

Fox fell silent. She had a terrible feeling that the snow was an omen – after all, there had been snow in her last vision. Snow that had turned to feathers - angel feathers.

"Who are you two gossiping about?" Bunny asked, plonking the tray of steaming hot-chocolate down. Catching the look on her sisters' faces, Bunny changed key and her face fell serious. "So is one of you going to tell me what is going on?"

"It's nothing!"

"So there is an *it* then, meaning *something* is going on."

"Leave it alone, Bunny!" Swan warned.

"No I won't leave it alone. You two have been having secret little chats for weeks now. Whispering in the hallway, hanging out together at lunch, sneaking in to each other's room in the middle of the night. You've got a secret and it's not fair to leave me out."

"Not fair! Don't be stupid, Bunny. You sound like a whining five-year-old. You don't need to know everything that goes on – some things are not your business."

"I'm not behaving like a five-year-old. You two are! Anyway, I know what it's all about! It's to do with Fox and her freaky…

Swan grabbed hold of Bunny's arms and dragged her into her seat with a cry.

"Why are you being such a bitch?" Bunny snarled at Swan.

Swan raised her hand as if to strike her sister, but instead she laid it on Bunny's arm. At her touch, she instantly calmed.

"We're trying to protect you because we love you," Swan said. "I know it's hard to feel left out, and you probably think we're being cruel, but we don't want you to get hurt."

Fox placed her arm around Bunny and pulled her into a hug. "We love you."

Bunny pushed her away. "Get off! Look, please just tell me what's going on. It's to do with the Ravenhearts isn't it?"

Swan and Fox exchanged concerned looks. "What makes you think that, Bunny?" Fox asked.

"Something Thalia said yesterday when I knocked into her."

"What did she say?"

"She said that I was dead – that we were all dead and it was just a matter of time until they buried us."

"Don't you think you should have told us?"

"I thought it was just Thalia being her usual bitchy self but it wasn't, was it? Something has happened."

"Look, I'll cut you a deal," Fox whispered. "If you can keep your nose out until Sunday then I'll tell you exactly what's going on."

Bunny took a moment to consider the proposal. “You promise you’ll tell me everything on Sunday?”

“Promise!” Fox said, holding out her little pinky finger to seal the pledge in the way they’d done since childhood.

“Do you also promise to tell me what’s going on between you and Will?” Bunny asked, giggling.

Fox gave her a playful shove. “I’ll tell you that right now. Nothing!”

By the time they moved outside to wait for their lift with Violet, the snow was falling thick enough to make Fox feel slightly motion sick. They would be cutting it fine to get back to Heargton before the roads became completely impassable.

Violet had had the foresight to drive the four-by-four BMW to work, offering them some snow protection and a lot more luxury than the school bus. Once all of them were in and the excited greetings finished, they settled down for the half-hour drive home. Bunny, sat next to Fox in the back, plugged herself into her iPod and Swan and Violet chatted quiet enough to make listening too much of an effort. Fox pulled out her phone and checked her text messages. She had thought that Jeremiah might have texted to say why he wasn’t in, but then again, why should he? It wasn’t as if she had any claim over him. She watched as the endless fields gradually hid themselves under a blanket of snow. She was lost deep in her thoughts when the sound of the radio being turned up jogged her out of them. Swan was staring over her shoulder at Fox, who was taking a moment to catch up on what the news report was about.

"Police and local residents are out searching for the toddler who is believed to have gone missing from St. Ursula's playgroup sometime this morning between ten and ten thirty. The two-year-old is described as blonde with blue eyes and was wearing a red snow suit when she was last seen. Fears are growing as the weather situation intensifies. Anybody with information that might be of use should contact Heargton Police office on…"

Swan flicked the radio off before the details could be given and waited for Fox to respond. The tension in the car was solid. Bunny pulled out her earbuds.

"What's happened? What's going on?" she asked.

Nobody answered at first, then Violet spoke. "Does the description match with your vision, Fox?"

Fox didn't want to respond in words, all she wanted to do was to cry.

"Did you see this happening, Fox?" Bunny asked, trying to play catch-up.

"Yes," Fox croaked. "The description matches the little girl in my vision. They've taken her to Heathmoor Cottage."

"You need to phone the police!" Bunny said, almost bouncing in her seat, "Doesn't she, Swan? Tell her she needs to phone the police." Bunny jabbed her finger towards Fox's phone. "Ring them!"

"It's no use phoning the police, Bunny."

"But why?"

"Because they wont get anywhere near Heathmoor Cottage. Fox and I tried to get up there the other day but the Ravenhearts have put a protection shield around the area."

"The Ravenhearts! Oh my God! They're involved in this? Did they kill Martha?"

Fox let out a heavy sigh, "This is exactly why I didn't want you to know, Bunny – you go over the top with things!"

Bunny threw herself back into the leather seats and pouted with her arms crossed. "You still see me as the baby in the family but you don't know me at all."

"Oh, Bunny, really! We've got more pressing matters than dealing with your ego at the minute," Swan snipped from the front seat.

"Really? Matters that involve a protection shield exactly like the ones I know how to break?"

All three of the Meadowsweet girls turned to face Bunny at the same moment, causing Violet to skid perilously before regaining control of the car just before it headed into the hedge.

"What do you mean you can break protection shields?" Violet asked. "That's powerful magic!"

"What? I'm not worthy of it?"

"Jeez, Bunny, are you due on your period or something!" Swan snapped. "Get over whatever your issue is and start trying to help us out here. How long have you been able to do this?"

"More to the point, how do you know you can do it?" Violet asked.

"Don't you remember how Mum used to stick us in protection shields as babies when she was doing jobs like pegging out the washing or when she wanted to go to the bathroom. She used to throw a protection shield over us in the same way most normal parents use a playpen."

Fox and Swan laughed at the memory. Mum's protection shields had sent the little Meadowsweets into full temper tantrums as they fought invisible bars. Now Bunny mentioned it, they had both forgotten how their mum used to despair at the antics of their baby sister, who managed somehow to escape the protection shield and wreak havoc throughout the house. It had seemed nothing more at the time than the cheeky antics of an over lively baby, but clearly it was Bunny's gift coming in very early; one that it seemed had not left her.

"I didn't really know I had the gift until about six months ago when I got myself into a stupid situation with a group of boys at a party?"

"What party?"

"Which boys?"

Bunny screwed up her nose. "It doesn't matter what or which, that's not the point. Anyway, things got a little out of hand. I'd had too much to drink and I didn't really know what was happening. One thing led to another and I found myself on my own with a group of college boys who clearly thought I was up for… Everybody was drunk so it's all a bit of a haze but one minute one of them is trying to pin me to the bed and the next minute they're shouting at each other at the end of the bed and banging their fists against this invisible barrier, just as if they were behind a glass window. After a couple of minutes of being completely freaked out, they left and I got home as fast as I could."

"Jeez Bunny, why didn't you tell us?" Swan asked.

"Because you two freak out about things like that – and you'd have told Mum."

"Damn right I…"

Violet interrupted, breaking up the escalating sibling squabble. "So you can make them as well as break them, Bunny?" Violet asked, still reeling from the revelation.

"Yep."

Violet glanced back at Bunny through the rear-view mirror. "It would seem we're going to need your help then."

Bunny flashed a satisfied smile and straightened herself up in her seat.

"Okay, so what's the plan then?" Bunny asked.

Silence filled the car as each of the girls thought about Bunny's question. Their original plan had been sketchy enough, which would have been okay given that they thought they had time on their side, but with news of the little girl being already taken, a sketchy long term plan was no longer going to cut it.

At last Violet said, "The news said that the villagers were out looking for the child. I suggest that when we get home, we wrap up warm, grab some searchlights, and join in with the search party. We'll head off through Raven Woods, past the Rookeries, and up around to the west of Heathmoor

Hill. We're less likely to bump into other members of search parties that way."

"You know that takes us through the grounds of Ravenheart Hall don't you?" Fox said.

"No matter," Violet replied. "It's not as if there's going to be anyone home."

Fox looked out across the fields that were now almost entirely lost. It was not the weather to be undertaking stealthy rescue missions. There would be evidence of their tracks everywhere, and it would be far too easy to get lost in the snow.

"Do you think we should call your sisters?" Swan asked Violet.

Violet took a moment to think. She sighed heavily before nodding her head. "Yes. I really didn't want to involve them, especially not Primrose; you know how fragile she is." She glanced at Fox in the mirror, "Your visit the other day sent her quite off on one, but I think we are going to need them both."

Fox fidgeted, "I'm sorry about Primrose, I didn't mean to…"

"It's alright, that wasn't a telling off. You just need to understand that Primrose is different from the rest of us. She feels things very keenly; she has acute empathy skills. When you speak with her, she isn't just hearing the words but she's reading your thoughts too – all of your desires and fears – even the ones you don't want to admit to yourself are open to her. I guess you must have been carrying around a lot of both when you went to visit her."

Fox could tell Violet was trying to communicate something to her without the others knowing, but the message was too faint. Instinct told her it was to do with Jeremiah but she could not fathom what. Violet watched for Fox's response in the mirror. It wasn't as she'd hoped. The smallest shrug of Fox's shoulders told her that her message had not got through.

Violet slowed the car down to creeping point. The salt-gritters hadn't got as far out as the small lanes surrounding Heargton, and the road was now only guessed at by the rows of spindly black-boned hedgerows. Despite only being early afternoon, the sepia-leaden sky had fallen impossibly low and Violet had to flick on her headlights to full beam. The effect was startling and changed the landscape from something familiar and safe to something alien and harsh.

"I really don't like this weather," Bunny said.

"No, it feels like the sky is falling in," Fox mused.

Violet leaned forward and tapped a button on the car computer screen. The sound of a ringing phone filled the car. After several rings, it was picked up by Primrose. The reception was poor and attempts at a detailed conversation were pointless. After several failed attempts at sentences, Violet resorted to shouting, "Heathmoor. Ravens." Before clicking out.

"Do you think she will understand?" Swan asked.

Violet nodded. "Oh, yes, the message was loud and clear."

They were still five miles from Heargton and at the rate of the snow fall, and the way it was settling on the road in front of them, it was a race against time as to whether they would make it by car or not. Fortunately, the four-by-four was better prepared than the car they saw stranded at the side of the road; its boot crumpled in by a hidden milestone post. The track of footprints was already fading into the distance and Fox hoped that whoever it was had managed to make it to the nearby pub without getting too cold, or lost. Eventually, hedgerows were replaced by woodland, marking the boundary of the village.

A police car was parked as sentinel on the road into the village. Seeing the four-by-four approach, two police officers got out and flagged Violet down. She stopped and dropped the window. After a brief exchange of questions about where they had come from and had they seen anything strange on their journey? The officers waved them through.

As they approached the well at crossroads, they saw it had once again become operations center. Several police cars were parked on the pavements and officers, wearing hi-visibility jackets, were coordinating the well-meaning villagers who had come to face the elements and search for the missing toddler. Each volunteer was being issued with a hi-visibility bib and a map.

Violet swung the car towards Meadowsweet Cottage and said, “We’ll head home and prepare. We’ll need warm clothes, a flask of tea, and some provisions should we be out overnight.”

It felt surreal, packing as if they were about to do nothing more extraordinary than a school day-trip – but there wasn’t really a special way of preparing for a potential coven battle and a fight against ancient powers of darkness. Tea, sandwiches, and a weatherproof jacket would have to do.

Wren was in the kitchen when they arrived. She greeted them with a visible relief that they had all managed to get home safely. Her face turned to one of concern as Swan informed her that they were off to help with the search for the missing girl. Their mother locked eyes with Violet and a silent communication ran between them. Sadly, Wren nodded her head and sighed heavily. Swan and Bunny failed to witness this interchange, as they were both already preparing provisions. Fox tipped her head quizzically at her mother, trying to work out how much she knew, but Wren had turned her attention back to the stovetop where she was making soup.

"You might as well take this with you in a thermos. It's terribly cold out there. I don't want you all to perish." Her mother's last word faded.

Fox made her way to her room to dress. She stripped out of her skirt and blouse but kept her woolen tights on, over which she pulled on a pair of black leggings and then a pair of black combats. She searched in the back of the wardrobe, finding her thick socks and pulled them on before lacing herself into her stiff walking boots. It truly felt like she was preparing for battle, and as she armoured herself against the cold, one item of clothing at a time, she mentally layered up her powers. She didn't honestly know whether the six of them were strong and skilled enough to take on the

Ravenhearts. The Ravenhearts still embraced their witchcraft, whereas it felt like the Meadowsweets had spent their lifetimes denying theirs. An uncomfortable anger towards her mother began to niggle. *Why hasn't your mother prepared you better? Why has she denied you your heritage?* the internal asked. Now it seemed their gifts had come in, despite Wren trying to ignore them. Fox had discovered that her sisters had powerful skills, but they were unstable and not properly tested – or under control. She'd also discovered that Violet and Swan had a knowledge of the Dark Arts, and Fox still didn't know quite how she felt about this.

When she'd finished layering up, she headed to the cedar wood box on her dressing table where she kept her special things: her tarot cards, her ebony handled athame, and her obsidian amulet - a gift designed to ward off evil spirits, which all three of the sisters had received from their grandmother upon their birth.

Putting it over her head, she looked into the mirror and offered up a silent incantation asking the Goddess for protection and for all of them to return home safely, including the Ravenheart sisters – for Fox did not want to return home with the blood of their enemy on her hands. The mirror rippled and Fox stepped back with surprise. Waves undulated across the glass until eventually it calmed and the surface was a flat opaque white. She recalled the scrying exercise with Swan and how hideously that little lesson had turned out. She tried not to look on the glass that was waiting expectantly for her, but in the end the pull of it was too strong and she stepped forward, bracing herself against the dressing table with her hands gripped firmly to each side. Slowly, she opened her eyes and let them see into the swirling mist.

It took her a moment to realise that far from being a useless exercise, she was looking up at the snow heavy sky. She tilted the mirror down, shifting the view and gasped when she saw the mirror fill with the image of Ravenheart Hall. The door of the house opened and Fox's sight journeyed into the imposing reception hall. She had never been there, but Ravenheart Hall was exactly as she had imagined. The whole place was silent except for the chiming of the clock. Fox wondered what she was missing; everything seemed normal. Just then, Jeremiah stepped out from a side door and walked across the hall before passing through another door. Fox shook her head trying to process what she had just seen. He certainly looked at home, dressed in sweats and a t-shirt with no shoes or socks. She continued to stare at the mirror, but nothing else came to her. The image faded back into the glass and left her with a reflection of her confused expression.

"What the hell?"

"What did you see?" Swan asked from the doorway. She was leaning against the frame as if she had been watching her for a while.

Fox startled and sent her perfume bottles scattering across the chest. "Nothing!" she said hurriedly and not in the least bit convincingly.

"You saw something," Swan said, walking into the room.

"No, no, I didn't. Just…" Her mind went blank, refusing to cooperate with a lie. She sighed in resignation. "I saw Jeremiah in the glass."

"Jeremiah Chase?"

Fox nodded. "He wasn't doing anything. It just took me by surprise, that was all."

"Well there must be a reason you saw him. What was he doing? Where was he?"

Fox shook her head and shrugged her shoulders to suggest she had no idea. "Come on, we've got stuff to do," she said, leading Swan away from the mirror. "We should try and get to the cottage before nightfall."

They returned to the kitchen, where their mother was filling up a large thermos with soup and Bunny was stuffing a medical kit into a rucksack. Violet had been loaned Wren's walking gear and was wrapped up and ready to go. To anybody else in the village they just looked like supportive members of the community offering to help.

The image of Jeremiah at Ravenheart Hall refused to leave Fox. A feeling of deep betrayal cut into her and it was laced with paranoia. She was cross at herself for falling for it all – falling for *him*. She had let herself believe for one moment that Jeremiah Chase wasn't the wicked-rich-immoral-bastard she'd first thought. That had been a mistake. He'd tricked her; playing that whole humble, reformed, misunderstood card. Now she was grateful that she hadn't shared a kiss with him. *Even though you've thought of little else since!*

Fox felt Swan's scrutinizing eyes on her. She knew something was up, but somehow it seemed that Fox had managed put a barrier up against her sister's usual mind raiding tactics.

"Everybody ready?" Fox asked, mainly as a way of distracting Swan from her thoughts.

Violet got up from the table, went over to Wren and wrapped her up in big hug. Fox watched curiously as Violet whispered something into Wren's ear and watched as her mother nodded her head and mouthed, "Okay!" before giving Violet a kiss on the cheek. Fox saw Wren secretly slip something into Violet's hand. Again, Fox had the feeling that their mother knew exactly what was going on. Wren followed her daughters to the kitchen door, telling them that she'd have a late supper waiting for them when they returned. It was clear that she was trying to act as normal as possible.

"Try to get back before ten, please, girls," she said. "I don't want you out too late in this weather."

They waved and Violet headed them to the police rendezvous point.

"Why are we going there?" Bunny asked.

"Because it needs to look like we're doing it properly."

"Won't it look suspicious?"

"It would look more suspicious if we get caught in the woods skulking about with no jacket or map like everyone else."

Bunny shrugged, she couldn't really see the point, thinking it would just add complications. She was proved right. After handing the girls their jackets, the officer attempted to put them into a group of men from the village; concerned that a group of girls should not be travelling the countryside on their own, which to be fair was a sensible point. However, worse than being bundled into company, they were then informed that their search area was to take place on the open farmland on the east side of the village; the exact opposite direction to where they needed to be.

Violet dipped her head and muttered to Swan, "This is really not good."

"Is there a problem with that?" the iron-haired officer snapped.

Fox stepped forward and smiled sweetly. "It's just that we think we could be much more useful searching Raven Woods. We know the area much better than the farmlands. We hang out there all the time and we'll notice if anything is out of the ordinary."

The officer stroked his beard, considering the argument. "I see what you're saying and we haven't yet sent a party out in that direction, but I really don't want you heading out on your own, ladies."

"How about I go with them?" one of the young male police officers offered. "I've got my radio and I'm armed," he said pointing to a can of CS spray tucked into his belt.

Fox rolled her eyes. *A can of CS spray is hardly going to be much use against the Ancient Ones*, the internal correctly observed.

Violet grasped at the opportunity. "There you go, see. We're going to be in perfectly safe hands, aren't we officer?" She offered her most winning smile and Fox watched with curiosity as Violet charmed the lead officer. Within seconds he'd had gone from steely control-freak to blushing servant.

"Okay then, but keep in touch by radio. I don't want anybody else going missing, hear me?"

He handed them their search pack, on the top of which was a photograph of the missing child. Fox winced at the sight of the pretty little creature with her mop of blond curls and bright piercing blue eyes. The photo showed her laughing at some unknown amusement.

"Come on, let's go," she snapped, pulling the group together and heading off in the direction of the woods. She hoped Violet had a plan on how to deal with their escort because she really didn't relish the thought of having to manhandle him to the ground and then being sprayed in the face with his trusted CS spray.

The sound of the snow crunching under foot set Fox's teeth on edge. It had always made her skin creep. Her jaw ached from being clamped so hard, but it wasn't just the cold, or the sensation under foot that caused the muscle to spasm in her cheek; it was the thought of Jeremiah Chase all at home in Ravenheart Hall. Anger clawed at her. *What the hell was he doing there?*

The boundary to the woods was now nothing more than a series of random black scratches against white earth and sky. There was no point in talking, as the snow was far too keen to steal their words; not that anybody felt like talking. Each of them was lost in the picture of Emily Stone – the little girl for whom they were going to be fighting. Swan's sense of direction was good and before they knew it they approached the ruinous gateposts of the Rookeries.

"I think we should take a look around in here," Swan said addressing the police officer.

The young officer suddenly looked nervous. "I'm not sure… it's not on our brief. Chief is sending police teams to search buildings. Civilians are meant to stick to searching open ground."

Swan had already squeezed her way through the safety fence and Bunny followed, leaving the officer little choice but to reluctantly follow whilst issuing pathetic attempts at taking charge of the quickly unravelling situation.

Once all the party was through, the officer found his voice.

"Stop! This is against orders. We need to sweep the woods and then report back."

With an alarming amount of authority, Swan said, "We don't need to take orders from your chief. We're entitled to go where we please, and it pleases us to check out the asylum."

She turned on her heels and headed towards the door, where she pushed aside one of the wooden planks and stepped in. The officer, still stuttering and blustering, trundled after her, pulling his coat tighter. The whirling wind made it impossible for anybody to really stand their ground and have an argument.

Bunny leaned in and whispered, "What the hell is going on?"

"I don't know," Fox replied. "I guess Swan has a plan about getting rid of our little escort problem."

"You don't think she's going to…"

Fox laughed. “No!” she snorted. The internal wasn’t quite as convinced, *Are you absolutely sure about that?*

“I guess we’d better go in after them,” Violet said, passing under the plank.

“I don’t like this,” Bunny said, looking around. “Something doesn’t feel right.”

“Come on.” Fox ducked under and beckoned Bunny in. “I don’t expect we’ll be more than a few minutes.

Fox had been right. It took less than five minutes for Swan to cast spells that sent the constable to sleep and to get a fire burning in one of the old fireplaces.

“Sleep tight, officer,” Swan whispered, tiptoeing from the room as the others trotted behind her.

“What did you just do to him?” Bunny asked.

“Just a little trick mother taught me when you decided to scream your way through the night – every night!”

“Blimey, talk about problem child!” Fox said, nudging Bunny’s arm and laughing.

“Right, we need to get a move on, the darkness is thickening,” Violet said, waving her hand at them. “Primrose and Rose are probably already at the meeting point.”

“Where are we meeting?”

“At the Ravenheart mausoleum on the far side of the lake.”

Fox wrinkled her nose, wondering how her cousins had such a good knowledge of the Ravenheart grounds. Their own mother had always forbid her and her sisters ever crossing the boundary onto the Ravenheart land; it was bad enough that they had to breathe the same air and go to the same school, she'd frequently complain.

Despite the snow and clouds, the night had grown full dark. Fox flicked her torch on and recoiled at the blinding white that bounced back. The woods were deathly quiet; not a thing stirred in the woods.

As Fox followed the beam of the torchlight she was hit by a sudden whooshing sensation. The air around her thickened. She pitched forward and folded in half, almost falling face first into the snow. The pressure inside her head felt like it would split it open. The sound of drumming beat violently against the soft tissue of her brain. She brought her hands tight to her ears and clamped them over them, hoping to eradicate the terrible beat of the drum. Then the screams started and it was as if they were burning her from the inside out. Fox opened her eyes to see that it wasn't the screams that were burning her but flames that licked at her legs. They were desperate to take hold of her. Shadows moved amongst the flames at her feet; dark and terrible beings, with teeth and claws that gnashed hungrily in anticipation of flesh and bone.

"Help me!" she tried to shout, but the words faded in her throat before they made it into the air.

A figure came through the flames. It was hard to see his face as the flames danced and flickered, causing a melting effect. Arms wrapped around her and pulled her out until she felt the cold air on her skin. She gasped in the fresh ice-air and rubbed her eyes, which were sore from the smoke. She opened them, expecting to look up on her rescuer, but it was Swan, who was stroking the hair from Fox's face and looking worried.

"Another vision?" she asked.

Fox nodded.

"Anything we should know?" Bunny asked.

Fox shook her head. "Just fire and flames, it was as if I were being burned alive."

She didn't tell them about the mysterious figure travelling through the inferno towards her.

"I have a really bad feeling about this," Bunny whispered. "I don't think we really know what we're getting ourselves into."

Violet looked at them. Worry etched across her face. Despite agreeing with Bunny full heartedly in her head, she smiled and said,

"Come on, we're stronger than they are. Just because they like to go around flashing their magic about, doesn't meant they're as powerful as they think they are. What they have in darkness, we outshine them with light. You need to hold on to that."

Swan sighed heavily. "Violet is right. Together we are strong. Everything is going to be okay. We'll all be home safely before the morning – including the little girl."

Fox looked at them and begged her heart to believe it, but there was something gnawing at her hope – it was the image of Jeremiah Chase walking barefoot through the rooms of Ravenheart Hall.

The Meadowsweets fell into a single line, making their way through the woods and towards the hill on top of which sat Heathmoor cottage; home of the legendary Heathmoor witches: killers of children, slayers of priests. Swan fell back and dropped her voice low enough for Fox to hear,

"Is there anything you haven't told me? Have you given me every detail?" Fox looked at her, unwilling to lie but not wanting to say more. Swan continued, "Because I have this terrible feeling that there's something you're not telling me and that *something* is very important."

Fox could not think that Jeremiah was important enough to matter in any of this and so she bit down on her lip and shook her head.

"There's nothing more. I've told you everything I have seen."

"Hmm," Swan said cynically.

Why can't she read your thoughts about Jeremiah?

Her sister's voice spoke loudly in her head, making her jump. "Because you don't hold Jeremiah in your head – he's held elsewhere."

Her implication was loud and clear. Fox still wasn't sure why she hadn't told Swan about Jeremiah being at Ravenheart Hall. Something had stopped her; something deep and intuitive.

*

Jeremiah looked out over the snow-laced grounds of Ravenheart Hall. It was bitterly cold. The window was doing a fair impression of being nothing more than a thin slice of ice. The snow was still too deep to drive through, but he wondered if he set out on foot whether he could make it to the village. Jeremiah's anxiety had reached the point whereby he had even tried the front door to ensure he hadn't unknowingly been made their prisoner. It had opened with ease and he had blown a sigh of relief through his tense lips.

Daniel said he was on his way, but in this weather that didn't offer much reassurance. After all, if Jeremiah couldn't even get three miles down the road in his Range Rover, what chance did his uncle have of getting from the station by taxi? Night was falling fast. One thing was for sure, Jeremiah did not relish the thought of spending the night at Ravenheart Hall. He had to get out and try and make it to somewhere safe. He listened hard to the sounds of the house. He was listening for the sisters but the house was as silent as the grave, except that was for the incessant ticking of the clock in the grand hallway. Like a metronome it offered a strange hypnotic effect. *Where could they be? What were they doing?*

He stepped away from the window and called out, "Hello!" Silence replied so he tried again, louder this time, placing his cold, naked foot on the first step of the stairs. "Hello, anybody there?"

He smiled weakly, aware of how much like a bad B-type horror movie it was all turning into. Another step, then another, and still silence. He was convinced that he was alone in the house, but he couldn't even guess where the Ravenheart sisters could have gone in such weather. Jeremiah was already halfway up the sweeping staircase. Every instinct in his body screamed at him to turn around and leave, but the sound of the clock was increasingly maddening and it disturbed his reason. It was coupled with the strangest feeling that something was pulling him up the stairs towards a fate that had been written many months ago – way back when his father had made the decision to exile him from his old life.

His stomach flipped and a wave of nausea swept over him. It sidelined him, having felt perfectly well just a moment before. He gripped his stomach, fighting the urge to throw up. He struggled up the last of the steps in search of his guest room and the bathroom. The upstairs corridor was an endless row of doors, and obstructing his way was the door of the laboratory, wide open as if in welcome.

He staggered in, knowing it was most likely a trap but unable to resist the temptation. With one hand still on his stomach, he grabbed the nearest large book and wedged it into doorframe with the hope that it might prevent the door from slammed (or possibly being locked) shut. The urge to vomit faded into a general sense of queasiness. He knew he was in the worst possible place. He knew it was madness to return to the room he should never have seen in the first place, but there was an answer here; he was certain of it. It was just a shame that he didn't know what the question was.

He scanned the room, taking in the same objects he'd seen on his first visit. Aside from the general spookiness of the collection, there seemed nothing specific that should be capturing his attention. His hand indiscriminately trailed across the objects on the workbench with the idea that his hand might discover something his eyes couldn't – which is exactly what happened. His fingers lingered over cool glass and crisp dry herbs until it hit the pages of a heavy book, where they tapped distractedly as he continued to gaze around the room. His fingers had told him loud and clear but he had not been listening. If he had just turned, he would have seen that his fingers danced over an image etched into the thick cream velum; it was the image of a young girl dressed in a simple robe, with a blood-stained bandage wrapped over her eyes. Flames crept up her dress from a pyre on the floor, and amongst the flames, demons danced.

Jeremiah removed his hand from the book and let his fingers find his temple where they pressed and squeezed until they offered some momentary relief from the pain that throbbed in his head.

"What am I looking for?" he whispered.

He turned towards the table, ignoring the book because something else had caught his eye. It was a map and it didn't take him more than a moment to realise with its cruciform road structure and the markings of the two big houses, that it was a map of Heargton. It was from some time ago by the looks of the paper and the hand-drawn quality of the markings. He bent forward to take a closer look, still not sure what it was that he was searching for but knowing that somehow he was a step closer towards understanding. There were several strange markings that had been added to the map; they were symbols that had been drawn next to some of the key Heargton buildings. He recognised The Green Man Inn and looked closely at the square with crossed lines running through it, which had been drawn next to it. Then there was Coldstone House, over which there was a heart broken into two parts. His eye travelled to the church and the drawing of the inverted crucifix, which although a little disquieting, was probably to be expected given the reputation of the Ravenhearts.

His finger tapped on a building, which although obviously important enough to have been marked with its own symbol, was one he didn't at first recognise. It was only after closer inspection that he realised it was the cottage linked to the Heargton witches. Nausea swept over him once more. He picked up the map and revealed the image of the blindfolded girl underneath. This time he didn't overlook it. The image was too familiar for that. It reminded him of Martha Paisley. Cogs started to whir in his mind but they still refused to fully engage.

Just then his cell rang, causing him to jump back from the table. It was unnaturally loud and he felt sure it would alert somebody (or something) to his snooping. He grappled at it, desperate to quiet it down.

"Hello," he whispered.

"Jeremiah, it's me, Daniel."

"Where are you?"

"Close. It's a nightmare though. Am going to try and make it on foot."

"Are you crazy?"

"There's nothing else I can do. I need to get to you. I've come prepared."

Jeremiah recalled the various times he had witnessed his eccentric uncle turning up at family functions in the most unusual and often dramatic way.

"What do you mean *prepared*?"

"It means, don't worry, I've got this."

"Sure!" Jeremiah replied with a heavy edge of sarcasm.

"Look, I'm going to be a bit slow but I am on my way. Hold tight and don't do anything stupid. I should be with you in the next couple of hours."

Out of reflex Jeremiah checked his watch. A couple of hours didn't sound too long, however a lot could happen in a couple of hours in a place like Ravenheart Hall. It put his uncle's ETA at around nine o'clock - late enough for it to be very dark and for the light of morning to still be a very long way away.

He sighed. "Which direction are you travelling? Maybe I can come out and meet you half way," Jeremiah offered.

"No point in both of us getting hyperthermia, my boy. I'll come to you."

"Take care."

"You too."

The phone went dead. Still holding the map, Jeremiah walked over to the small window that looked out over the woods and onto the hilly moorlands beyond. The snow impeded his visibility, but he knew that the notorious little cottage sat out there on top of the moor; like a black bird of death, it perched over the village, waiting…

According to the village accounts, the Heargton witches had been so cloaked in evil that after they were hanged above the burning pyres, it took three days for their bodies to burn to ash. Others said their bodies were so full of magic that other witches had come and stolen the bodies to use in powerful, demon-raising rituals. There was a lot of *saying* and not a lot of *knowing*, but one thing most people agreed on was, the witches had never really left Heathmoor Cottage.

Somewhere amongst the mess of clues and local legend, lay the truth. Martha Paisley had been laid out ritualistically, dressed like the image of the girl in the book. It was clear she had been the victim of some horrendous ritual killing, and that whatever that ritual had sought to achieve, it had failed. There would be another victim, of that he was sure. Somehow, if this book was to be believed, the killing of Martha Paisley was connected to the Ravenheart sisters, and it had from the marks on the map, he had a strong feeling that it was something to do with the Heargton witches. If that was the case, what was the chance of the Meadowsweets also being involved? It was clearly a question his uncle and other higher powers were also asking.

He studied the map hard, committing it to memory before returning it to the table. He paused at the door and looked both ways before progressing back into the corridor and down the stairs. He went to the kitchen and put on his shoes, hoping that he would find some warm clothing hanging in the hallway cupboard so he could make his escape without catching his death.

He was in luck, the cupboard was stocked with a good range of waxed country jackets and woolen scarves. Not exactly hip and happening, but warm and weatherproof. He picked the largest of the jackets and put it on, pulling one of the soft cashmere scarves from the peg. His flesh crept with the thought of wearing the clothes of murdering witches, but he was in no position to get all sensitive about it. He needed to get out of there, and he needed to do it without dying. He headed towards the door and clicked it open, cursing the deep snow and the fact that it was going to happily announce the direction of Jeremiah's flight. At first he tried to sweep over his footsteps but it was far too laborious and when he looked back it did little more than making his track even more conspicuous, as well as taking an impossibly long time. If he were lucky, the snow would continue to fall at the rate it was and would cover his tracks before the Ravenhearts spied him – not that they probably didn't have other magical way of tracking him down.

He walked towards the woods, compelled by a strange force of virtue to head towards the dark little cottage. Until he had come to Heargton, Jeremiah had never been into that whole destiny, esoteric rubbish – he'd believed in money, soccer, love, and good times. Now he was traipsing across ancient English woodlands, searching out supernatural horrors on a whim strong enough to lead him through a violent snowstorm and to ignore his uncle's instruction to stay put and keep out of trouble.

The going was tough. It would take at least an hour at the rate he was travelling, but at least he was warm enough. Within moments of entering the treeline he became disorientated and understood just how hard, and foolish, his task was going to be.

16

Violet had been right, Primrose and Rose were already waiting for them behind the mausoleum. They were both dressed in black skinny jeans and black woolen cloaks. Whether the effect was intentional or not, Fox couldn't help but smile on seeing them; there was no mistaking their witch status in that garb. On seeing them approach, Rose lifted her black leather clad hand and offered a wave. Snowflakes had wound their way into her impressively straight blond hair.

"Hello!" she said in a far too cheery way. You'd never guess that she was moments from battling with a rival coven. Something about her attitude was pleasantly reassuring.

"Anything to report, sister?" Violet asked.

"Nope, not a dickie bird. All very quiet indeed."

"Good," Violet wrinkled her nose, "I mean not good. Quiet means that they're already in position, doing…" her words trailed off as none of them wanted to think on the horrors that might already be happening.

"Indeed."

"Any other activity?" Fox asked.

"We thought we saw movement about twenty minutes ago, but the weather has made it a bit difficult for proper surveillance. We put it down to a deer or something. It was certainly nothing to worry about; no negative vibes."

Fox looked at them intensely and wondered if it had been Jeremiah they'd seen.

"So what's the plan then?" Rose asked.

For a moment or two, they all looked to one another to provide the answer. It seemed nobody had really got that far. Bunny surprised them all by suddenly speaking up.

"I guess we just walk right up to the protective shield, let me wave my wand at it and then we…"

Her light humorous tone could not last the entire sentence. Whichever way events played out there was a serious risk one of them might be hurt or worse still…

Swan jumped in, taking charge of the conversation. "I don't think we can really plan how we're going to do this until we've been up and taken a look,"

"They'll be waiting for us. They'll be able to see us coming," Fox added, thinking back to the time she had been caught scrying.

"We can do something about that," offered Primrose, pulling out a small silver mirror from inside her cloak.

"What's that?" Bunny asked nervously. Her anxiety was understandable; the object was giving out very strong vibes and they didn't feel all white.

"It was passed down to me," she muttered in reply.

Fox noted that this seemed to be the first that either of her sisters had known about it.

"That's not…?" Violet stopped, her face furrowed in concern. "I didn't believe it really existed. I mean I've read about it but I never thought…" her voice trailed off. "I thought it had been destroyed. Why have you kept this to yourself, Prim?"

Fox had tired of trying to work out what the magical object was and of the sibling fight about to erupt. She put out her hand to touch it briefly before snatching her fingers back.

"So what exactly is it?"

Prim pulled it protectively close to her chest so that it was out of Fox's reach.

"I really don't like this Prim," said Violet, spinning on her heel and turning her back as if to walk away.

"It's a traveller mirror," whispered Swan. "It allows you to carry hidden people with you – it works a bit like the Trojan Horse."

"How is that possible?" asked Bunny who was excited by the prospect of using a "real" and powerful magical object.

Primrose knelt down on the floor and placed the mirror on top of the snow. It was no bigger than the size of a large footstep and was made in roughly the same shape. "You step into the glass and it holds you so that the carrier can transport you with them."

"Whoa, that is totally awesome!" Bunny said with her foot already poised to take a step. Swan pulled her back sharply.

"How many people can it hold?" she asked.

"I don't know exactly but I think it's no more than eight."

"Eight!"

Primrose nodded. Her fingers were still protectively resting on the handle.

"Problem solved then," Bunny said, clapping her hands together.

Violet turned her attention back to the group, her ineffectual protest over. "I think it's about time you also told them about the dangers of the traveller mirror."

Primrose shifted uncomfortably and shrugged. "It's not really worth worrying about is it? I mean it sounds dramatic but it's highly unlikely to happen."

"What is?" Fox asked.

Rose stepped forward, breaking her unusually silent stance. "If the mirror gets broken and you're inside of it, then you're trapped for eternity. Your soul fractures like the shards of glass across time and space."

"Oh," Bunny emitted the sound over a gulp in her throat. "Nothing to worry about then!"

Fox slipped Swan a knowing look. The mirror, despite clearly having survived hundreds of years more than they'd all thought, was still only a fragile piece of glass. It would only take Primrose slipping on the snow or some minor incident that lead to them all being in serious peril.

"I don't know about this," Fox said, "I'm with Violet on this one. I really don't think it's a good idea. Too much could go wrong."

"It's a stupid idea!" Violet said viciously. "One of us would have to carry it and the Ravenhearts would see them. They're not stupid; they'd guess that something odd was going on."

"Agreed," Rose said, stepping towards Prim, "but she could wear this," she said removing a green stoned ring from her hand and holding it out. "Then they wouldn't see her. She'd also be protected from any scrying or psychic identification."

Violet threw her hands up in the air with exasperation. "For the sake of the Goddess, does anybody else have an ancient, and possibly dark-art, object lurking about their person, which they've happened to forget to share?"

Prim and Rose shared a look that tried to look contrite but that couldn't quite hide a subversive smile. Violet held out her hand to inspect the ring.

"And this would work?" she asked. "Prim could carry us in the mirror and be invisible by wearing this?"

"That's pretty much how it would go," Rose confirmed.

"Wouldn't it be better if I carried the mirror?" Bunny asked.

The rest of them turned to her with surprise. The very last person they all thought best for the job was Bunny. It wasn't just that she was the youngest, but she'd hardly earned the reputation of being sensible and responsible over the last few years. She noted their look before they each replaced it with a patronising smile. Now wasn't the time for sulking and so she sucked in her breath and said,

"Nobody else here has the gift of shield breaking, do they?"

They each looked at each other, hating to admit that Bunny had a point. Nobody knew for certain exactly how the mirror worked but they all guessed that a witches power could not operate from within it.

"Well, I guess that settles it then." Bunny said. "Jump in. I promise to be careful." Her smile left each of them with a slight feeling of mistrust.

Fox eyed up the innocuous little mirror in much the same way you might a potentially deadly snake. Nothing about it felt good; not the silent, creepy little mirror, or the thought of having her soul shattered. And what about the million questions? *What's going to happen to your physical body? What if you can't get out? Will it hurt? Surely it will hurt; all that molecule warping, or whatever it is that is going to happen.*

Swan glanced at her with heavy eyes that communicated a shared anxiety. There was only so much time they could afford to waste on weighing up all the possible consequences, and being that nobody really knew the answers, worrying about them was a waste of time.

"You will be extra careful won't you, Bunny? You know how things have a habit of..." Swan's sentence trailed off. It wasn't a smart idea to wind Bunny up when she had your life literally in her hands.

"Of course I'll be bloody careful! Just get in and stop dithering. If that little girl is dead by the time we get there, it will probably be the result of wasting these minutes."

Fox wasn't entirely convinced that Bunny had intended her rhetoric to be so motivating, but it did the trick nevertheless. Prim stepped forward and reached out her boot-clad foot. Where the toe made contact with the glass, it buckled and liquefied. Fox couldn't take her eyes off it. Prim pressed her weight down through her foot and gasped as the mirror swallowed it up. Within the blink of an eye and a swirl of her cloak, Prim had completely disappeared. Fox leaned forward and looked down into the glass where she saw Prim standing perfectly unscathed, smiling and waving as if nothing more weird was happening than she was beckoning her reluctant cousins into a slightly chilly swimming pool.

Swan took a deep breath and exclaimed, "Here goes!"

Just before she fully slipped through the glass, she gave Bunny a warning shot that dared her to mess it up. Bunny ignored it. Rose and Violet followed, leaving Fox to last. A position she'd really hoped not to find herself in.

"Well I guess this is bye for now!" Fox said, stepping her right foot onto the glass.

The sensation was just like plunging into cold water. It didn't hurt but it wasn't exactly pleasant either. She was very pleased when she hit the bottom and the feeling passed. Inside, the mirror was a surreal but surprisingly boring space; nothing like Alice in *Through the Looking Glass*. There was a slight swaying sensation and Fox guessed it was the motion of Bunny picking up the mirror and walking with it. It wasn't a comfortable thought, despite the reassurances that had been given.

Bunny slipped the mirror into her coat pocket, plunging the Meadowsweets into darkness. Now all they could do was wait for Bunny to navigate her way through the snowy woods, break down the shield and release them, hopefully still giving them the advantage of surprise. Swan was in no doubt that once through the shield, they would not be afforded the gift of time to plan a fail-safe plan. Their attack needed to be swift and aggressive – the highest-risk approach. She felt inside her pocket for her crystal pendant and looped it around her neck. The action drew the curious but silent question of her fellow passengers.

A ripple effect went around the seated circle as each of the Meadowsweets checked their personal arsenal of weapons and protective talisman. Each one knew that despite the crystals, metals and magic charms, it would ultimately all come down to the use of their wits.

*

The way through the woods was difficult and Jeremiah was beginning to regret ever starting such a foolish trip. A voice in his head growled that there was absolutely no reason for him to be getting involved in any of this head-screw shit. Only, alongside this voice was another; it told him that the reason for ignoring his uncle's warnings and for walking towards a life threatening situation was Fox Meadowsweet. That quirky little creature had somehow got under his skin. He now understood that although he had felt his love for Rachel had been very real at the time, he had simply been playing at being in love.

Every footstep in the snow of Raven Woods was another point of learning for Jeremiah. He would be a much wiser man by the time he arrived.

*

It was with a huge sigh of relief that each of the Meadowsweets stepped out from the confines of the glass. Bunny flashed them a large told-you-so grin of triumph.

"Did you do it? Did you break the shield?" Swan asked anxiously.

Bunny cocked her eyebrow. "Of course."

"Do you think they know we're here?"

Prim closed her eyes. She was concentrating hard.

"Is she seeking?" Swan asked.

Violet responded by lifting her finger to her lips and instructing them to be silent. They all obeyed, except for Fox, who had been plunged into her own vision.

The Ravenhearts were far too preoccupied to notice the arrival of the Meadowsweets. They were in the middle of a terrible row. Fox couldn't make out exactly what it was that they were arguing about, but Nigella was in a red and dangerous rage.

"No," Fox answered, pulling away from the vision. "They don't know we are here yet but we need to act quickly."

Primrose opened her eyes. "The child is still alive and unharmed. She's sleeping peacefully in a cradle, although we haven't got much time –

they've already dressed her in white linens and gotten her ready for the ritual."

The thought of it sent a shiver through each of them.

"Plan?" Fox asked.

Violet spoke. "I think we should split into pairs." She raised her arms and offered instructions like an airhostess. "A pair should approach each side of the barn in flanking motion and then Swan and I will head straight forward. The weather is in our favour; it will obscure us until we're close enough to gain their attention." She took her athema from inside her pocket and crouched down close to the soft snow, using it to draw out the battle plans. Each of them huddled in closer to see. "They'll see the two of us approaching and hopefully assume that as we are the eldest, we've come alone. We'll lure them out and then you guys can cut in from behind. Circling them like this." Almost as fast as she drew the line, the falling snow obscured it.

"Bunny," she looked directly at her, "I'd like you to wear the ring and sneak into the barn. Get the baby and place her into the mirror, then take the door at the far end of the barn that leads out onto the moors and then down into the woods. Move swift and quiet. Head back to Wren. She'll be waiting for you."

Bunny nodded. It was clear she was enjoying her new status and responsibilities.

"What if only two of the sisters come out?" Swan asked.

"Then Prim will go in with Bunny. That will ensure that we outnumber each point two to one, giving us good odds."

"Okay," Swan said. There was little else they could do in the time they had and with the minimum resources they held.

"Let's get this show on the road," Swan said, sighing heavily.

Violet divided them up so that Prim and Bunny headed off in the Eastern direction and Fox was paired with Rose to head off in the Western, leaving, as planned, the two eldest to head straight on.

Just as they were about to move forward, the snow, which had until this point been an unwelcome hindrance but now promised to be useful, eased until there was barely a flurry, dramatically exposing the three pairs of black-clad Meadowsweets against the stark whiteness.

"Great!" Fox muttered under her breath. "Anything you can do about that, Swan?"

Before Swan could answer, a large raven settled on top of the barn and distracted them all. He ruffled his feathers and cawed out across the bleak landscape. It was a very bad omen. Rose and Fox huddled down and made their way swiftly into position. She watched Violet and Swan stride towards the barn. They looked magnificent and proud with their chins held high. For the first time, Fox truly began to understand the power that ran through their veins.

From behind them, a large flock of birds burst out of the treetops. Something in the woods had disturbed them. Fox refused to be spooked. It was probably just a deer or a wild pig. The distance to the barn was not far in reality, but in Fox's imagination, waiting with every breath for something terrible to emerge from its doors, it seemed to take forever. As Fox looked towards her advancing sisters, her heart fell. There were three clear tracks in the snow betraying their battle tactics. The Ravenhearts would see them immediately. Fox stepped out from the side of the barn, and took up position in full view of the door. When Violet turned to her and threw her a questioning look, Fox just nodded to the tracks. The message was clear. Plan B then – only they hadn't discussed what plan B might be.

Just then, Fox had an idea. Admittedly it was a little bit crazy, but it might just work in disguising the tracks made by Bunny and Prim who were taking position on the other side of the barn. She turned to Rose and said,

"Follow my lead and dance!"

Fox danced across the snow, swerving and diving so that the string of footprints created a dazed and higgled path. It took Rose a moment to understand what on earth Fox was doing, but once she caught on, she too danced across the snow, zig-zagging and weaving so that the over all effect was that a hundred people had just passed through the area. Fox returned to position and looked at the mess they'd made in the snow. It would do. Because Fox knew the path that Prim and Bunny had travelled she was convinced that their tracks were still glaringly obvious, but they might just get away with it; especially if they could keep the Ravenheart sisters busy. Fox slinked back into shadows of the barn and waited.

The dreadful raven perched on top of the roof cried out again. Fox wished she had a stone to hurl at the disgusting creature. *That would teach it to shut its nasty little beak.*

They all stood for a moment not knowing what to do. They'd all perhaps envisaged the Ravenhearts would hear them coming and open the door in greeting, then charge out in force to face the foe, but nothing happened, which left them in the rather puzzling predicament of how to get the action going.

Violet glanced at Swan and flashed a smile, "Do you think we should just walk up and knock on the door?"

Swan snorted a nervous little laugh. "Maybe we should have called ahead and made sure they were home."

"Oh, they're home all right; I can smell the cheap trashy perfume from here," Violet sneered. Swan was surprised to hear her otherwise incredibly tolerant cousin emit a hint of bitchiness and cracked a wry smile.

"I guess we could go for something a little more Hollywood."

"What have you got in mind?"

Swan pulled her rowan-wood wand from her back pocket. "I've been experimenting a little bit lately, with some quite delightful little tricks." Her sentence was punctuated by the spectacle unfolding in front of them. A channel of snow rose up out of the ground, giving the strange impression of an albino snake. As the energy pulsed down the length of the body, the mass swelled until the shape became a large fist ready for knocking. When it came within distance of the door, the snow rose up and the snow-fist rapped three times hard on the door before collapsing into a shower of fluffy snowflakes.

Violet nodded her head and twisted her lips in appreciation. "Classy!"

Holy shit! Fox shook her head to make sure she hadn't been hallucinating. It seemed everybody had been doing some secret magic studies, everyone that was except for her. Whilst Swan and Bunny had obviously been secretly practicing their wand magic, Fox had been... *Yes, what have you been doing? Playing the clichéd love-triangle with Jeremiah Chase and William Harrington, that's how you've been spending your time.*

"Ridiculous," she muttered.

"Pardon?" asked Rose, who like Fox was still a little shocked from Swan's display.

"Nothing," Fox mumbled.

There wasn't time for Rose to press her further because just as expected, the doors flew open and out came the eldest of the Ravenheart sisters followed by Thalia and the middle sister, Nigella, completing the arrow-head effect.

They paced forward a couple of steps and then stood their ground, clearly they were pretty pissed at having been interrupted. The eldest, Lilith stared Violet and Swan down with little success.

"How did you get through?" Lilith asked, scanning the area to work out the extent of the threat. She seemed satisfied that there was little to worry about.

"Sorry, I guessed your powers were strong enough to see us coming," Violet taunted.

Nigella put her hand on her hip and pouted. "What do you want?"

"Don't play games, Lilith. You know exactly what we want."

"Well I'm afraid we can't oblige."

The middle sister, Nigella stepped forward, cocking her head and threw her chin out defiantly, "Why don't you just turn around and head on home before one of you gets hurt or… worse." She flicked a vicious little smile that reminded Fox of sharp pins. "We're happy to let this one go, for old times' sake, but we shall not be giving you a second chance."

Violet stepped forward, her right hand tucked into her coat. "That's not the way this is going to happen."

She drew her wand out and held it straight in front of her as if it were a gun. Swan followed suit, lifting hers so that both tips pointed in the direction of the Ravenhearts. Thalia let out a tinkling, sarcastic laugh,

"Aw bless them, they've clearly been swotting up by watching episodes of *Charmed*, how sweet!"

Fox saw Swan's wand waver ever so slightly. Swan was hopeless when being mocked. Feelings of humiliation crippled her on the inside. Fox wondered if Thalia had seen the monstrous snow-

hand whether she would be mocking the power of the Meadowsweet wands or not.

"All we want is the child, and then we'll walk away," Violet said with a voice as steady as rock.

"We all know that *isn't* the way it's going to be," Lilith replied. "Even if we give you *this* child, we'll harvest another, and then you'll be back here making the same impudent demands, and so on and so on, until one of us snaps with the banality of it all and zaps somebody, causing all hell to break out and every Meadowsweet girl to be crushed under a Ravenheart heel."

"In your dreams," Swan retorted.

Fox rolled her eyes; this was turning into a farce. Then she was hit by a vision clear and sharp.

Bunny had the child in her arms and was heading towards the back door. *So that was what all the schlock dialogue has been about - keeping the Ravenhearts talking.* Prim was behind Bunny, searching out the door handle but it was locked. Moving the child had disturbed her and she let out a small animal-like mewl. Thalia's attention snapped behind her,

"What the hell?" she shouted. The other two sisters allowed their eyes to flit momentarily to the events behind them but they were not foolish enough to let their eyes leave the Meadowsweet sisters for longer than necessary. Fox's attention moved from the vision to the scene in front of her. It was as if some cosmic scissors had suddenly severed the threads that had been holding them all in a position of sanity.

Thalia flew round, heading off towards Bunny and Prim. Just as Nigella was about to turn heels and head off to support her sister's attack, a bright beam of light flew out of Swan's wand. As the light travelled out across to Nigella, it turned into a length of binding chord, which wrapped its way tighter and tighter around Nigella's ankles until eventually she fell to the floor.

"You've done it now, bitch!" Lilith screamed as her hand flew forward. A large bolt of bright blue energy flew across the distance, hitting Swan full force in the chest. It was enough to cause her to fly backwards and hit the ground in an undignified heap. Fox could see the pain etched across Swan's face, despite the fact that she was struggling back to her feet trying to pretend that it was nothing.

Nigella, now free from the ropes, was raging. She marched up to Violet and Swan, uttering a whole stream of obscenities. Unsure of what to do with no physical weapon being brandished, Swan and Violet held fast and waited. A foolish mistake, for as Nigella charged forward, something solid formed in her shadow. By the time she traversed the space between them, a snarling black panther slinked alongside her, with its head nestled close to its mistress' thigh. Nigella's hand patted the beast on top of its head, and then urged it forward into attack with the command,

"Devour!"

The beast lunged at Violet, causing her to stagger and swerve. She had been too quick, and the panther's jaws clamped around air. In the next vicious leap, it went straight to her shoulder and sunk its teeth in. Realising it had missed the prize of the jugular, the panther snarled and gnashed, lunging forward in another attempt. This time it hit closer to home and Violet felt the mixture of hot saliva and warm blood mix with the hard enamel of fangs. The pain was blinding. A scream tunneled through her. As the panther started to shake its head and tear out Violet's soft flesh, Swan struck the beast with a spell, causing it to momentarily spasm and yelp before lunging into another frenzied attack. Violet's cries grew weaker.

From the barn, Bunny's shouts dominated the scene. Whatever was happening in there, it wasn't good. Fox was torn between rushing to the aid of Violet, whose bright red blood spattered the snow like glinting rubies, or heading towards Bunny who was clearly fighting her own battle – and by the sound of it, possibly losing. Before she could choose, Fox saw Swan raise her wand high in the air. The night sky channelled down into a swirling vortex above its tip. The mass grew denser and darker, and Fox shuddered as she understood that her sister was calling on the negative energies of the universe: she was summoning black magic to defeat black magic. Seeing that Swan had the situation in hand, Fox fled to the barn to assist with Bunny.

There's another reason you're heading in the opposite direction though, isn't there? the internal said. *You're afraid of her!* Fox glanced back, to see her sister, awesome and powerful, cloaked in darkness. The swirling mass of air had become something solid and monstrous. It was her sister's demon, a reflection of the latent darkness within, formed from the death and decay found within the balance of nature. Once the demon was fully formed, Swan struck her wand down in the direction of the panther, which now slunk backwards into its own bones. It understood a greater power had entered the theatre. The demon flew down on the pitiful creature. Just as Fox was about to enter the barn to the sound of the panther's death throes, something in the distance moved, causing her to stop and turn back towards Swan and Violet.

Lilith watched the whole episode between Nigella and Swan Meadowsweet with fascination. She had completely underestimated the Meadowsweets. Never in her wildest imaginings had she thought a Meadowsweet, a Guardian, no less, would resort to the use of dark arts. She wasn't sure if she was impressed or disappointed; there was something noble in having your enemy on an opposing side. With Nigella's denizen defeated, and Swan Meadowsweet's terrifying demon stalking the ground between them, there was little she could do. She looked over to the barn, where her youngest sibling was still fighting off the other Meadowsweets; by the sound of it, the battle was fierce. An almighty cracking sound preluded the collapse of part of the roof. Looking up to the full moon, Lilith saw that the time was now. If they were ever to reach their end goal, she had to put an end to this overblown playground scrap as soon as possible. She ran in the direction of the barn.

*

Jeremiah stopped at the sound of something bloody and monstrous up ahead in the shadows of the forest. The sound of snarling filled the air with the strange resemblance of thunder. Whatever lay ahead did not belong to reality but nightmares. He looked up through the mess of branches to the navy-blue sky. It offered no answer. The snowfall had at least stopped a little while ago, leaving the earth quiet and soft. The woods were heavy with nighttime, reminding him of the lines from Shakespeare, “Nor heaven peep through the blanket of the dark.” The words rang round his head in the voice of a ghost and he shivered with their presence. In the distance, a bright flash of light bounced off the snow and cast coloured lights of green and orange into the sky. He really didn’t want to move towards the unearthly chaos that was going on beyond the trees, but nevertheless he found that his feet continued to step one in front of the other, leading him towards whatever horrors lay ahead.

A rustling noise behind him made him stop and turn. Something was moving towards him. He dipped behind the fattest tree at hand and peered round it. It was pointless; the shadows were too full. Jeremiah tried to calm his heavy breaths. White clouds of hot breath betrayed his whereabouts. He leant his head back against the tree, wishing that somehow he could melt into it. The rustling stopped, the creature also becoming aware that it was not alone. *Great*, Jeremiah thought, *Trouble in front of me, trouble behind me – that's the story of my life.*

The low hoot of an owl travelled through the scraggly trees. Jeremiah's ears alerted to the noise and dared for a moment to hope that everything might be okay. Then it sounded again and he sighed with relief; he'd recognise that call anywhere. He cupped his hands together and returned the call.

Satisfied that he was in the company of friend he stepped out into view.

"Uncle Daniel," Jeremiah whispered urgently, "how did you find me?"

His uncle flashed him a condescending grin and nodded his head in the direction of the imprinted footfalls. "You really have to ask," he said, approaching his nephew and wrapping him up in a strong side-hug. "I thought I told you to stay put."

Jeremiah shrugged his shoulders. "Yeah about that – I'll explain later." He looked back in the direction of the eerie light show and the cracking sound of high-voltage energy. "Is that ….?" Jeremiah didn't need to finish his sentence before Daniel nodded and replied,

"Sure is, we've got to hurry. They have a child and if we don't act now, then there's a chance we will be too late to save her." A terrible whooshing sound filled the air and both men looked up to see a black tornado began to spin wildly in the air above the clearing.

"What in God's name is that?" Jeremiah asked, his eyes wide with confusion.

"That's not good. Normally I'd tell you to wait here for me, but I might need your help with this. Come on," he said, already heading off.

Jeremiah was forced to jog in order to catch up, a task made more difficult by his eyes' refusal to stop watching the swirling mass of black air. It became increasingly opaque, taking on form and substance like a living thing. Its wicked presence was palpable even from a distance.

"Is that…" Jeremiah stumbled over the words he could never have imagined himself asking. "Is that magic?"

"Yes, dear boy - of the very blackest kind." Daniel stopped, causing Jeremiah to nearly fall over him. Daniel pulled off his knapsack and rummaged around it until he finally located what he was searching for. He withdrew a set of long distance night vision goggles. "Whoever is summoning that force needs to be destroyed on the spot. It is demonic."

Jeremiah let the words hang in his thoughts. "Destroyed." Jeremiah's world had suddenly tilted into the realm of insanity. He didn't get long to consider the consequences of what they were about to do, as another flash of light followed by a blood-curdling growl erupted into the air.

Daniel explained, "My guess is that there are battling covens; it's probably a power match to claim the ritual. Knowing which covens live in this territory, my guess is that it is probably the Meadowsweets and Ravenhearts."

Daniel set off in the direction of the clearing, leaving Jeremiah skittering behind him. Impulsively he felt the need to defend the Meadowsweet sisters, but he wasn't sure he could – not until he'd seen with his own eyes what the hell was going on. As Daniel continued his potted briefing of the enemy, Jeremiah remained silent. His Uncle was talking about them all as if such names should be alien to him, as if they were nothing more than names plucked from some genealogy book, but they weren't; he knew both families well. For Christ's sake, he went to college with some of them, he'd watched them eat soggy egg sandwiches in the canteen and scribble down their maths homework in fear of gaining a detention, he could hardly believe that all along they'd been a powerhouse of dark magic and black rituals.

"Historically," Daniel continued, "the Meadowsweets have declared themselves as Guardians, which are like guardians against the dark arts, practicing only white magic. It has meant that the higher powers have turned a blind eye, whilst engaging in more urgent matters. The Ravenhearts, well let's just say, their bloodline has a little more nefarious reputation. It was thought that the last 'intervention' by our establishment might have taught them a lesson – clearly not.

"So the Medowsweets are safe then?"

Daniel turned on his heel. "Safe? What a strange word to use. What do you mean?" he asked shaking his head.

"You said that they were Guardians. That they only practiced white magic – so that makes them on our side, right?"

Daniel coughed out a laugh and shook his head. "No, my dear boy, they are still *witches*. That still makes them mistresses of deception and deceit. Who knows what their true nature really is? There's been rumor of certain activities within both covens over the last year that have not gone unnoticed by the…"

"What kind of practices?" Jeremiah asked.

He didn't get his answer. They had reached the boundary of the woods and had a full view of the carnage taking place; at the center of which was Swan Meadowsweet with her wand held high in the air above her. Forces of darkness twirled and danced above it like a macabre ballet dancer until it shaped into the form of a large black beast that flew through the air towards another creature cowering on the ground.

Before Jeremiah could stop himself, he uttered the low cry of, "No!"

*

The dark demon, having done its job of tearing out the panther's throat, once again took its ethereal form of dark mist and turned itself into a reverse vortex before being sucked up into the starry night. Daniel was already charging towards its mistress with his bible extended out in front of him like a shield. Swan Meadowsweet turned to see his approach. Her golden tresses and milk-blond skin gave her an almost angelic luminosity.

"Turn, witch and face your judge and redeemer!"

Swan was startled by the presence of the man striding towards her; his ridiculous eyewear gave him a slightly comical look. However, the closer he got, the less funny he appeared, and Swan responded defensively, raising her wand in his direction. Fox saw the man draw out a pistol from the leather holder behind his back and all at once, the world seemed less certain.

"Mistress of darkness, you must be destroyed," he called.

Swan looked panicked, and clearly the man could sense her volatility. Fox started to walk towards them. Somebody had to try and stop the madness. With every step Fox took, flashes of the possible future assaulted her. The visions stopped her properly being able to see what was happening. The sound of the pistol firing kicked her instincts, and she sped across the distance towards the travelling bullet. She grasped at it, moving through the air like some highly trained goalkeeper. The heat of the bullet seared the flesh of her skin and she felt pain beyond what she thought possible. She fell to the ground and her hot burning flesh hissed against the snow.

She had no idea what had just happened, all she was aware of was the pain, and the feeling of acid-burning metal in her palm. She dropped the bullet into the snow; still not believing that she had managed to cover such a distance and catch a moving bullet. She was not alone in her incredulity. All three of them turned to each other in amazement. Swan, gathering her wits about her, reached down and pulled Fox to a standing position.

Daniel, unsure of what powers he was really facing, searched out Jeremiah, alerting Fox's attention to the boy standing at the edge of the trees. Her heartbeat jumped out of synch and the sensation was almost as painful as her hand.

"Jay!" the man shouted, beckoning for him to advance towards the barn, "Go and find the child."

Fox watched Jeremiah run off in the direction of the barn, which was also filled with chaotic activity. It sounded as if all Hell itself was breaking loose; and there was a real possibility it was.

After a moment of hesitation, Jeremiah ran off in the direction of the barn. All of Fox's instincts urged her to follow him, knowing there was no chance of him surviving the battle raging between the two covens. But the strange, unknown man continued to stand in front of her sister with a look of destruction in his eye.

Swan held out both hands in submission; her defensive panic turned to an eerie calm. She tilted her head in innocence.

"Please, it's not what you think. Please, I need to tend to my cousin. It really isn't what you think," she pleaded. Tears traced down her cheeks.

At her feet, Violet let out a faint moan. Violet's hand, which had been stemming the blood flow, had now fallen from her neck and a steady scarlet puddle grew in the snow. The man looked down at the girl dying on the ground but no sympathy registered on his face.

"Silence, witch, your kind does not deserve compassion. I know black magic, and I know what needs to be done."

"But please," Swan begged, "she's innocent. She was trying to help the child." Her voice dropped, "I was trying to help the child."

The man's hand relaxed on the pistol and he let it fall to his side. Swan's charms were powerful. But just as Fox was about to sigh a breath of relief, he returned the pistol to its original position, aimed directly at Swan's heart.

"How about a deal?" Swan offered. "You let me help my cousin and I'll hand myself over to you willingly, without a fight?"

"No!" Fox cried. "You can't do that, you've done nothing wrong."

The man looked into Swan's eyes and it was as if he were able to see right into her soul.

"Very well," he nodded, "and you understand the fate that awaits a witch who calls forth demons?"

Swan nodded solemnly before dropping to her knees and laying her hands over Violet's wound. Fox locked eyes with the man, hoping that he could feel her feelings of hatred towards him.

"She's not a black witch. She's not demonic!" she cried, but his face was stern.

"Are you denying what we all witnessed?" he asked.

Fox had no answer. She still wasn't sure what it was her sister had summoned, or how she'd gained the powers or knowledge to do so. Before she could answer, a scream came from the barn and with it, a bright burst of red light that gave the impression the barn had exploded into fire.

Swan turned to Fox and said flatly, “You need to go and check on Bunny.”

Fox looked briefly at her and then turned to the barn. Dark shadows crawled all over the red-lit barn; minions were seeping out of whatever portal the Ravenhearts had managed to open.

“You need to check that Bunny got away. It doesn’t look good,” Swan said.

Fox reached out for her sister with her thoughts, but there was nothing; all receptors were down. Swan saw the look of doubt in her sister’s eyes and begged her to go.

“Please, go and save Bunny. I’ll be okay, honestly, I’ll be okay.”

Fox knew she was trying to convince herself as much as anybody else.

The scene inside the barn was chaotic. Flames licked the walls and minion demons slid amongst them. Prim and Lilith were locked in a fierce battle; equally matched in powers it would simply be a matter of who got distracted or tired the first. Explosions of energy burst all around them, scratches covered each of their faces. The psychic trauma flowing between the two of them caused their limbs to flail and jerk. Fox looked at Prim and knew that there was nothing she could do to help; any interference would probably cause more damage than good.

It took Fox several moments of searching before she caught sight of Bunny and the child. The mirror lay shattered on the floor. Fox had no time to ask what had happened. The baby was held above the heat, flames and demons in a protective bubble – the work of Bunny, who was near the door, battling with Nigella and holding her own admirably. Nigella was bent double, trying to undo a knot of rope that Bunny had managed to cast around her waist. The rope was tightening, causing Nigella to emit a small squeak and a mouthful of expletives.

A voice in Fox's ear caused her to turn.

"Take the child and go." It was Jeremiah.

She looked at him, her eyes wide with confusion. "Why are you here?" she mouthed.

"There's no time for that now. Just take the baby and go. I'll follow you later."

Fox turned back to the fight between Bunny and Nigella. It was all under control. Nigella was now tied tightly to one of the supporting beams and her wand lay uselessly out of reach. Even with her extensive powers, there looked no danger of her breaking Bunny's binding spell.

Bunny lifted her wand in the direction of her cousin Prim and a blinding white light of energy broke through the flames and bathed her cousin in energy-rich power. The surge was enough for the spell she was building and within moments, Lilith fell ungracefully to the floor. Her wand splintered into two, and minions swarmed over her like lice, nipping at her skin. Lilith phased out, disappearing from in front of them.

Fox rushed to Prim's side. "Where's Thalia?" she asked.

Prim looked around before shrugging. "I don't know, I thought she was outside with you."

Suddenly there was a scream, and Nigella burst out of the bonds and ran towards Bunny and the child. Jeremiah saw her intention and ran towards her at speed. They collided in a messy and brutal, bruising heap. As Jeremiah fell, the palm of his hand fell flat against Nigella's chest and she let out a blood-curdling scream before falling deathly quiet in a faint.

Bunny cradled the child to her. She felt surprisingly heavy sitting on her hip.

"Do you think it's finished?"

"For now," Fox said.

"And Violet?" Prim asked.

"Rose and Swan are with her," Fox replied.

With the disappearance of Lilith and with Nigella unconscious, whatever power the minions of the Ancient Ones were feeding off, faded. The light in the barn returned to its normal ink-blue, and everything stilled. Fox, Bunny, and Prim left Jeremiah behind and walked out back towards the bloody scene outside.

At first, Fox couldn't process the scene in front of her. Violet still lie on the ground, with Rose's cloak spread over her, giving the impression of some dark fallen angel. Rose crouched by her side, moving her hands up and down over her sister's body, a white healing light emitted from the palms of her hands. Swan was not there, and neither was the man.

Fox scanned the tree line, although it was difficult to see anything beyond the heavy darkness of the night. "Where's Swan?" Fox asked.

"She went with him – that man," Rose said stonily. "There was no way to stop her. They headed over there." She nodded her head offering direction.

Fox's turned to the ruins of the cottage. It had once probably been a pretty place, but now it was scared and ugly.

A blinding pain hit Fox in the middle of her forehead and if it hadn't been for Jeremiah running up behind her and catching her in his arms, she would have fallen face first into the snow.

Screams ricocheted around her head. They were her sister's. Flames were everywhere. They scurried up the base of the wooden pillar that her sister was tied to. She had been stripped of her warm winter layers, and was shivering against the cold, in just her white vest and jeans. Her boots scrabbled against the pile of wood underneath her. It took Fox a moment to work out where about he had taken her. It looked like the half rotten framework of an outbuilding. The wood piled at the bottom of her feet suggested it was …

Fox gasped in the ice-cold air and her eyes flew open. "The woodshed! He's taken her to the woodshed."

Fox's eyes searched the ramshackle group of buildings. To the side of the cottage was the one that looked most likely. She took flight, leaving Jeremiah behind her. She stopped only when she felt her sister's body under her fingertips and the heat of fire nipping at her skin. Despite Fox's desire to hold on to her, Fox's body refused to stay and be burned. She changed tactic, removing her coat and battering at the flames that were reluctantly eating the damp wood. All she succeeded in doing was fanning them, so that smoke rose and little flames rose up and nibbled at Swan's boots.

"Fox?" Swan croaked, opening her eyes. "Go!" Swan whispered.

His voice came from the shadows from where he was watching. "Your sister is right – you should go."

The flames rose higher, and Swan started to cry. There was no time left. Voices erupted behind them.

Bunny, with the sleeping child still on her hip, came jogging in. Seeing Swan, she started to scream, but the sound wouldn't come out. Her chest rose and fell, and Fox could see that she was at risk of full-blown panic attack. The child moved in her arms; its sleep disturbed, despite the powerful sleeping spell.

"Bunny, get out! Take the child outside now!" Fox commanded.

Prim arrived at the door, and after surveying the scene, grabbed Bunny and forcefully guided her outside. Already a wall of flames blocked Swan from view. Her cries turned into screams. Everything happened too quickly. In a moment of insanity, Fox lunged forwards towards the flames, but just as they kissed her cheek and palms, strong arms circled her waist and dragged her backwards. The cold winter air nearly stung her blistered hands as much as the flames. Jeremiah's voice boomed around her,

"Stop it, Uncle! Stop it! This is wrong! It's all wrong!"

Fox, who'd been kicking and struggling against him, now collapsed against his arms, sobbing.

"It's too late, Jay. It's the price she must pay. She knew that," his uncle said stonily.

Rose stood behind them. She watched on in silence. Despite the horror, it would have been wrong to leave Swan to endure it alone. The flames spread.

"We need to get out!" Rose said. "The whole barn is going to go up." Already the flames were spreading into the damp wood and the space was rapidly filling with smoke, causing them to cough. Confident that his job was done, Jeremiah's uncle led them outside.

He walked them over to where Bunny was stood, cradling the child to her chest like a comforter. Bunny's eyes were wide with grief and pain, but she wasn't seeing; although her body stood there, her spirit had retreated somewhere safe and far away. When Jeremiah's uncle held out his arms to receive the child, Bunny handed her over automatically without looking at him.

He headed in the direction of the footpath that would take them down to the main road and back to Heargton – where the child's distraught mother would be waiting. Sensing his nephew was not following behind, he turned and raised a questioning eyebrow. Jeremiah simply replied,

"I'll catch up with you later."

It was clear that Jeremiah's apparent closeness to the Meadowsweet girl was both unexpected and disapproved of. Not that Jeremiah cared about his uncle's stance on the situation. *He's no better than my father!* he thought.

Rose and Prim still tended Violet. They were both crying silently. Fox reached for Bunny's limp fingers and laced them with her own. She didn't know if Bunny could feel her, but she needed to hang on to her and stop her leaving too. Jeremiah stood by her side. His arms folded across his chest. His head bowed. Despite being desperate to take hold of Fox's other hand, whatever intimacy had been between them earlier, it had passed. In its place was an impenetrable wall.

They stood and watched the barn burn, knowing that somewhere inside were the remains of Swan Meadowsweet. It took almost two hours for it to finally collapse into a smouldering heap of timber and ash. Snow fell, quenching the last stubborn flames.

"It is finished," Fox whispered.

"Yes," Jeremiah replied. His voice was thick with regret. He knew that there would be no forgiveness. Whatever could have been between the two of them had died alongside her sister.

"We need to get back," Prim said, gently placing her hands on Fox's shoulder. "We need to let your mother know. There are things that need to be done in the hours following a witch's..." she stopped and changed focus. "We need to get your hands treated before there is permanent damage."

Fox nodded and squeezed Bunny's hand. The Meadowsweet cousins headed slowly towards the footpath, supporting Violet's frail body between them. Seeing her cousins leave, Bunny snapped back into her body and said to Jeremiah, "Take Fox home!"

Fox turned to her. "Why? I can't leave you here."

"Please," she whispered. "I need some time alone."

"I really don't think that's a good idea."

It wasn't just that Fox didn't think Bunny should be left alone with her grief, but there was also the possibility that the Ravenheart sisters might return and seeing Bunny alone, think it a good opportunity to execute revenge.

"There's something I need to do," she said enigmatically.

"We're not leaving you, Bunny," Jeremiah said.

She stopped at the sound of his voice. "Don't you speak to me! No one of your blood ever speak to me again!" She spat her words out viciously.

Jeremiah flinched from them.

Fox turned to him. "You never answered my question."

"What question?"

"What are you doing here?"

He sighed heavily, and implored her, "I'm not here for the reason you think I am."

Fox challenged him with her eyes.

"I bumped into Daniel in the woods. I was coming… I was coming for a different reason."

"Which was?"

Jeremiah coughed uncomfortably. He really wanted to tell her that he had been coming for her, to be by her side and protect her, but he couldn't.

He'd failed. He'd worse than failed. In the end, it hadn't been the Ravenhearts that had harmed her, it had been his own kin. His face crumpled with thoughts. Too many thoughts.

"I see!" she said, not really seeing at all.

"No, no you don't," he said, shaking his head. "I hate them. I hate them all; my father and my uncle."

Fox and Bunny exchanged looks.

"You are one of them," Fox said.

Jeremiah shook his head. "Not any more. Not after…" he stopped, unable to decide precisely on which of their unforgiveable deeds he should choose as reason for the divorce he now felt.

Bunny weighed up the sincerity in his voice and seeing that there was no way he was going to leave her to do what she needed, she sighed heavily and said, "Very well, but if you are to stay, you will need to seal a blood bond – you will need to make a sacred vow that you will not speak of what you are about to see." As she said it, she hoped this might be enough of a threat to finally get him to leave.

However, Jeremiah nodded his head. "I need to be here."

Fox threw him a glance before asking Bunny, "What's going on? I don't understand what's happening."

Bunny ignored her. "Jeremiah, you do understand that the bond between a witch and a Witch Hunter is very powerful? You know that once it is made, it cannot be unmade. You will become enemies forever locked together."

Jeremiah shook his head. His forehead creased with confusion. "Witch Hunter? I don't... I don't know what you mean."

It took a moment for Bunny to comprehend. "Oh my word, you don't know – do you?"

"Know what?" Fox asked.

"That you're a Witch Hunter. That's why you were able to petrify Nigella. Your hand must have pressed against the space above her heart."

Jeremiah shook his head. "No. You're wrong. Uncle Daniel is the Witch Hunter, not me. I don't believe in all that..." the sentence faded. He was about to say that he didn't believe in all that supernatural rubbish, and yet, the events of the evening had been real, very real.

Bunny was increasingly agitated. Her feet jabbed against the snow. She had work to do and really didn't have time to spend filling a Chase on his own blood history.

"I haven't got the time for this. Make a choice. Either make the bond between our blood or leave."

There was a moment while Jeremiah tried to process everything he'd been told. A choice? He didn't even know what that really meant. All he knew was that he didn't want to leave Fox. As he had no intention of ever taking up the role of a Witch Hunter, what harm could such a pledge hold? He nodded his head. "I'll make the bond."

Bunny grabbed at his hand and drew out her anathema. The blade glinted in the moonlight. She stabbed the point into the soft flesh of his palm and he winced as she dragged it across his skin. Blood welled from the cut. Bunny was just about to draw her own blood when Fox shouted, “Stop!”

They both turned to look at her.

“Make the bond with me,” she said holding out her hand. “It’s me that brought the Chase blood to our door – they should be my responsibility.”

Bunny shook her head. “But you don’t understand what bargain you’re making.”

“It’s one that you were going to make.”

“Yes, but I have my reasons. What are yours?”

Fox looked at her sister with new sight. She shuffled and sighed with exasperation. “Just do it, Bunny!” she said nodding to her hand.

Reluctantly, Bunny cut her sister’s palm. It didn’t hurt as much as Fox thought it would, but that was probably the result of the burns, which still stung viciously. Taking both of their hands, Bunny pressed them together, incanting a spell under her breath. As their blood mingled, an extreme pain tunneled through Jeremiah’s veins. The pain was so acute that he could no longer stand and his knees buckled under him.

Visions flooded Fox’s mind. Jeremiah’s whole personal history unveiled itself to her – and this is how she learned that Jeremiah Chase truly loved her.

When she saw this, her instinct was to pull away her hand, but Bunny wasn’t finished and she continued to hold them together. Fox wondered if it was two-way traffic, and which of her secrets Jeremiah now knew. She wondered if he had learned how much she hated him.

"It is done," Bunny said, dropping their hands. "Come on," she said addressing Jeremiah. "You might as well make yourself useful."

They walked up to the ruins of the woodshed. Despite the snow, they were still too hot. Bunny bent down and took her wand from her pocket. She placed the tip of it in the snow and they watched as ice spread up and over the steaming piles of charred wood. Convinced it was cold enough, Bunny began pulling at the burned timbers.

"Don't just stand there!"

Fox and Jeremiah began pulling at the wood too. It didn't take long before they could see something underneath. Nestled in the middle of the flames, curled up in a ball and surrounded by a wobbling transparent shield, was Swan; giving the surreal impression of a baby curled up in its amniotic sack.

"Oh, my word!" Fox exclaimed. "How…?" her words trailed off at the miracle sight in front of her. Swan's clothes and hair were burned away, and she was covered in black soot but she looked peaceful, as if she were sleeping.

"I guess your uncle wouldn't be too pleased about this," Bunny said. "Now you understand why you had to make the bond. Your uncle can not know of this."

Jeremiah nodded. "I understand. You have my word that no one shall hear of this from me."

Bunny stared at him intensely and shook her head slowly. "We have no need of your word, Jeremiah; we have your blood."

Jeremiah shuffled uncomfortably. He still didn't truly understand what she meant by this, but the way Bunny said it suggested his pledge might come to be something he regretted at a later date. Subconsciously, he flexed his hand, as if he to hide the ugly red scratch and undo it.

As they continued to move away the burned logs and ashes, Fox asked Jeremiah, "So this is what your uncle does for a living? I've heard of Witch Hunters, but I didn't think they really existed."

Jeremiah let out an awkward laugh. "That's a bit like me and witches. I mean I've always known that Daniel was a Witch Hunter, but I didn't ever really think that the witches he dealt with were actual witches. I thought they were nut-jobs with over active imaginations and a sadistic murderous streak."

"So you've met the Ravenhearts then!" Bunny said, cracking a reluctant smile.

The mention of the Ravenhearts prompted his memory of an earlier comment Bunny had thrown away.

"What did you mean when you said I 'petrified' Nigella?" he asked.

Bunny seemed surprised by the question. "When you touched the space above her heart, you stopped it, of course."

Jeremiah's forehead wrinkled.

"The same with the lips. If a Witch Hunter presses his lips to a witch, it stops her breath. If the touch in either case is brief, then it will simply petrify the victim, but if it is longer, then death will ensue." Bunny scowled, "Hasn't your father told you how this all works?"

Fox blushed at the memory of the kiss that never was. What would have happened if she and Jeremiah had kissed? Would she now be dead? For some inexplicable reason a feeling of loss emerged rather than relief.

"My father?" Jeremiah asked.

"Yes. The Witch Hunter blood is passed down the paternal line," Bunny replied.

"But my father isn't a Witch Hunter – it's my uncle."

Bunny wrinkled her nose. "But your father must be one too – if your uncle and father share the same father, which I guess they do – and his father before him?"

Jeremiah snorted. The thought of his corporate fat-cat father living the alter-ego life of a Witch Hunter – all leather jackets and Holy water didn't seem likely – *a hired assassin is more my father's style,* he thought bitterly.

"But just because you're born a Witch Hunter, doesn't meant you have to actually go hunting down witches – does it?" he offered.

Bunny shrugged. "I think it's probably a bit like witchcraft – you don't get a choice when your gifts come in."

Jeremiah had a million questions that he wanted to ask, but their conversation was cut short by the surreal sight in front of them. With an adequate space cleared, Bunny retracted the shimmering protection shield, exposing Swan's curled body to the cold air. She shivered when the snowflakes touched her naked skin. Normally Jeremiah would have found the situation a little embarrassing, but this wasn't – it was no more embarrassing than seeing a naked new born; only rather than the joy and wonder that accompanies birth, this perverted version felt sad and injurious.

Swan's eyes fluttered open and took in the scene slowly. She was trying to determine if she were still alive or whether she had passed through to another world. Fox bent down and inspected her closely. She was shocked at the damage that they had earlier underestimated.

Bunny let out a low, "Oh my God!" at the sight of Swan's cheek pressed against the embers. An angry red burn covered most of her face and neck, her hair had mostly burned away, and what was left, was so brittle that it threatened to blow away in the wind. Although Bunny had been surprisingly brave until this point, she now turned back into the baby sister. Tears brimmed her eyes. She held out her wand with a wavering hand and closed her eyes, silently mouthing a secret incantation. With the shimmering shield now gone, the sweet sickly smell of burning flesh hung in the air.

Swan opened a swollen eye-lid and looked straight at them with the eye of an injured animal. Fox dropped her voice so that it was barely more than a whisper,

"We should have asked Rose to stay; her powers of healing are stronger than ours."

Bunny's voice wobbled. "I thought I'd done it in time. I thought I'd saved her."

"You did Bunny – you did save her!"

Fox smoothed the hair out of Swan's eyes, at which Swan let out a small cry.

"Ssh, Swan, it's going to be okay, darling, it's going to be okay." Fox offered these reassurances knowing in her heart that everything was going to be far from okay.

*

Getting her home was going to be almost impossible, Jeremiah thought. He stumbled up onto the base of the pyre and made to move her, stopping when he saw the injurious state she was in. He tried to hide his expression but he hadn't been quick enough.

"We should call an ambulance," he offered. "She looks really fragile."

"And say what exactly, Jeremiah?" Fox snapped. "That our sister has been burnt at the stake by a deranged Witch Hunter who mistakenly believed she was in league with the Devil?"

Jeremiah fell silent and shrugged his shoulders. There was nothing he could say to make things better. From that point on he did exactly as he was told.

Swan screamed out at the sensation of Fox's coat being wrapped around her and Jeremiah's arms pushing their way underneath her. Despite her slight appearance, it still took Jeremiah by surprise to discover just how heavy she was. He stumbled, almost dropping her. He had no idea how he was meant to carry her all the way back to

Meadowsweet Cottage. Sensing his anxiety, Bunny said, “Don’t worry, we’ll share the load.” There was something in the way she said it that led him to believe there would be some magical assistance. He turned to Fox, trying to understand just who these weird sisters were and what power they truly held.

17

The walk back to Meadowsweet Cottage was all the harder because of the snow. It covered the track and caused Jeremiah to veer off and stumble on the embankments. However, true to Bunny's promise, Swan magically felt lighter the longer he carried her and the further they walked the slower the sisters became, as if burdened by a heavy weight. They made their way in silence through the night.

Eventually, they made it to the boundary of the village. With the child safely returned and the search parties called off, the police had headed back to HQ, leaving the village eerie and still. As they travelled, the snow disguised their approach to the cottage. Silently, Fox thanked the Goddess for her small mercies. The sound of Wren's sobs bled through the door of Meadowsweet Cottage.

"The cousins must have told her," Bunny said flatly.

Fox lead the way and found the women assembled in the kitchen. Violet was laid on the sofa. A patchwork quilt had been thrown over her in a bid to have her rest, but she wasn't sleeping – she was staring wide-eyed out across the floor to a spot in the corner of the room. She looked completely traumatised. The other women were sat around the table, linked hand by hand creating a circle of strength and comfort. With sound of her remaining daughters returning, Wren looked up towards the kitchen door. Fox had steeled herself for the intense emotional field but was almost physically held back from the kitchen by the force of it. Wren stood, breaking the circle and the energy dipped, allowing first Fox, then Bunny and eventually Jeremiah and his precious bundle to step into the kitchen.

It took Wren a moment or two to fully understand the sight of Jeremiah carrying her eldest child in his arms,

"You brought her home," she cried, and then she was running across the space, her arms outstretched to receive her baby. She gasped when she saw Swan's eyes open at the sound of her mother's voice.

Words filled the kitchen as the cousins tried to work out how the miracle had happened,

"Impossible! How?" they asked.

"None of that matters," Wren whispered. "She's home and she's safe."

Swan emitted a small mewling sound that suggested a failed attempt at crying. The sound transformed Wren back into her busy, efficient mother-hen, and after giving Jeremiah instructions to carry Swan upstairs to her room and lay her on the bed, she began gliding around the kitchen gathering up armfuls of lotions and apparatus that she might need. Taking her lead, Prim and Rose sprang into action boiling water in the kettle and recovering bandages and balsams from the pine dresser. After a few hectic minutes Rose and Wren headed upstairs with everything they needed to undertake the healing ceremonies that would go on throughout the night.

With nothing left to do, Fox collapsed into one of the rickety kitchen chairs and looked at her blistered hands properly for the first time. It was as if she had forgotten to find them painful, and now seeing them, the memory came flooding back. She winced and Prim sat down beside her.

"I'm not much of a healer, I'm afraid," she said, standing back up and heading off to get a bottle of balsam from the dresser.

She returned, sat, and lifted one of Fox's damaged hands into her own, applying the cold cream into the burn. The relief was immediate. Prim had much better healing powers than she'd led Fox to believe. The feeling of blissful relief that flooded over her skin was almost too much and it unlocked her defenses so that she began to cry. Jeremiah reached out a supportive arm, intending on pulling her into a sideways hug, but she shouldered him away.

"I don't want you here," she said. "I want you to go now."

Prim stood and made her way to the dresser on pretense of looking for something. She purposefully buried her head in one of the low cupboards.

Jeremiah began to protest, "You don't understand, I'm in…" but Fox painfully raised her hand to stop him.

"Deep down, I knew from the very moment I saw you that you would bring us harm. I never want to see you again. You're not welcome here. Go back to Coldstone House – it's where your kind belong!"

Prim heard the pain in Fox's voice and she knew the agony Fox felt was not just from her burnt hands but because Fox loved Jeremiah – even if Fox had managed to almost convince herself otherwise.

Reluctantly, Jeremiah stood and made towards the door.

"If that's what you wish." He went to say more but thought better of it and left.

Fox listened for the sound of the front door shutting and when it slammed shut, a door inside her own heart slammed shut too.

Prim returned and resumed her rhythmic task in silence.

"I hate that boy!" Fox said with a simmering rage.

Prim didn't respond but thought, *If only it were as simple as that.*

18

Lilith and Thalia flew through Ravenheart Hall at speed, packing for their flight. A couple of hours had passed since their failed attempt at summoning the Ancient Ones and still Nigella had not yet returned home. The sisters were not unduly worried; Nigella had a habit of ditching the scrap to come back a few hours later with the chief's head on a stick. Nigella (Lilith hated to admit) was possibly the strongest of the three of them – it was a strength that came from a distinct pleasure in cruelty. Thalia hoped for all their sakes that Nigella had tracked down the Witch Hunter and executed suitable revenge; the sound of Swan Meadowsweet's screams as she burned refused to leave Thalia's ears. It was one thing a witch slaying another, but quite a different thing when a witch's death was at the hands of a bible-wielding Witch Hunter.

It didn't take much to deduce that the Witch Hunter accompanying Jeremiah had to be Daniel Chase, one of the most feared Witch Hunters of modern time. Even now, the name Daniel Chase was whispered amongst the covens. The Chase blood was reputed to be very powerful. *Just imagine if you could harvest it?* Thalia thought. A smile stroked the corner of her lips.

And then there was the matter of Jeremiah Chase. Despite Lilith's warnings, he hadn't seemed such a threat – and yet… the power of Chase blood ran through his veins too. With that thought, Thalia's breath caught in her lungs and her stomach contracted. *Stupid girl! Stupid girl!* she shook her head. How could she have missed that? Her memory flicked back to a scene in the barn full of flames and minions and chaos – and to Jeremiah and Nigella on a collision force. She needed to go back to the barn. She ran through the halls of Ravenheart Hall calling for her Lilith, but she was nowhere to be found.

*

Lilith had warned her sisters of Jeremiah Chase the moment she had set eyes on him. His beauty betrayed the threat that ran through his veins. It was well known amongst the covens that the Chase brother that sat as head of Chase Enterprises was no real Chase (the offspring of some spiteful affair) and so not being of Witch Hunter blood, his son, Jeremiah, had been discounted as any kind of threat – that was until Lilith had laid eyes on him. As soon as she had seen him, she knew that the boy was a Witch Hunter. It had been in the colouring of his eyes, the structure of his bones and in his otherworldly beauty. When she saw him standing next to his "uncle" her suspicions had been confirmed. There was no question that Jeremiah

Chase and Daniel were father and son. The question was, did the boy know? If he didn't, he soon would.

She had left Thalia packing and returned to the farm alone. She had heard Nigella telepathically calling for help when she had fallen, but it had been impossible to reach her. All she could hope was that Jeremiah hadn't touched the space above Nigella's heart.

The fight with the Meadowsweets had been a lot more vigorous than she had anticipated, and she had been left feeling weaker than she'd like. If her sister was petrified, it would take a lot of energy to bring her back.

The farm was deathly quiet except for the caw of the crow, which despite everything that had happened still sat guarding his territory. Lilith headed towards the barn ignoring his warning cry. The smell of woodsmoke and another unpleasant, sweet, repellent smell still hung heavily in the air. Lilith shuddered at the thought of the Meadowsweet witch burning; the burning of a witch broke a natural order and although the Ravenhearts and Meadowsweets would never be friends, they did at least now share a common enemy. Bonds of allegiance had been built on less.

The barn door was ajar. Lilith peered into the gloom. It was dimly lit by several naked bulbs hanging on black flex. They flickered with the movements of moths that repeatedly flew into them. Other than the moths, there was no sign of life. Lilith scanned the room with mounting expectation. The sight of a black leather boot caught her attention. There was no mistaking its owner. She flung the door back and ran in, falling in a heap beside the motionless body of Nigella. She picked up her sister's wrist with the desperate hope of finding her sister petrified and nothing more.

It was worse than she had feared. There was no pulse. Nigella was dead.

Lilith gasped. She had seen Jeremiah collide into her, and seen them fall to the floor, but she had been sure that Jeremiah did not know to press his hand against her heart. Lilith reached out to the buttons of her sister's blouse. She needed to confirm what she already knew. An ugly, black, heart-shaped bruise showed that her heart had bled out.

"I guessed you'd be here. Did you know? About Jeremiah that is?"

Lilith turned to Thalia and raised an eyebrow. "So you worked it out too."

"Too late though."

"Yes too late. We were both too late," Lilith said sadly.

"So she is…?" Thalia asked, not believing it.

"We need to send her on," Lilith said.

Thalia fought back tears; they were not only from grief, but from rage - a tornado of rage that she could feel building in the pit of her stomach.

"No. It's too soon. We need to do it properly. We need to complete the rituals," Thalia protested.

"We haven't got time. Chase knows our bloodline is still active - he'll be coming for us. We have to go."

"Let him come," said Thalia defiantly. "I'm not scared of him."

Lilith stared at hard and then nodded her head towards Nigella's corpse, "Really? You're not scared of the blood that did this to your own sister - your sister who was twice as powerful as you?"

Her eldest sister's words stung and intensified her anger. She knew that she was right.

"That's why we need to go to Mexico," Lilith said, soothing her sister's temper. "We need to bide our time, gather our intelligence and find out what we are really dealing with. You've heard the rumours. Then we'll be the one's who are hunting him."

"Why Mexico?"

"I've been talking to the High Council. They told me that Daniel Chase was in Mexico last month and he slayed the Merinion Coven – all of them."

Thalia's eyes widened. "How did we not know of this?"

"It's been kept as quiet as possible. The Council didn't want there to be panic spread amongst the covens."

"But the Merinions? Surely that can't be. They're one of the oldest covens in the world."

Lilith nodded sagely. "Times are changing. No one is safe."

A heavy silence fell between them. With Nigella dead it already felt that some deep and powerful magic connected to their bond of three had left them.

"I don't want you to send her on yet," Thalia said. "I'm not sure that it's time. Something is telling me that she isn't done yet."

"What you're feeling is denial. She's dead. There's nothing more we can do."

"Please," Thalia begged. "Place her in the Palace. Let her rest there until we get back from Mexico and things are over."

Nigella took a moment to think. The Palace was a magical place that existed between temporal and spatial dimensions; it sounded a lot prettier and nicer than it was. In reality it was a dark and cavernous grey space in which a cold wind blew and spirits haunted. Christians called it Purgatory, the no-man's land between Heaven and Hell. It was a space in which the dead half-existed. It was not a place that she wished to send her sister to, not when there was the promise of her living in the luxury of Hell as one of His own.

Thalia's voice dropped to a whisper, "Please, just till we get back."

Nigella looked at her sister intensely, reading her face. Something more than a reluctance to let her sister go was going on in her sister's head. Instinct told her that Thalia was just a conduit for a greater message, and so she found herself nodding in agreement. She sighed heavily. "Okay, as you wish - but just until we get back."

"Thank you."

Both girls took position either side of their sister's body and each took a hand of the other until the circle was complete. Nigella's hand felt hard and cold like marble and both sister's wished for the sensation to be as brief as possible. Touching death was ugly and felt contagious. They closed their eyes and began a low, undulating chant.

The lights above them flickered.

They called on the spirits of the Palace to recover their sister's body and hold her safe.

The barn door blew open hard and slammed against the wall. A cold wind circled bringing a light frosting of snow with it. It turned until it seemed to take on a more solid form and the snowflakes traced the outline of a being. The entity found Nigella's body and hovered above it, drawing her in molecule by molecule until her body had completely faded away into the wind. Then the entity bolted at speed for the door and was gone. The lights stopped flickering, the barn door eased shut, and the temperature returned to its settled cold.

The sisters dropped their hands and opened their eyes to stare at the empty space beneath them. Nigella was gone and now it was time for them to flee.

19

It was after midnight when Jeremiah returned to Coldstone House. His aunt had already gone to bed but his uncle sat in the library waiting for him. He was sat in the chair nearest to the fading fire. He had a large tumbler of Scotch in his hand and looked heavy with troubles.

Jeremiah crept in. He knew that his refusal to follow Daniel home would be seen as a betrayal. It was better to face him now rather than wait the long hours of night for the morning. Jeremiah coughed nervously from the door.

"I was beginning to worry," Daniel said.

"I was… I was…" Jeremiah stumbled over his explanation. It wasn't until he began to speak that he realised just how angry he was at his uncle. The image of Swan Meadowsweet drenched in flames assaulted his senses. Pain seared his head and he squeezed the bridge of his nose between his thumb and his forefinger. It offered little comfort. The desire to walk over to his uncle and punch him rapidly increased. Jeremiah breathed deeply, but rather than calming him, it added oxygen to the fire raging in him. He strode across the room, his hand gesticulating wildly whilst he tried to find the words. He was used to feeling this sense of contained rage in the presence of his father, but not his uncle. Daniel was meant to be the one who never let him down, his mentor, his solid rock of dependable love and understanding, but now…

Sensing his nephew's unpredictable mounting anger, Daniel stood and placed the tumbler onto the mantle piece.

"You're upset?" Daniel asked softly. "I understand. It's never a pleasant experience; trust me, it gives me no joy."

"Upset! Upset!" Jeremiah spat. "I've just watched you murder my friend's sister - in cold blood. You tied her up and you set her on fire!"

"It's what has to be done."

"Has to be? What do you mean? Who says it has to be done? The voice of a God you don't even believe in?"

"You know how it is, Jay. It's my calling."

"No, I don't know how it is. I don't understand this stupid *calling* business. You're a paid executioner, nothing more! Don't try and make it sound more noble than it is!"

"I can't expect you to understand, Jeremiah. If I could have chosen a different path, trust me, I would have – something like stunt driving, or being a cattle driver, or a treasure hunter is more my style, wouldn't you agree?" Daniel dared a wry smile but Jeremiah wasn't taking the bait. Daniel sighed. "But I didn't get to choose."

"What do you mean, you didn't get to choose?" Jeremiah asked, still fighting the urge to launch into nuclear meltdown.

Daniel shrugged. "It's hard to explain – I'm not even sure that I understand it all myself, but it's in our history; there's something in our blood that... compels us."

"Us?"

"It really is about time you paid more attention to the family stories. They're important – they define who you are."

Jeremiah snorted. "Yes, Aunt Penelope has been doing a pretty good job but I'm beginning to guess that there is a lot more I really ought to..."

Daniel raised his hand to stop him. "Not tonight, Jeremiah. Not tonight."

Sensing he was no longer in physical danger, Daniel reached for his glass. It was a mistake. Jeremiah was not finished. Before he knew what he was doing, he knocked the glass from his uncle's hand. It landed into the embers of the fire and the alcohol caused the flames to flare up dramatically.

"Yes tonight! I'm fed up with all this bullshit! I want to know who I am. Bunny said that I was a Witch Hunter? Like all true Chase blood – and yet, my father..."

Daniel's eyes flicked to Jeremiah. He hadn't been expecting the turn in the conversation.

"Your father is not a Witch Hunter," Daniel finished the sentence for him.

Jeremiah's stomach lurched, the room span. All of a sudden, everything in the room that was solid and substantial became nothing more than wisps.

"He's not my father, is he?"

Daniel shook his head. How he wished he still had a mouthful of liquor to wash down the truth. “No, he’s not.”

“No! No! No! This can’t be happening!” Jeremiah paced in a circle, grabbing at his hair. His head couldn’t take any more of the day.

“It’s you, isn’t it! It’s you!” Jeremiah was somewhere between screaming and crying. He stopped and pulled himself up to Daniel, knocking him on the shoulder with the flat of his hand.

“Go on, hit me? Would that make you feel better?”

Jeremiah eyeballed him. Part of him felt that hitting him was exactly what he wanted to do. He felt his hand itch as it flexed in and out of a clenched fist. The anger was sliding into a simmering, cooler feeling of hate.

“I think it would be better if we sat and talked. Shall I pour us a drink?” Daniel asked walking towards the decanter.

“I don’t want to talk. There’s nothing to say,” Jeremiah replied turning and heading towards the door.

Daniel called after him, “Jeremiah, stay away from the Meadowsweets. Things are not done yet.”

Jeremiah turned and flashed him a dark look of defiance. “I mean it Jay.” Daniel continued, “Whatever is between you and that Meadowsweet witch, pack it up and lock it away. It will come to no good.”

*

If his uncle said more, he didn't hear it. Jeremiah had already left him behind and was making his way up the stairs. Paulina was sat on the top step waiting for him. He stopped and smiled at her, "Hey, you."

She stood and reached out her hand to touch him on the arm in a display of sympathy, but now he knew Paulina was not of the living world, his mind no longer played the physical trick and it passed right through him. It returned sadly to her side. Her face fell with the understanding that she'd never be able to offer him the warmth of human compassion again.

He left her standing on the stairs and walked on. They each had to bear their own losses. When he glanced behind him, she'd faded away to wherever it was that she went when she wasn't manifesting. He hoped it was not to the horrors of the Rookeries.

Closing the door behind him, he headed to his desk. He was exhausted but the last thing he wanted to do was sleep. He knew that as soon as he closed his eyes, the images of that night would replay themselves in an unending nightmare. If he thought he'd escape them by staying awake then he'd been wrong. Images hit him rapidly like the bullets of a machine gun.

Snow and strange lights.

Fire and sliding shadows, like demons dancing over the walls.

The baby, impossibly held in a shimmering, iridescent bubble.

Thalia's sister, charging at him. The force of impact. The feel of her hard body under his, and her hitting her head so that she passed out.

Then there had been the sound of Fox screaming and he'd been running, running faster than he'd ever ran before. He ran towards the flames and the realisation that amongst the flames was Swan Meadowsweet - and she was burning.

But she didn't die.

20

Wren sat down at the kitchen table. She was exhausted. The kitchen was dark except for the small, warm light above the cooker, and it gave the familiar space a sense of otherworldliness. She had been up all night tending to Swan's burns, nursing her daughter's skin in the hope that her attentions might lessen the ugliness of the scarring that was sure to result. Of course there was always the option of magical intervention – but the price of beauty was high. Vanity involved dark magic, of the oldest kind, and it never ended prettily. No, her beautiful daughter would have to endure her scars for the rest of her life, and wear them as experience in the same way that most people have to carry their scars on their heart.

Wren felt tears creep down her face. She would do almost anything to smooth those burns from her daughter's face and place them onto her own. That was a mother's love. She had done all she could, laying the cooling herbal balsams over the skin, stopping the fire from eating deeper into flesh. She'd laid hands, and uttered incantations, sang lullabies, and wrapped her firstborn tenderly in bandages, reminding her achingly of when she had swaddled her as a baby.

The sound of the kettle reaching temperature diverted her thoughts. The whistle sang and she knew she had to move because if she didn't stop to deal with it then there was nobody else to.

It was times like these that highlighted how lonely the life of a witch really was. When she had been young and living amongst her sisters she could never imagine a time when she would ever have to deal with anything alone. Then there had been the "accident," when their youngest sister had died. When the accident had happened, she thought that she would literally die from a broken heart. The pain was made worse by the guilt. She had never accepted that she wasn't entirely to blame; after all, it had been her fault that they'd opened up the portal. They'd been foolish, barely more than curious children – but the Ancient Ones didn't care about that; all that mattered was that the conduits were powerful enough to keep the door open for them and they had been – once the sacrifice had been made – once their baby sister had been pulled into the portals of Hell. Their mother and aunts had arrived just a few moments too late, sealing up the portal and sending the two remaining sisters home whilst they "dealt with the mess."

After that fateful night, she had never returned to Heathmoor Cottage or the moors that surrounded it. She'd made a solemn vow never to use magic again, and until tonight she had kept that vow.

When Thomas had arrived and swept her off her feet, giving her three beautiful daughters, she thought that maybe she could finally move on and put an end to the Meadowsweet's witchcraft legacy. She married Thomas in St. Ursula's Church; a Meadowsweet woman had never married before, not alone taken part in any form of church service. She changed her name to his, becoming Mrs. Weston. She tried to break with tradition in every way. She even put the cottage on the market, but nobody wanted to live in a house with so much superstition surrounding it. The girls followed swiftly and then it was as if Thomas' role had been played out. He died the night after Bunny was born. He was returning home from the hospital in his battered red Fiat on the northern road when he swerved to miss an animal in the road. He was killed on impact. Some in the village believed he was a victim of the Highwayman hauntings. Wren knew better. Thomas' death was punishment for her childhood curiosity – it would seem it was an endless debt.

She shook the memories away; they were too painful, even now, and certainly too much to think on tonight. She poured the tea and watched the steam curl and twist. It made her think of potions; the kind that her mother had taught her before she'd foolishly thought she could deny her blood, and lost her way making cosmetics for rich women who wanted to buy their spirituality in a bottle. But now, darkness was beating its wings and evil had already touched her daughters. It was time to visit the sanctuary and dust off the cauldron. It was time she gave her daughters a proper education.

21

Jeremiah Chase stood at the window and looked out onto the pure white grounds and to the woods beyond. The events of the evening had shaken him to the core. He no longer knew who he was. He no longer wanted to know. He was afraid of what he might learn.

He looked down at his hands and pulled them closely for examination. How could it be that his very touch could kill somebody? He traced the outline of his lips with his fingertips and sighed sorrowfully. Those lips would now never kiss Fox Meadowsweet, and there was nothing more that he wanted to do than kiss her because out of all this madness, one thing had become perfectly clear – he had fallen in love with her.

22

Fox pulled the duvet up over her head. She wanted to nestle down and block out all the horrors she'd seen. She knew that she was in shock; the events of the evening had been traumatic enough to shake even the most steely of hearts. She also knew that she should cry it all out, but the tears wouldn't come because they were held back by too much anger. The sound of Swan's cries floated through the walls and under the door adding to Fox's own pain. Fox reached over and grabbed her earbuds from the side table. She wanted to escape it all; the image of Swan burning, the panther tearing at Violet's throat, the minion shadows, and Jeremiah… she especially wanted to escape thoughts of Jeremiah.

She desperately wanted to phone Will but he had his own troubles and now really wasn't the time to make demands on him. Even though her head reasoned all of this, her heart wished that he were here beside her now, wrapping her safely up in his arms.

Her phone beeped alerting her to an incoming message. Her heart rose with the hope that through some kind of witchcraft, Will had felt her need for him. She flicked onto the messages and her heart sank again. It was Jeremiah. Her curiosity outweighed her principles and she pressed the envelope. It flipped open to reveal three simple words,

I love you.

She threw the phone to the end of the bed – out of the way of temptation. Then the tears came, and they burned.

THE END

Read the Opening of The Forest of Adventures (Book One of The Knight Trilogy)

PREFACE

SLEEP IS FOR the innocent. For the guilty, the night is a time when we are fearful prisoners locked tightly behind heavy eyelids. We look asleep but we're not – we're living in nightmares, and it leaves us exhausted and half crazy. This is the punishment for our crimes.

It always starts the same, with the thick scent of wildflowers and sun-warmed earth lulling me into a false sense of peace. It doesn't last. Too soon it fades, replaced by the sinister iron-stench smell of blood blending with mud and the sweeping sounds of sharpened metal striking the sky. On hands and knees, I crawl forward. My palms slip on the grease of the rain-soaked earth and my dress is so heavy with rain, that I'm dragged even lower; sliding serpent like towards him.

He looks at me with his cheek half-buried in the earth. His eyes stare blankly. I can't tell if he's dead or still dying. I think I hear him whisper my name and I stretch out a hand but I can't quite reach. Death breathes on my bones. Flowers of red-ice bloom over my heart. I wake, gasping for air as if I've been drowning.

The pain is exquisite, the pain is love.

1. BEGINNING

Blake Beldevier started college on the first day of the January term. He arrived with the snow. Perhaps looking back this should have served as an omen: a warning to anybody foolish enough to fall in love with him that they ran the risk of having their heart turned to ice.

Nothing could have prepared me for the first time I saw him. He walked in to the common room, took a seat and started reading *The Times*. It wasn't for this weirdness that I noticed him – although it would normally have been enough – but because of his breath-stealing beauty. It was the sort of beauty that snaps a secret part of you to attention and reduces you to the beast you are at heart. It was a rough and rugged beauty; a colouring of the skin, a face that had been hewn from a remote and wild cliff face; a darkness of the eyes full of latent storms and solitude. He was more beautiful than any other boy I'd ever seen in my seventeen years.

All of this I saw in an instant but it was enough. A sickening current swelled in my stomach. I felt dizzy and stars erupted in front of my eyes. It was as if I'd been hit by a force of freezing ocean air that physically knocked the breath from my lungs. The book I was holding, a thing of exquisite and private joy previous to this moment, flapped limp in my lap, revealing itself as the faded and battered thing it was. Now, here in front of me, sat something more divine than anything an author could create.

By the time I'd managed to regain the appearance of someone who was actually sane – flicking through the pages of my book to give the impression I'd been reading and had hardly noticed him – he'd gone to his lesson.

Sam, who'd been sat at my side throughout all of this, was completely oblivious to these seismic shifts. He was too busy scribbling down the last two answers of his Math homework. As I got up to leave for my lesson, he took hold of my right hand and kissed the well of my palm. His love was solid and reliable. It was for its purity and simplicity that I loved him. Sam was clear waters and instinctively I understood that Blake Beldevier was the swirling waters of a deadly current.

The sense of treachery I felt as I walked to my literature class was as overwhelming as the force that had been the meeting of Blake. It felt as if I had an iron scarf wrapped around my throat, and where Sam's love usually offered a warm contentment, for the first time in the two years we'd been together, his love felt like it was choking me.

The English block was at the far side of the college grounds, and for this I was unusually grateful. The biting wind and the ice-rain that spliced my skin seemed a fitting punishment for the torrent of fire Blake had caused in me. Perhaps it was a taste of the pain that all of us would come to feel.

The English classroom was on the third floor and almost empty when I arrived. Condensation streamed down the windows of the overly hot classroom, which melted the view into the flat, dull, grey of the winter sky. It was comforting to look at something bland and unexciting. The classroom filled without my notice, but this escape didn't last for long.

"May I sit here?" he asked in a hushed tone, clearly embarrassed that he'd arrived late to lesson.

My heart quickened. I reasoned with myself that this seat, one of several available, had been chosen because of its closeness to the door, and was in no way related to my existence. After several disappointing minutes, I realised my reason was right – he hadn't even registered me.

The English teacher, Mr Dwell, was a flamboyant creation; a relic of some previous age of leather volumes, cream teas and cigars. He reminded me very much of my own Uncle Josef and so whilst others took delight in mocking him, cruelly impersonating his slight lisp and his portly walk, I felt an affection for the old man and loved the time I spent in his slightly out-of-sync world.

Literature was my favourite subject and the lessons normally held my entire attention. But unlike other, more ordinary days, today the close scent of Blake's warm body caused my thoughts to bounce all over the place and the words on the page to blur.

"Miss Singer, is there a problem?" Dwell's soft Scottish voice filtered through as if it were travelling through water.

By the time I'd resurfaced, the moment had passed and the class were searching through their copies of Hamlet to find where we'd ended last lesson. Whilst I had been dancing around in my own little daydream, Dwell had selected people to read. Thankfully I wasn't one of them. The 'To be or not to be?' passage was now being read by an unfamiliar voice.

Hamlet's words sat easy in Blake's mouth, giving the impression he was reading from memory, or like an actor who had learnt his lines. And rather than murdering Shakespeare's verse, like we normally did, his voice fitted the iambic pentameter with ease. It created intensity to the language that until this moment, I'd struggled to understand. I lost myself in the music of the reading, jolting back to the room when he suddenly faltered and become unsettled in his movements. He turned to me, his eyes flickering with something like recognition. I noticed with embarrassment that my arm was touching his. There was something terrifyingly captivating in the fact that I couldn't feel him; as if he simply didn't exist.

The creepy thought that maybe he didn't jumped on me. I looked around the classroom, desperate for somebody else to prove he wasn't a figure of my overactive imagination. An ice-spider took a leisurely crawl across my spine. Blake's eyes locked onto mine and looked right into the heart of me. Moving a finger to his lips, he motioned me to silence, as if I had just stumbled across an impossible secret. A smile flitted across his mouth. At that moment, the strongest impulse to kiss him grabbed me and if it hadn't been for the sound of the bell, then maybe madness would have won out.

Before the bell even had a chance to finish ringing, I'd packed as speedily and clumsily as a frenzied criminal about to skip the country. I wondered how it was possible to lose your sanity in the space of an afternoon. All my instincts screamed at me to run, to get away. But something else, something deeper, richer, sweeter, wanted me to stay and move closer. And even though a siren was wailing through my head telling me that this boy was dangerous, all I could think about was kissing those lips.

*

Thankfully, Sam's class had been released early for good behaviour. He stood outside the English block, car keys swinging in one hand, two paper bags containing a late lunch in the other. He greeted me like a dutiful puppy, falling into step by my side and sending the sandwiches on a perilous flight as he swung his arm around my shoulders.

"What's up, Sweetie-Pea? You're white as a ghost!" Sam's voice was full of concern.

"Nothing," I lied unconvincingly. "I think maybe I'm going down with something. Look do you mind if we rain-check this evening? I need to get my head down and rest."

I flashed him a reassuring smile but it felt like a lie. Sam made a valiant attempt at hiding his disappointment. He hated his home, not that Sam really considered it a home. It was merely a place where his drunken father happened to live. At Sam's house there was no space he could call his own. He slept on a pull out sofa bed and all his books and belongings lived either in his college bag, on the backseat of his battered mini or at my house. It couldn't have been more different from the warm, eccentric home my mum, Martha, had created for me. As an illustrator of children's books, she'd magically extended the fairy-tale into the fabric of our own house, meaning it looked part museum, part library, and part falling-down shack.

Even though Sam had his own 'glorified cupboard' at ours, I needed space to think about how I was going to handle the arrival of a certain Mr Beldevier. I couldn't do that with Sam so close. There were many girls at college who would find my situation crazy. Sam was attractive, blonde and athletic. He stopped just short of being magazine-handsome, but he was sparkly and good and it drew the attention of other girls to him. I'd had to put up with their jealousy throughout our time together which had been made more vicious because we were an unlikely couple in every way. I was quiet; he was life and soul of the Rugby club. I read; he played the drums. I was Art and English; he was Maths and Physics. In almost all ways we were our own clichéd opposite.

Judging from the quiet journey home, I guessed Sam had already felt the first shifts begin. He dropped me off outside home and leant over, placing his finger under my chin and lifting my lips to his. Usually I loved to fall into his kiss then afterwards look deep into his gorgeous, sea-blue eyes. They were eyes that were soft and full of the promise of love. Tonight when I looked into them, grey shadows flickered across the violet blue, and I couldn't shake the horrible feeling that a great storm of sadness was about to take hold.

2. FIRE & ICE

The morning's lessons were slow but not slow enough; Double Art History followed by Biology. I didn't even know why I was taking Biology. It had seemed like a good idea at the time and as it was the one subject that Sam and I took together, I hadn't found a good enough reason for chucking it in. But even though slow, I couldn't escape the inevitability of lunchtime coming, and after lunch my English lesson.

By the time Sam and I made it to the canteen, the others had managed to grab a table before the uniform-wearing locusts descended. Daisy and Joe had their heads together in deep conversation about the upcoming ski-trip and although not an official pair like Sara and Matt, it was obvious to all of us, apart from them, that they were made for each other.

Daisy however, was currently wasting her time on a guy from Falmouth Art College who Sam and I had met once, and instantly disliked. We recognised a creep when we saw one. Sadly, Daisy was besotted with him and spent most of her lessons staring out of the window doodling love hearts with their initials entwined in them. I'd found it hard to hide my disapproval and general urge to puke.

Sara and Matt had been together over a year and because Matt was Sam's best friend, we at first tolerated Sara and had since, in a funny and unlikely kind of way, come to like her. Although completely different in almost everyway to Daisy and me, who'd been friends since primary school, Sara added a certain glamour to our otherwise misfit group. Sara was always perfectly preened as if she'd just stepped off of some American High School series with her blonde hair, legs that went on forever and light healthy tan that she had even in the depths of winter.

We made our way through the canteen system, grabbing limp sandwiches and hot chocolate (the only thing drinkable from the vending machine) and started to snake our way through the slightly damp-dog smelling lower school. Before we had quite made it, Joe shouted out across to Sam, "Tell her Sam – she won't have it. Wasn't I James Bonding the Blacks last year?"

"Sure, Joe, just like Bond." Sam nodded sarcastically and winked at Daisy causing her to collapse into a fit of giggles.

"You're so full of it," she said, elbowing Joe so that his sandwich missed his mouth and splattered mayonnaise on his cheek, furthering his humiliation.

Before Sam could take a seat, a small, still immaculately uniformed Year Seven, which we believed to be Matt's brother no matter how often he denied it, swerved in from the side and plonked his skinny bum down on the chair.

"Oi! Out Weasel Head!" Sam said with full sixth-form menace.

"No chance. You snooze you lose, Moose Nose." Weasel-Boy issued this insult as he stuffed a handful of Daisy's chips into his mouth.

Before Sam could respond in defence of his

nose, Weasel-Boy dived straight into conversation with Matt, giving the impression of a small, orange cement-mixer and leaving Sam with nothing to do but stand with his tray in one hand and quietly feel his nose with the other.

"Matt, we wants to know if you can help us out on Wednesday after school? Merrik says we can play a set at the Year Seven disco but we need some help from the Sixth-Formers."

Sam glowered at Matt, and Joe shook his head in a dramatic 'noooo' action.

"Sure thing, Little-Man," Matt said as he extended a clenched fist out to power-pound the ginger haired rat. "Count us in. My man Joe will come and help out as well." Matt thrust two thumbs up in Joe's face.

The little ginger kid moved off the seat and as he did, he looked at Joe and flashed him a large sarcastic smile of latent child menace before skipping merrily back to his table where he was greeted with a collection of high fives from equally rodent-like small boys.

"Matt, why do you do it man? They drive me potty!" Joe said hitting the palm of his hand to his head. "And they're getting cheekier. I'm sure we weren't that cheeky when we were in lower school."

"It's the decline of man, Joey-Boy," he replied taking a swig of coke from his can as if dramatically concluding a complex point of philosophy.

Matt and Joe had achieved an almost unprecedented *cool* status amongst the Lower

School boys because of their recent performance at the school Charity Gig. Their band, *The Space Cadets,* had finished their set, rather controversially, by performing the now iconic anthem adopted by most of the year eight boys, which included the inspired lyrics;

'School ain't no place for learning books,
Maths with Rogers really sucks,
I like to imagine how Smithy… cooks.

Needless to say, the young and very pretty Food Technology teacher, Ms Smith, had been less than impressed when the Year Eight boys had taken to singing it at the top of their voice, replacing the carefully crafted last word. I suspected that had been Matt's intention all along.

Sara and Daisy had moved onto planning our usual Friday night gathering and were in full-animated flow. I took the last empty seat by the window, which gave me a clear view out onto the playing fields. At this time of the year, when the day never really got going and the dawn bled into twilight, they were eerily grey and empty. A fine layer of frost still coated the blades of grass from the night-frost and a low heavy fog had settled so that even the huge, black skeletal oak trees looked more like shadows than anything of solid. I lost myself in it, mentally armouring myself for my next meeting with Blake. I'd always been the first to scoff at the idea of 'love at first sight'. I'd thought that only idiots believed you could look at somebody and feel instantly as if your heart might implode. Sam and I had spent many conversations shaking our heads and sighing heavily at Daisy's habit of falling headfirst for some nut-job. We'd prided ourselves on being the fortune tellers of complete car-crash relationships and yet… I sighed heavily. Then there was Blake Beldevier and the crazy thing that had happened in English. My skin prickled at the memory of his ghost-like presence.

I'm not sure where I was in my thoughts when I heard *the* noise, but even though the canteen was bursting with the noise of over excited kids, there was a sound, way beyond the glass, that grabbed my entire attention and made every other noise fall quiet.

Impossible as it was, the thunderous sound of a charging horse travelled towards me as if riding on the mist. Its hooves pounded the hard winter earth like the beating of a war-drum and it beat in perfect sync with the rhythm of my heart. I was in no doubt that it was coming directly towards me, and directly towards the plate-glass window of the canteen. Panic surged and my body, preparing itself for impact, started to fold in on itself. I gasped and shut my eyes waiting for the explosion of glass. Nothing happened. The sound abruptly stopped. Opening one eye, I glanced back to the table expecting to see everybody in the same shock and panic as me but they were all still involved in their own conversations and totally oblivious to the events outside the window.

"Did you hear that?" I asked to no one in particular.

"Yeah, I think there is a storm coming."

"It wasn't thunder," I whispered. "It's the wrong time of year." A series of disinterested shrugs spread through the group.

Outside the window, I expected to see the animal close up; its warm breath misting the window and its rider in shock but there was nothing; just a shifting of the fog through which I was sure I could see the shimmering glint of metal.

"Mina… Mina... Earth calling Mina! What do you fancy? Blood and gore or something more romantic?" Daisy pulled me to attention, snapping me out of my bizarre hallucination.

"What?" I asked having no idea as to where we were in the conversation.

"Film. Friday. Romance or gore?"

Without taking my eyes from the window, I responded robotically, "Gore definitely – no contest." I turned to look at her briefly.

"Really, do we have to?" Sara chimed in. "I hate all that stalker-killer stuff. It is always freaks me out so I can't sleep. What about the new Anniston film, you know the one about some love triangle?"

Sara, true to form, flicked her expensively highlighted hair as if this might somehow seal the deal. Clearly it was a move that got Matt to agree to anything she wanted. The very thought of seeing a film about love triangles made *me* want to freak!

"Mina?"

"Really, I don't mind – I'll go along with everyone else." As I said it, I was already thinking up the excuse of a coursework deadline.

By the time the lunch bell went, I'd decided I was going to bail on the afternoon, ensuring no more weird aftershocks from the Blakequake.

Feeling slightly pathetic about it, I convinced myself that Blake wasn't the only reason I had a headache. It wasn't entirely untrue; I couldn't get the sound of the horse's galloping hooves out of my head. Only now the sound seemed to have altered ever so slightly to be more like the beating of somebody else's heart nestling along side my own.

*

I didn't tell Sam I was leaving early because he'd only have worried and fussed. He'd also have insisted on giving me a ride home and I really wanted to try and walk off the fever that was burning.

I wasn't long into town when I began to regret the really foolish decision to walk. The dry-ice day had grown thick and heavy with sleet, and having had a lift with Sam in the morning, I was completely underdressed and now violently shivering. Weighing up the very real possibility of freezing to death before I made it home, I took a turn into the bookshop, tempted by the warm yellow lights and the thought of the thick, velvety hot chocolate they served whilst you lost yourself in big saggy sofas.

Within minutes of sitting down, hot chocolate warming my frozen hands, the bell above the shop door went. Bent over, and fleeing the miserable weather outside, Blake entered. "Damn it!" I muttered. Clearly he too had decided to skip the afternoon lesson with Mr Dwell.

He stopped at the door, wiped his feet and shook out the snow-rain from his dark curls before pulling himself up to his full six-foot height. With one hand, he undid his coat and with the other he loosened his scarf, which looked bizarrely more like the remains of an old flag then the more usual woollen number. Despite a really conscious attempt to ignore him, I couldn't help but check him out head to toe.

Unlike me, he was dressed for the cold weather, wearing a simple but obviously expensive pair of jeans and a thick black jumper beneath his thigh length woollen coat. His clothes gave the impression of subtle wealth and, although simple in their design, it was obvious they were of serious quality. Sleet hung to the fine, soft wool of his navy coat, almost like someone had threaded small diamonds into the weave. Even at this time of the year he had a slight tan, the kind of tan that is burnt in by wind and activity. He flashed a smile in response to something the pretty sales assistant said and made his way towards the literature section.

He didn't spend long looking. He seemed instinctively to find whatever it was he was looking for. His hands moved deftly along the spines of the books and I caught myself thinking about how his hands would feel running themselves over my thighs. The delicious thought made me blush and the sudden rush of blood to my cold cheeks caused a strange prickling of my skin.

I watched him pull out several versions of the same text, *Tennyson's Collected Works*, and then he settled on the one with the image of Waterhouse's Lady of Shalott on its cover. His finger traced the outline of her face and he offered a wry smile, as if smiling at some private joke. Suddenly he went rigid, aware that this private moment was being watched. I tried to look casual, despite my pounding heart, my blushing cheeks and quickening breath; as if somehow, I hadn't noticed him and this sudden recognition was as much of a surprise to me as it was to him.

"Hello, it's Mina, isn't it?" he asked softly with a slight lilt in his voice.

"Yes, hi!" I cringed inside as my voice came out in a strange, almost strangulated squeak.

"Are you alright? You're shaking."

I blushed as I imagined the state I looked, red and blotchy from the cold. "I forgot my coat," I said as my heart hammered in my chest.

Instantly, without a moment's hesitation he started to slide out of his coat. "Here, borrow mine. I've got the car outside."

I was about to protest but before I could, he'd already deposited the coat on my lap. It weighed a tonne. The lining was as red as blood.

"I can't borrow your coat, you barely know me," I said.

"Don't be ridiculous; you can give it back to me in class tomorrow."

"Talking of which, why aren't you there now?" I asked.

"Well I could ask you the same question." He smiled. "I guess we've caught each other out."

"I guess so." I found myself blushing like an

idiot with a smile that almost hurt.

"Well, I'd better get going," he said, tapping the book. "I've got a lot to catch up on by the looks of it. Nice to meet you again, Mina Singer; I look forward to seeing my coat in lesson tomorrow."

With that he headed towards the counter to pay. In his place lingered the smell of wild-flower meadows and the warm smell of sun-kissed barley fields. I returned to my hot chocolate, strangely curious about the physical effect Blake had on me; I was trembling.

"Sorry to disturb you again," Blake's voice startled me, causing me to spill some of my hot chocolate, narrowly missing the expensive wool of his coat, "but it's started to snow quite heavily. Would you like me to drive you home?"

I flushed hot and wondered if he could see me blushing.

"No, really. No, it's fine. I've... I've..." I stammered, trying to think of a reason that might sound slightly believable. I changed track and with an embarrassing amount of over-enthusiasm, blurted out, "It's snowing? That's great! I LOVE snow! All that... white flaky stuff. Brilliant!"

He raised an amused eyebrow and smiled. "As you wish, My Lady. See you tomorrow."

As he left I could hear him amusedly muttering to himself, "*White flaky stuff. Brilliant!*"

I sat there no longer cold. The fire of total humiliation had warmed me up a treat.

3. HYACINTHS

I arrived home just after the dark had settled in for the night. Mum had switched on the fairy lights in the trees, giving the narrow garden an otherworldly feel. Unlike the usual feeling of magic, tonight it exaggerated the concern I had about my rapidly sliding sanity. The snow had given the garden the look of a wild and dangerous wood and I found myself huddling down the garden path as if to avoid the wicked witch. It was only when I heard the deadlock of the red front door click behind me that I took the chance to stop and breathe.

Home, as always, was warmly lit. Dusty, our ancient and cantankerous cat came into the small hallway, swirling his way around my ankles and purring a welcome that was really a poorly disguised demand for supper. I slipped out of Blake's coat and folded it up into as small a ball as it would go, trying to force the bright red lining out of sight. All the way home the coat had almost sent me half demented with the warm spiced smell of his body and I was strangely grateful that the house was filled with the rich smell of roast chicken in the hope that I could now be free of it.

Mum was sat huddled between her desk and the wood burning stove and Sam was sat at the dining table with several science textbooks sprawled out. He had his headphones in and hadn't noticed me come in. Standing outside of the half-open door and looking in at the peace and warmth of the room, I felt a sudden wave of guilt, which felt like a distressing blend of love and claustrophobia all rolled into one.

Mum stretched, removed her glasses and stood up before making her way to the kitchen. As she passed Sam, she placed a hand on his shoulder. It was the action of a mother who loved her son dearly. *One big happy family!* Something about it all suddenly freaked me and I took a step back knocking over Martha's umbrella and sending it skittering to the floor in a noisy commotion.

"Mina, is that you? Run up and wash your hands. I'm about to serve supper and don't forget to feed Dusty before we eat."

As if my guilt couldn't get any worse, I pushed my bedroom door open to find a small bunch of hyacinths lying on top of my pillow. A small card had been slotted into the top of them on which Sam had written in his spider-like handwriting the simple and yet most important of all words, *I love you!* I lifted the flowers to my nose and breathed in their pretty sweetness. Immediately the events at the bookshop flooded back to me.

Sam was not usually so showy in his feelings. He wasn't given to corny clichés and often took the piss out of the sort of grand gestures Matt made to Sara on an almost daily basis. However, the simplicity of the flowers and the inscription showed that Sam was aware that something was wrong, and he cared about it enough to put it right. I knew he deserved to be loved and not hurt and I promised to put things right. But even as I made the promise, I knew it wasn't one that I'd be able to keep. Something had changed and it wasn't going to change back.

I pulled on my deep emerald jumper, which was Sam's favourite and looped my string of green glass beads around my neck. Sam had bought them for me on my last birthday. He said they matched the colour of my eyes and I loved them, yet tonight when I looked at myself in the mirror they reminded me of a beautiful noose.

*

Dinner was already on the table by the time I arrived downstairs and Sam was lighting the candle with a firelighter lit from the wood burner. With his spare hand he went to reach out and take mine but stopped as if thinking better of it. Instead he cracked an awkward smile before saying,

"Hello, stranger. I'd started to think about sending out a search party." His voice was trying to put on a comic edge but it was tense. I smiled and shrugged, unable to give him either an unhurtful or rational explanation as to where I'd been. He deserved better than a lie. "Thought maybe you had been kidnapped by aliens or that you'd finally made good your promise to run away with the circus."

I could barely meet his eyes, thinking that there was nothing more genuinely painful then when somebody you loved tried to hide their hurt and confusion with a joke.

I hoped a half-truth would satisfy him. "I went to the bookshop." He nodded. I panicked. "Thank you for the flowers, Sam. They're really lovely.

Look I…" but before I could finish, Mum busied into the room carrying the gravy and interrupting my apology.

Dinner was chatty, a result maybe of all of us trying to hide the weird atmosphere. Mum fired questions at Sam and me in quick succession, and Sam, seemingly satisfied that things were hopefully on their way back to normal, was happy to indulge her.

By nine o'clock, Mum had already gone up to bed, book in one hand and a cup of tea in the other, and Sam was on the sofa under the throw and flicking through the T.V channels. I snuggled in beside him, feeling the warm certainty of his body. Out of habit my hand traced the muscles of his forearm causing him to turn towards me. He smiled and leant over, kissing my cheek before putting his arm around me and pulling me in. His lips found mine with the ease of familiarity. Sam was a good kisser, firm and soft all at once. Being together for almost two years, he'd perfected his skills and when he kissed me, it was easy to believe that the world was a silent place and that we were the only two people in it.

This evening was no different and as he kissed me I could feel all the doubt and uncertainty heal over with warm acceptance and love. I felt the comforting contact of skin on skin as his hand moved under my clothing, his kiss becoming more urgent as we headed towards a place I wasn't ready for. I pulled away but Sam moved himself so that I was pinned to the sofa with nowhere to go. Panic hit me as his kisses became increasingly aggressive. All at once *everything* was wrong. I pulled my face away as best I could, putting my hands out in defence.

"What the hell are you doing?" I shout-whispered.

He looked at me, almost as shocked as I was and pulled himself away to the far end of the sofa.

"I'm so sorry, Mina – that was really out of order. I don't know what came over me."

I stood up and looked down on him crumpled at the edge of the sofa, his eyes filmed with water as he fought back tears.

"What the hell was that all about?" I said, pulling down the bottom of my top.

"I'm sorry, I got carried away. I'm sorry, I didn't mean to – shit, I've really messed this up. I just wanted to check that everything was okay."

"What? You thought that the best way to check that was by forcing the situation?"

"I didn't mean to… *force*…. God, Mina, don't use that word, it's not as if I was going to… as if I was going to do *that* to you. I love you. I just thought maybe you wanted me to… Shit, I don't know what I thought!"

The situation was spiralling quickly out of control and I knew that whatever Sam had been thinking, it wasn't that he'd meant to hurt me. The whole day had been weird and it was no real surprise we'd ended up here.

"It was a mistake, Sam; I'm not happy about it but I know you wouldn't hurt me. I'm going to bed. We need to sleep on this and we'll talk about it tomorrow." I pressed a tight smile. "Night,

Sam."

As I went through the door I heard Sam whisper, "I'm sorry. I love you."

From upstairs in my room, I could hear the sound of the television travelling through the white painted floorboards and in order to drown out the ghost, I stuck in the ear buds of my iPod and turned the volume up to the borderline of pain. The deep rhythmic drums of *Florence and the Machine* drowned out Sam's presence but they didn't make me feel any better, for as I lay there, I realised with startling clarity that falling out of love with someone was like pulling a plaster – shockingly painful but surprisingly quick.

The deep, rich scent of the hyacinths filled my room and it was so overpowering that it made it almost sickening to breathe. Opening my window to let in the cold air seemed to have little effect and seeing no alternative, I took hold of them roughly by their slender green necks and threw them out into the night sky where they fell into the garden below and scattered across the navy-green grass like grounded stars.

*

All that night, I was attacked by dreams that made no sense. Dreams full of blood and mud, of cold grey, glinting steel and a winter sky cut through with a flock of cawing black birds. And even though I couldn't see her, I knew the old crone was there; standing at the side of my bed, her one crone hand pressing the air from my lungs, the other injecting my heart with a terrifying love poison. “A storm is coming! A storm is coming!” she croaked. And I knew that she was right; it would be the storm to end it all. When I woke, breathless and half terrified at the breaking of the dawn, I felt I’d been through the ravages of battle.

The Forest of Adventures by Katie M John

ABOUT THE AUTHOR

Katie M John is the author of the UK bestselling Teen series, 'The Knight Trilogy'. She lives in London with a handsome giant and two very naughty, cheeky mud-puddle fairies. She can be found hovering around Twitter and Facebook when she should be writing.

You can find out more about Katie and her books at www.katiemjohn.com

You can e-mail her at katiemjohn@yahoo.co.uk

She is the author of the following books.

THE KNIGHT TRILOGY
The Forest of Adventures
Immortal Beloved
Star Fire

Beautiful Freaks

When Sorrows Come

THE MEADOWSWEET CHRONICLES

Made in the USA
Charleston, SC
28 November 2016